The Red Court Farm by Mrs Henry Wood

COMPLETE IN TWO VOLUMES

Ellen Price was born on 17th January 1814 in Worcester.

In 1836 she married Henry Wood, whose career in banking and shipping meant living in Dauphiné, in the South of France, for two decades. During their time there they had four children.

Henry's business collapsed and he and Ellen together with their four children returned to England and settled in Upper Norwood near London.

Ellen now turned to writing and with her second book 'East Lynne' enjoyed remarkable popularity. This enabled her to support her family and to maintain a literary career.

It was a career in which she would write over 30 novels including 'Danesbury House', 'Oswald Cray', 'Mrs. Halliburton's Troubles', 'The Channings' and 'The Shadow of Ashlydyat'.

Sadly, her husband, Henry died in 1866.

Ellen though continued to strive on. In 1867, she purchased the magazine 'Argosy', founded two years previously by Alexander Strahan. She was a prolific writer and wrote much of the magazine herself although she had some very respected contributors, amongst them Hesba Stretton and Christina Rossetti. Although she would gradually pare down writing for the magazine she continued to write novel after novel. Such was her talent that for a time she was, in Australia, more popular than Charles Dickens.

Apart from novels she was an excellent translator and a writer of short stories. 'Reality or Delusion?' is a staple of supernatural anthologies to this day.

Ellen Wood died of bronchitis on 10th February 1887. Her estate was valued at a very considerable £36,000.

She is buried in Highgate Cemetery, London.

A monument to her in Worcester Cathedral was unveiled in 1916.

Index of Contents

VOLUME I

CHAPTER I

Introduction

On a certain portion of the English coast, lying sufficiently convenient to that of France to have given rise to whispers of smuggling in the days gone by, there is a bleak plateau of land, rising high above the sea. It is a venturesome feat to walk close to its edge and gaze down the perpendicular cliffs to the beach below—enough to make a strong man dizzy. A small beach just there, called the Half-moon from its shape, nearly closed in by the projecting rocks, and accessible only from the sea at high water; at low water a very narrow path leads from it round the left projection of rock. It was a peculiar place altogether, this spot; and it is necessary to make it pretty clear to the imagination of those who read the story connected with it. The Half-moon itself was never under water, for the tide did not reach it, but the narrow path winding round to the left was; and that rendered the half-circular beach unapproachable by land at intervals in the four-and twenty hours. A few rude steps shelved down from this Half-moon to a small strip of lower beach underneath, whose ends were lost in the sea. The projecting rocks on either side, forming as may be said the corners of the Half-moon, went right into the sea. Those on your right hand (standing face to the sea) cut off all communication with the shore beyond, for a depth of water touched them always. Those on the left extended less far out, and the narrow path winding round them was dry when the tide was down. It thus arose that the Half-moon could be gained by this one narrow path only, or by a boat from the sea.

For all practical purposes it might just as well have been unattainable. Not once in a month—nay, it might be said, not once in twelve months—would any human being stray thither. Not only was there no end to be answered in going to it, but the place was said to be haunted; and the simple villagers around would sooner have spent the night watching in the church's vaults than have ventured to the Half-moon beach between sundown and cockcrow. The most superstitious race of men on the earth's surface are sailors; and fishermen partake of the peculiarity.

Turning round on the plateau now—it is called the plateau just as the beach below is called the Half-moon—with our backs to the sea, we look inland It is only the plateau that is high; the coast itself and the lands around lie rather low. On the left hand (remember that our hands have been reversed) a long line of dreary coast stretches onwards, not a habitation to be seen; on the right lies the village—Coastdown. Fishermen's huts are built on the side and top of the cliffs, not there so perpendicular; small cottages dot the low-lying grass lands; and an opening in the one poor street (if it can be called such) of the village, shows the real useable beach and the few fishing craft moored to it.

Standing still on the plateau, our backs to the sea, the eye falls on a landscape of cultivated plains, extending out for miles and miles. The only house near to the plateau is exactly opposite to it—a large redbrick house built in a dell. It may be a quarter of a mile distant from the edge of the plateau where we stand, but the gradual descent of the grassy land causes it to look very much nearer. This is the Red Court Farm. It is a low, long house, rather than a high one, and has been built on the site of an ancient castle, signs of whose ruins may be seen still. The plateau itself is but as wide as about a good stone's throw; and on its lower part, not far from where it joins the lands of the Red Court Farm, and the descent is rather abrupt, rises a dilapidated circular stone wall, breast high, with a narrow opening where the door used to be. This is called the Round Tower, and is supposed to have been the watch-tower of the castle.

The Red Court stands alone, the last house of the colony, some distance removed from any; its gates and door of entrance are at the end of the house, looking to the village. The nearest building to it is the small old church, St. Peter's, standing in the midst of a large graveyard dotted with graves; with its portico-entrance, and its square belfry, grey with age, green with patches of moss. The high road, advancing from the open country behind—it's hard to say whence, or from what bustling cities—comes winding by the entrance gates of the Red Court Farm with a sharp turn, and sees two roads branching off before it. It takes the one to the right, bearing round to the village, passes through it, and goes careering on to Jutpoint, a small town, some four or five miles distant, having the sea on the right all the way. The other branching road leads past the church to the heath, or common, on which are situated the handful of houses, all of moderate size, inhabited by the gentry of the place.

The only good house was the Red Court Farm. Thornycroft was the name of the family living in it. Mr. Thornycroft owned the Red Court and some of the land around it; and he rented more, which he farmed. Many years ago a gentleman had come down to look at the place, which was for sale, and bought it. He was named Thornycroft. His two sons, Richard and Harry, were fine powerful young men, but wild in their habits, and caused some scandal in the quiet place. Previous to the purchase, the house had been known as the Red Court, it was supposed from the deep red of the bricks of which it was built. Mr. Thornycroft at once added on the word "Farm"—the Red Court Farm. A right good farmer he proved himself to be, the extent of the land being about three hundred acres, comprising what he rented. Within a very few years of the purchase Mr. Thornycroft died, and Richard, the eldest son, came into possession. In the following year Richard also died, from the effects of an accident in France. Both the brothers were fond of taking continental trips, Richard especially.

Thus the place came into the hands of Harry Thornycroft, and he entered upon it with his wife and little son. His ostensible residence since his marriage had been in London; but he had stayed a great deal at the Red Court Farm. A second son was soon after born, and some five or six years later another boy and a girl. Mrs. Thornycroft, a gentle, ladylike, delicate woman, did not enjoy robust health. Something in her face and manner seemed to give the idea that she had an inward care—that skeleton in the closet from which so few of us are quite free. Whether it was so or not in her case none could tell. That Harry Thornycroft made her a fond and indulgent husband—that they were much attached to each other— there could be no doubt of. Her look of care may have arisen solely from her state of health; perhaps from the secret conviction that she should be called away early from her children. Years before she died Coastdown said she was fading away. Fade away she did, without any very tangible disorder, and was laid to rest in a corner of the churchyard. To those who know where to look for it, her large white tombstone may be distinguished from our standing-place on the plateau. That grief had been long over, and the Red Court itself again.

Mr. Thornycroft was a county magistrate, and rode in to Jutpoint, when the whim took him, and sat upon the bench there. There was no bench at Coastdown; but petty offenders were brought before him at the Red Court—partly because he was the only gentleman in the commission of the peace living at Coastdown, partly from the fact that he was more wealthy and influential than all the other residents put together. A lenient justice was he, never convicting when he could spare: many a fine, that he himself had imposed from the bench at Jutpoint, was mysteriously conveyed out of his pocket into the poor offender's to save the man from prison. To say that Justice Thornycroft—the title generally accorded him—was beloved in Coastdown, would be a poor word to define the feeling of the poorer people around. He had a liberal hand, an open heart; and no person carried a tale of trouble to him in vain. His great fault, said the small gentry around, was unreasonable liberality. Never was there a pleasanter companion than he, and his brother magistrates chuckled when they got an invitation to the Red Court dinners, for they loved the hearty welcome and the jolly cheer.

The two elder sons, Richard and Isaac, were fine towering men like himself—rather wild both, just what Harry Thornycroft and his elder brother had been in their young days. Richard was dark, stern, and resolute; but he would unbend to courtesy over his wine when guests were at table. The few who remembered the dead elder brother said Richard resembled him much more than he did his father, as is sometimes seen to be the case. Certainly in countenance Richard was not like the justice. Isaac was. It was his father's fair and handsome face over again, with its fine features, its dark-blue eyes, and its profusion of light curling hair. There was altogether a great charm in Isaac Thornycroft. His manners were winning; his form, strong and tall as Richard's, had a nameless grace and ease that Richard's lacked; and his heart and hand were open as his father's. The young one, Cyril, was less robust than his brothers—quiet, gentle, very much like his dead mother. Cyril's taste was all for books; to the out-of-door life favoured by Richard and Isaac he had never been given. Richard called him a "milksop;" Isaac would pet him almost as he might a girl; all indulged him. To Richard and Isaac no profession was given; as yet none was talked of for Cyril. The two elder occupied themselves on the land—ostensibly, at any rate; but half their time was spent in shooting, fishing, hunting, according to the seasons. "A thriving farm the Red Court must be," quoth the neighbours given to gossip, "for the old man to keep all his sons to it." But it was well known that Mr. Thornycroft must possess considerable private property; the style of living would alone prove that.

A broad gravel drive led straight from the gates to the entrance door. There were different gates and entrances at the back of the house, serving for farm vehicles, for servants, and for people on business generally. The kitchens and other domestic apartments were at the back, looking on to the various buildings behind—barns, stables, and such like. The further end of the stables joined some of the old ruins still standing—in fact, it may be said that part of the ruins were used as such. The young men kept their dog-cart there—a large, stylish affair, capable of containing no end of dogs—and the fleet, strong, fine horse that usually drew it. The front of the house (as already seen) faced the plateau and the sea—a wide handsome frontage enclosing handsome rooms. And it is quite time we entered them.

Through the portico, level with the ground, and up the two steps into the long but somewhat narrow hall—very narrow at the back, and shut in by a door—doors opened on either side of it. The first room on the right was the dining-room—a spacious apartment, warm and comfortable, bright pictures on its dark wainscoted walls, a rich Turkey carpet giving luxury to the tread. The windows were at the end, looking towards the village and the church belfry; and the fireplace was opposite the door. Passing up the hall, the next room was called familiarly the justice-room. Here Mr. Thornycroft sat when offenders were brought before him, and here he saw his farming people and kept his papers. Beyond this was the staircase, and a door, still on the right, opening on the passage leading to the domestic apartments. On the left-hand side of the entrance-hall was the large drawing-room, its windows facing the front; beyond it a smaller and plainer one, always in use. A snug little parlour adjoined this, in which Miss Thornycroft took her lessons: all these three faced the front. The door at the back of the hall opened on a passage and to some rooms used only by the gentlemen. The passage ran through to a side entrance, which was just opposite that portion of the stables built on the old ruins—this was convenient, since the young men, who had a habit of coming in at all hours of the day and night, could put up their horse and dog-cart and let themselves in with their latch-keys without sound or movement penetrating to the family and household.

It is with the study, or Miss Thornycroft's parlour, that we have to do today. Its window is thrown open to the hot July sun—to the green lawn and the shrubs underneath—to the bare plateau beyond, on whose edge a coastguardsman was pacing on duty—to the sparkling sea in the distance. The paper of the room was of white and gold, pretty drawings and landscapes in water-colours adorning it. Some of them had been done by Miss Thornycroft, some by her late mother. The carpet and chairs were green; the piano, cabinets, and other furniture were handsome; the white curtains waved in the gentle breeze—altogether it was a room pleasant to look upon.

Seated on the music-stool, her face to the door, was a little middle-aged, brown woman, unmistakably French, without her tongue, which was going fluently, a look of reproach on her naturally placid face. It was Mademoiselle Derode, the governess, resident now some five years at the Red Court. A simple-minded woman, accomplished though she was—good as gold, and timid as her own nature. Richard Thornycroft had related to her some of the ghostly tales connected with the Red Court—or rather with its immediate environs—and she would not have stirred out at night alone for the world. Her chamber window when she first came faced the plateau; after hearing the stories she begged and prayed to be removed into another. Mrs. Thornycroft, alive then, complied with a sad smile, and reproved Richard in her gentle manner for saying anything. If whispers were to be believed, these same ghostly rumours were even then helping to kill Mrs. Thornycroft.

Mademoiselle Derode was en colère this morning with her pupil. French, German, English; good music, harp, and piano; drawing and painting; she was thoroughly versed in all, and had as thoroughly taught. For her age, Miss Thornycroft was an exceedingly well-educated girl, but apt at times to be a rebellious one. In fact she was growing quite beyond the control of the little governess.

The young lady stood by the table facing the window—a tall, very handsome girl of nearly sixteen, with her brother Isaac's fair skin and bright features, and a suspicious look of Richard's resolute lip. She wore a blue muslin dress, blue ribbons in her fair hair; her pretty hands were tossing, not in play but petulance, a large white rose, broken short off from its stalk; her well-shaped head was thrown back; her light clear blue eyes looked out defiantly.

"As if there could be reason in it!" spoke mademoiselle in her quaint but well-pronounced English. "You did but the little half of your lessons yesterday; the other day before it you went out without saying to me the one word; and now this morning you want to go out again. You will not do any one little thing! I say, Miss Mary Anne, that it has not reason in it."

"I promised Captain Copp I would go, mademoiselle. Mrs. Copp will be waiting for me."

"And I promise you that you cannot go," returned the governess, decisively. "My faith! you go, you go, you go; yesterday, today, tomorrow; and where are your studies? I might as well take my departure; I am of no longer use."

"I wish I was that douanier," spoke the young lady with an angry stamp, looking out at the preventive man pacing the edge of the plateau.

"I wish you were—for one day; you would soon wish yourself back again into yourself, Miss Thornycroft. Will you sit down and begin your studies?"

"No; it is too hot to work. German would give me the headache today, mademoiselle."

"I wish your papa, Monsieur the Justice, was at home. I would appeal to him."

"So would I. I wish he was! Papa would not make me do lessons against my will."

"Will you come into the other room to your harp, then?"

"No," reiterated Miss Thornycroft. "When I don't want to work, I can't work; and, excuse me, mademoiselle, but I won't. There! I am invited out today, and I want to go. Mrs. Sam Copp is going to Jutpoint, and she is to take me."

Mademoiselle got up in despair. Day by day, she saw it well, her authority was getting less.

"Miss Mary Anne, hear me! I will not have you go. I defend you to quit the house."

Mary Anne laughed disobediently.

"I shall go if Captain Copp comes for me, mademoiselle."

Mademoiselle wrung her hands.

"I will go and find Mr. Richard. He is master here when the justice is not. I will lay the case before him and say, 'What am I to do with this rebellions child?'"

She quitted the room on her search. Miss Thornycroft went to the window and leaned out, wishing herself once more the preventive man, or anybody else who had not a governess. At that moment she saw her brother Isaac go running on to the plateau from the direction of the village, stand a minute talking with the coastguardsman, and then come vault ng down towards the house. It has not been mentioned that a line of light railings enclosed the plateau below the round tower—a boundary line between it and the Red Court grounds. Isaac Thornycroft leaped the railings, and saw his sister. She called to him in a voice of earnestness; he came round to the front entrance and entered the room.

Handsome in his careless grace, and bright as the summer's morning. He wore light cool clothes, his linen was curiously white and fine; looking altogether, as he always did, a noble gentleman. Richard would be in coarse things, unbrushed and shabby, for a week together; the brothers had quite opposite instincts.

Mary Anne went up to him with a pleading voice and tears in her eyes, all her assumption of will gone.

"Oh, Isaac!—dear Isaac! won't you help me? You are always kind."

"My little dove! what is t?"

She told her tale. Her engagement with Captain and Mrs. Copp, and mademoiselle's cruel hardheartedness. Isaac laughed outright.

"Cruel hardheartedness, indeed! worse than that of Barbara Allen. My pretty one!" he whispered, stooping until his lips touched her cheek.

"Well, Isaac?"

"Put on your things, and I'll smuggle you off. Quick"

She needed no second warning. In two minutes, down she was again, a white mantle on her shoulders, a straw hat with its blue ribbons shading her fair bright face. Isaac took her out at the front door, just before Mademoiselle Derode got back again.

"I have sent for your brother, Mr. Richard, Miss Mary Anne, and—Ella n'est pas ici?"

Mademoiselle called, and looked in this room and that. She had not finished when Richard strode in, his face dark and stern as usual, his shoes and gaiters dusty, his velveteen waistcoat buttoned close up, his coat soiled. He had been helping to fill in a pond.

"Lessons! of course she must learn her lessons. Where is she, mademoiselle?"

Mademoiselle was arriving at the conclusion that she was nowhere. One of the housemaids had seen her dress herself, and go downstairs. Of course she had gone. Gone in disobedience! Richard went back to his pond, and mademoiselle sat down and folded her arms.

In the course of an hour Mr. Thornycroft came in. A handsome man still, upright and grand; his features fair and pleasant, his smile rather free, no grey as yet mingling with his still luxuriant hair. Mademoiselle carried her grievance to him; as she had been obliged to do more than once of late.

"It is not to complain of her, monsieur; I'm sure you know that, I love her too well; but in her own interest I must speak. She is at the age when she most needs guidance and control; and she is showing that she has a will of her own, and will exercise it! It was always there."

"I suppose it was," said the justice. "I have a will myself. Richard and Isaac have wills."

"If I can no longer be obeyed, monsieur, better that I should go back to my little home in France, and make a place for a governess who will have control."

"No, no," said Mr. Thornycroft, very quickly. "That would not do. I'll have no fresh governess here."

"But what is to be done, monsieur?"

"I'll think of it," said Mr. Thornycroft.

CHAPTER II

Robert Hunter and his Wife

In the midst of the pretty and exclusive village of Katterley, an inland spot, from twenty to thirty miles away from the sea, there stands a charming residence, half-cottage, half-villa, called Katterley Lodge. Its rooms are warm in winter, cool in summer; it rises in the midst of a lovely garden, in view of magnificent scenery; and the sweetest roses and honeysuckles entwine themselves on its walls.

The evening August sun—July had just past—shone full on its entrance gate; on a lady, young and fair, who was leaning over it. She may have been about three-and-twenty, and she was dressed in white, with ribbons in her hair. There was a remarkable refinement and delicacy in her face, her manners, in her appearance altogether; and her soft dark eyes had a sad expression. Did you, who may be reading this, ever observe that peculiar, sad look—not a passing sadness, or one caused by present care—but a fixed mournful look, implanted in the eyes by nature? It is not a common expression, or one often seen; rely upon it, when you do see it, it is but an index that the spirit is, or will be, sad within.

Sauntering up the road towards the gate, encumbered with a basket, a rod, and other apparatus pertaining to the fishing art, strode a gentleman, carelessly switching the hedge as he passed it. No sad expression was there about him; rather the contrary. He was of middle height, very slender, with a frank pleasant face given to laughing, and dark auburn hair; his manner was light, his speech free and careless. Her face sparkled, at his approach, and she opened the gate long before he had gained it.

"What sport, Robert? What have you brought?"

"Brought you myself," was the gentleman's reply, as he passed in at the gate she held wide. "Thank you. How much is the toll?'

As he bent to take the "toll," a kiss, she glanced shyly in his face and blushed—blushed brightly; although she was his wife of nearly three years' standing. In a retiring, impassioned earnest nature such as hers, it takes a great deal ere love can die out—a convulsion sometimes. With her it had not begun to die.

His name was Robert Frederick Hunter. His wife liked the second name best, and generally called him by it, but as other people adhered to the first it may be best to do so here. His career already, young though he was, had seen changes. Reared in middle-class life in the North of England, practically educated, rather than fashionably, he had served his articles to a civil engineer. Ere they were quite out, and he free, a small fortune came to him through a relative. Mr. Robert Hunter thought he could not do better than take to a red-coat, and he purchased a lieutenancy in a home corps. Nearly simultaneously with this, he met with Clara Lake, of Katterley. He fell in love with her; at least he fancied so; she most unmistakably did with him, and the preliminaries for a marriage were arranged. Her father made it a proviso that he should quit the army; and that they should live with him after the marriage at Katterley Lodge. Robert Hunter assented, sold out, and the marriage took place. When his wife's father died shortly after, it was found that Katterley Lodge and money amounting to four or five hundred a year were left to her, with a condition that Mr. Hunter should take the name of Lake. So he was mostly called in Katterley, Lake, or Hunter-Lake; elsewhere he was as before Hunter. Just for the present we will call him Lake, but it must not be forgotten that Hunter was his real name.

Mr. Lake opened his basket as he got in and displayed the contents—some fine trout. Two were ordered to be dressed, and served with the tea. On the days of these fishing expeditions, Mrs. Lake dined early. Occasionally she went with him. Not very often. The sport wearied her, and but for him at whose side she sat, it would never have been endurable. "Sport, indeed!" she used laughingly to say, "I'd as soon be at a funeral."

"What have you been doing all the afternoon, Clara?"

"Oh, reading and work ng; and wishing it was time for you to come home."

"Silly girl!" laughed he, as he played with her curls. "Suppose I should be brought home to you some day fished out of the stream myself; drowned and dead."

"Don't joke, please," was her reply, given in a low voice.

"It had like to have been no joke this afternoon. I all but overbalanced myself. But for a friendly tree I should have been in; perhaps done for."

"Oh, Robert!" she exclaimed, the bright rose fading out of her cheeks.

"And there's a fierce bit of current there, and the river is at its deepest, and the mill-wheel a stone's throw lower down," he continued, as if he enjoyed the sport of teasing her; which perhaps he did. "I was an idiot never to learn to swim."

"Did you slip?" she asked in a half-whisper.

"No; I was leaning too forward and lost my balance. Oh, Clary! you are a little coward at best. Why your heart is beating fast; a vast deal faster than mine did, I can tell you. And where have your roses gone?"

She looked up with a faint smile.

To be affected in this manner, to agitation, merely at the recital of the possible danger, now past, was what Mr. Lake did not understand Neither did he understand the depth of her love, for no sentiment in his own heart echoed to it; the time for love, with him, had not come.

"It is simply foolish, child, to feel alarm now," he said, looking at her gravely.

"You must not go again, Robert."

The remark called forth a hearty laugh. "Not go again! What am I to do, then, until shooting comes in?"

What, indeed? Robert Lake was an idle man. One of those whose unhappy lot it is (the most unhappy lot on earth) to be obliged to "kill" time, or else find it hang on their hands with a heavy weight. To a man born to idleness, cradled in the lap of luxury, it is bad enough; but to Robert Lake, brought up to industry, it was simply unbearable. He was skilled and clever in his profession, and he loved it; the misfortune of his life was having the money left to him; the great mistake his quitting his profession. He saw it now; he had seen it nearly ever since. Another mistake, but a smaller one, was his retiring from the army; as he had entered it, he ought to have kept in it. That fault was not his, but old Mr. Lake's. Lieutenant Hunter was on a visit at his sister's when he met Clara Lake, also staying there, the heiress in a small way. They fell in love with each other; he, after his temperament, carelessly and lightly, a species of love that he had felt for others, and would feel for more; she with all the fervour, the lasting depth of an impassioned and poetic nature. When he came to speak of marriage, and the father—an old-fashioned man who had once worn a pig-tail—said "Yes, upon condition that you quit soldiering and settle down with me—I cannot part with my daughter," Robert Hunter acquiesced without a word of murmur. Nay, he rather liked the prospect; change of all sorts bears its charm of magic for the young. And he was very young; but a year or so older than his wife. They settled down in Katterley Lodge; he to idleness, and it brings danger sometimes; she to happiness, which she believed in as real, as a bliss that would last for ever. If there were a man more perfect than other men on earth, she believed her husband to be that man. A charming confidence, a safeguard for a wife's heart; but sometimes the trust gets rudely awakened. One great grief had come to Clara Lake—she lost her baby; but she was getting over that now.

How intolerable idleness had been to Robert Hunter at first, none save himself ever knew. Over and over again visions of resuming his work as a civil engineer, came pressing on him. But it was never done. In the first year of their marriage came old Mr. Lake's long illness and death; in the second year came the baby and a prolonged illness for Clara; in the third year, this, the idleness had grown upon him, and he cared less to exchange it for hard work. It is of all evils nearly the most insidious.

All the year long, from January to December, living at Katterley Lodge with nothing to do! And he was really beginning not to feel the sameness. Their income, about six hundred a year in all, was not sufficient to allow of their mixing in the great world's fair, the London season; and one visit only had they paid the seaside. The pretty cottage, with its roses and its honeysuckles for a bower, and fishing for recreation in the summer season! It had a monotonous charm, no doubt; but the young man's conscience sometimes warned him that he was wasting his life.

The tea and the fish came in, and they sat down to it, Mrs. Lake remarking that she had forgotten to mention his sister had been there.

"What has she come over for?"

"To see the Jupps. Some little matter of business, she said."

"Business with the Jupps! Gossiping, rather, Clary."

"She said she should remain to tea with them. I wanted her to come back and take it with us; I told her there would be some fish. The fish was a great temptation, she said, but she must stay at the Jupps'! Who's this?" continued Mrs. Lake as the gate was pushed open with a hasty hand "Why, here she is!"

"And now for a clatter." He alluded to his sister's voluble tongue, but he got up and went out to greet her, table-napkin in hand It was Mrs. Chester, his half-sister. She was ten years older than he, twenty times older in experience, and rather inclined to be dictatorial to him and his gentle wife. Her husband, a clergyman, had died a few months back, and she was not left well-off in the world. She had just taken a house at Guild, a place about seven miles from Katterley; though how she meant to pay expenses in it, she scarcely knew.

"Well, Clara! here I am back again!" she exclaimed as she came in; "like a piece of bad money returned."

"I am so glad to see you!" returned Mrs. Lake, in her warmth of courtesy, as she rose and brought forward a chair and rang the bell, and busied herself with other little signs of welcome.

Mrs. Chester threw off her widow's bonnet and black silk mantle. Her well-formed face was pale in general, but the hot August sun made it red now.

She was a little, restless woman, inclined to be stout, with shrewd grey eyes and brown hair, and a nose sharp at the end. The deep crape on her merino gown looked worn and shabby; her muslin collar and cuffs were tumbled. She told everybody she was twenty-eight; Mr. Lake knew her to be four-and-thirty.

"Such a mess it makes of one, travelling in this heat and dust!" she exclaimed rather fretfully, as she shook out her skirts and pulled her collar here and there before the chimney-glass. "I've nothing but my bonnet-cap here; you won't mind it."

It was a bit of plain muslin with a widow's gauffered border. Mrs. Chester untied the black strings of it as she turned round and fanned herself with her handkerchief.

"Did the fish bring you back, Penelope?" asked Mr. Lake.

"Not it. When I got to the Jupps' I found they were going to have a late dinner-party. They wanted me to stay for it. Fancy! in this dusty guise of a costume. How delicious those fish look!"

"Try them," said Mr. Lake, passing some to her. "I have not caught finer trout this season. Clara has some cold fowl in the house, I think, if you have not dined."

"I dined before I came over—that is, had a scrambling sort of cold-meat meal, half dinner, half lunch. Robert, I should like you to catch fish for me always."

"How are you getting on with the house, Penelope?" he asked. "Are you straight yet?"

"Oh, we are getting on. Anna's worth her weight in gold at that sort of thing. She has been used to contrive and work all her life, you know."

"She might be used to worse things," said Mr. Lake.

"I have got a—visitor coming to stay with me," resumed Mrs. Chester, making a pause before the word visitor, and then going on with a cough, as if a fish-bone had stuck in her throat.

"Who is it?"

"Lady Ellis."

"Lady Ellis!" echoed Mr. Lake, unaware that his sister had any one of the name on her visiting list. "Who on earth is Lady Ellis?"

"Well, she is a friend of the Jupps'."

"Oh. And why is she going to visit you?"

"Because I choose to ask her," returned Mrs. Chester, in a reproving tone meant for the public benefit, while she gave her brother a private kick under the table. "She is a widow lady, just come home from India in the depth of her sorrow; and she wants to find some quiet country seclusion to put her poor bereaved head into."

Mr. Lake concluded that the kick was intended as a warning against asking questions. He put a safe one.

"Is she staying with the Jupps?"

"Oh dear, no. She went to India a mere child, I fancy. She was very pretty, and was snapped up by some colonel, a K.C.B., and dreadfully old."

"Ellis by name, I presume?" carelessly remarked Mr. Lake, as he looked for another nice piece of fish for his sister's plate.

"Colonel Sir George Ellis," spoke Mrs. Chester, in a grandly reproving tone, as if the title were good for her mouth. "He is dead, and Lady Ellis has come home."

"With a lac of rupees?"

"With a lack of rupees,' retorted Mrs. Chester, rubbing her sharp nose. "Sir George's property, every shilling of it, was settled on his first wife's children. Lady Ellis has money of her own—not very much."

"And why is she coming to you?"

"I have told you. She wants quiet and country air."

"Will she pay you?"

"Pay me! Good gracious, Robert, what mercenary ideas you have! Do you hear him, Clara? Oh, thank you; don't heap my plate like that, though I think I never did taste such fish. The Jupps have been praising her to the skies, one trying to out-talk the rest Never were such talkers as the Jupp girls."

"Except yourself," put in Mr. Lake.

Mrs. Chester lifted her eyes in surprise.

"Myself! Why, I am remarkably silent. Nobody can say I talk."

He glanced at his wife as he suppressed a smile. The matter in regard to Lady Ellis puzzled him—at least, the proposed residence with Mrs. Chester; but he supposed he might not inquire further.

"Should you like to take home some trout, Penelope?"

"That I should. Have you any to give?"

"I'll have them put up for you, the fellow brace to these. Mind the youngsters don't get the bones in their throats."

"They must take their chance," was the philosophical reply. "Children were never sent for anything but our torment. I am going to pack the two young ones off to school."

"Have you further news from the Clergy Orphan School about James?"

"News! Yes. It is all cross together. There's not the least chance for him, they write me word, at the election in November; I must try again later. And now, Clara, I want you and your husband to come to me for Sunday and Monday. Will you promise? I came over purposely to ask you."

Mrs. Lake did not immediately answer.

"You can come on Sunday morning in time for church, and remain until Tuesday. I don't ask you to come on Saturday evening; we shall be busy until late. The Jupps are coming."

"All of them?" asked Mr. Lake.

"Not all. I don't know where I should put them. Some of the girls: Mary and Margaret for two; and Oliver. I have three spare bedrooms nearly ready."

"Three spare bedrooms? And you grumbling about the purse's shallowness!"

"Allow me to manage my own affairs," said Mrs. Chester, equably. "You will say 'Yes,' will you not, Clara? I want to show you my house; you have never seen it."

Clara Lake did say "Yes;" but at the same time there was a feeling in her heart prompting her to say "No." She neither listened to it nor gave way to it; and yet she was conscious that it was there, as she well remembered afterwards.

"And now I must be going," said Mrs. Chester, putting on her bonnet and mantle. "You will come with me to the station, Robert?"

They started together: he carrying the basket of fish: and walked slowly. As he remarked, they had plenty of time.

"I know it," she said. "I came on early to talk to you."

"About Lady Ellis and her projected visit?" he quickly rejoined. "I thought there was some scheme agate by the kick you gave me."

"Robert, I must scheme to live."

"I think you must if you are to keep three spare bedrooms for visitors."

"I am left a widow, Robert, with a fair amount of furniture, and a wretched pittance of two hundred a year. How am I to live like a lady and educate the children?"

"But why need you have taken so large a house?"

"What am I to do? How am I to eke out my means? I cannot lose caste. I can't go and open a shop; I can't turn Court milliner; I can't begin and speculate in the funds; I can't present myself to the Government or the Bank of England directors, and make a curtsey, and say, 'Please, gentlemen, double my income for me, and then perhaps I can manage to get along.' Can I?" added Mrs. Chester, fiercely.

"I never said you could."

"No; I have only got my own resources to look to, and my own headpiece to work upon. It has been ransacked pretty well of late, I can tell you. The first idea that suggested itself to me was to educate Fanny at home with Anna Chester's help, and to get half-a-dozen pupils as well, on the plan of a private family. But I hated the thought of it. I have no nerves and no patience; and I knew I should be worried out of my very existence. Besides, education gets more fantastical every day, and I am not up to the modern rubbish they call requirements: so I said, 'That won't do.' Next I thought of getting three or four gentlewomen to live with me, on the plan of a private family. Quite as visitors, you know; and the longer I dwelt on the scheme the better I liked it. I thought it would be a pleasant, social way of getting on; and

I determined to carry it out. Now you know why I have taken a large house, and am putting it into good order."

"That is, you are going to take boarders?"

"If you choose to put it in that plain way. You are so very downright, Robert. Lady Ellis is the first coming."

"How did you hear of her?"

"Never you mind," returned Mrs. Chester, who did not choose to say she had advertised. "Friends are looking out for me in London and elsewhere. I have had some correspondence with Lady Ellis, and she comes to me the middle of next week. She wants quiet, she says—quiet and country air. A most exquisite little hand she writes, only you can't read it at sight."

"Have you references?"

"Of course. She referred me to some people in London, and also in Cheltenham, where she is now staying. In her last letter she mentioned that the Jupps of Katterley knew her, and that's the chief thing that brought me over today. Mind, Robert, I did not tell the Jupps she was coming to me as a boarder: only as a visitor. 'She writes me that you know her,' I carelessly said to the girls, and they immediately began to tell all they did know, as I knew they would."

"What did they say?"

"Well, the whole of it did not amount to much. At first they persisted they had never heard of her, till I said she was formerly a Miss Finch, having lost sight of her when she went to India. They are charmed to hear she has come back Lady Ellis, and think it will be delightful for me to have her with me."

"Unless you can get more boarders, Lady Ellis will prove a source of expense to you, Penelope, instead of a profit."

"You can't teach me," retorted Mrs. Chester. "I mean to get more."

"What is she to pay you?"

"Well, you know, Robert, I can't venture upon much style at first, wanting the means. I am unable to set up men-servants, and a service of plate, and a pony carriage, and that sort of thing: so at present my terms must be in accordance with my accommodation. Now what should you think fair?"

"I? Oh, nonsense! Don't ask me."

"Lady Ellis is to pay me a hundred pounds if she stays the year; if not, ten pounds per month. Now you see if I get four at that rate, permanent inmates," went on Mrs. Chester, rapidly, "it will bring my income up to six hundred pounds, which will be comfortable, and enable one to live."

"I suppose it will."

"You suppose it will!" snapped Mrs. Chester, who was resenting his indifferent demeanour. "It is as much as you and Clara possess. You live well."

"We have none too much. We spend it—all."

"And more imprudent of you to spend it all! as I have often thought of telling you, Robert Hunter. I wonder you can reconcile yourself to live up to the last penny of your income, and do nothing to increase it. How will it be when children come?"

"Ah, that's a question," said he, giving the fish-basket a twirl.

"You may have a large family yet; you are both young. What sort of a figure would your six hundred a year cut when everything had to come out of it? A dozen children to keep at home, and find in clothes, and doctors, and sundries, and a dozen children to provide for at school, would make your money look foolish."

"Let's see," cried he, gravely; "twelve at home and twelve at school would make twenty-four. Could you not have added twelve more while you were about it, and said thirty-six?"

"Don't be stupid! You know I meant twelve in all. They may come, for all you can tell; and they'll require both home expenses and school expenses, as you will find. It is a sin and a shame, Robert, for a young capable man like you, to live an idle life."

"I tell myself so every other morning, Penelope."

She glanced at him, uncertain whether he spoke in jest or earnest. His dark-blue eyes had a serious look in them, but there was a smile on his pleasant lips.

"If you don't think well to take up civil engineering again, try something else. There's nothing like providing for a rainy day; and a man who lives up to his income cannot be said to do it. You cannot be altogether without interest; perhaps you might get a post under Government."

"I'll apply for the lord-lieutenancy," said he. "The place is vacant."

"I know you always turn into ridicule any suggestion of mine," again retorted Mrs. Chester. "You might get into the board of works, and leave the lord-lieutenancy for your betters. There's the train, shrieking in the distance. Don't forget Sunday. I wish you and Clara to see how nice the house looks."

"All right, Penelope; we will not forget. But now I want to know why you could not have given your explanation before my wife."

"Her pride would have taken alarm."

"Indeed you cannot know Clara if you think that."

"I know her as well as you," returned Mrs. Chester. "I shall acquaint neither her nor the Jupps of the terms on which Lady Ellis is coming."

He said no more. To keep the fact from the clear-sighted, sensible Jupps would be just an impossibility; and he meant to tell his wife as soon as he got home. They passed through the waiting-room to the platform. Mrs. Chester took her seat in one of the carriages; he handed in the basket of trout, and stood back. Just before the train started, she suddenly beckoned to him.

"Robert," she began in a low voice, putting her head out at the window to speak, "I'm going to give you a caution. Don't you carry on any of that nonsensical flirting with Rose Jupp, should you ever happen to be together in the presence of Lady Ellis. You make yourself utterly ridiculous with that girl."

He looked very much amused. "A couple of sinful scapegoats! I am astonished you ever have us at your house!"

"There you are, mocking me again. You may think as you please, Robert, but it is excessively absurd in a married man. I saw you kiss Rose Jupp the other day."

He broke into a laugh.

"Anything of that before Lady Ellis would be an awful mistake. It might frighten her away again."

"Oh, we will both put on our best behaviour for the old Begum. Do not let doubts of us disturb your sleep, Penelope."

"She is not old, but I daresay she knows what propriety is," sharply concluded Mrs. Chester as the train puffed off. And Mr. Lake, quitting the station, went home laughing.

He found his wife in a reverie. The feeling, that she had done wrong to promise to go to Mrs. Chester's, was making itself unmistakably heard, and Clara tried to analyse it. Why should it be wrong? It was difficult to say. Sunday travelling? But she had gone several times before to spend Sunday with Mrs. Chester, gone and returned the same day; for Guild Rectory, where Mrs. Chester had lived, was short of bedrooms. No, it was not the idea of Sunday travelling that disturbed her, and she could find no other reason. Finally she gave up the trouble of guessing, and her husband came in.

"Were you not too early for the train, Robert?"

"I should think so. Penelope confessed that she wiled me out to talk of her plans. I'll tell you about them directly. What do you think she wound up with, Clara, just as the train was starting?"

He had sat down in a large armchair, and was holding his wife before him by the waist.

"With an injunction not to flirt so much with Rose Jupp! Which is absurd in itself, she says, and might frighten away the grand Indian Begum."

Clara Lake laughed. She was accustomed to witness her husband's free rattling manners with others, but not a shadow of jealousy had yet arisen. She believed his love to be hers, just as truly and exclusively as hers was his; and nothing as yet had shaken the belief.

CHAPTER III

Clara Lake's Dream

[Footnote 1: The dream is not fiction: it is but transcribed, even to the minutest particular]

It was certainly a singular dream, well worthy of being recorded. Taken in conjunction with its notable working out, few dreams have been so remarkable. At least, if it may be deemed that subsequent events did work it out. The reader must judge.

Mr. and Mrs. Lake retired to rest as usual, eating no supper. When they had fish or meat with tea, supper was not served. On this evening he drank some wine-and-water before going to bed; she touched nothing. Therefore it cannot be thought she suffered from nightmare.

It was a singular dream; let me repeat the assertion. And it was in the earlier part of the night that it visited her. How soon after she went to sleep, how late, there were no means of knowing.

Part of the evening's doings came to her again in her sleep. She thought that Mrs. Chester called, went on to the Jupps' house, returned to drink tea, and gave the invitation to go to her house at Guild on the Sunday—all just as it had been in reality. Clara also thought that she felt an insuperable objection to go, in spite of having accepted the invitation. Not the vague idea that had presented itself to her awake, the half-wish that she had not made the engagement, but a strong, irrepressible conviction that the going would bring her evil—but accompanied with a conviction, a knowledge, so to say, that she should go, that it was her fate to go, and that she could not avoid it. She dreamt that Mrs. Chester had departed, and that she was discussing the point with her husband They were in a kitchen, a large kitchen quite strange to her, and were standing by a small, round, dark-coloured table in its middle. The fireplace, as Clara stood, was behind her; the window, a wide one, with an ironing board underneath it, was in front; a dresser with shelves was on her left hand; and there were several doors, leading she did not know where. Altogether, the kitchen looked large and bleak, something like those we see in farm-houses: and, seated on a chair to the right, apparently engaged in sewing, and taking no notice of them, Clara suddenly saw Mrs. Chester. She and her husband were discussing earnestly—to go, or not to go. It appeared that both felt some evil was impending, but yet both knew they should go and encounter it, in spite of the hesitation: and yet Clara seemed to feel that her husband could have helped her to remain if he would. "What excuse can we make for declining?" she seemed to say to him, and then they both thought over various pleas, but none appeared to answer, and they came to the final conclusion that go they must; which they both had known throughout would be the conclusion. All the time they spoke, Mrs. Chester was sitting in her chair, listening, but taking no notice; and upon arriving at the decision Clara and her husband parted, he going towards one of the kitchen doors, she towards the window; but so sharp was the conviction that she was rushing upon evil, that she awoke.

Clara thought it a curious dream—curious because it represented what had actually occurred, and the bent of her own feelings; curious also because it was so unusually vivid, so like reality. She got out of bed quietly, not to disturb her husband, struck a wax match, and looked at the hanging watch. It was exactly three o'clock.

But the dream was not yet over. She went to sleep again, taking up the thread almost at the point where she had left it. She remembered all that had passed, both of dream and reality; she remembered that she awoke in the certainty that she could not go beside the dreaded expedition; all that was plain in this, her second sleep, but she now began making strenuous exertions to escape. She did not see her husband again, but Mary Ann and Margaret Jupp had joined Mrs. Chester, and the three seemed to be forcing her to go. Not by force of violence, but of argument, of persuasion; and she still seemed to know that they must prevail, that to withstand at the last would be beyond her power.

The time appeared to change to the morning of departure: or rather, with that inconsistency peculiar to dreams, it appeared to be the morning of the departure without having changed. Still she strove against it; not saying why, not hinting that she feared evil; of that, she had only spoken with her husband; but striving, not to go, by every possible argument, and by passive resistance. And—strange inconsistency!—it appeared that if she could have told them the reason of her reluctance, her dread of evil, all would have been well; but it was precisely to them she must not and dared not tell it.

To any who may fancy the description of the dream unnecessarily spun out, the small details too much dwelt upon, I would say just a word. It is difficult to shorten that real dream of midnight sufficiently for it to be told within reasonable bounds. No pen can trace its particulars as they appeared; no power of language describe them as they were pictured. And now to resume it.

Mrs. Chester and the Miss Jupps urged her to depart; were waiting for her. Clara Lake resisted. "There!" she suddenly exclaimed to them, "we cannot go. It is past ten: we have let the hour go by, and the train is gone." "Oh!" said Mrs. Chester, "we can get a carriage and overtake it." She went out with them—resistance appeared to be over; she felt that it was over, and that she could not help herself—went out to look for a carriage. They ran about, down lanes and in the open fields, and could not see one; but a butcher's cart came up in the lane; one of them said that would do as well as a carriage, and they all got into it. They seemed to fly, going along at a fearful pace, but through a most dreary-looking country, the skies gloomy, the scenery barren, and the road muddy, so muddy that it splashed up upon them as they sat: there were also shallow, dismal ponds through which they drove. All this haste seemed to be to catch the train, but suddenly a noise was heard behind them, and it was known that it was the train: they had gone so fast as to outstrip it. Their cart stopped to wait, and Clara, when the noise came close, looked behind, but could only distinguish something black which whirled by them, turned round, came back, turned again, and pulled up. "Why, it is a hearse!" she screamed out (but in surprise, not fear), to Mrs. Chester. Yes, it was a hearse, all black, and two men sat upon the box. Clara looked out, expecting to see the rest of their party on it, but there was no one but the two men: the one she could not see, for he seemed to hide his face; but she caught, fixed upon her, the strangely black eyes of the driver, the blackest eyes she ever saw in her life: of the rest of his face she remembered nothing. "Come," said he, "there's no time to lose;" and they all four descended from the cart. Clara got on to the hearse first, and was settling her cloak around her, when she heard the cart drive off, taking the road home again; and, seated in it as before, were Mrs. Chester and Mary and Margaret Jupp. "Why don't you come with me?" she called out; "why are you going back?" "No," said Mrs. Chester, "that hearse is for you, not for us;" and they drove off. The hearse also drove off the contrary way, and Mrs. Lake found herself sinking into its interior. She was calm enough for a moment, but suddenly she knew that she had been entrapped into it, and that she was being taken to her burial.

With a dreadful scream she awoke.

The scream awoke Mr. Lake. She was bathed in perspiration, and shaking as in an ague fit. In vain he asked what was the matter, whether she was ill: she could not speak to tell him, and it was several minutes before she was able in any degree to overcome the fright, or relate it to him.

Robert Lake had no belief in dreams; was given to scoff at them; but he had too much regard for his wife to attempt to scoff then, in her extremity of distress and agitation. He got up and lighted a lamp, for though morning was glimmering it could not be said to be yet light.

"I am quite certain that it is sent to me as a warning," she exclaimed; "and I will not go on Sunday to Guild."

"I never knew before that you could believe in dreams," he answered.

"I do not believe in dreams; I have never had any particular dreams to believe in. But you must acknowledge, Robert, that this one is beyond common. I cannot describe to you how vivid, how real everything appeared to me. And it was not one dream; it was two: that at least is unusual. The second dream was a continuation of the first."

"The one induced the other. I dare say you saw a hearse pass yesterday?"

"I have not seen a hearse for ever so long," she answered, still shivering. "But, go to your sister's, I will not. Thank heaven! though the power to refuse was not mine in the dream, it is in reality."

But that it was not the time to do it, he could have laughed outright at the superstitious folly. He spoke pleasant, loving words to her, almost as one would to a frightened child, trying to soothe her back to tranquillity.

"Clara; consider! the very fact of your being able to act as you please, which it seems you could not do in the dream, ought to convince you how void of meaning it was."

"I will not go to Mrs. Chester's," was all she reiterated, with a strange sigh of relief—a sense of thanksgiving that the option was assuredly hers.

"Wait for the morning sun," said he. "You will be in a different mood then."

She did not rise so soon as usual. She had got to sleep again at last, first of all making a firm inward resolution that no persuasion, no ridicule, no "morning sun"—in whose cheery rays things indeed wear a different aspect from what they do in the dark and weird night should suffice to alter her determination. The warning against going she fully believed to have been sent to her, and she would abide by it.

Mr. Lake waited breakfast for his wife. She came down in her delicate muslin dress, looking as pretty as usual. At first she made no allusion to the past night; neither did he—he hoped it was at an end; but when breakfast was about half over, she glanced up at him in her rather shy manner, speaking in a low tone.

"I have a request to beg of you, Robert—that you will not mention this dream to any one. I will make some other excuse for not going to Guild."

"Dream!" cried he, speaking with his mouth full. "Why, Clary, I had already forgotten it. And so will you before the day shall be over."

She shook her head.

"I shall send word to Penelope that I cannot go."

Mr. Lake put down his knife and fork and gazed at her in astonishment. To his sober, practical mind, his careless nature, this in truth savoured of the ridiculous.

"Clara, you will never be so foolish! I gave you credit for better sense. Dreams are all very well in their places—to amuse old women and children—but in these days they should not be allowed to influence actions. You can see the bright sunshine, the busy work-a-day world around you, and yet you can retain remembrance of a ridiculous dream! I thought dreams passed away with the night."

"Of course a great part of the vivid impression has passed with the night," she replied, confessing what was the actual fact; "but I will abide by the night's impression, nevertheless. I look at it in this light—my remaining at home can hurt no one, it cannot bring harm in any way, while my going may bring me harm; we cannot tell. I am fully decided," she continued, in a firm tone; "and do you eat your breakfast and cease staring at me."

"Perhaps you fear the train will come to grief, and pitch us all into coffins made to fit your hearse."

"Well, I don't know," returned Clara. "If I did get into the train on Sunday morning, I should be unusually pleased to find myself safe out of it again."

Mr. Lake said no more; in this frame of mind reasoning was useless. But he felt persuaded the fancy would wear away, and his wife go contentedly enough with the rest of them.

Nothing more was said that day, which was Friday. On the next day, Saturday, two of the Miss Jupps called on Clara, full of the following morning's excursion. A large family was that of the Jupps—six sons and six daughters, all living. The sons were out in the world—one in the army, one in the navy, one in the church, one reading for the bar, one here, one there; Oliver, the youngest of them, was just now at home. The six daughters were all at home, and marrying men seemed to fight shy of so large a host. Social, pleasant, chatty girls were they, the youngest two-and-twenty, the age of the eldest locked up in the church's register. Mr. and Mrs. Jupp were a quiet, inoffensive couple, completely eclipsed by their sons and daughters; not that any were undutiful, but the old people belonged to a bygone age, and were scarcely equal to the innovations of this. Mr. Jupp had once been high sheriff of the county: it was the one great event of the Jupps' life, imparting to them an importance which their pride never quite lost sight of. They lived in a large house abutting on the street of Katterley, about five minutes' walk from Mr. Lake's.

Mary Ann and Margaret Jupp had come to gossip about the proposed Sunday excursion. They were pleasant, voluble girls (to pay them the compliment of still calling them girls), with light hazel eyes and reddish hair. The sisters were all much alike—these two, the eldest; Louisa and Rose, the youngest. They had on flimsy skirts, nankeen-coloured jackets, and straw hats. They sat in the shady room open to the trailing honeysuckles, talking to Clara.

"Our plans are changed," spoke Mary. "Oliver, Louisa, and Rose go tomorrow, returning home to sleep, and I and Margaret go over the next day."

"We think it would be so truly unconscionable to inflict four of us on Mrs. Chester at once, with her few servants, that we have written to tell her we will divide ourselves," interrupted Margaret, who liked to have her share of tongue. "Mamma says she wondered at our thoughtlessness when she heard us making the bargain."

"Mrs. Chester would not have made a trouble of it," answered Clara. "She is not one to put herself out of the way."

"No, she is very good; but it would have been imposing on hospitality," said Mary Jupp. "For that very reason, as mamma observed, we ought to spare her. So Louisa and Rose spend Sunday with her; I and Margaret Monday; Oliver goes both days."

"But you will remain for Tuesday?"

"No. Until she has her house in complete order it would be unfair to trouble her with night guests. You and Mr. Lake of course will remain the whole time. And now to deliver Louisa's message. Shall they call for you here tomorrow morning, or will you be at the train?"

"I am not going," replied Mrs. Lake.

"Not going!" echoed Mary Jupp. "Good gracious! Why not?"

"It is not quite convenient. Mrs. Chester does not expect me."

"But she did expect you!" exclaimed Mary, in wonder. "Oliver saw Mr. Lake that night after he had taken Mrs. Chester to the train, and he told him you were going. Did you not?" she added, appealing to Mr. Lake, who sat perched on a side table doing something to a fishing-line.

"All right," nodded he.

"Yes, we did promise; but since then I have altered my mind, and have written to Mrs. Chester," said Clara. "I shall go later, when she is more settled."

"Well, I never heard of such a thing!" cried Margaret Jupp. "Oliver and the girls will be in a way! I don't think they care to go but for the pleasure of your company. Mr. Lake, why have you changed your minds?"

"Ask Clara," returned he, without looking up. "It's her affair, not mine."

The delicate pink in Clara Lake's cheeks grew a shade brighter as the two ladies looked at her and awaited the explanation. Not choosing to mention the dream, she was at a loss for any sound plea to make.

"I seem to have a prejudice against going tomorrow," she said, feeling how lame were the words. "And—and I wrote to Mrs. Chester, telling her not to expect me."

"How very odd!" cried Margaret Jupp. They were keen-sighted, those girls, and felt sure there was some suppressed reason.

"The truth is, my wife has taken it into her head that Sunday travelling is sinful," cried Mr. Lake, partly to help Clara out of her dilemma, partly in the indulgence of the mocking spirit he liked so well. "If we do venture to go tomorrow, in the teeth of the sin, she thinks the engine will infallibly burst and blow us up."

Mrs. Lake felt vexed. It was precisely the fear her imagination induced her to take. Unable to conceive any other probable danger, she was unconsciously casting doubts on the safe convoy of the train. But she had not confessed it to him.

"Do not talk nonsense," she said to her husband; and Mary and Margaret Jupp looked from one to the other, not knowing what to think.

"My dear Mrs. Lake, they get to Guild for morning service, you know," spoke Margaret. "I don't see any great harm in going just that little way on a Sunday morning."

"Robert is very stupid to say such things," returned Mrs. Lake, driven into a corner. "I did not think anything about its being a sin. The sin is not my objection."

"The train runs whether we passengers go in it or not; so that our staying away is not of the least benefit in a religious point of view," logically argued Mary Jupp. "Do pray go, Mrs. Lake."

"Not tomorrow," Clara gently said, shaking her head.

"Can't you induce her, Mr. Lake?"

"I! I have wasted all my powers of oratory; I have tried persuasion; I have hinted at an illegitimate application of my riding-whip, and all in vain. She's harder than a brickbat."

The young ladies laughed. "Dear Mrs. Lake, you must go, if only to oblige us. Think of the disappointment to Louisa and Rose."

Clara remembered her dream: how Mary Ann and Margaret (the very two of the sisters now present) had striven in it to persuade her. The recollection only served to render her more firm. They began to fear that there would be no prevailing, and felt half inclined to be offended. "And yourself, Mr. Lake? Do you also remain at home?"

"Not I. I don't live in fear of the boiler's treachery."

"Of course I do not wish to prevent my husband's going," said Mrs. Lake, hastily.

"Though you know you would rather I did not," he rejoined.

"Well, of course, if there is to be—as you say, though I don't—a bursting of the boiler, it would be as bad for you to be in it as for me," she said, affecting a light laugh. The truth was, she did wish he would not go; she knew that she should feel more easy; though she would not ask him to remain, lest it might seem selfish. The Miss Jupps rose to leave.

"I hope you will think better of it," said Margaret. "Louisa was saying this morning how glad she was Mrs. Lake was going. She has been counting on you."

"Ah, well—she had better count upon me instead," cried Mr. Lake, as he left his seat to attend them to the gate. "And mind you give my love to Rose, and tell her I shall be a bachelor for the day."

"Don't forget that," put in Clara.

The two ladies walked away, commenting on what had passed. Clara Lake was a poor actor, and her manner had betrayed that the true reason had not been spoken. Margaret said she should put it down to "caprice;" but both acknowledged that they had never known Mrs. Lake capricious before.

Never did a more lovely day dawn than that Sunday in August. Not another word upon the subject had been exchanged between Mr. Lake and his wife since the visit of the Miss Jupps; she shunned it, feeling half ashamed of herself for her persistent folly; he had given the matter up for a bad job. After breakfast they stood together, looking from the open window. The church bells rang out; Mr. Lake's time for departure was drawing near.

"I must not miss the train," he carelessly observed. "'Twould be a pity to lose the excursion such a morning as this."

"It is a most beautiful day," she sighed. "I almost envy you."

"Clara," he said, turning to her with a sudden seriousness of manner, "I ask you to be yourself. Lay aside this folly, and act as a reasonable woman ought. Put on your things and come with us."

She moved closer to him and spoke deprecatingly, "Do not be angry with me, Robert; I believe I am doing right to remain away. I must remain."

"Well, of all the simpletons that ever walked, you are about the worst," was his complimentary rejoinder as he caught up his gloves. "Good-bye, Clary," he added, stooping to kiss her.

"Oh, Robert, I hope you will come back safely!" she said, clinging to him as if she feared he was going away for ever; and the tone of her voice, full of mournful wailing, struck upon the ear of her husband.

Nevertheless he went off laughing, telling her not to fear—that he'd come back with all his legs and wings about him.

On the platform he met Louisa and Rose Jupp under the convoy of their brother. "Then actually Mrs. Lake is not coming!" exclaimed Louisa.

"And I have only come to see you off," was Mr. Lake's response. "I am not going on to Guild."

"Oh, you barbarous deceiver!" quoth Rose. "Where are you going?"

"To church, as a respectable individual of modern society ought."

"I tell you what, Lake," interrupted Oliver Jupp, a dark, short young man, quiet and sensible, "this is not fair. These girls entrapped me into taking them, on the strength that you were to be one of the party, and it's too bad to shuffle off it."

"So it is," returned Mr. Lake. "But you must talk to my wife about it. I am the most hopelessly henpecked husband your worst fancy ever pictured; Caudle was nothing to it."

The train went smoothly off, and Mr. Lake returned home. His wife was leisurely attiring herself for church. She started when she saw him. "Why, Robert, what has happened?"

"Nothing. The boiler has not gone up yet; that calamity is expected to take place midway between here and Guild."

"Why have you come back?"

"I came back because I have got a silly child for my wife," he said, standing in front of her, and speaking half tenderly, half severely. "One who would have worried her foolish heart into a fever, had I gone, believing I should never come back alive."

She wound her arms round him and pulled his face down to hers in her fervent love, her tears falling upon it. "Oh, my darling! my dearest! you don't know how happy you have made me!" she passionately whispered. "How shall I thank you for giving way to my foolishness? I should have been in unhappy suspense all day long."

"I shan't give way to it the next time," cried he, as he kissed away her tears. "And I have told the girls what a henpecked husband I am, the slave of a capricious tyrant. Jupp won't be in a hurry to marry after my warning example before his eyes."

"The next time!" she repeated, with a sad smile. "Robert, there will be no next time. I shall never have such a dream again."

The Jupps went grumbling all the way to Guild. That is, the young ladies grumbled, and their brother listened. The disappointment was really great. Mr. and Mrs. Lake were great favourites with everybody; just those people that make society brighter for their presence.

"Margaret says Clara Lake was taken with a capricious fit."

"Nonsense, Louisa!" spoke Oliver, at length. "She has too much innate good feeling for caprice. Mrs. Chester has been at her domineering ways, I expect, and frightened her poor little sister-in-law."

Guild reached, they found their way to Mrs. Chester's house, which was just outside the town, some ten minutes' walk from the station. It was a pretty place—old-fashioned but commodious; standing in the midst of a productive garden, with windows opening to a large lawn. It used to be called Guild Farm; Mrs. Chester had already changed that, and rechristened it "Guild Lawn." She had it at a cheap rent. There were two houses on the farm, and the farmer who rented the land lived in the other: to let this was so much gain to him. Guild Rectory, where Mrs. Chester had hitherto lived, was at the opposite end of the town.

The Reverend James Chester, her late husband, had been a poor curate for the greater portion of his life. He, his first wife (who was a cousin of the Jupps), and their only child, Anna, had lived on his country curacy of one hundred a year. He had no residence; and none, save themselves, knew the shifts they had been put to—the constant scheming and contriving they had been forced to exercise to live as gentlepeople and keep up appearances out of doors. His wife died; and, close upon it, the bishop gave him the living of St. Thomas, at Guild. Its emoluments were a small house and three hundred a year—great riches, in the eyes of the Reverend James Chester. He next married Penelope Hunter, who had two hundred a year of her own. Three children were subsequently born, Fanny, Thomas, and James. When the girl was ten years old and the youngest boy six, Mr. Chester died; and Mrs. Chester was left with Anna and her own children on her hands, a little good furniture and her two hundred a year to bring them up upon. So—as she told her half-brother—she had to scheme to live: she took this house, and hoped that would help her to do it.

"Well, and now what's the reason that Robert and Clara have not come?" began Mrs. Chester, without any other greeting, as she stood, bonnet and mantle on, to receive her guests. "I should like to know what Clara means by it! I had the coolest letter from her!—just putting off her visit to a future time, without saying with your leave or by your leave."

Fine nuts for the Miss Jupps to crack! They hastily recounted what had passed at their sisters' interview with Mrs. Lake, and her husband's words at the train in the morning. There was no time for more.

"If you ask my opinion," said Louisa Jupp, as they hurried off to the nearest church, "I should say that Mrs. Lake has acquired an objection to Sunday travelling."

"What a crotchet!" concluded Mrs. Chester. "I never quite understood my brother's wife."

CHAPTER IV

The Accident

It was a fine night, though not unusually light, for there was no moon, and the heavens looked a little misty, as they do sometimes following on a hot August day.

The nine o'clock train dashed into Guild, received its waiting passengers, and dashed on again.

Amidst others, the Miss Jupps and their brother entered it, having finished their day's visit to Mrs. Chester. They took their seats in the middle compartment of a first-class carriage, and happened to have it to themselves. The young ladies sat with their backs to the engine, he with his face to it.

"The Lakes would have had a pleasant day had they come," remarked Louisa. "You may rely upon it her objection lay in its being Sunday. Perhaps she is growing religious."

"What an awful lookout for Lake!" spoke up Mr. Jupp, from his corner.

"Oliver!" reproved the young ladies.

"She'll stop his liberty and his cigars," persisted Mr. Oliver: "there are no such martinets under the sun as your religious wives. Talking about cigars, would it affect your bonnets, girls, if I lighted one now?"

They screamed out together. They would not have their loves of new bonnets poisoned and blackened with cigar smoke; they'd never be fit to go on again. 'And you must not smoke in these carriages," added Louisa: "we are near Coombe Dalton station, and the guard would see you."

"Pretty wives you'll make when you are married," remarked Oliver. "Afraid of cigar smoke!"

The caution, or the bonnets, caused Oliver Jupp to keep his cigar-case in his pocket. Coombe Dalton station, an insignificant one, was about midway between Guild and Katterley. The train did not stop at it. Oliver leaned from the window to take a survey of the route.

"We are close to it," said he; "yonder are the lights. Halloa! what's the red light flashing up and down for? That ought to be a green."

"If a red light is waving in the green's place, there must be danger," said Rose, quickly. "Red is the danger signal."

"There's no danger. If the light indicated danger the train would come to a standstill; it is going on at the same speed."

Scarcely had the words quitted Oliver Jupp's mouth when—they scarcely knew what occurred. There was a shriek from the whistle, a shock; and a shriek, not from the whistle, but from human beings in their terror. The train came to a standstill and they with it: they and their carriage were not hurt or inconvenienced; the carriages behind them were not hurt, nor the carriages immediately before them, but the foremost carriages— What had happened?

Unstopped, and dashing on in its speed and recklessness, the engine had dashed into some obstruction on the line, a little past Coombe Dalton station. It ran up a bank, gave a dance, and was forced back on the line, falling sideways, and the three foremost carriages, next to the break van, were dragged with it. The two first, third-class ones, were greatly injured; the third, a second class, less so. Oliver Jupp, with other male passengers, was speedily out of his carriage, running forward to see what assistance he could render to those, his ill-fated fellow-creatures, some of whom were groaning in the death agony.

What a scene it was! The dark night; the hissing engine, mad instrument of death, but harmless now; the torches brought forward from the station to throw light upon the calamity; the figures, some dead, some dying, lying in the midst of the wreck; the scalded, the wounded, the bleeding; the silent and the still, the moaning and the helpless, the shrieking and the terrified! Not here, gratuitously to harrow feelings and sympathies, will the worst details be given; and, adding no little to the distress and confusion prevailing, was the uncontrollable alarm of the uninjured passengers, escaping from their carriages and running hither and thither, uncertain where to go or what to do. Katterley (as well as other stations) was telegraphed to for medical assistance.

Meanwhile Robert Lake and his wife had spent an exceedingly sober day. With the passing of the chance of danger, Clara's opinion experienced a sort of revulsion; and she began to think—not so much of how foolish she had been, but of how foolish she must appear in the eyes of her practical husband She said nothing; it was the wisest plan; and he had not alluded to it in any way. Quietly the day dragged on, and they sat down to supper in the evening; the dinner hour on Sunday being two o'clock.

It was at this juncture that Mary Jupp burst in without any ceremony whatever, neither bonnet on her head nor shawl on her shoulders. The news of the accident had spread like wildfire and penetrated to the house of the Jupps. Of course it had lost nothing in carrying; and Mary Jupp fully believed she should never see her sisters or brother again alive.

"Oh, Mr. Lake!—and you to be sitting here quietly at supper! Have you not heard the news?"

They rose up: they saw the state of alarm and agitation she was in. Clara caught the infection, and looked as frightened as her impromptu visitor. Mr. Lake was calm, cool; man in general is so.

"What news?" he asked. "What is it?"

"There has been an awful accident to the train at Coombe Dalton. No particulars positively known, that we can learn, but people are saying half the train's killed and the other half wounded."

"Sit down, sit down," said Mr. Lake, taking her trembling hands. "What train? How did the news come?"

"Why, our train!" returned the excited girl, bursting into tears. "The train that Oliver and Louisa and Rose must be in. Oh, Mrs. Lake! was it true that you had a presentiment of evil happening to it?—was that really your reason for declining to go?"

Clara, deathly pale, had sought the eyes of her husband She was overwhelmed with astonishment and dismay; with a feeling that she could not describe and had never yet experienced. Had they really escaped danger, accident, perhaps death, from that strangely vivid dream of warning? Her faculties seemed bewildered.

"How has the news reached Katterley?" repeated Mr. Lake, drowning the words about the dream, for he was conscious that a thoughtless slip of his had given the clue to Miss Jupp.

"By telegraph," she answered; "and one of the porters ran up to our house to tell it, knowing Oliver and the girls went to Guild this morning and took return tickets. The station here is already besieged by a crowd. Poor papa is pushing his way through it."

Mr. Lake caught up his hat, when at the same moment who should come in but Oliver Jupp. Mary seized upon him with a cry.

"Now don't smother me," cried he to her. "First of all, we are all right; you see I am, and Rose and Louy are safe and well inside Coombe Dalton Station. My father sent me in to tell you; he said you were here; and he is gone home to reassure them."

"But, Jupp, how did you get to Katterley?" questioned Mr. Lake.

"I came on a stray engine. I thought they would all be in fits together at home, and I took the opportunity offered, of coming on to stop the alarm. The first person who laid hold of me at the station was the poor old governor, pretty nearly in a fit himself. It's an awful accident, though."

"How was it?" "Are many hurt?" "Did the boiler really burst?"

"If you all reiterate questions at me at once, how am I to answer? Very few are hurt, comparatively speaking. The engine went into something, a truck or trucks I believe, and there was a smash. The two first carriages, both third-class, are—nowhere, and the passengers I won't tell you about, Lake, before these two girls, for it would spoil their night's rest. The next carriage, a second-class, was damaged, and its inmates are bruised, but not much, I think."

"And what of the rest of the train?" breathlessly inquired Clara.

"Nothing. The carriages came to a standstill on the line, and we got out of them."

"Are you sure there is no first-class carriage injured?" she continued.

"Certain. So to speak, there has been no accident to the rest of the train, beyond the delay and fright."

Mr. Lake looked at his wife and smiled. "So you would not have been one of the injured, Clary, had you been in the train."

She shook her head. "We have not the full particulars yet. Oliver may be deceived."

"It is exactly as I tell you, Mrs. Lake," said Oliver Jupp. "There is no further damage."

"Are you going back to Coombe Dalton?"

"Yes, as soon as I can. But I thought it well to come on and let you know the best and worst. Lake, will you go with me?"

"Of course," he answered.

The two young men went out together. Mary Jupp ran home, and Clara waited the return of her husband.

It was long past midnight when he came in. They sat up talking over the accident; the details which he had learnt, and seen. Oliver Jupp had been quite correct in his limit of the damage. Mrs. Chester (taking up the suggested notion that Clara Lake had stayed away because it was Sunday) had sent a very pressing invitation for her and her husband to come on the following day, Monday, with the two elder Miss Jupps. Mr. Lake delivered it to her.

"Will you go, Clara?"

"Will they go?" she rejoined. "Will they venture?"

"Venture!"

"After this accident?"

"I do not see why they should not. An accident two days running would be something remarkable. What about your dream?"

"Oh, I will go, Robert. Yes. The dream has done its office and I shall be ever thankful for it."

She spoke the last words reverently. Mr. Lake looked at her with surprise.

"Clara, don't encourage that fancy of yours," he gravely said, his voice taking almost a stern tone. "To be superstitious at all argues a want of common sense; but to be foolishly superstitious is a great deal worse. No reasonable being, wife of mine, would indulge that."

"What do you call being foolishly superstitious?"

"The remark you have just made—that the dream had done its office, and you should ever feel thankful for it—is an illustration. Had you gone to Guild this morning, you know quite well that we were not to have returned until Tuesday, therefore should not have been in the train to-night."

"Something might have occurred to cause us to return," she interrupted.

"Granted—for the sake of the argument. We should have travelled in a first-class carriage, as you know; and there is no first-class carriage injured."

He paused and looked at her. She could not deny anything he said, and kept silence.

"Therefore, what possible bearing that dream could have had upon the accident, or where could be the utility of the warning, which, as you declare, it conveyed to you, not to go to Guild, I cannot see."

Neither, it must be confessed, did Clara herself see it; but she did not lose her faith in the dream. Rather believed in it all the more firmly, in what her husband would have called a manner void of all reason.

The dream, as she looked at it and expressed it, had "done its work;" and she anticipated the excursion on the morrow with renewed pleasure, springing from a sense of relief.

Alas, alas! Poor short-sighted mortals that we are! The working out of the ill, shadowed forth, was only just beginning.

The morning rose brilliantly; rather too much so, taken in conjunction with the heat; and the day, as it wore on, promised to be one of the hottest on record.

Katterley station was in a bustle not often experienced at the quiet little place. People, idlers and others, crowded it, bent on a journey of curiosity to Coombe Dalton. The deaths from the accident now numbered several, and excitement was rife. Report came that the real cause of the calamity was giving rise to dispute: on the one hand it was said that the driver of the train had dashed through Coombe Dalton station, regardless of the warning red light, held up as a signal that he should stop; on the other it was maintained that no red light had so been held.

The twelve o'clock train came steaming into the Katterley station, where it would stay its accustomed three minutes, and those going by it looked alive. A very few passengers got out; a vast many rushed up to take their places. People were flocking to Coombe Dalton en messe; and would be flocking there until public curiosity was sated.

A porter held open the door of a first-class carriage for a party who were struggling on to the platform, one running before another; it consisted of two gentlemen, three ladies, and a maid-servant. The porter knew them well and touched his cap; Mr. and Mrs. Lake, Oliver Jupp, and his two eldest sisters.

"Let us have the compartment to ourselves, if you can manage it, Johnson," said Oliver in an undertone. "The day is too hot for crowding."

"Very well, sir," replied the man. "I dare say I can contrive it."

"But now whereabouts is this carriage?" called out one of the ladies, in a hasty and rather shrieking voice, as she looked to the right and left; "because, if it's not just in the middle, I won't get in. I'll never put myself towards either end of a train again as long as I live."

"Step in, step in," cried Oliver to her. "You are all right."

"Make haste, miss," added the porter. "The time's up."

"Of course it's up," repeated the young lady, who was no other than Mary Ann Jupp; "and I wonder it wasn't up before we reached it. This comes of putting off things till the last moment. I told you all the clocks were slow and we should be late. If there's one thing I hate more than another, it's the being obliged to rush up and catch a train at the last moment! No time to choose your carriage—no time to see or do anything; they may put you in the guard's van if they please, and you not know it until you are off. I dare say we have come without our tickets now. Has anybody thought of them?"

In reply, Oliver Jupp held up the six bits of cardboard for his sister's satisfaction, and the party settled themselves in their seats; the maid-servant, who was Mrs. Lake's, entering last.

"Why, Elizabeth, is that you?" exclaimed Miss Jupp. "I declare I never saw you."

"Didn't you, miss?" replied the girl, who was very tall and thin. "I walked behind you from our house."

"I thought it better to bring Elizabeth," interposed Clara Lake, who was looking unusually lovely in her summer dress—white muslin with a blue sprig upon it. "Mrs. Chester's servants will be glad of help with so many of us to wait upon."

"Mrs. Chester is the best manager of a house I ever saw," cried the Miss Jupps in a breath. They wore alpaca gowns of very light green, and hats trimmed with velvet. "Fancy!" added Margaret, "only two servants, and one of those you may almost call a nurse, for the children require plenty of attending to, and yet things seem to go on smoothly. I can't think how she contrives it."

"Trust to Mrs. Chester for contriving," said Mr. Lake. "She has to do it. Besides, you forget Anna."

The carriage held eight. Elizabeth sat at the farther end, the seat next to her and the seat opposite to her being empty. She kept her head close to the open window, looking out. Railway travelling was rare in her experience. The rest chatted eagerly, giving themselves up to the pleasure of the moment. Something was said about the previous day's sojourn at Guild.

"I hear it was a delightful party," Mrs. Lake remarked to Oliver Jupp.

"We wanted you and Lake to complete it," he answered. "It was too bad, Mrs. Lake, to declare off, after having promised to go. There was an uncommon nice girl spending the day there. She's to be there again today, I fancy."

"Who was that?" inquired Mr. Lake, briskly, who had a propensity for liking "nice girls."

"Don't know who she was, or anything about her," replied Oliver. "Your sister called her Lydia, and I did the same."

"It was a Miss Clapperton," interrupted Margaret Jupp. "Louisa and Rose were telling me about her this morning; they took an immense fancy to her."

"Clapperton?—Clapperton?" repeated Mr. Lake. "Oh, I know; a fresh family who have come lately to Guild. Penelope said she was getting intimate with them. You shall not pick out nice girls for me, Jupp, if you call her one. I saw her once: a young Gorgon in spectacles, with prominent eyes."

"That's Nancy Clapperton, the near-sighted one," corrected Mary Jupp, who was one of those ladies who like to put the world to rights. "It was her sister who was there yesterday, and she is a charming girl. Louy and Rose both say so."

"I hope she'll be there today, then," said Mr. Lake.

"She is to be there; but don't you and Oliver quarrel over her. He monopolized her yesterday, I hear."

"We'll go snacks," said Mr. Lake. "Or else draw lots: which shall it be, Jupp? When does the old Indian Begum make her entry?"

"For shame, Mr. Lake! You do turn everything and everybody into ridicule," exclaimed Margaret. "I'm sure I think she will be a delightful acquisition; so pleasant for your sister to have a visitor."

"Well, when does she come? Nobody says she won't be an acquisition—for those who can stand Begums. I knew one once, and she was awful. She had gold teeth."

Margaret Jupp turned to Clara.

"Why don't you keep your husband in better order? He is incorrigible."

"I fear he is," was the answer, given with a gay smile.

"Very strange!" cried Mr. Lake. "I can't get an answer to my question: I think it's somebody else that's incorrigible. When—does—the—Begum—arrive? I hope that's plain enough."

"Mrs. Chester was talking of her yesterday to me," interposed Oliver Jupp. "The Begum is expected to make her entrance on Wednesday or Thursday."

"When the house shall have been cleared of us sinful people," added Mr. Lake. "We are not good enough for an Indian Begum. What do you know of this one?"

"As good as nothing," answered Margaret Jupp. "That is, of late years. Papa and mamma used to know old Mr. and Mrs. Finch. He was a lawyer somewhere in London, and Angeline was the daughter."

"Angeline!"

"That's her name. Isn't it a fine one?"

"Very," said Mr. Lake. "The baptismal people must have foreseen she was destined to be a Begum."

The arrival at Coombe Dalton interrupted the conversation. Slackening its speed, the train came to a standstill. They inquired of a porter how long it stayed, and understood him to say "ten" minutes. So they got out, and heard almost immediately the train puff on again. The man had said "two." Looking at each other in consternation, a laugh ensued. The next train came up at three o'clock, and they could only wait.

Plenty of time now to examine the scene of the accident. They were not the only spectators. The battered engine, the débris of the carriages were there still—not on the line, but drawn away from it.

"In shunting some trucks on to the other line, one of them broke down, and could not be got off before our train came up," explained Oliver Jupp. "The engine ran into it, and—we were done for."

"But how dreadfully careless of the people at the station to allow your engine to run into it!" exclaimed Margaret. "They ought to have signalled your train to stop."

"They did signal it," interrupted a strange voice at her elbow, and Margaret turned to see the stationmaster, who was known to her brother and Mr. Lake. "The red lights were exhibited at the station, and a switchman waved the red signal light up and down, all to no purpose. You observe that post," he added, pointing to an iron post or pillar close to them, for he perceived she looked as if she scarcely understood him: "that is the night signal-post. When the line is clear, a green light is exhibited on it, as a notice that the trains may pass; but when it is not clear, a red light is substituted, and no train must proceed when the red light is there. Not only was the red light shown there last night, but the switchman, alarmed at the train's coming on so quickly, seized it, and waved it to enforce attention. The driver took no notice, and came dashing on to destruction."

"Was he killed?" inquired one of the bystanders, a knot of whom had gathered round.

"No," replied the stationmaster; "and his escape is regarded as next door to a miracle. He was flung from the engine, lay motionless, and was carried off for dead; but it appears he was only stunned, and is nearly well this morning. He'll have to stand his trial, of course; and a good thing for him if they don't bring it in 'Wilful Murder'—for that's what some of these careless engine-drivers will come to one day."

The official spoke with a good deal of acrimony. If the blame did not lie with the driver, it lay with him, and some hot dispute had been going on already that morning.

"Does the driver deny that the red light was up?" asked Mr. Lake.

"He denies it, and stands to it," said the aggrieved stationmaster. "He says the green lights were up as usual. The man's a fool."

"He had taken something to obscure his vision, possibly?"

"Well, no. I don't think he had done that. He is a sober man. It is a case of carelessness: nothing else. They go driving on, full pelt, never looking at the signals. On these quiet lines of rail, where there's not much traffic, the danger signal is not exhibited for weeks together. They get accustomed to see the other, and it becomes to them so much a matter of course that it must be there, that they forget to look at it at all. That, in my opinion, must have been the cause of last night's work, and I see no other possible way of accounting for it."

He turned back to the station as he spoke, and a gentleman, who had drawn near, held out his hand to greet the Lakes and the Jupps. It was Colonel West, an acquaintance who resided at Coombe Dalton.

"Oh, colonel," exclaimed one of the young ladies, "what a shocking accident this has been!"

"Ay, it has. Seven picked up dead, and four more gone this morning; besides legs, and arms, and backs broken. It is awful to think of."

"And all from one man's recklessness!" added Mr. Lake, with more severity, more feeling, than he generally suffered himself to display. "As the stationmaster says, they'll not be brought to their senses, these drivers, until some of them are convicted of wilful murder. I hope the man who drove the train last night will get his deserts."

The spectators generally, including Oliver Jupp, had strolled off in the wake of the stationmaster, he being the one from whom most news was to be expected, and their curiosity was craving for it. Colonel West, a keen, sensible man of fifty, brought himself to an anchor before Mr. Lake, touching him on the waistcoat to command attention.

"Let me disabuse your mind, at any rate. I hear they are putting the blame on the driver; but he does not deserve it, and they must be doing it to screen themselves. I know nothing of the man; I never saw him in my life until this morning; but I shall stand between him and injustice."

"In what way? what do you mean?" Mr. Lake inquired.

"They say at the station here that they exhibited the danger signal, red, and that the train dashed on regardless of it," said Colonel West. "I went to the inn this morning where some of the wounded are lying, and there I found the driver—as they told me he was—on a mattress on the floor. 'How did this happen?' I said to him. 'I don't know how it happened, sir,' he replied; 'but I declare there was no red signal up to stop me; the green light was up as usual.' That was the first I had heard about the red light," continued the colonel; "but I find the man said true, and that the whole blame is laid upon him. Now it happens that I was in my garden last night when the smash came, just over on the other side of the line, and I can bear the man's assertion out. It was the green light that was up, and not the red."

"Shameful!" exclaimed Mr. Lake, rising up at once against the injustice in his impulsive way. "I hope, colonel, you will stand by the man."

"You may be sure of that. I'd transport a reckless driver for life, if I could, but I would never see an innocent man falsely accused."

Having nothing to do with themselves, they strolled into the village, such as it was, the colonel with them. At the door of the small inn, whose floors had been put into requisition the previous night, on the green bench running under the windows, sat the driver of the engine, his head tied up with a white cloth and his arm in a sling. Colonel West introduced him: "Cooper, the driver." Cooper was a man of notoriety that day.

"Why, Cooper!" cried Mr. Lake in surprise the moment he saw the patient, "was it you who drove the engine last night?"

"Yes, sir, it was me," replied Cooper, standing up to answer, but sinking back at once from giddiness. "And I can only say I wish it had been somebody else, if they are going to persist in accusing me of causing the accident wilfully."

Mr. Lake knew him well. He was a young man, a native of Katterley, of very humble origin, but of good natural intelligence and exemplary character. It was only about a month that he had been promoted to be a driver; before that he was a stoker. "I need not have speculated on whether the driver was overcome by strong liquor, had I known who it was," said Mr. Lake.

"He tells me he never drinks," interposed Colonel West.

"Never, sir," said Cooper. "Water, and tea, and coffee, and those sort of things but nothing stronger. I had a brother, sir, who drank himself to death before he was twenty, and it was a warning for me. This gentleman and these ladies knew him."

Mr. Lake nodded acquiescence. "So they say the red light was up, do they, Cooper, and you would not see it?"

"I hear they are saying so at the station, sir; but it's very wrong. There was no other light up but the one that is generally up, the green. Should I have gone steaming on, risking death to myself and my passengers, if the danger light had been up? No, sir, it's not likely."

"Did you look at the signal light?" inquired Mary Jupp, who was always practical. "Perhaps you—you might, you know, Cooper—have passed it without looking just for once."

"I did look, miss; and I couldn't have been off seeing it last night, for it was being swung about like anything. 'What's up now,' I said to myself, 'that they are swinging the lamp about like that?' and I thought whoever it was doing it, must have had a drop too much."

"But don't you think you might from that very fact have suspected danger?" questioned Mr. Lake.

"No, sir, not from the green lamp. If they had wanted to warn me of danger, they should have swung the red. Any way, I'd rather have given my own life than it should have happened when I was driver."

"Cooper, I saw the green light swung as well as you; and I shall be happy to bear my testimony in your favour at the proper time and place," said Colonel West. "It is quite a providential thing that I happened to be in my garden at the time."

"Thank you, sir," said the man, earnestly, the tears of relief and emotion rising to his eyes.

Whiling away the time in the best way they could, they got back to the station a few minutes before the train for Guild was expected. The accident was the topic of conversation still.

"I have seen the driver," remarked Mr. Lake to the stationmaster. "I know him well, a sober, steady man. He persists still that the red signal was not exhibited; that it was the green."

"Oh, he does, does he?" returned the stationmaster. "He had better prove it. Of course, when they are at their wit's end for an excuse, they invent anything, probable or improbable."

"Cooper is not a man to invent. I am sure he is truthful."

"Let him wait till the inquest," was the significant reply.

The train came in, and they were taken on to Guild station. From thence they found their way to Mrs. Chester's, losing Oliver Jupp on the road.

"You disagreeable, tiresome things! what brings you here at this late hour?" was the greeting of Mrs. Chester, as she stood at the door, in no amiable mood, to receive her guests. "You knew we were to have dined at three o'clock, and taken dessert and tea on the lawn, I have been obliged to order the dinner to be put back."

"It was the train's fault," said Mr. Lake. "It deposited us halfway and left us."

"Of course you must put in your nonsense, Robert, or it wouldn't be you," retorted Mrs. Chester, who could be objectionably cross when put out, especially to him. "Come along with me, girls, and take your things off. Dinner will be on the table in twenty minutes."

She led the way to the staircase with scant ceremony. Mr. Lake touched her arm.

"A moment, Penelope, just to answer me a question. Is Lydia Clapperton here today?"

"Yes," was Mrs. Chester's answer, delivered impatiently. "Why?"

"Where is she?"

"In the garden, I think—or perhaps with the children. What do you want to know for?"

"Only to get the start of Oliver. He monopolized her yesterday, I hear."

"Where is Oliver?" demanded Mrs. Chester, suddenly remembering that he had not come.

"Oh! he went into the town to buy cigars, or something of the sort," responded Mr. Lake, as he turned to the garden, glad perhaps to get out of the reach of his sister's anger. That something besides their late arrival had put out Mrs. Chester was self-evident.

Across lawns, over flower-beds, behind trees, went Robert Lake, in search of the beauty that to him was as yet a vision—Lydia Clapperton. Good chance—or ill chance, just as the reader may deem—took him to a small summer-house at the end of a shady shrubbery, and in it he discerned a lady sitting; young and pretty, he decided in the semi-light. The lattice was trellised with the green leaves of summer flowers; roses and clematis clustered at the door.

He thought, looking at her in the subdued shade, that she must be four or five-and-twenty. Her dress was young—young for daylight. A rich black silk with a low body and short sleeves, edged by a ruche of white crape, a jet chain on her white neck, and jet bracelets. She had very decided aquiline features, thin and compressed lips. Her eyes were such that would have been called beautiful or hideous, according to the taste or fancy of the spectator: they were large, bold, and intensely black. Her hair was beautiful: a smooth purple black, very luxuriant, and disposed in an attractive manner round the head.

Mr. Lake took a private view through the interstices of the green stalks across the lattice.

"It is Lydia Clapperton," he said to himself; "and a fine girl!"

"There she is!" he began aloud, in his free and somewhat saucy manner—a manner that women like, when displayed by an attractive man—as he bared his head to enter the summer-house, and held out his hand with an abandon of all ceremony.

That she was surprised into the putting forth her hand in return, was indisputable. She had been intently bending over some fancy-work, netting; and she lifted her head with a start at the greeting, and let fall the work.

Mr. Lake took her hand; she looked up at him and saw a gay fascinating man, gentlemanly in the midst of his freedom. Drawing back her hand she sat down again, perfectly self-possessed.

"I told Mrs. Chester I should come and look for you," he said, in explanation. "I have the pleasure of knowing your sister, so we need not wait for a formal introduction."

"And you?" cried the lady, looking puzzled.

"You have heard, no doubt, of Mrs. Chester's brother, the scapegrace. She never gives me too good a word. I am out of her books again, through keeping her and the dinner waiting."

It happened that the young lady had never heard of Mr. Lake, as a scapegrace or otherwise. She did not say so, and went on with her netting work.

"Mrs. Chester has been wondering at the non-arrival of some friends she was expecting."

"And fuming at it too," returned Mr. Lake, with a light laugh. "We had an adventure. Getting out at Coombe Dalton in the supposition that there was plenty of time, the train went on without us. I am really sorry, though, for it has delayed your dinner."

"Oh that is nothing," was the answer, spoken in a spirit of politeness. "I would rather not dine at all than dine alone."

Mr. Lake sat down on the bench, took up her scissors, and seemed inclined to make himself at home. She glanced at his bright blue eyes, dancing with light gaiety and with admiration of her fair self.

"I think nothing is more pleasant than a country-house filled with visitors," she observed, tying a sudden break in the silk of her work, and holding out her hand for the scissors to cut the ends off.

"When they can do as they like," added Mr. Lake. "We shall remain until tomorrow night or Wednesday morning, I believe, and must make the most of it. And you—do you remain long?"

"My stay is quite uncertain."

"At least I hope you will be here until Wednesday. After that there'll be nothing to stay for; all the pleasure and the freedom must end; liberty will be replaced by restraint."

His tone had become serious. She paused again in her work, and lifted her eyes to speak.

"What restraint?"

"Mrs. Chester has sold her liberty to a Begum. Surely you must have heard of it! An old Indian Begum, who is coming to stay here, and takes possession the middle of the week. We must all be upon our good behaviour before her. No fun to go on then."

"An Indian Begum!" uttered the young lady, staring at him.

"Nothing less formidable, I assure you. She is expected to make the journey from town on an elephant. I shall draw a sketch of her after dinner for private circulation: shawls, fans, woolly hair, and propriety. She's a widow; the relict of a Sir George Ellis; we must not so much as whisper before her."

The lady laughed.

"Mrs. Chester has laid down rules for our conduct," he went on, in a rattling sort of fashion. "The last time I was at Guild she saw me snatch a kiss from a pretty girl who was staying with her; and a few days ago she appeared at my house with an inquiry of what I supposed my Lady Ellis would think of such conduct. You have no conception what a nightmare this Begum is to me—this old relict of a K.C.B."

"Really I don't wonder. Shawls, fans, woolly hair, and, an elephant! Old and ugly! Did you say ugly?"

"As if a Begum could be anything else! Not that her ugliness or beauty could affect one; but her interfering with the liberty of a fellow—that does it."

"But—according to your version—it is Mrs. Chester who seems to be interfering; not the Begum."

"It is all the same; excepting that, for Mrs. Chester we should not care, and for the Begum, I suppose, we must. I did think of getting a few days' fishing here this charming weather, but that's over now. I shall never stand that Begum—twirling one's thumbs before her; and speaking in measured monosyllables."

The young lady bent over her netting; she had made a long stitch. Glancing up, she saw those attractive eyes fastened on her. 'Mrs. Chester seems to wish to keep you in order," she remarked, bending them again.

"She does. It is her vocation. I listen to her pretty dutifully, and when her back's turned have a good laugh over it. Allow me to try and get that knot undone for you; it is giving you trouble."

"Why, what do you know about netting?" she asked, gaily.

"A great deal. I netted a boy's fishing-net once. Those long stitches are the very plague."

"A fishing-net!" she laughed. "Well, perhaps you did; but what do you think you could do to this fine silk: you, with your man's fingers?"

"I can try, so as to save the trouble to you." He bent as he spoke, and attempted gently to draw the work from her. She kept it tight. It really looked as though they had no objection, either of them, to lapse into a flirtation, when at that moment voices were heard, and Mr. Lake looked up. Passing across the shrubbery, by an intersecting walk, was Oliver Jupp, with a young lady by his side. She turned her head, and stood still for a moment, calling out to Mrs. Chester's children, who were behind, so that Mr. Lake had a view of her face.

"Who the deuce has Jupp picked up now?" murmured Mr. Lake, in a half-whisper. "She's an uncommon pretty girl." The lady also looked at them, letting her netting fall on her lap.

"Do you know who that young lady is?" he asked.

She disengaged the string from her foot, got up, and looked from the door. Mrs. Chester's children ran across the shrubbery with fleet feet and noisy tongues, and the sound of their voices faded away in the distance.

"It is a Miss Clapperton. Mrs. Chester introduced her to me by that name. Lydia Clapperton, I think, she called her."

Mr. Lake stared in his surprise. "That Lydia Clapperton!"

"Mrs. Chester certainly called her so."

"Why, then—who are you?"

"I? Oh, I am the Indian Begum; but I did not come on an elephant."

His pulses stood still for a moment. But he thought she was playing a joke upon him.

"You are not—you cannot be—Lady Ellis!"

"I am indeed. The old relict of Colonel Sir George Ellis, K.C.B."

Never in all his life had Robert Lake been so taken to, never had he felt more thoroughly confused and ashamed. The hot crimson mounted to his temples. Lady Ellis had sat down again, and was quietly going on with her work.

"I humbly beg your pardon, Lady Ellis," he said, standing before her as shamefaced as any convicted schoolboy. "I cannot expect you to accord it to me, but I most sincerely beg it."

"I think I must accord it to you," she answered, in a pretty tantalizing sort of manner. "Your offence was not against me, but against some fabled monster of your fancy. You shall sketch her still after dinner for private circulation."

The sound of a gong as she spoke gave notice that dinner was ready. Mr. Lake held out his hand with hesitation.

"Will you ratify your pardon, Lady Ellis? Will you promise to forget as well as forgive? I shall never forget or forgive myself."

She frankly put her hand into his as she rose. "I have forgiven; I will promise to forget. But then, you know, you must not convert me into a nightmare."

"You a nightmare!" he impulsively cried, some of his old lightness returning to him. "If you are, it will be one of a different kind: a nightmare of attraction," he gallantly added, as he offered her his arm. "What did you think of me? Did you take me for a wild animal just arrived from the savage islands?"

"No," said Lady Ellis; "that is what you took the Begum for. I found you were under a mistake as soon as you spoke of my sister. I have no sister. But what about your intention of fishing here? I am sorry that I should frustrate it."

He bit his lip; he could not conceal his annoyance. "I thought you promised to forget," he softly whispered.

"And so I will."

"When did you arrive?"

"Only an hour or so ago. Just in time to dress for dinner."

Leaving Lady Ellis in the drawing-room, he ran upstairs in search of his wife, and found her in the chamber which had been assigned them—a pleasant room, looking towards the lawn. She was at work: making a doll's frock for Fanny Chester.

"How hot you look!" she exclaimed, as her husband entered. "Your face is crimson."

"My brain is also," he replied. "What do you think?—Lady Ellis is here."

"Mrs. Chester told us so. She had a note from her this morning, and she herself arrived at two o'clock."

"Clary, I called her the Begum to her face."

"Oh!"

"I don't know what else I didn't call her: old and ugly, and a nightmare; and said she was coming on an elephant. In short, I did nothing but ridicule her. You see, I took her for that Lydia Clapperton."

Mrs. Lake's face turned red in its turn. She was of a refined, deeply-sensitive temperament, ever considerate of the feelings of others.

"What apology can you possibly offer, Robert? How can you make your peace?"

"I have made it already. She seems thoroughly good-natured, and saw the thing as it was—a misapprehension altogether. I'd rather have given a hundred pounds, though, than it should have happened. Why couldn't Penelope open her mouth and tell me she had come and was in the garden?"

He was splashing away at the water, having turned up his cuffs and his wristbands to wash his hands, evidently not on very good terms with himself. His wife put the doll's frock into her little ornamental basket and stood up to wait, watching him brush his hair. Then they were ready to go down.

"Clara."

"What?" she asked, turning round to him.

"Don't speak of this to any one, my darling. It really has annoyed me. I do not suppose Lady Ellis will."

"Of course I will not." And he bent his hot face over his wife's, and kissed it by way of thanks. "What is she like?" asked Clara.

"Young, and very good-looking."

A knock at the door. Mr. Lake opened it. There stood a fair girl of fifteen or sixteen, with soft brown eyes and a pale gentle face. Her hair, of a bright chestnut-brown, was worn plain, and her voice and manners were remarkably sweet and gentle. It was Anna Chester, Mrs. Chester's step-daughter. There was a sort of patient weary look about the girl, as if she had long had to do battle with care; her black merino dress, rather shabby, was only relieved by a bit of quilled white net round the throat, and plain stitched linen bands at the wrists.

"Mrs. Chester sent me to tell you that dinner is being taken in."

"We are ready for it. Here, Anna, wait a moment," added Mr. Lake, drawing her in and shutting the door. "What brings that Lady Ellis here? I thought she was not to come until Wednesday or Thursday."

"Neither was she," answered Anna. "It put us out very much this morning when we got her letter, because things were not ready. But we did the best we could."

"That accounts for Penelope's sharpness," remarked Mr. Lake. "But she could not have come from Cheltenham this morning, Anna!"

"No, from London. She left Cheltenham on Saturday, she told, us, and wrote from London yesterday."

"Now then, you people!" called out Mrs. Chester's voice from the foot of the stairs.

"Come along, Anna," said Mr. Lake.

"Oh, I am not going to dine with you," was the girl's answer. "There would be nobody to see that things went on properly, and to wash the forks and spoons."

For Mrs. Chester had not sufficient forks and spoons to serve for all her courses without washing. The dinner was made more elaborate than it need have been, in honour of the first appearance of Lady Ellis at table. Anna Chester spoke cheerfully, with patient meekness, as if it were her province to be put upon; and Robert Lake muttered an angry word in his wife's ear about Mrs. Chester's selfishness.

In the corridor they encountered Mary and Margaret Jupp, and all descended together. The party was going into the dining-room; Mrs. Chester had momentarily disappeared; Oliver was laughing with Lydia Clapperton; Mr. Lake went up to him and claimed to be introduced; the Miss Jupps seized upon Lady Ellis with greetings and reminiscences of old times; and altogether there was some confusion. Clara Lake, naturally retiring, slipped into the dining-room behind the rest, and took her seat unobtrusively by the side of Fanny Chester. So that it happened she was not introduced to Lady Ellis. That Indian widow, casting her roving eyes around, heard her called "Clara" once or twice by Mrs. Chester, and took her for the governess. A young curate in a straight coat down to his heels, made the tenth at table.

"Mamma said I was to dine here," whispered Fanny, confidentially to Mrs. Lake, "or else there would have been an odd number."

Mr. Lake took the foot of the table, and had Lady Ellis on his right. They talked together a great deal. Altogether it was a very social dinner, plenty of laughing. Anna Chester washed up spoons and forks outside the door, kept the little boys in order, and saw to things generally.

Dinner over, they went on the lawn, where a table was set out with wine and fruit and cakes. But none of them seemed inclined to sit down to it at first; preferring to disperse in groups, and flit about amidst the walks and flowers. Oliver Jupp appropriated Lydia Clapperton, and Mr. Lake was perfectly content that it should be so. For himself he was everywhere; now with Mary Jupp; now with Margaret; now with his sister; and now, and now, and now with Lady Ellis. Chiefly with her: and she by no means objected to the companionship. In short it was a delightful, unceremonious, laisser-aller sort of gathering, with Mrs. Chester seated in her weeds to play propriety, whilst her young boys, left to themselves, got into as much mischief as they possibly could.

"And so you found yourself restless at Cheltenham?" remarked Mr. Lake, as he and Lady Ellis emerged once more in the open ground from some one of the many side walks.

"I get restless everywhere. India suited me best. It may be different, perhaps, when once I settle down."

"I never saw Cheltenham. It is a charming place, according to report."

"At this season it is nothing but heat and dust. I did intend to stay there until the middle of this week; but I couldn't do it. I could not, Mr. Lake. So I went up to London on Saturday night, and wrote word to your sister that she must expect me on Monday."

They were crossing the lawn. Seated now near Mrs. Chester, at the table, was Clara Lake, who had been beguiled indoors by Fanny Chester to the doll's frock. That important work being accomplished, Clara had come out again. Lady Ellis—her black lace shawl draped artistically round her shoulders, and her very brilliant black eyes darting their glances here and there, fixed their light upon Clara.

"Who is that young lady, Mr. Lake?"

He looked surprised, and then smiled. "Don't you know?"

"I don't know who she is. I know that she is one of the very boldest girls I ever saw."

"She bold!" returned Mr. Lake, in marked astonishment, while a flush darkened his cheek. "You are mistaken, Lady Ellis."

"Bold; and unseemly bold," repeated Lady Ellis. "I speak of that young lady who is now sitting by Mrs. Chester. Some of them called her 'Clara' at dinner. I thought she might be the governess, but she seems to take too much upon herself for that."

"I understand of whom you speak. But why do you call her bold?"

Lady Ellis was silent for a moment, and then lifted her head. "When we have lived in India, have travelled—in short, have rubbed off the reserve and rusticity which experience of the world only can effect, we like to speak out our opinion, and call things by their right names. Half an hour ago you were with her in that walk, talking to her; she held your arm, and she suddenly clasped her other hand over it, and kept it there, turning her face up to yours with what looked very like ardent admiration. It struck me as being not—not seemly."

Mr. Lake coughed down a laugh. "She has a legal right to look in my face as ardently as she pleases: and you may fully believe me when I assure you that from her you will never witness aught unseemly. That young lady is my wife.'

"Your—wife!" echoed Lady Ellis, taken utterly by surprise.

"My own wife." His saucy blue eyes gazed into those amazed black ones, enjoying their confusion with an exceedingly saucy expression. Lady Ellis burst into a laugh.

"Well, I suppose I must beg your pardon now. We all seem to be letting ourselves in for mistakes and blunders. I thought she was a young girl, and I did not know you were married."

"She does look young," he answered, his eyes following his wife's pretty figure, as she went towards the house with Mrs. Chester; "nevertheless she has been my wife these three years."

"You must have married early. Is it wise, think you, of a man to do so?"

"Wise?—In what respect?"

"Repentance might come. Men scarcely know their own minds before thirty."

"A great many of us risk it."

They sat down at the dessert-table, and Mr. Lake helped her to some wine and fruit. One of the little boys ran up and clamoured for good things in the absence of his mother. Lady Ellis privately thought that children did not improve the social relations of the world.

Mrs. Chester had taken Clara to look at what she called the domestic arrangements, which in reality meant the kitchens and back premises in general. Encountering Miss Jupp as they went, she turned to accompany them.

"Had you come at the time you ought, I should have shown you over the house before dinner," grumbled Mrs. Chester, who could not forget the upsetting of her plans.

"Of course we were very sorry," spoke Mary Jupp. "It is so tiresome to put back one's dinner after it is at the fire. I should have been more cross than you, Mrs. Chester."

"What with one thing and another, I have been cross enough today," confessed Mrs. Chester, giving a jerk to her widow's cap, which never kept on two minutes together, wanting strings. "First of all, this morning, came Lady Ellis's letter to upset me, and with nothing ready for her!"

"Why did she come today?"

"Some whim, I suppose. It was a courteous letter of excuse—hoping I should pardon her, and begging me not to treat her as a stranger. How very handsome she is!"

"Her features are handsome," rejoined Mary Jupp; "but their expression's bad."

"Bad!" cried Mrs. Chester.

"I think so. There's nothing good or kind in them; and she's eaten up alive with vanity. You must take care of your husband, Clara, for she seems to covet his admiration."

Clara Lake, who was in advance, looked back and laughed merrily.

"How can you put such notions in her head?" spoke Mrs. Chester, severely. "Robert Lake's manners with women are in the highest degree absurd; but there's no need for his wife to be reminded of it to her face."

"I don't mind being reminded of it, Mrs. Chester. It means nothing."

"Of course it does not. I only hope Lady Ellis will not take offence at him. What age is she, I wonder—five-and-twenty?"

"Five-and-thirty, if she's a day!" spoke Mary Ann Jupp, in her strong decision. "She is made-up, you know—cosmetics and that, and dresses to look young. But just look quietly at her when the sun is on her face."

"But she cannot be that age."

"I think she is. I will ask mamma when I get home: she knows."

The subject dropped. Mrs. Chester took them round the house, and in at the back door, showing one thing, explaining another. The larder and the dairy were first entered.

"That is what was once the dairy," observed Mrs. Chester. "Of course, I want nothing of the sort, not possessing cows. It will do to keep herbs and pots and pans in. This is the kitchen," she continued, turning into a large, convenient room on the right of the boarded passage.

"Why, it is like print!" exclaimed Mary Jupp, in her hasty way. "There's not a speck of dirt about it; everything is in its place. How in the world have they got it into this order so soon after dinner?"

"This is the best kitchen," explained Mrs. Chester; "they cook in the other. Don't you see that there's no fire? We shall use this in winter, but while the weather is so hot, I like the cooking done as far from the sitting-rooms as possible. Farm-houses generally have two kitchens, you know. The other is in the yard. You can come and see it."

They went out of the room, but Clara did not. She stood rooted to the spot, like one in a trance, rather than a living, breathing woman. She glanced here, she glanced there; at the doors, the large window, the fireplace; at the furniture, and position of everything. Her breathing came softly; she pressed her brow to make sure she was awake.

Mrs. Chester and Mary Jupp came back, and she had not stirred: her cheek was pale, her hands were clasped, she looked very like a statue. Mrs. Chester began explaining where the several doors led to: one down to the cellar, one to the coal-house, one to the dairy, and one to a china closet; four in all, besides the entrance door. Both of them were too busy to notice her.

"Are you coming, Clara?" asked Miss Jupp, as they went out.

"Directly," she replied, speaking quietly. "Mary, I wish you would find my husband, and tell him I want him here for a minute."

"You want to show him what a model place it is," cried Mrs. Chester, complacently. "Do so, Clara. He will never have such a kitchen in his house."

Mary Jupp delivered the message to Mr. Lake, who was still at the table, and peeling a pear for Lady Ellis. The objectionable boy had disappeared. He came away when he had finished his job, leaving the two ladies together. Mrs. Chester had hastened in dire wrath after the other of her mischievous young sons, who was climbing up a prickly tree, to the detriment of his clothes.

"I had no idea until just now that Mr. Lake was a married man," observed Lady Ellis to Mary Jupp, as she leisurely eat her pear.

"No! Then whom did you suppose Mrs. Lake was?"

"I did not suppose anything about it; I did not know she was Mrs. Lake. Have they been married long?"

"About three years."

"Ah, yes; I think he said so. Any children?"

"There was one. A beautiful little child; but it died. Do you not think her very lovely? It is so sweet a face!"

Lady Ellis shrugged her shoulders. "She has no style. And she seems as much wrapt up in her husband as though they had been married yesterday."

"Why should she not be?" bluntly asked Miss Jupp. "I only hope when I am married—if ever that's to be—that I and my husband shall be as happy and united as they are."

"As she is," spoke Lady Ellis. "I would not answer for him."

Mary Jupp felt cross. It occurred to her that somebody might have been whispering tales about Mr. Lake's nonsensical flirtation with her sister Rose: and purely innocent nonsense, on both sides, she knew that to be. "Young Lake is one of those men who cannot live without flirtation," she observed, "who admire every woman they meet, and take care to let her know it. His wife can afford to laugh at it, knowing that his love is exclusively hers."

Lady Ellis drew down the corners of her mouth and coughed a little cough of mocking disbelief; for which Mary Jupp, upright and high-principled, could have scolded her for an hour.

"So very old-fashioned, those notions, my dear Miss Jupp. Love!"

"Old-fashioned, are they?" fired Mary.

"A woman hazards more than she perhaps bargains for, when she ties herself, for better or for worse, to one of these attractive men: but of course she must put up with the consequences."

"What consequences?" exclaimed Mary Jupp, feeling herself puzzled by the speech altogether.

"The seeing herself a neglected wife: the seeing others preferred before her—as she must inevitably do when her own short reign is over."

"Had you to experience that?" sharply asked Mary Jupp, intending the question as a sting.

"I!" equably returned Lady Ellis. "My husband had nothing attractive about him, and was as old as Adam. I spoke of the wives of fascinating men: others may humdrum on to their graves, and be at peace."

"I don't see what there is to fascinate in young Lake. He is light-headed and careless, if that means fascination."

"Ah," superciliously remarked Lady Ellis, playing with her jet chain.

They were interrupted by Margaret Jupp, who came up with Mrs. Chester. The young lady, hearing of the expedition to the kitchens, was not pleased to have been omitted, so Mrs. Chester was going to do the honours again.

"I think there's nothing so nice as looking over a house," said Margaret. "Kitchens have great interest for me."

"I suppose I may not ask to be of the party?" interposed Lady Ellis, looking at Mrs. Chester.

"Certainly you may: why not?" And they slowly strolled across the lawn on the expedition.

Meanwhile Mr. Lake, in obedience to the summons, had found his wife in the large kitchen. She was still standing in the middle of the floor, just as though she had been glued to it.

"Did you want me, Clara?"

"Do come here," she whispered, in quite an awestruck tone. And Mr. Lake, wondering a little, stepped up and stood beside her. Clara, touching his arm, pointed to different features of the room, turning about to do it.

"Do you see them, Robert? Do you remember?"

"I have not been in the kitchen before," was his answer, after a pause, looking curiously at the room and then at her.

"It is the kitchen of my dream!"

"The what?" exclaimed Mr. Lake.

"The kitchen I saw in my dream."

He barely stopped an irreverent laugh. What he saw upon her face arrested it.

"It is," she whispered, her voice sounding strangely hollow, as though some great physical change had taken place within. "I described its features to you that night, and now you may see them. We—we are standing in the same position!" she burst forth more eagerly, as if the fact had but that moment occurred to her. "See! I was here, you on that side me, as you are now; here was the small round dark table close to us; there is the large window, with the ironing-board underneath it; there, to the left, are the dresser and the shelves, and even the very plates and dishes upon them—"

"Of the precise willow pattern," put in Mr. Lake.

"There, behind us, is the fireplace; and around are the several doors, in the very self-same places that I saw them," she continued, too eager to notice or heed the mocking interruption. "I told, you it looked like a farm-house kitchen, large and bleak: you may see that it does, now."

"I shall begin to think that you are dreaming still," he returned.

"I wish I was! I wish I had never seen in reality the kitchen of that dream. I did not at the first moment recognise it. When I came in with Mrs. Chester and Mary Jupp, the place struck me as being familiar, and I was just going to say to them, 'I must have been here before,' when my dream flashed upon me, like a chill. I felt awestruck—sick; I feel so yet."

"This beats spirit-rapping," said Mr. Lake. "Let us lay hold of the table, and see whether it won't turn."

"Why will you turn it into mockery?" she resumed, her tone one of sharp pain. "You know that dream seemed to foretel my death."

"I declare to goodness, Clara, you will make me angry!" was his retort, his voice changing to severity. "What has come over you these last few days?"

"That dream has come over me," she replied, with a shiver. "I thought it was done with; done with by the accident of last night; and now the sight of this kitchen has renewed it in all its horror. If you could, only for one minute, feel as I am feeling, you would not wonder at me."

Her state of mind appeared to him most unaccountable: not foolish; that was not the word; far worse than foolish—obstinate and unreasonable. Never in his life had he spoken so sharply to her as he spoke now. Perhaps his recent intercourse with that equable woman of the world, Sir George's relict, had given him new ideas. "I should be sorry to feel it, even for a minute; I should be ashamed to do so: and I feel ashamed for you. What did you want with me?"

"To show you the kitchen. To tell you this."

He gave vent to an impatient word, and turned angrily to the door. She, her heart bursting, went forward to the window. Just so had it been in the dream; just so had they seemed to part, he going to the door and she to the window; just so had been her sharp conviction of coming evil. Mr. Lake looked back at her; she had laid her head against the wall near the window: her hands drooped down; in her whole air there was an utter agony of abandonment. His better nature returned to him, and he walked across the kitchen. As he drew her face from the wall he saw that it was white, and the tears were running down her cheeks.

"Clara," he exclaimed, as he took her to himself, "must I treat you and soothe you as I would a child?"

"No, treat me as your wife," she passionately answered, breaking into a storm of sobs.

He suffered her to sob for a few moments, until the paroxysm had spent itself, and then spoke; in a tone of remonstrance, it is true, but with deep tenderness. "Is it possible that you can allow a foolish superstition, a dream, to cause this wild grief?"

"It is not the dream that is causing the grief. You are causing that: you never so spoke to me: when I said it might foretel my death, you turned my words into ridicule. It is as if you do not care whether I live or die."

"Clara, you know better. What can I do for you? How can I soothe you?"

"Do not speak to me in that tone again."

"My dearest, I will do anything you wish in reason; you know I will, but you must not ask me to put faith in a dream. And if my voice sounded harsh—why, it would vex any man to find his wife so foolish."

"Well, well, it shall pass; I will not vex you with it again. If any ill does come, it must; and if not—"

"If not, you will acknowledge what a silly child you have been," he interrupted, kissing the scalding tears from her face.

"Silly, and superstitious, if you will," she whispered, "but not a child. I think I am less a child at heart than many who are older. Robert, if you ever grew unkind to me, I should die."

"That I never shall, my darling."

Standing outside the half-open door, taking a leisurely survey through the chink, was Lady Ellis, having come noiselessly along the passage matting; not purposely to deceive, she was not aware there was anything to see, but her footsteps were soft, her movements had mostly something cat-like about them. She saw his face bent on his wife's, and heard his kisses, all but heard his sweet words; heard quite enough to imagine them. An ugly look of envy, or something akin to it, rose momentarily to her pale features. Legitimate love such as this had never been hers. Mr. Lake was what she had called him, an attractive man. He had that day paid her attentions, said sentimental nothings to her in a low voice; and there are some women who would fain keep such men to themselves, whether they may have wives or not; nay, their having a wife is only an inducement the more. Was Lady Ellis one?

The smile changed its character for that of mockery. It flashed into my lady's mind that this little domestic scene was one of reconciliation after dispute, and that the dispute must have had its natural rise in those recent attentions paid to herself. The voices of Mrs. Chester and Margaret Jupp were heard approaching, and she made her safe way back to them.

"Let it pass, let it pass, Clara," Mr. Lake said hastily to his wife, hearing the voices also. "My dear, there is no reason in your fear. What harm do you suppose can arise from your visit here? There is no chance of a breakdown again as we go home."

"It is just that—that I cannot see any probability of harm. But I gave you my word just now to say no more about the matter, and I will keep it."

"Come and walk in the air, it will do you good. Your eyes are as red as if you had been crying for a day, Clara."

Lady Ellis pushed the door open and came in, followed by the others. Mrs. Chester began expatiating upon the conveniences of the kitchen, its closets and cupboards, and Mr. Lake and his wife slipped away. My lady, looking from the window, saw him pass it towards the kitchen garden, his wife upon his arm.

CHAPTER V

Red, or Green?

The inquest on those killed by the railway accident took place on the Tuesday morning. Numbers were attracted to the spot, impatient to hear the evidence. Reports had been busy as to the conflicting nature of the testimony expected to be given, and excitement was at its height. While one party openly asserted that Cooper, the driver, was falsely trying to "whiten" himself, and so avoid punishment for his carelessness; the stationmaster was less loudly accused of having been the one in fault, and with "taking away the man's character."

Amidst the crowd, meeting at Coombe Dalton, were Mr. Lake and Oliver Jupp: the one went from Guild, the other from Katterley. Oliver Jupp, with his sisters, said adieu to Mrs. Chester on the Monday evening, and returned home: Mr. Lake and his wife stayed at Guild. Curiosity or interest in the proceedings, or opposition in their own opinions, took them both. Mr. Lake felt certain that Cooper spoke truth in saying the green light was exhibited, not the red; would have been ready to stake his life upon it. Oliver Jupp, relying upon his own eyesight, upheld the side of the stationmaster. Each one had maintained tenaciously his own opinion when discussing the affair at Mrs. Chester's; and they would not have missed the inquest for the world.

In the largest room that the small inn at Coombe Dalton could afford, the coroner and jury assembled, and proceedings commenced. About the cause of death there could be no doubt; and it needed not the testimony of old Dr. Marlow, of Katterley, who had been the first doctor to arrive at the spot on the Sunday night, to prove it. However, the requirements of law must be obeyed, and he was there with sundry of his brethren. Next came the evidence as to the cause of the accident.

The stationmaster, one porter, and a "switchman," comprised the officials who had been at the station on the Sunday night. They all gave their testimony in a very positive and unequivocal manner: that the red lights were exhibited to give warning of danger, and that the train, in reckless defiance of the red, came dashing on, and so caused the catastrophe.

"What was the danger?" officially inquired the coroner.

"Some trucks were on the line just beyond the station, and had to be shunted," replied the stationmaster. "Three minutes would have done it; and the train would not have been kept waiting longer than that, had it only stopped."

"What brought the trucks on the line just as the train was expected to pass?"

"They couldn't be shunted before, because the coal waggons were in the way."

"Why were the coal waggons there just then?"

"Because an engine had gone on and left them there."

And so on; and so on—engine, and coal waggons, and shunting, and trucks. It was like "the house that Jack built." Nobody had been in fault, apparently, or done anything wrong, except the miserable train that had dashed on to its destruction, and its still more miserable driver, Matthew Cooper.

Cooper came forward and asked leave to give his evidence. The coroner cautioned him; he thought he had better not; it might be used against him. But Cooper persisted; and he stood there to say what he had to say, his pale face, surrounded by its bandages, earnest and anxious.

"I'll say nothing but the truth, sir. If that is to be used against me, why I can't help it. I'd not tell a lie even to screen myself."

He took his own course, and gave his evidence. It was to the effect that the green lights were exhibited as usual that night, not the red. The coroner felt a little staggered. He knew Cooper to be a steady, reliable, truth-telling man. One of the witnesses observed, as if in continuation of what Cooper had just said, that "Mat Cooper wouldn't tell a lie to screen himself from nothing." The coroner had hitherto believed the same.

"Did you look at the lights?" he asked of Cooper.

"I looked at both, sir. The lamp that was at the near end of the station, and the lamp on the signal-post beyond it."

"And you say they were the green lights?"

"That they were, sir. The same green lights that are always up. He had taken the light off the post, and was swaying it about, and I couldn't conceive what he was doing it for."

"But here are three witnesses, the stationmaster and the two men, who have sworn that the red signals were up, and not the green," persisted the coroner. "It is very strange that you should maintain the contrary."

"The three may be in a league together to say so, and hide their own negligence," audibly interposed the voice of some zealous partisan from the most crowded part of the room. Upon which the coroner threatened to commit anybody so interrupting, for contempt of himself and the court.

"All I can say is, sir, that there was no difference, that night, in the lights from those exhibited on other nights," returned Cooper. "They were the green lights, and not the red; and if I had to die next minute, I'd say it."

Which was altogether unsatisfactory to the coroner and puzzling to the jury. Most of them knew Cooper well, and would have trusted him; his voice and face, now as he spoke, bore their own testimony to his truth. On the other side, the three station people, who were not to be discredited, gave him the lie direct.

"Did you see the red light swung about?" continued the coroner.

"No, sir. I saw the green; and I couldn't think what it was being swung about for."

Cooper held to this, and nothing more could be got from him—that is, nothing to a different effect. He would have descanted on its being the green light until night, had the coroner allowed him. When he was done with, a gentleman presented himself for examination. It was Colonel West.

"Can you state anything about this matter, Colonel?" asked the coroner, when he had exchanged bows with the voluntary witness.

"Yes, I can, if you will allow me to be sworn." And sworn he was.

"In anxiety to see justice done to the driver, I have come here to offer my testimony," began the colonel, addressing the coroner and jury. "I am enabled to state that the light exhibited on the signal-post, and which the man took down and swayed about, was green. When the driver asserts that it was not red, he speaks the truth."

Some excitement. The coroner drew in his lips, the jury put their heads together. Colonel West stood bolt upright, waiting to be questioned.

"Were you at the station?" inquired the coroner of the witness.

"No; I was in my garden, which is precisely opposite the signal-post on the other side of the line. I was walking about in it, smoking a cigar. I heard the train approaching, and I saw the man take the lamp off the post, lean forward, and swing it about, evidently to attract attention. A minute afterwards the accident happened."

"And you say this was not the red light?"

"It was not. It was the light that is generally up, the green."

The coroner gave an expressive look at the stationmaster, which spoke volumes, and the latter looked red and indignant. Colonel West reiterated his assertion, as if willing that all should be impressed with the truth, and with the injustice attempted to be dealt to Cooper. Then he stood down.

There ensued a commotion: at least, if numerous tongues can constitute it. The coroner interposed to stop it and restore order. When the noise had subsided, Oliver Jupp was standing by the table in Colonel West's place. One of the jury inquired of him why he was put forward.

"I don't know," returned Oliver. "Somebody pushed me up. I happened to mention that I saw the light in question exhibited and swayed about: I suppose it is for that."

"Oh, you saw it, did you," said the coroner. "Swear this witness."

Oliver Jupp took the oath accordingly, and the coroner began.

"Which light was it, the red or the green?"

"The red."

There was a pause. Perhaps more than one present thought of the old fable of the chameleon. The room fixed its eyes on Oliver Jupp.

"From whence did you see it?" demanded the coroner.

"I was in the train returning from Guild. As we got to Coombe Dalton station I looked out at the window, and saw a red light being waved about. I remarked it to my sisters, who were in the carriage with me, and one of them observed that if it was the red light there must be danger. The accident occurred almost as she spoke."

"Are you sure it was the red light, sir?" inquired one of the jury, all of whom had been so particularly impressed with Colonel West's evidence.

"Certain."

"And of course he could have no motive in saying anything but the truth," remarked the juryman to another, who seemed in a state of perplexity.

"I a motive!" haughtily observed Oliver, taking up the words. "I am put here simply to state what I saw, I expect; neither more nor less. I am sorry to give evidence that may tell against Cooper, who is respected in Katterley, but I am bound to say that it was the red light."

"Don't you think you might have been mistaken, sir?" came the next query; for Oliver Jupp's word, a young and little man, bore less weight than Colonel West's, who counted five-and-fifty years, and stood six feet two in his stockings.

"I was not mistaken. It was the red light."

Colonel West was recalled. What else could they do in the dilemma? He stood forward, and Oliver Jupp hid his head amid the ignoble crowd close behind.

With an apology for the apparent doubt, the same question was put to him. Did he think he could have been mistaken in supposing the light was the green.

"Not a bit of it," the colonel answered, with good-humoured equanimity. The lights exhibited that night were the same that always were exhibited—green. The light he saw swayed about was the green.

"Well," exclaimed the coroner, "there's hard swearing somewhere."

And hard swearing there certainly appeared to be. As a spectator audibly remarked, "one could not find an end out of it." The coroner got impatient.

"It is impossible at the present stage to come to any satisfactory conclusion, gentlemen of the jury," he observed; "and I think we had better adjourn the inquiry, when other witnesses may be forthcoming."

Adjourned it was accordingly for a fortnight.

"But for Colonel West they'd have had it all against me," remarked Cooper, who was feeling himself wronged.

"But for Colonel West there'd have been no further bother," cried the aggrieved stationmaster, who thought Cooper ought to have been committed for trial on the spot.

It was certainly singular that the only two witnesses, apart from those interested, should testify so positively in exact opposition to each other. As the spectators poured out of the inquest-room, they formed into knots to discuss it. Neither the one nor the other had any interest to favour the station people or to screen Cooper; and, indeed, both were above suspicion of anything of the sort. Colonel West had never before heard of Cooper; Oliver Jupp knew him, and was evidently sorry to give evidence against him. On the other hand, Oliver Jupp did not know the stationmaster, while Colonel West was friendly with him.

"Will you go back with me to Guild, and stay the rest of the day?" asked Mr. Lake, putting his arm within Oliver Jupp's.

"Can't," returned Oliver. "Promised them at home to get back with the verdict as soon as it was over."

"But there is no verdict."

"All the same; they'll want to know the why and the wherefore."

"As if you could not keep the girls waiting for once!"

"It's not the girls, it's the old folks; and Guild has no charms for me today. Lydia Clapperton's gone."

Mr. Lake laughed. "I say, Jupp, how could you swear so hard about the lights?"

"They swore me. I didn't ask for it."

"I mean against Cooper."

"You would not have me say the light was green when it was red?"

"Colonel West says it was green; he was close to it."

"Moonshine," quietly repeated Oliver. "What on earth causes him to say it I can't make out. Look there"—holding out the end of the cigar he had lighted, and was smoking—"what colour do you call that?"

"Red. All the world could tell that."

"Why don't you say it's green?"

"Because it is not green."

"Just so. Neither was the red lamp."

"Cooper is a reliable man; I don't believe the poor fellow would tell a lie to save himself from hanging; and Colonel West is of known honour; both of them assert that the lights were green."

"I swear that the light exhibited and swung about was red," retorted Oliver Jupp. "There; let it drop. Are you and Mrs. Lake coming home to-night?"

"No. It was uncertain what time I might reach Guild after the inquest, and Mrs. Chester seized upon it as a plea for urging us to remain another night. She wants us to stay for the week, but I don't think we shall. Clara seems rather averse to it."

They parted at the station. Oliver Jupp taking the train for Katterley: and with him we have nothing more to do at present. Mr. Lake got into the train for Guild.

Upon arriving at Mrs. Chester's he found the house empty. Going from room to room in search of them, he at length came upon Anna Chester, mending socks and pinafores.

"Where are they all?"

"I think they have gone to see the late rose show," she said; "there's one in the town today."

He stood by while she folded some pinafores she had finished. Her hands were quick; her sweet face was full of patient gentleness.

"It is not the right thing for you, Anna."

"It is pleasant work. I have been obliged to be useful all my life, you know."

"I don't mean that. Why should you be left at home, while they all go to a flower-show?"

A bloom, bright as any rose in the famous show, shone in the girl's cheeks. She loved flowers, and looked up with a happy expression.

"Perhaps time will be found for me to go tomorrow; mamma said so. It will be only sixpence then."

"And today it's a shilling, I suppose?"

"Yes."

Mr. Lake nodded his head once or twice in a rather marked manner, but did not give utterance to his thoughts, whatever they might be. Anna resumed.

"I do all the work I can—of sewing and other kinds. It has cost mamma so much to get into this house, with the new things she has been obliged to buy, that she says she is nearly ruined. With Lady Ellis here, and only two servants, we could not get along at all but for my looking to everything."

Mr. Lake went off muttering something about Penelope's selfishness. That Anna was put upon quite like another Cinderella he had long known, and his sense of fairness rose up against it.

"If the girl was a tyrant she'd not have stood it for a day," he cried, as he flung himself down on a bench and raked the gravel with his cane. "A meek temper is a misfortune."

A short while, and he heard the keys of the piano touched in the drawing-room; a soft, sweet, musical voice broke out gently in song. He knew it for Anna's. She had finished her work, and was snatching a moment for music, having come in to get the table ready for tea. The open piano tempted her. Mr. Lake listened through the song—an old one; and put his head in at the window as she was rising.

"Sing another for me, Anna."

She started round with a blush. To believe you are singing for yourself, and then to find you have an audience, is not agreeable.

"Oh, Mr. Lake! I did not know you were there."

"Just another, Anna."

"I cannot sing for you. I know only old songs."

"They are better than the new ones. The one you have just sung, 'Ye banks and braes,' is worth any ten that have been issued of late years."

"I feel quite ashamed to sing them before people; I am laughed at when I do. Lady Ellis stopped her ears this morning. Papa loved the old songs, and he did not care that I should sing new ones; so I never learnt any."

He took up a book of music much worn, "Old songs," as Anna called them. Her mother used to sing them in her youth, and the Reverend James Chester had learnt to love them. "Robin Adair," "The Banks of Allan Water," "Pray Goody," "The Baron of Mowbray," "She never blamed him," "The Minstrel-boy," and many others.

It was in his hand, and Anna stood looking over his shoulder, laughing at what Mrs. Chester sometimes called the "ancient bygones." On the table lay a drawing that Anna had done, betraying talent; the more especially when it was remembered that she could never sit to that, or anything else, for five minutes at a time. Up and down continually: called by Mrs. Chester, called by the children, called by the servants. She had never had a lesson in drawing in her life, she had never learnt to sing; what she did do was the result of native aptitude for it.

Mr. Lake had the drawing in his hand when the party entered, trooping in unceremoniously through the window, the children first. Lady Ellis's black-lace shawl was draped around her in its usual artistic fashion, and she wore a bonnet that could not by any stretch of imaginative politeness be construed into a widow's. Clara was with her, her refined face bright and radiant. The two were evidently on good terms with each other.

Mrs. Chester did not enter with them. Her household cares worried her, now that things must wear a good appearance for the new inmate, Lady Ellis. She came in presently from the hall, a cross look on her face, and spoke sharply to Anna. Selfish naturally, made intensely so by her struggle to get along, Mrs.

Chester appeared to think that for her step-daughter to be in the drawing-room and not in the kitchen, though it were but for a few minutes in the day, was a heinous crime.

"Robert," she said, addressing her brother, "I wish you'd come up to my room while I take my bonnet off. I have a letter to show you."

He followed her dutifully, just as he used when he was a little boy and she a woman grown. Mrs. Chester's room, which she shared with Fanny, was small and inconvenient. Sweeping a host of things off a chair to the floor in her untidy way, she graciously told him he might sit there, but he preferred to perch himself on a corner of the dressing-table.

"I'm torn to pieces with indecision and uncertainty," she began, taking a letter from a drawer. "I begin to think now it might have been better had I adhered to my first thought—that of taking pupils. Only look at the thing I have missed!"

He held out his hand for the letter, which she struck as she spoke. In her dictatorial manner she preferred to read it to him, and waved his hand away.

"The Red Court Farm, Coastdown.

"MADAM,

"I have been advised to write to you by my friends here, Captain and Mrs. Copp. They think you are making arrangements to receive half-a-dozen first-class pupils to educate with your own daughter. I am in search of something of the sort for my daughter, Miss Thornycroft, and it is possible that your house may be found suitable. She will require the best advantages, for which I shall expect to pay accordingly.

"With your permission I will drive over one of these first days and see you.

"And I am, madam,

"Your obedient servant,

"HARRY THORNYCROFT.

"Mrs. Chester."

"Who is Harry Thornycroft?" were Mr. Lake's first words when her voice ceased.

"I should have been as much at fault to know as you, but for a note Anna has had from Mr. Copp, giving a little explanation. Mr. Thornycroft is the great man of Coastdown, it seems; a county magistrate, very influential, and very rich. Mrs. Copp thinks he would pay quite two hundred a year with his daughter."

"And Mrs. Copp—who is she?" repeated Mr. Lake. "And where in the name of geography is Coastdown?"

"We shall never get on if you bother like this," returned Mrs. Chester, irascibly. "Mrs. Copp and Anna's mother were related, and Coastdown is a little place on the sea, about two-and-twenty miles from here.

Only fancy—only think—two hundred a year with the first pupil! If I only got three others at the same terms there'd be eight hundred a year at once—a thousand with my own income. It would be quite delightful."

"But that's reckoning your chickens before they are hatched."

"I might have known that you'd throw some mocking slight upon it," was the angry retort.

"No mocking slight at all, Penelope. I do not mean it as such. Of course, if you could get four or six pupils at two hundred a year each, it would be a jolly good thing. Only—I fancy pupils on those terms are not so readily picked up."

"One, at any rate, seems ready to drop into my hands. Should Miss Thornycroft not be placed with me after this, I shall look upon life as very hard."

"Can't you take her, should they offer her to you, and trust to good luck for finding others?"

"Then what am I to do about Lady Ellis?"

"Keep her also, if she will stay."

"But she would not. I sounded her this morning. Not as if I had a personal interest in the question. Anything like a school was her especial abhorrence, she said. She'd not enter a house where teaching was carried on for the world."

"So that you have to choose between the young lady with her two hundred a year and Lady Ellis?"

"In a sense, yes. But I have a difficult game to play. It strikes me that at the very first mention of a probable pupil Lady Ellis would take fright and leave. Now, you know, Robert, I have not got Miss Thornycroft yet, or even the promise of her; and it might happen that the negotiation would drop through. Where should I be in that case, with Lady Ellis gone?"

"On the ground, fallen between two stools," was Mr. Robert Lake's irreverent answer.

It angered Mrs. Chester; but she had an end to serve, and let it pass.

"I want you and your wife to do me a favour, Robert. Stay here for a week or two with us, paying me, of course; you know what my circumstances are. My heart would be good to keep you, but my pocket is not. I am so afraid of Lady Ellis finding the place dull. She has come for a month to see how she likes it. I forget whether I told you this yesterday. On Monday, when we were talking together after her arrival, she said to me, 'You will allow me to stay a month to see if the place will suit me: if it does, we will then make our agreement.' What could I say?"

"And you fear it may not suit her?"

"I fear she will find it dull. She said this morning she thought the house would be triste but for the presence in it of Mr. and Mrs. Lake. Now, you do me a good turn, and stay a week or two."

"I'd stay fast enough, Penelope—there's the fishing; but I don't know about Clara. You must talk to her."

"You must talk to her," returned Mrs. Chester. "Nobody else has a tenth of the influence over her that you have."

"I'll see," said Mr. Lake, alighting from the dressing-table. "We'll stay a day or two longer, at any rate: I know I can promise that."

Mr. Lake went straight to his wife, and recounted to her, word for word as nearly as he could recollect, what Mrs. Chester had said. There was nothing covert in his disposition: his fault, if it was a fault, was undisguised openness. But he did not urge the matter one way or the other. Clara looked grave at the proposition, and he left it to her.

"I said we would remain a day or two longer, Clara. I thought you would not object to that, as it is to do her, as she fancies, good."

"I don't mind staying to the end of the week, Robert, now we are here. We will go home on Saturday, if you like."

"All right." And Mr. Lake strolled away in his careless lightness.

CHAPTER VI

Justice Thornycroft's Visit

The days passed pleasantly enough: Lady Ellis made herself agreeable, Mr. Lake was always so; and Clara nearly forgot her dream. On the Friday morning, a hot but cloudy day, Mr. Lake went out to fish. Lady Ellis and Fanny Chester strolled after him; and Mrs. Chester took the opportunity to—as she phrased it to herself—"tackle" Clara. That estimable and managing matron beguiled the young lady into the quiet and secluded nursery—a room above, that the children were never in—and there burst into a flood of tears over her work, the darning of a tablecloth, and laid her unhappy case bare in the broad light of day.

"Only another week after this, my dear Clara! If you would but consent to stay! Think what my position will be should Lady Ellis quit me!"

Clara hesitated. Just the same instinct arose within her against staying at Guild, that in the first instance, the evening before the dream, had arisen against going to it. But she was gentle, young, pliable; it seemed to her that refusal would be an unkind thing, and she could not form her lips to say it.

"Would another week's stay make so very much difference to Lady Ellis, think you, Mrs. Chester?"

"My dear good soul, it would make all the difference. She'll have become accustomed to the place then, and will not care to leave it."

"Well—I will talk to Robert when he comes in."

"Of course—if you wish. But you know, Clara, the decision lies entirely with you. He will do what you suggest. Now, my dear, do picture to yourself the difference in our positions, yours and mine, and be hard-hearted if you can. You with your happy home to return to, your three servants, and your six-hundred a year; and I with my poor pittance, my toiling life, and my heap of children!"

Mrs. Chester showered tears upon the tablecloth in her lap, and Clara Lake felt that she was in for it.

"If you and Robert will remain two weeks with me from the day you came, I shall be thankful.—My goodness me! who's that?"

Mrs. Chester alluded to the clatter of some steps on the stairs, and the entrance of two ladies. Unfortunately for Clara Lake, they were Mary and Margaret Jupp. In high spirits, and with their usual volubility, they explained that they had a commission to execute at Guild for their mother, which gave them the opportunity of paying a flying call at Mrs. Chester's.

Not so very flying; for the young ladies took off their bonnets and made themselves comfortable for an hour or two. Mrs. Chester—craftily foreseeing what valuable allies these would prove—melted into tears again, and renewed her request to Mrs. Lake. Abandoning pride and its reticence, she openly explained what a boon to her, poor distressed woman, it was that she was craving for, and avowed her poverty, and the terms on which Lady Ellis had come to her. The Miss Jupps had known all about it before, as Mrs. Chester knew, but she took advantage of the situation.

They did the same. In their open good nature, and they had no other motive, they urged Clara to the promise. On the one hand, there would be the service to Mrs. Chester; on the other, a delightful holiday for Mr. and Mrs. Lake. Borne along on the stream of persuasion, assailed on all sides, Clara Lake felt that all power of resistance was taken from her, and she yielded to the stream.

Yielded to the stream, and gave the promise.

The Miss Jupps were clapping their hands at the victory, when Mr. Lake entered. Mrs. Chester explained the applause, by saying that dear Clara had promised to remain a fortnight at Guild.

"Have you?" he asked, turning to his wife.

"Yes; I have been over-persuaded," she replied, with rather a sickly smile.

The Miss Jupps applauded again, and a happy thought struck Mr. Lake; or an unhappy one. You can decide which as the history goes on.

It had been in contemplation to throw out a bay window in their dining-room at Katterley. A dark room and rather small, Mr. Lake and his wife had both decided that it should be altered. This, as it seemed to him, was the very time to set about the alteration. They had thought of deferring it until spring, but it would be a good thing over; and he intended to have some of his Yorkshire friends up for Christmas. Approaching his wife, he spoke to her in a low tone.

"Begin the alteration now!—while we are here!" she exclaimed, in surprise. "But, Robert! how long will they be over it?"

"About a fortnight. They may begin and end it in that time."

"Do you think so?"

"I'm sure so," he answered, carelessly and confidently. "I'll make Peters put it in his contract. Why, Clara, what is it? just the throwing out of a window? They might do it in a week if they chose. But just as you like, my dear."

Again, hearing the conversation, Mrs. Chester and the Miss Jupps joined in, taking wholly Mr. Lake's view of the matter. The only one who spoke with an interested motive was Mrs. Chester: the others were as honest as the day in what they said—honest in their inexperience.

And Clara was borne down once more in this as in the last, and agreed to the alteration being begun.

"It won't be much more than putting in a fresh window frame," decided Margaret Jupp.

No more shilly-shallyings now, no more questions of whether they should go or not. Mr. Lake went over that same afternoon to Katterley, in attendance on the Miss Jupps; saw the builder, Peters, and had the work put in hand On the Saturday he and his wife both went over, to return in the evening.

It was a sultry midday. Lady Ellis sat on the lawn under the shelter of a spreading lime-tree, whose branches had been more redolent of perfume a month or two ago than they were now.

The sky was cloudless, of a dark hot blue; the summer petals, clustering on the flower-beds, opened themselves to the blistering sun. Lady Ellis was alone with her netting. She wore a black silk gown and little cap of net, all the more coquettish for its simplicity, its plain lappets hanging behind. Her work proceeded slowly, and finally she let it fall on her knee as one utterly weary.

"What a life it is here!" she murmured in self-commune. "Say what they will, India is the paradise of women. Where means are in accordance; servants, dress, carriages, horses, incessant gaiety, it may be tolerable here; but where they are lacking—good heavens! how do people manage to exist?"

"The world has gone hard with me," she resumed after a pause. "Two years of luxury to be succeeded by stagnation. I'd never have married Colonel Ellis—no, though he did give me a title—had I supposed his money would go to his children and not to me."

Another pause, during which she jerked the netting-silk up and down.

"And this house? shall stay in it? But for that young man, who is rendering it bearable, I don't think I could. This managing clergyman's widow, with her flock of young ones, she is a study from nature—or art. Ah well, well! a month or two of it, and I shall go on the wing again."

Closing her eyes, as if weary with the world's view, Lady Ellis remained perfectly still, until the sound of rapidly advancing wheels aroused her. Looking up, she saw a very handsome carriage, a sort of mail phaeton, dash up to the gate. The gentleman driving got out and assisted down a girl of fair beauty, who had sat by his side; the groom having sprung round to the horses' heads from the seat behind.

They came up the path, and Lady Ellis looked at them. An exceedingly fine man, of middle age, tall and upright, with a handsome face still, and clear blue eyes. The girl was handsome too, she wore a beautiful dress of training silk, and a hat with blue ribbons. We have met them before—Mr. and Miss Thornycroft.

Looking about, as if seeking for the door of entrance, or for some one to receive them, their eyes fell upon Lady Ellis. She could do nothing less than advance to the rescue. Missing the turning that led by a shady path to the door, they could see only windows. Mr. Thornycroft raised his hat.

"I have the honour of speaking to Mrs. Chester?"

Lady Ellis laughed slightly at the supposition, and threw back her head, as much as to say it was a ridiculous and not flattering mistake.

"No, indeed. I am only staying here."

Mr. Thornycroft bowed in deprecation; Miss Thornycroft turned her head slightly aside and took a look at the speaker. There was a slight contraction on that young lady's queenly brow as she turned it back again.

Out of an upper window, surveying the new guests, surveying the carriage being driven away by the groom to the nearest inn, was the head of Mrs. Chester; her cap off, her hair untidy, a cross look in her wondering eyes. Who were they, these people, interrupting her at that unseasonable hour? Strange to say, the truth did not strike her. They were underneath the windows, and she could take her survey at leisure.

Lady Ellis, quite capable of doing the honours of reception, ushered them into the drawing-room through the open window. At the same moment Anna Chester came forward in her poor frock and with her sweet face. Mr. Thornycroft had laid a card on the table, and she glanced at it in passing. Her manners were calm, self-possessed, gentle; an essentially ladylike girl in spite of the frock.

"I will tell mamma that you are here," she said, when they were seated; and she quitted the room again.

"Had I seen that young lady first, I should not have committed the mistake of taking you for Mrs. Chester," spoke Mr. Thornycroft in his gallantry.

Lady Ellis smiled. "That young lady is not Mrs. Chester's daughter, however. Mrs. Chester's children are considerably younger."

Anna meanwhile was going upstairs. Mrs. Chester, doing something to the inside of a bed, had her black dress covered with fluff, and her hair also. She turned sharply round when Anna entered.

"Mamma, it is Justice Thornycroft."

What with the startling announcement—for Mrs. Chester took in the news at once—and what with the recollection of her own state of attire, Mrs. Chester turned her irritability upon Anna. It was provoking thus to be interrupted at her very necessary work.

"Justice Thornycroft! What in the world possesses you to call the man that, Anna Chester?"

"Mrs. Copp called him so in her letter to me, mamma.'

"Mrs. Copp's a fool," retorted the bewildered lady. "Justice Thornycroft! One would think you had been bred in a wood. Who do you suppose uses those obsolete terms now? What brings him here today?"

She put the question in a sharp, exacting tone, just as f it were Anna's business to answer it, and Anna's fault that he had come. Anna quietly went to a closet and took out Mrs. Chester's best gown.

"To come on a Saturday! Nothing was ever so unreasonable," groaned Mrs. Chester. "Here's all the flock and the down out of the bed, and I covered with it. Look at my crape! Look at my hair! I took off my cap because those bothering lappets got in my way."

"You will have your gown changed in two minutes, mamma, and I will smooth your hair."

Mrs. Chester jerked the gown out of Anna's hands. One of those active, restless women, who cannot bear to be still while anything is done for them, was she; and began to put it on herself, grumbling all the while.

"Nothing in the world ever happened so contrary. Of all things, I wanted, if these Thornycrofts did come over, to keep them from Lady Ellis. Once let her get an inkling of their business, and she'd be off the next day. And there they are, shut up with her. I dare say she knows it all by now."

"Oh, mamma, it is not likely Mr. Thornycroft would speak of it to her."

"Indeed! That's your opinion, is it? Give me the hair-brush."

She brushed away at her hair, Anna standing meekly by with a clean cap ready to put on. Mrs. Chester continued her catalogue of grievances.

"It is the worst day they could have come. All things are at sixes and sevens on a Saturday. The children are dirty, and the plate's dirty, and the servants are dirty. They must have luncheon, I suppose—or dinner, for that's what it will be to them, coming this long drive. Mr. Thornycroft can possess no sense to take me by storm in this manner. Anna, I hope you did not proclaim to them that you were a daughter of the house," she added, the thought suddenly striking her.

Anna's face flushed. She had spoken of Mrs. Chester as "mamma," and when she went in Lady Ellis had said, "This is Miss Chester." Under the stern gaze now bent upon her, poor Anna felt as if she had committed some not-to-be-atoned-for crime.

"In that wretched frock of yours! You have not the least sense of shame in you, Anna. Over and over again I have said you were born to disgrace me. Why could you not have passed yourself off for an upper maid or nursery governess, or something of that sort? Or else kept out of the way altogether."

It never struck Anna Chester that the reproach was unmerited; it did not occur to her to petition for a better frock, since that one was so shabby. She had a better, kept for Sundays and rare holidays; to put it on on a week-day, unless commanded to do so, would have been an astounding inroad on the order of things. Reared to self-sacrifice and privation, that sacrifice and privation that a poor clergyman—a good, loving, but needy gentleman, must practise who has the care of those poorer than himself—Anna Chester had lived but to love and obey. When her father gained his living (that looked so wealthy in prospect), and the new wife—this present Mrs. Chester, now bending her eyes condemningly upon her—came home close upon it, Anna's habit of submission was but slightly changed. Formerly she had yielded wholly to her father in her intense respect and love; now she, had to yield to her stepmother in exacted, unquestioning obedience. She never thought of repining or rebelling. Brought up to think herself of no earthly consequence, as one whose sole mission in life it was to be useful to others, doing all she could for every one and ignoring self, it may be questioned if any young girl's spirit had ever been brought to the same state of perfect discipline. Never in her whole life had Anna rebelled at a request or resisted a command; to be told to do a thing was to obey. But for her naturally sweet temper, her utter want of selfishness, and the humble estimation imparted to her of herself, this could hardly have been. She stood there now, listening repentantly to the reproaches, the disparaging words of her second mother, and accepted them as her right. That lady, a very pharisee in her own opinion, gave a finishing twitch to her widow's cap, to her collar, to the "weepers" on her wrists, took the broad hem-stitched handkerchief that Anna held in readiness for her, and turned to leave the room.

"What shall I do now, mamma?" came the meek question.

"Do?—ay to be sure," continued Mrs. Chester, recalled by the words; "why, you must go to the kitchen and see what sort of a lunch can be sent up. I had ordered the cold fowl and ham with salad, and the cold mutton for you and the children. The mutton must be hashed now; very nicely, mind; you can cut it up yourself: and the veal cutlet that was intended in for dinner, must be dressed with herbs, tell Nanny; and some young potatoes. The tart can come in and the cream, and—and that will do. I shall make it our dinner, apologizing privately to Lady Ellis for the early hour, and call it luncheon to the Thornycrofts."

"Are the children to be at table?"

"Certainly not. What are you thinking of? You must keep them with you. The miserable thing is that Elizabeth went back with the Lakes this morning; she's so respectable a servant to be seen behind one's chair in waiting. Tell Dinah to put on her merino gown, and make herself tidy."

Away went Mrs. Chester to the drawing-room, the cares of the many orders and contrivances on her shoulders, and away went Anna to the kitchen to see to the execution of them, to aid in their preparation, to keep in quietness by her side (an exceedingly difficult task) the noisy children. Little did Mr. Thornycroft, bowing to the comely and well-dressed widow lady who introduced herself as Mrs. Chester, think of the trouble the advent of himself and his daughter was causing.

Mrs. Chester had accused him of possessing no sense. He possessed plenty, and also tact. As Mrs. Chester remained silent as to the object of his visit, ignoring it apparently altogether; rather boasting of how glad she was to make their acquaintance, to see them there for a day's change; he said nothing of it either. Mrs. Chester was on thorns though all the while, and talked rather at random. Lady Ellis was content to sit displaying her charms, and to put in a word or a smile here and there. Mr. Thornycroft said something about going to the hotel for luncheon.

"Oh, but surely you will remain and take luncheon with me?" said Mrs. Chester, with as much empressement as though she had a larder full of good things to send up.

"Would you prefer that we should do so?" asked Mr. Thornycroft.

He put the question quite simply. Luncheon and other meals were provided for so munificently in his own house, it did not occur to him that his remaining could cause embarrassment in Mrs. Chester's. That lady answered that it would give her great pain if they departed, and Mary Anne Thornycroft took off her hat. Turning to place it on a side-table, she saw a very fine piece of coral there, shaped something like a basket.

"Oh, papa, look at this!" she exclaimed. "It must be the fellow-piece to the one at Mrs. Connaught's."

"What Connaughts are those?" asked Lady Ellis, briskly. "I knew a Mrs. Connaught once."

This Mrs. Connaught, who had lived about two years at Coastdown, proved to be the same. Lady Ellis noted down the address in her pocket case.

Later, when all had dispersed, Mrs. Chester seized on her opportunity.

"I think we can have a few minutes alone now, Mr. Thornycroft, if you wish to speak to me. May I flatter myself that your visit today is to make arrangements for placing your daughter under my charge?"

"Madam, I came today not to make arrangements,—that would be premature,—but to ascertain if possible whether such arrangements would be suitable," he replied in his open manner. "I do wish very much to find an eligible home for my daughter, where she may complete her education and be happy. Captain and Mrs. Copp,—some connexion of yours, I believe?"

"Of my late husband's," interposed Mrs. Chester, quickly, as though not willing to claim connexion with Captain and Mrs. Copp; "that is, of his first wife's. I don't know them at all."

"Ah, indeed; very worthy people they are. Well, madam, Mrs. Copp spoke to me of you; The widow, she said, of the Reverend James Chester, of Guild. I had some slight knowledge of him in early days. You were intending to take some pupils on the plan of a private family, Mrs. Copp said, and she thought it might suit Miss Thornycroft."

"Yes," replied Mrs. Chester, scarcely knowing what to reply in her uncertainty of plans, "I did think of it."

"And do you wish still to carry it out?"

"Yes, oh yes; if I could get the pupils."

"I had better tell you what I require for my daughter," observed Mr. Thornycroft. "She must be in a family where the habits and arrangements are essentially good; not the scanty, coarse provision generally pertaining to a school. She must be well waited on, well fed, well treated; her companions must be the daughters of gentlemen; her education must be continued on the same liberal scale as that on which it has been hitherto conducted. And I should wish her to get from the lady principal that good, conscientious, careful training that is rarely given except by a mother."

"Is she well advanced for her age? In music, for instance?" asked Mrs. Chester, after a pause.

"Very well. She plays the harp and piano, sings, and has begun harmony. German and French she speaks well; but, all that you can inquire into yourself. In saying that her education must be liberal, the word is sufficiently comprehensive."

"And for these advantages what sum would you be prepared to pay?"

"Whatever was asked me, madam, in reason—in reason, of course. I am at my ease in the world in regard to money, and shall certainly not spare it on my only daughter."

Mrs. Chester's mouth watered. She was sure she had heard of such a thing as three hundred a year being asked in a case like this, and given. Time enough for terms, though, yet.

"Miss Thornycroft has hitherto been educated at home, I believe?"

"She has; but she is getting beyond the control of her governess, Miss Derode, and I think she would be better at school for the next year or two. A good soul, poor Miss Derode, as ever lived, and thoroughly accomplished; but Mary Anne has begun to laugh at her instead of obeying her. That won't do, you know."

Mrs. Chester sat twirling the crape of her dress between her fingers in thought. Presently she looked at Mr. Thornycroft.

"Have you thought of any sum that might be suitable—for the advantages you require?"

"I should think about two hundred a year. I would give that."

"Very fair," murmured Mrs. Chester. "Of course, any little extras—but that can be left for the present. I should like much to take her."

"For this sum I should expect commensurate advantages," continued Mr. Thornycroft, in his straightforward, candid way. "At present I do not see—you will forgive me, madam—that you are at all prepared for such a pupil. You have no pupils, I think?"

"Not yet."

"And I should wish my daughter to have companions, young ladies of her own age—just three or four, to reconcile her to being away from home, the notion which she does not at all relish. A resident governess would also be essential—unless indeed the lady superintendent devoted her whole time to them."

"Yes, yes; a resident governess, of course," mechanically answered Mrs. Chester.

What more might have been said was arrested by the entrance of the youngest child, his pinafore and mouth smeared with treacle. Clamouring for bread and treacle, Anna had given him a slice to keep him quiet. In the midst of eating it he had broken away, ungrateful boy, and rushed into the presence of Mrs. Chester. Dinah, who had not got on her merino gown yet, or made herself tidy, came and carried him, kicking, away again. Mrs. Chester was depressed by the accident, and sat subdued.

"I think, madam, that if you carry your intention out, the better way will be for you to write to me as soon as you are ready to receive pupils," said Mr. Thornycroft. "I will then consider the matter further, and decide whether or not to send you my daughter. There is no great hurry; Miss Derode has not left us."

"You will not promise her to me?"

"I cannot do that, Mrs. Chester," was the answer, given with prompt decision. "Until I see that arrangements would be suitable, that the home would be in all respects desirable, I can say no more."

Mrs. Chester sighed inwardly, and felt from that moment she must resign hope—Miss Thornycroft and her liberal pay would not be for her. But she suffered nothing of this to appear, some latent aspiration might be lingering yet, and she rose up gaily and shook Mr. Thornycroft's hand in a warmth of satisfaction, and said the matter, left so, was all that was to be desired.

And then they took the luncheon—Mrs. Chester, Lady Ellis, Mr. and Miss Thornycroft. Some fruit was set out on the lawn afterwards, and coffee was to follow. Lady Ellis did the honours of the garden to Mr. Thornycroft, nothing loth; walking up this path with him, down that; halting to sit on this rustic bench, entering that shady bower. A very charming woman, thought Justice Thornycroft.

Miss Thornycroft was left to the companionship of Mrs. Chester. And that young lady, with the freedom she was accustomed to make known her wishes at home, asked that Anna Chester might join them.

"I promised Mrs. Copp to take word back of her welfare, and what sort of a girl she was," said Mary Anne. "How can I do so unless I see her?"

With outward alacrity and inward wrath, Mrs. Chester disappeared for a moment, and sent a private telegram to Anna that she was to dress herself and come out. In five minutes the girl was with them. She came with the coffee. Her black silk dress (made out of one of Mrs. Chester's old ones) was pretty; her face was flushed with its refined, delicate colour, her brown eyes sparkled with their soft brilliancy, her chestnut hair was smooth and pretty. Essentially a lady was Anna now. Justice Thornycroft, coming up then for the coffee with Lady Ellis, took her hands in his and held her before him.

"My dear, I can trace in you a great likeness to your father. It is just the same refined, patient face."

Ere the words were well spoken, the brown eyes were wet, the sweet lips were quivering. The loss of her father, so intensely loved, had been Anna's great grief in life. A chance reminiscence, such as this, was more than she could bear.

"Did you know papa, sir?" she asked, looking bravely up through the tears.

"I knew a little of him many years ago, and I once or twice saw your mother. You must come and pay us a visit at Coastdown."

A glad light in the gentle face.

"I should like it very much, sir. Mrs. Copp has already invited me to go to them; but I cannot be spared."

"You must be spared; I should like you to come," spoke Mary Anne, imperiously, with the tone of one who is not accustomed to have her slightest wish disputed. But the waiting coffee and Mrs. Chester turned off the subject.

The clock was striking five when the punctual groom appeared with the carriage. Down it came with grand commotion, its fine horses fresh after their rest, and stopped at the gate. The whole party escorted Mr. and Miss Thornycroft to it: Mrs. Chester and Anna, the children, tidy now and on tolerable behaviour, Lady Ellis and her fascination. Promises of future friendly intercourse were exchanged. Mr. Thornycroft gave a positive undertaking to drive over again and spend another day, and they took their places in the carriage. Away went the horses in a canter, rather restive; the justice, restraining them, had enough to do to raise his hat in farewell salutation; the groom had a run ere he could gain his seat behind. And they started on their long drive of three-and-twenty miles.

At the same moment, appearing from an opposite quarter, came Mr. and Mrs. Lake and Elizabeth on their return from Katterley. They were near enough to see the carriage go swiftly off, but not to distinguish its inmates. Mrs. Chester and the rest waited for them at the gate.

"Have you had visitors, Penelope?" asked Mr. Lake.

"Yes. And very cross and contrary I felt it that you were not here," continued Mrs. Chester, who was proud of her good-looking brother. "It is Mr. Thornycroft and his daughter—they have been with us ever since twelve o'clock. To think that you were away! I am sure Clara would have liked Miss Thornycroft."

To think that they were away!—that the two ladies spoken of did not meet! One of them at least would deem it a chance missed, a singular fact, in the years to come.

CHAPTER VII

Going Fishing

A chilly evening. The hot days of August have passed away; this is October, and the night is turning out raw and misty. But in Mrs. Chester's house warmth and light reign, at least in the inhabited rooms of it.

In one of them, a moderate-sized, comfortable apartment, whose windows opened to the ground, the large fire had burned down to a red glow, after rendering the atmosphere unpleasantly warm; and a lady, seated in a lounging chair, had pushed it quite back, so that she was in the shade both from the light and the fire. A look of perplexity, of care, sat on her face, young and lovely though it was; even in her hands, as they lay listless on her lap, there was an air of abandonment. But that the room was growing dusk and dim in the autumn twilight, that sadness might not have been suffered to show itself, although she was alone.

It was Clara Lake. Her thoughts were buried in a painful retrospect—the retrospect of only the two past months. They had brought grief to her: as the summer did to the unhappy girl, told of in that beautiful ballad Anna Chester sometimes sang, "The Banks of Allan Water."

Had any one warned Clara Lake the previous August, when she came to Mrs. Chester's for a two days' visit, that the sojourn would not be one of days but months, she had simply disbelieved it. Even when the term was extended to a proposed fortnight—a fortnight in all—she would have laughed at the idea of staying longer. But she had stayed. She was here still. Nevertheless, things had so turned out; all easily and naturally, as it seemed, to look back upon. As it seemed to her now, sitting in her chair, and tracing the course of past events.

The alteration in their house at Katterley, as proposed by Mr. Lake, and which was to be completed in ten days or a fortnight, was begun in due course—the throwing out of the dining-room by means of a bay window. He and his wife went over one day to see the progress of the work. It was then suggested—whether by the builder, by her husband, by herself, or by all three jointly, Clara could not to this hour recollect—that, to make a complete job of it, the window in the chamber above should also be thrown out. The additional expense would be comparatively little, the improvement great; and it was agreed to on the spot. Orders were also given for the drawing-room and their own chamber to be painted, repapered, and decorated.

"Won't it take a long time?" Clara suddenly asked.

"About a month, if they work well; certainly not more," replied Mr. Lake.

He must have known little of workmen, to speak so confidently. Builders, carpenters, painters, decorators, are not famous for working themselves thin through over-hurry. The popular saying, "If once you get them into your house, you never get them out," seemed to be exemplified in this one instance. Here was October come in, and Katterley Lodge was as far off being ready for reception as ever.

It would have been a slight grievance, the detention, to Mr. and Mrs. Lake—not any, in fact, to him—for Mrs. Chester's house was an agreeable one, and they had no home ties; but Lady Ellis was making the stay insupportable to Mr. Lake's wife.

Tolerably young, showy, very handsome according to the taste of many, exacting attention, living but in admiration, and not scrupulous how she obtained it provided she got it, Lady Ellis had begun to cast her charming toils on the careless and attractive Robert Lake in the very first hour of their meeting. Not to eat him up; not intending certainly to be eaten herself; only to be her temporary slave, pour faire passer le temps. In that dull country house, where there was no noise or excitement but what arose from its children, Lady Ellis wanted something to make the time pass.

Mr. Lake was perfectly ready to meet her halfway. One of those men who, wife or no wife, consider a flirtation with a pretty woman—and with one not pretty, for the matter of that—a legitimate occupation in their idle life, he responded to her advances gallantly. Neither of them had any idea of plunging into shoals and quicksands; let us so far give both their due. A rather impressive clasp of the hand; a prolonged walk in the glowing beauty of the summer's day; an interchange of confidential talk, meaning nothing—that was the worst, thought of by either. But then, you see, the mischief is, that when once these things are fairly embarked in, the course entered upon and its midway post reached, down you glide, swimmingly, unwittingly; and it is an exceedingly difficult matter to turn back. Good chance (to call it so here), generally sends the opportunity, but it is not always seized upon.

The flirtation began. There were walks in the morning sun, shady garden chairs for rest at noontide, lingerings in the open air by twilight, that grateful hour after a sultry day. There were meetings indoors, meetings out; singing, talking, netting, idling. Mr. Lake went fishing, his favourite pastime just now, and my Lady Ellis would carry his luncheon to him; or stroll down later, wait until the day's sport was at an end, and stroll home with him. One or other of the children was often with her, serving to satisfy the requisites of propriety, had friends been difficult.

None were so. For a whole month this agreeable life went on, and nobody gave it a care or a thought. Certainly Clara did not. She was accustomed to see her husband's light admiration given to others; never yet had a suspicion crossed her mind that he had more than admiration to give. That his love was exclusively hers, to be hers for ever, she believed in as fully as she believed in heaven.

Well, the month passed, August; and September was entered upon. The flirtation (to call it so for want of a better word), had grown pretty deep. The morning walks were frequent; the noontide restings were confidential, the twilight lingerings were prolonged to starlight. The songs became duets, the conversation whispers; the netting was as often in his hands as hers, and the silk purse did not progress. Mr. Lake drove Lady Ellis out in the stylish little open carriage, conveniently made for two persons and no more, that he was fond of hiring at Guild. One day Fanny Chester went with them; my lady's dress got crushed, and of course the inconvenience could not be allowed to occur again. Twice a week she rode with him, requiring very much of his care in the open country, for she said she was a timid horsewoman. In short, they had plunged into a whirligig round of days that was highly agreeable to the two concerned.

Sharp-eyed Mrs. Chester—nearly as sharp as Lady Ellis herself, but more honest—saw quite well what was going on. "Don't you go and make a fool of yourself with that woman, Robert!" she said to him one day, which sent Mr. Lake into a fit of laughter. He thought himself just the last man to do it. And on went the time again.

Imperceptibly—she could not remember how or when it first arose—a shade of annoyance, of vexation, stole upon Mrs. Lake. Her husband was always with Lady Ellis; except at meals and at night, he was never with her; and she began to think it was not quite right that it should be so. Crafty Mrs. Chester— honest enough in the main, but treacherous in this one matter—was on thorns lest Clara should take alarm and cause an outbreak; which would not have done at all. She did what she could to keep alarm off, and would have to reconcile it to her conscience in later days. Mr. and Mrs. Lake paid her well, and that was also a consideration.

"Clara, dear, it is so good of your husband to help me," she would say, or words similar. "He has never been a true brother to me until now. Were it not for him I am sure Lady Ellis would die of ennui in this place. He keeps her amused for me, doing what he can to make her days pass pleasantly. I shall be ever thankful to him."

Once, and once only, Clara went to the fishing stream after them. It was a mile and a half away, the one they had gone fishing in that day. They! Lady Ellis had a costly little rod now, bought for her by Mr. Lake, and went with him. Clara, having nothing better to do in the afternoon, uneasily conscious of the advent of incipient jealousy arising in her heart, thought she would join the party. Her husband had never asked her to do so at any time; upon her hinting that she should like to fish too, he had stopped the idea at once: "No, she would be too fatigued." Mrs. Lake, it was true, was not strong; heat and fatigue knocked her up. Mrs. Chester had been crafty from the first. One day in the early stage of the affair, seeing her husband and Lady Ellis sitting together in the shade at noontide, Clara was innocently stepping out at the window to sit too, when Mrs. Chester interposed to prevent it. "Good gracious, Clara! don't go stealing out like that. They may think you want to hear what they are saying—out of jealousy." And the word "jealousy" only caused an amusing laugh to Clara Lake then; but she remained indoors. Well, on this afternoon, she started for the stream, taking Master James Chester in her hand Master James abandoned her en route, going off on his own devices, and she was alone when she reached them. A deliciously shady place she found it; the chance passers-by beyond the trees at the back few and far between. Both were sitting on the bank, attending to their lines, which were deep in the water. They looked round with surprise, and Lady Ellis was the first to speak.

"Have you come to look after us, Mrs. Lake?"

Innocent words, sufficiently courteous in themselves, but not in the tone with which they were spoken. There was a mocking undercurrent in it, implying much; at least, Clara fancied so, and it brought the red flush of shame to her cheeks. Open, candid, ultra-refined herself, to spy upon others would have been against her very nature. It seemed to her that in that light she was looked upon, as a spy, and inwardly resolved not to intrude again.

James Chester made his appearance in the course of time, and Clara set off home with him. They asked her to stay until the sport was at an end; her husband pressed it; but she could not get over that tone, and said she would walk very quietly on, that they might overtake her. Master James went off as before, and Clara thought of the interview. "There was no harm; there can be none; they were only fishing," she murmured to herself. "What a stupid thing I was!"

"Where's Jemmy?" asked Mrs. Chester, coming forth to meet her.

"I'm sure I can't tell. He ran away from me both in going and returning. It was not my fault. He does not mind anybody a bit, you know."

"Why did you not wait to come home with Robert and Lady Ellis?"

"I don't know. I wanted to get back, for one thing; I was tired. And I don't much think Lady Ellis liked my going."

"My dear Clara, you must not take up vague fancies," spoke Mrs. Chester, after a pause. "One would think you were growing jealous, as the boys and girls do. Nothing can be in worse taste for a lady, even when there may be apparent grounds for it. In this case the very thought would be absurd; Lady Ellis is ten years older than your husband."

And so, what with one thing and another, Clara was subdued to passive quietness, and Mr. Lake and Lady Ellis had it all their own way. But her suspicions that they were growing rather too fond of each other's company had been aroused, and she naturally, perhaps unconsciously, watched, not in the unfounded fancy of an angry woman, a jealous wife, but in the sick fear of a loving one. She saw the flirtation (again I must apologize for the name) grow into sentiment, if not to passion; she saw it lapse into concealment—which is a very bad sign. And now that October had come in and was passing, Clara Lake's whole inward life was one scene of pain, of conflict, of wild jealousy preying upon her very heartstrings. She had loved her husband with all the fervour of a deeply imaginative nature; had believed in him with the perfect trustingness of an innocent-hearted, honest English girl.

She sat in her chair there in the drawing-room, drawn away from the fire's heat, her eyes fixed on vacancy, her pretty hands lying weary. What was that heat compared to the heat that raged within, the mind's fever?

"If it could but end!" she murmured to herself; "if we could but go back to our home at Katterley!"

Strange to say—and yet perhaps not strange, for the natural working out of a course of events is often hidden to the chief actor in it—the dream and its superstitious dread had faded away from Clara's memory. Of course she had not forgotten the fact; whenever she thought of it, as she did at odd times, its features presented themselves to her as vividly as ever. But the dread of it was gone. When day succeeded day, week succeeded week, bringing no appearance of any tragic end for her, accident or else, that could put her into a hearse, the foreboding fear quite subsided. Besides, Clara Lake looked upon the accident to the railway-train that Sunday night as the one that would have killed her had she only been in it. So the dream and its superstition had become as a thing of the past.

Lonely, dispirited, unusually low, felt she this afternoon. Mr. Lake had gone over in the morning to Katterley to see how their house was progressing, and she began to wonder that he was not back. They had taken dinner early that day, and Lady Ellis had disappeared after it. When Mr. Lake was away she would invariably go up to her room after dinner, saying she had letters to write. Shrewd Fanny Chester, taking after her quick mother, said my lady went up to get a nap, not to write. Mrs. Chester was in the nursery, where she had a dressmaker at work, making clothes for her children; Anna was helping; and Clara was alone.

It may as well be mentioned that the mystery attaching to the cause of the railway accident had not been solved yet. The coroner and jury had met regularly once a fortnight since, and as regularly adjourned the inquest. In the teeth of Colonel West's most positive testimony, it was impossible to bring in a verdict against Cooper, the driver; in the teeth of Oliver Jupp's, it was equally impossible to exonerate him. No other witnesses, save the parties interested, appeared to have seen the lights that night. The public were fairly nonplussed, the coroner and jury sick to death of the affair. The young person now working for Mrs. Chester was Cooper's sister.

The red embers were fading down nearly to blackness, when Fanny Chester came bursting into the room to Clara in her rather boisterous manner. Clara aroused herself, glad perhaps of the interruption to her thoughts.

"Is it you, Fanny? Where are they all, dear?"

"Mamma's at work in the nursery. She's running the seams, and showing Miss Cooper how she wants the bodies cut. Anna's there too. Have you seen Uncle Robert?"

"Uncle Robert is not back yet, Fanny."

"Yes, he is," replied the young lady, who at all times was fond of her own opinion.

"You are mistaken," said Clara. "He would have come in to me the first thing."

"But I saw him. I saw him in the garden ever so long ago. Lady Ellis was with him. They were at the back there, walking towards the shrubbery."

Indisputable testimony; and Clara Lake could have bitten her tongue for saying "He would have come to me the first thing," although her audience consisted only of a child. Mr. Lake was to have brought her some book from home that he had forgotten the previous time; she was ardently longing for it, and thought he would at least have come straight to her and delivered it.

"Will you please reach me one of those old newspapers up there," proceeded Fanny. "Mamma sent me for it. She wants to cut a pattern."

Giving the child the newspaper she asked for, Mrs. Lake shut the door after her and drew to the window, her heart beating rebelliously. "So he was back ever so long ago, and solacing himself with the sweet companionship of Lady Ellis." As she stood there, looking out on the darkening gloom—fit type of the gloom within—Clara asked herself the serious question, Was this constant seeking of each other's society but the result of accident; of a nonsensical liking which meant really nothing, and would pass away; or was it that they were really in love with each other, and she losing her place in her husband's heart?

An impulse—a wild impulse—which she could not restrain, and perhaps did not try to, led her to open the glass doors and step out: some vague feeling in her unhappy mind, making itself heard amidst the inward tumult of wishing to see with her own eyes whether the child's information was true. It might not have been her husband; it might have been the curate, or Oliver Jupp, or that big Mr. Winterton, all of whom were fond of coming and of walking with Lady Ellis when they got the chance; and she would go and see. Pretty sophist! Poor Clara knew in her inmost heart that it was Robert Lake, and no other: instinct told her so. Had she given herself a moment's time for reflection, she would probably not have gone. To an honourable nature—and Clara Lake's was essentially such—the very idea of looking after even a recreant husband is abhorrent. But jealousy is the strongest passion that can assail the human heart, whether of man or woman. Under its influence we do not stop to raise questions of expediency.

The raw fog pervading the air struck upon her with a chill as she came out of the heated room. She had nothing on but a thin muslin body, and shivered quite unconsciously. What cared she for the cold or the heat? Had she been plunged into a bath of ice she would not have felt it then. On she went, sweeping round the lawn in the dusky twilight; for it was not dark yet—keeping close to the trees, that their friendly shade might shelter her from chance eyes. Fanny Chester's words, "Going towards the shrubbery," serving for her guide unconsciously, she made for the same place.

Well, what did she find or see? Nothing very dreadful, taking it in the abstract; but quite enough to fan the jealous indignation of a wife, especially of one who loves her husband.

The shrubbery appeared to be empty; and Clara had, gone half way down it, past one of its cross openings, when, from that very opening, sounds of voices and footsteps advancing struck upon her ear. Retreat was not expedient: they might see her pass; and she darted into a deep alcove the shrubs had been trained to make, before which ran a bench. Cowering almost into the very laurels, she stood there in sick fear. Never had she intended to get so near, and almost wished for the earth to open and bury her alive rather than she should be seen. Her heart beating with a wild shame, as if she had been caught in some great crime, there she had to stay.

On they came in their supreme unconsciousness, turning into the shrubbery, and alas! towards the verdant alcove. Clara's eyes were strained to look, and her poor breath came in gasps.

They were arm-in-arm; and Mr. Lake held one of my lady's hands, lightly toying with its fingers. He was speaking in low, tender tones—the same tones which had been given to her before their marriage, and had won her heart for ever. What he was saying she could not in her agitation tell, but as they were passing her, going from the house, you understand, not to it, Lady Ellis spoke.

"Robert, it is getting dark and cold."

Robert! Had she known his wife was listening! It might have made no difference.

"The dark will not hurt you," he said, louder. "You are with me."

"But it is damp also. Indeed, since I returned from India, I feel both the damp and cold very much."

She spoke in a timid, gentle tone: as different from her natural tones, as different from those she used to any but him, as can well be imagined. That she had set herself out to gain his love seemed a sure fact. How far Lady Ellis contemplated going, or Mr. Lake either, and what they may have anticipated would be the final upshot, how or where it was to end, was best known to themselves. Let it lie with them.

"There's a shawl of yours, I think, Angeline, in the summer-house. Sit you there while I get it."

He left her on the bench, behind which his wife was standing: they touched each other within an inch or two. Clara drew in her breath, and wished the earth would open. Lady Ellis began a scrap of a song, as if she did not like being alone in the darkness. Her voice, whether in singing or speaking, was loud and shrill, though she modified it for Mr. Lake. An antediluvian sort of song: goodness knows where she could have picked it up. Perhaps the stars, beginning to twinkle above, suggested its recollection to her.

"As many bright stars as appeared in the sky,
As many young lovers were caught by my eye;
And I was a beauty then, oh then,
And I was a beauty then.

"But now that I'm married, good what, good what!
I'm tied to a proud and fantastical fop,
Who follows another and cares for me not.

"But when I'm a widow I'll live at my ease,
I'll go all about, and I'll do as I please,
And take care how I marry again, again;
And take care how I marry again."

She had time to sing the three stanzas through, repeating the last line of the first and third verses as a refrain.

Mr. Lake came back swinging the shawl on his arm—a warm grey woollen one. "All right at last, Angeline. I could not find it, and had to strike a fusee for a light. It had slipped behind the seat. I began to think you must have carried it away today."

"I did not know it was there," she answered.

"Don't you remember throwing it off last evening when we were sitting there, saying you felt hot? Now be quiet: I'll wrap you up myself. Have you any pins?"

She had risen, and he put the shawl on her head and shoulders; then turned her round and pinned it under her chin, so that only her face was visible. With such care!—oh, with such care!

"You are taking as much trouble as though I were going to stay out for an hour!"

"I wish we were."

"Do you? What would your wife say?"

"Nothing. And if she did—what then? There, you can't feel the cold now."

"No; I don't think I can."

"But what am I to have for my pains?"

She made no answer. In truth, he did not wait for it. Bending his own face on the one he held up, he left a kiss and a loving word upon it: "My dearest!" A long and passionate kiss, as it sounded in his wife's ear.

Lady Ellis, perhaps not prepared for so demonstrative a proceeding, spoke a rebuke. He only laughed. They moved away; he retaining his arm around her for a lingering moment, as though to keep the shawl in its place; and their voices were dropped again to a soft sweet whisper, that scarcely disturbed the stillness of the murky autumn night.

Very different from the tone of that wail—had any been near to note it—when Clara Lake left her hiding-place; a low wail, as of a breaking heart, that came forth and mingled with the inclement evening air.

Some writer has remarked—and I believe it was Bulwer Lytton, in his "Student"—that to the vulgar there is but one infidelity in love. It is perfectly true; but I think the word "vulgar" is there misplaced, unless we may apply it to all, whether inmates of the palace or the cottage, whose temperament is not of the ultra-refined. Ultra-refined, mind! they of the sensitive, proud, impassioned nature, whose inward life, its thoughts, its workings, can never be betrayed to the world, any more than they themselves can be understood by it. Alas for them! They are hardly fit to dwell on this earth, to do battle with its sins and its cares; for their spirit is more exalted than is well: it may be said, more etherealized. The gold too highly refined, remember, is not adapted for general use. That the broad, vulgar idea conveyed by the word infidelity, is not their infidelity, is very certain. It is the unfaithfulness of the spirit, the wandering of the heart's truth to another, that constitutes infidelity for them; and where such comes, it shatters the heart's life as effectually as a blast of lightning shatters the tree it falls on. This was the infidelity that wrought the misery of Clara Lake: that other infidelity, whether it was or was not to have place in the future, she barely glanced at. Her husband's love had left her: it was given to another; and what mattered aught else? The world had closed to her; never again could she have, as it seemed, any place in it. Henceforth life would be a mockery.

She returned shivering to the house—not apparently with the cold from without, but from the chill within—entering by the glass doors. The fire was nearly out; it wanted stirring and replenishing. She never saw it, never noticed it; but crept upstairs to her own room to hide herself. We cannot follow her; for you may not doubt that the quarter of an hour she stopped in it she had need to be alone, away from the wondering eyes of men.

Only a quarter of an hour. Clara Lake was not one of your loud women, who like their wrongs to be proclaimed to the world, and punished accordingly. In her sensitive reticence, she dreaded their betrayal more than any earthly thing. So she rose from her knees, and lifted her head from the chair, where it had lain in utter abandonment of spirit, and smoothed her hair, and went out of her room again to disarm suspicion, and was her calm self once more. At that same moment, though she knew it not, Mr. Lake and Lady Ellis were slowly strolling across the grass to enter by the same glass doors, their promenade, which they had been taking up and down the broad walk since quitting the shrubbery, having come to a decorous end.

CHAPTER VIII

Catching a Chill

The warm light from the open nursery door flashed across Clara Lake's path in the corridor, and she went in. Mrs. Chester was running some slate-coloured breadths together, the lining for a black frock for Fanny. Miss Cooper sat at the table equally busy. She was a steady, industrious young woman, as well-conducted as her brother, the unfortunate engine-driver; and many ladies employed her at their houses by day.

"Is it you, Clara?" cried Mrs. Chester, looking up. "I'm coming down. I suppose you are all wondering what has become of me? Is tea on the table?"

"I—I don't know; I have been in my room," replied Mrs. Lake, taking a low chair near the fire.

Anna, with her quick ear of discernment—at work apart from the rest, with very little benefit of the candles' light—turned round and looked at Clara, as if something in the tone were unnatural; disguised. But she said nothing. Clara seemed absorbed in the fire.

Light, quick steps were heard on the stairs, and Robert Lake dashed in, a gay smile on his face. "Pretty housekeepers you are! The drawing-room fire's gone out."

"The fire gone out!" repeated Mrs. Chester, in consternation. "What will Lady Ellis say? Clara, dear, what could you have been thinking of? You should have rung for coals."

"It was a good fire when I left it," murmured Clara, believing she spoke in accordance with the truth.

"And the fire was all red coals, and the room as hot as could be when I went in for that newspaper," put in Fanny Chester.

"Run, Fanny, and tell them to make up the fire again, and to put in plenty of sticks," said Mrs. Chester. "Has Lady Ellis not been sitting with you this afternoon, Clara?"

"In her own room, no doubt, writing letters. I hope she is there still. So you have got back, Robert," Mrs. Chester added, turning to her brother.

"Safe and sound," was Mr. Lake's response, as he stood surveying the table and the work going on. "What are you so busy over, all of you?"

Mrs. Chester, bending her eyes and fingers on a complicated join, inserted from consideration of economy, did not take the trouble to answer. Mr. Lake went round to his wife.

"How are you by this time, Clary?" he lightly said; as, standing between her and the table, he bent down to the low chair where she sat, and kissed her forehead.

It was a cold kiss; a careless matter-of-fact sort of kiss à la matrimony. She made no response in words, or else; but the hot crimson dyed her cheeks, as she contrasted it with a certain other kiss bestowed by him on somebody else not long before; that was passionate enough; rather too much so. Had he noticed, he might have seen his wife press her hand sharply upon her bosom; as if she might be trying to hide its tumultuous throbbing.

"And how does the house get on, Robert?" asked Mrs. Chester, lifting her head to speak.

"Slower than ever. You'll have us here until Christmas, Penelope, according to the present lookout."

"I hope I shall; although Clara"—turning towards her—"does seem in a fidget to get back."

Clara seemed in a fidget about nothing, just then; she was sitting perfectly still, her face and her eyes cast down. Robert Lake ran on, in his own fashion, turning his attention upon the dressmaker now.

"Working for your life as usual, Miss Cooper! What is that you are cutting out? A pair of pantaloons for me?"

"It's a pair of sleeves, sir."

"Oh, sleeves; I feared they'd hardly be large enough. By the way, when is that inquest to be brought to an end?"

"I wish I knew, sir," she answered.

"And nothing has been decided in regard to your brother yet!"

"No, sir. It is very hard."

"It is very strange," returned Mr. Lake—"strange there should be this contradiction about the lights. Each side is so positive."

"I am quite certain, sir, that Matthew would not say what was untrue, even to save himself; therefore, when he says it was the green light up, I know it was the green."

"Precisely the same thing that I tell everybody. I have unlimited faith in Cooper."

"And there's Colonel West to bear out what he says, you know, sir. The colonel would not say the green light was up, if it was not."

"No. But then, again, Oliver Jupp and the station people maintain it was the red," said Mr. Lake, remarking upon the fact that had puzzled him all along. "For my part, I think there was a little sleight of hand going on. Some conjurors must have been there in disguise. Now gentlemen and ladies, walk up; the performance is just going to begin. The celebrated Signor Confusiani has taken his place, and is entering on his mysteries. He transforms colours by the help of his magic wand In looking at the green, you perceive it change to red; in looking at the red, it at once passes into blue."

They all laughed, except Clara. She sat still as before, her eyes fixed on the fire.

"You see, sir, the worst of it is that Matthew is kept out of employment all this time," said Miss Cooper. "They have suspended him. He and his poor young wife are at their wits' end nearly, over it. Two months now, and not a shilling coming in."

"Yes, it is very bad," returned Mr. Lake, speaking seriously for once. "There's a baby too, is there not?"

"Yes, sir. Three weeks old."

"I suppose you give them your earnings."

"I give them what I can, sir; but I have my mother to keep."

"Ah," concluded Mr. Lake, abandoning the subject. "Have you been for a walk today, Clara?"

"No."

"You ought to take her, Robert; she scarcely ever goes out now. You might have come back earlier and done it. Lady Ellis did not have a walk today, failing you. Why did you not come sooner?"

"Couldn't manage it, Mrs. Chester."

"But—when did you come?" suddenly resumed Mrs. Chester, after a pause of thought. "You must have come back in the afternoon. There's no train at this hour."

"Oh, they put on a special one for me."

"Don't be stupid," retorted Mrs. Chester. "You must have been back some time."

"Have it your own way, Penelope, and perhaps you'll live the longer."

"Uncle Robert, you know you were back ever so long ago," interposed Fanny Chester, who had just come into the room. "You have been staying in the garden with Lady Ellis."

"What's that?" cried Mr. Lake.

"I saw you. You were both of you going towards the shrubbery."

He caught hold of the little speaker by the waist, and swung her round. "That's the way you see ghosts, is it, Miss Fanny! Take care they don't run away with you! How could you see me in the shrubbery, pray, if I was not there."

"Be quiet, Uncle Robert; put me down. Mamma there's a good fire in the parlour now, and the tea-tray is carried in. And Miss Cooper, I was to tell you they are waiting tea for you in the kitchen."

Mrs. Chester, shaking the threads from her black gown, left the room, Fanny went with her, and Miss Cooper followed. Tea was a thankful boon to the weary, hard-worked dressmaker. Anna never quitted her work until the last minute, and sat on, drawing one of the candles a little nearer to her. Robert Lake began speaking to his wife of the progress of their house; or rather, the non-progress. Clara—the one dreadful certainty giving rise to other suspicions—wondered whether he had bribed the men to retard it. He had not done that, however; he was not one to commit wrong deliberately.

"Seriously speaking, Clara, I do think we shall not get back before Christmas."

She had determined upon saying something; what, she hardly knew. But when she tried to speak, the violent agitation that the effort brought, impeded all utterance. And perhaps the presence of Anna Chester acted as a restraint. She glanced up at him and opened her lips; but no words came; her throat was beating, her breath troubled.

"Clara! you have turned quite white. Are you ill?"

"I—I feel cold," was all she could say.

"It is a cold, nasty night," remarked Mr. Lake, giving no further thought to the matter, or supposing that there was cause to give it. "The tea is ready, I think; that will warm you."

He took one of the candles off the table and went to his room to wash his hands. Anna Chester laid down her work and approached Clara.

"Dear Mrs. Lake, something is troubling you," she said in her gentle manner, as her sweet eyes glanced deprecatingly at that care-betraying face. "Can I do anything for you—or get you anything? Shall I bring you some tea up here?"

"Hush, Anna! No, it is nothing—only that I am cold. Thank you all the same."

"You are looking so pale. Pale and sad."

"I don't think I have been very well lately, Anna. Let me be quiet, my dear, for a few minutes, will you? my head aches."

Anna Chester, with the delicacy innate in her, quitted the room, setting things a little straight on the work-table in passing it. When Mr. Lake came back, Clara was sitting just as he had left her. Putting down the candle, he came close up, making some trifling remark.

She would have given the world to be able to say a word to him; to ask whether she was to be second in his heart; second to that woman; but she simply dared not. Her agitation would have become unbearable, and ended in an hysterical scene.

"Are you not coming to tea, Clara?"

"Presently."

He looked at her with a keen eye. She was odd, he thought.

"What's the matter, Clara? You seem dull this evening."

There was no answer. Mrs. Lake had her hand pressed upon her throat and chest, striving, though he knew it not, to still the agitation that all but burst its bounds.

"Where is the book?" she presently asked.

"What book?"

"The one you were to bring for me; that you forgot last time."

"Oh, to be sure; here it is," he said, taking it from his coat pocket. "I did not forget it this time, you see."

"You might have brought it to me when you first got back," she reproachfully said.

"Well, I have not been back long. You are shivering; what makes you so cold?"

"Oh, I don't know."

"Perhaps you have been asleep; one does shiver sometimes on waking. Come along, Clara; tea will do you good."

She rose and followed him down. Mrs. Chester was pouring out the tea, and Lady Ellis, in her black silk gown with its low body and short sleeves, and the ruche of white crape, causing her to look girlish, years younger than she was, sat on the sofa. She had several evening dresses, but they were all black, and all made in the same simple style. Sir George had not been dead twelve months yet; but she had never worn a regular widow's cap—it would have spoilt her hair, she told them. The pretty white net things she wore in a morning were but an apology for one. Very fine, very silky and beautiful did her purple-black hair look that night, and Robert Lake playfully touched it as he sat down beside her.

The children's meal-table, at which Anna Chester used to preside in a little room, was done away with, the two boys having gone to school, so that Anna and Fanny were present as usual this evening. There was plenty of talking and laughing, and Clara's silence was not noticed—save perhaps by Anna Chester.

After tea, when Anna and Fanny were gone away again, Mr. Lake and Lady Ellis began chess: in one way or other they generally monopolized each other's evenings. Sometimes it would be with music; sometimes at écarté, which she had taught him; often at chess. The small table was drawn out, and they sat at it apart. Mrs. Chester was doing some embroidery-work this evening; Clara sat alone by the fire reading; or making believe to read.

But when she was unobserved the book dropped on her lap. Nobody was looking at her. Mrs. Chester's profile was towards her, but she was fully engrossed with her work; her husband's back was turned. Only Lady Ellis was in full view, and Clara sat studying her face and the glances of her large and flashing eyes.

How long silence had reigned, except for the remarks exchanged now and again between the chess-players, perhaps none of them could have told, when one of those subtle instincts, alike unaccountable and unexplainable, caused Mrs. Chester to turn suddenly to Clara Lake. What she saw made her start.

"Clara! What is the matter?"

Mr. Lake turned quickly round and regarded his wife. The book lay on her knee, her cheeks were scarlet as with incipient fever, her whole frame was shaking, her eyes were wild. That she was labouring under some extraordinary attack of terror appeared evident to all. He rose and came up.

"You are certainly ill, my dear!"

Ill, agitated, frightened—there could be no question of it. Not at once did she speak; she was battling with herself for calmness. Mrs. Chester took her hand Lady Ellis approached with dark and wondering eyes. Clara put her hands before her own.

"It is a nervous attack." said Mrs. Chester. "Go and get some wine, Robert, or some brandy."

He was going already, before she told him, and brought back both. Clara would take neither. Awfully vexed at having caused a scene, the mortification enabled her to throw off the symptoms of illness, except the shivering. Lady Ellis, with extreme bad taste, slipped her hand within Mr. Lake's arm as they stood watching her. He moved forward to speak, and so dropped it.

"You must have caught cold, I fear, Clara. Had you not better take something warm and go to bed?"

She lifted her eyes to his, and answered sharply—sharply for her.

"I shall not go to bed. I am well now."

"Colds are sooner caught than got rid of, Clara. If you have take one—"

"If I have, it will be gone in the morning," came the sharp interruption. "Pray do not let me disturb your game."

Contriving to repress the shivering by a strong effort of will, she took up her book again. They returned to the chess-table, Mrs. Chester went on with her embroidery, and so the night went on: Clara, outwardly calm, reading sedulously—inwardly shaking as though she had an ague-fit. Even to herself it was evident that she had caught a violent cold.

"I shall send you a glass of white-wine whey," spoke Mrs. Chester, when Clara at length rose to go upstairs, declining to partake of the refreshments brought in. "And mind you lie in bed in the morning. There's no mistake about the cold."

"How could she have caught it?" exclaimed Lady Ellis, with a vast display of sympathy; and Clara bit her tongue to enforce silence, for she could scarcely forbear telling her. My lady, taking her unawares, gave her a kiss on the cheek.

"Drink the whey quite hot, my dear Mrs. Lake."

Clara, her mind full of Judas the false and his kiss, went upstairs alone; she preferred to do so, she told them, and shut-herself in her own chamber. When Elizabeth appeared with the white-wine whey, and left it, she noticed that her mistress had not begun to undress.

Neither had she when Mr. Lake came up, nearly an hour afterwards. They had lingered in the dining-room—he, Mrs. Chester, and Lady Ellis. He was very much surprised. She sat by the fire, wrapped in a shawl, with her feet on the fender.

"Why, Clara, I thought you were in bed and asleep!"

There was no answering remark. Mr. Lake, thinking her manner more and more strange, laid his hand kindly on her shoulder.

"Clary, what ails you to-night?"

She shrank away from his hand, and replied to his question by another.

"Why is it that our house is not ready?"

"That is just what I asked of the workmen today, lazy dogs!"

"We can go back to it as it is. Some of the rooms are habitable. Will you do so?"

"What in the world for?" he demanded. "We are very comfortable here, Clara; and, between ourselves, it is a help to Penelope."

"We must go back. I cannot stay."

"But why? Where's the motive?"

She drew her shawl closely round her as if she shivered again, and spoke the next words with a jerk, for to get them out required an effort of pain. What it had taken to nerve her to this task so far, she alone knew.

"What is there between you and Lady Ellis?"

"Between me and Lady Ellis!" echoed Mr. Lake, with all the carelessness in life. "Nothing at all. What should there be?"

She bent towards him and whispered.

"Which is it—which is it to be, I or she?"

"To be—for what?" rejoined Mr. Lake, really at a loss.

"Which of us is it that you love?" she wailed forth; and indeed the tone of her voice could be called little else than a wail.

"Clara, you are growing foolish."

"Don't put me off in this false way," she vehemently uttered, roused to passion by his indifference. "Why are you always with her, stealing walks and interviews?—why do you give to her your impassioned kisses, and call her by endearing names? Robert, you will kill me!"

He put the heel of his boot on the bars to push down a piece of refractory coal, probably debating with himself what he should answer.

"Considering that you are my wife, Clara, and that Lady Ellis is but a chance acquaintance, I think you might be above this nonsense."

"Have you forgotten my dream?" she resumed, in a low tone. "Have you forgotten that my coming to this house seemed to shadow forth my death?"

"That dream again, of all things!" exclaimed Mr. Lake in open surprise, involuntary sarcasm in his tone. "I thought it was done with and dismissed."

"I have been thinking of it all the evening."

"Then I'd not confess it," he said, dropping either by accident or in temper the hair-brush he had taken in his hand "And the notion of my kissing Lady Ellis! and calling her—what did you phrase it?—endearing names? That's the best joke I have heard lately."

She fixed her gaze steadfastly upon him; there was something in it which seemed to say she could convict him of falsehood, if she chose; and his eyes fell beneath hers.

"What has come over you, Clary? You must be turning jealous! I never knew you so foolish before."

"No," she answered, in a tone of pain, "never before, never before."

"And why now? There's no occasion for it."

"I will not descend to explanation or reproach," she said, after a pause; "you may ask your own conscience how much of the latter you merit. I shall go home tomorrow; I dare not stay in this house with that woman. Do you understand me, I dare not. You can accompany me if—if— Robert, you must choose between us."

He did not speak for a minute or two; and when he did, it was in a careless tone, as though he wished to make light of the matter altogether.

"Of course if you have made up your mind to return to an uncomfortable home, half pulled down, we must do so. I am sorry for the caprice, for we shall be choked with paint and dust."

"Very well. We go tomorrow. I will send Elizabeth over early in the morning, to get things straight for us."

She rose as she spoke, and began to undress. His eyes fell upon the tumbler. Taking it up he held it to the light.

"I do believe this is your whey! It is quite cold. To drink it like this would do you no good."

"Oh, what does it signify?" she answered; as if that and all things else were utterly indifferent to her.

Mr. Lake quitted the room without speaking. By and by he came back with another glassful, quite hot.

"Now, Clara, drink this."

She refused at first; it would do her no good, she said; but Mr. Lake insisted upon it. He was her husband still, and could exact obedience.

But the morrow brought no journey for Mrs. Lake. It brought illness instead. With early morning Mr. Lake got up and aroused the house, saying that his wife was ill. She had awoke so exceedingly suffering—her breath impeded, her face and eyes hot and wild—as to alarm him. Mrs. Chester hastened to her bedside, and the nearest doctor was summoned in haste and brought to the house. He pronounced the malady to be inflammation of the chest and lungs, and forbade her to attempt to leave her bed. He inquired of Mrs. Lake if she knew how she had taken it, and she told him, after a pause of hesitation, that she had gone out of doors from a warm room the previous evening without putting anything on, and the damp cold must have struck to her.

Yes; it was so. As the sight she had gone out to witness struck a chill to her heart, so did the cold and damp strike a chill to her frame. Once before, five or six years ago, she had caught a similar chill, and inflammation had come on in the same rapid manner. The doctor observed that she must be especially predisposed to it, and privately inquired of Mrs. Chester whether any of her relatives had died of consumption. "Yes," was the answer, "her mother and her brother."

Mr. Lake went to Katterley and brought back the gentleman who had attended her from infancy, Dr. Marlow, an old man now. He was a personal friend of theirs as well as medical attendant. He saw no cause for anxiety, he said to Mr. Lake; that she was very ill there was no doubt, but not, he thought, ill unto danger.

"She has a good constitution, she has a good constitution," urged Mr. Lake, his tone of anxiety proving that he wished to be reassured upon the point.

"For all I have ever seen to the contrary," replied Dr. Marlow. "She must be more prudent for the future, and not subject herself to sudden changes of temperature."

"She found the drawing-room very hot, and went from it into the cold night-air. It opens with glass doors. And if you remember, doctor, last night was raw and foggy. At least, it was so here; I don't know what it may have been at Katterley."

So spoke Mr. Lake. But it never entered into his carelessly-constituted mind to wonder why his wife had gone out; or whether, having gone out, she might by some curious chance have come unsuspected across the path of himself and another.

For three weeks Mrs. Lake never left her bed. The inflammation had taken strong hold upon her. A nice time of it those two must have had downstairs! Robert Lake, genuinely sorry for her illness in itself, for her prolonged seclusion, was quite an exemplary attendant, and would pass half an hour together in the sick-chamber, indemnifying himself by several half-hours with somebody else. Mrs. Chester of course saw nothing; nobody on earth could be more conveniently blind where her interest was concerned, and it would be unprofitable to her to lose or to offend Lacy Ellis. Clara lay and imagined all that might be taking place, the sweet words, the pretty endearments, the confidential interchange of feeling and thought: it was not precisely the way to get better.

The maid Elizabeth was her chief attendant; Anna Chester sat with her often. Mrs. Chester, bustling and restless in a sick room as she was elsewhere, was better out of the chamber than in it. To none of these did Clara speak of her husband; but when Fanny ran in, as she did two or three times a day, Clara would ask questions if nobody was within hearing.

"Where's Mr. Lake, Fanny?"

"Oh! he's downstairs in the drawing-room."

"What is he doing?"

"Talking to Lady Ellis."

The answers would vary according to circumstances; and Fanny, too young for any sort of suspicion, was quite ready and willing to give them. "He is reading to Lady Ellis;" or "He is out with Lady Ellis;" or "He and Lady Ellis are sitting together by the fire-light;" just as it might chance to be. Twice Lady Ellis went with him to Katterley, and gave Mrs. Lake on her return a glowing account of how quickly the house was getting on now.

Well, the time wore away somehow, and Mrs. Lake got better and took to sit up in her room. The first time she went downstairs was an evening in November. She did not go down then by orders; quite the contrary. "Not just yet," the doctor had, told her in answer to an inquiry; "in a few days." But she felt very, very dull that afternoon, sitting alone in her chamber. Mrs. Chester and Anna were busy downstairs, making pickles—in the very kitchen that Clara had seen so minutely in her dream; Elizabeth had gone on an errand to Katterley, taking Fanny Chester, and Robert did not come up. She knew he was at home and sat feverishly expecting him, but he never came. Very lonely felt she, very dispirited;

tears filled her eyes repeatedly, uncalled for; and so it went on to dusk. Had everybody abandoned her? she thought, sitting there between the lights.

The shadows of the room, only lighted by its fire, threw their sombre darkness across, taking curious shapes. A long narrow box, containing ferns and seaweed, stood on a stool in front of the hearth; as the shadow of it grew deeper on the opposite wall in the rapidly fading daylight, it began to look not unlike a coffin. As this fancy took possession of her, the remembrance of her dream with all its distressing terror suddenly flashed into her mind; she grew nervous and timid; too frightened to remain alone.

Wrapping herself up in a grey chenille shawl, as warmly as her husband had wrapped another that recent bygone night, she prepared to descend. She was fully dressed, in a striped green silk, and her pretty hair was plainly braided from her brow. The lovely face was thin and pale; the dark eyes were larger and sadder than of yore; and she was very weak yet.

Too weak to venture down the staircase alone, as she soon found. But for clinging to the balustrades, she would have fallen. This naturally caused her movements to be slow and quiet. She looked into the dining-room first; it was all in darkness; then she turned to the drawing-room, and pushed open the half-closed door. Little light was there, either; only what came from the fire, and that was low. Standing over it she discerned two forms, which, as she slowly advanced with her tottering steps, revealed themselves as those of her husband and Lady Ellis. She was in her usual evening attire: the black silk gown with the low body and short sleeves, and some black ribbons floated from her hair. Mr. Lake's hand was lightly resting on her neck; ostensibly playing with the jet chain around it, and touching her fair shoulder. Talking together, they did not hear her entrance.

"You know, Angeline," were the first words audible—when at that moment he seemed to become conscious that some one had entered to disturb the interview, and turned his head. Who was it? Some muffled figure. Mr. Lake strained his eyes as it came nearer, and sent them peering through the semidarkness. The next moment he had sprung at least five yards from "Angeline."

"Clara! How could you be so imprudent? My dear child! you know you ought not to have left your room."

Pushing aside Lady Ellis with, it must be confessed, little ceremony, he dragged a couch to the warmest corner of the hearth, and took his wife in his sheltering arms. Placing her upon it, he snatched up a cloth mantle of Mrs. Chester's that happened to be near, and fenced her in with it from the draught, should there be any. Then he sat down on the same sofa, edging himself on it, as if he would also be a fence for her against the cold. That his concern and care were genuine, springing right from his heart, there could be no question. My Lady Ellis, standing on the opposite side to recover her equanimity, after having stirred the fire into a blaze, and looking on with her great black eyes, saw that.

He bent his head slightly as he gazed on his wife, waiting in silence, not saying a word further until her breath was calmer. Very laboured it was just then, perhaps with the exertion of walking down, perhaps with mental emotion.

"Now tell me why you ventured out of your room," said he, making a prisoner of one of her hands, and speaking in a tender tone.

"I was dull: I was alone," she panted.

"Alone! dull! Where's Penelope? where's Anna? I thought they were with you. Elizabeth, what is she about?"

She did not explain or answer. She lay back quietly as he had placed her, her eyes closed, and her white face motionless. For the first time Robert Lake thought he saw a look of DEATH upon it, and a strange thrill of anguish darted through him. "What a fool I am!" quoth he to himself, the next moment; "it's the reflection of that fire."

"My dear Mrs. Lake, I should only be too happy to sit with you when you feel lonely," spoke Lady Ellis, as softly as her naturally harsh voice would allow. "But you never will let me, you know."

Clara murmured some inaudible answer about not giving her trouble, and lay quiet where her husband had placed her. He kept her hand still; and she let him do it. He stole quick glances at her wasted features, as if alarm had struck him. She never lifted her eyes to either of them.

The announcement of dinner and Mrs. Chester came together. When that lady saw who was in the drawing-room lying on the sofa, like a picture of a ghost more than a living woman, she set up a commotion. What did Clara mean by it? Did she come out of her room on purpose to renew her illness? She must go back to it again. Clara simply shook her head by way of dissent, and Mr. Lake interposed, saying she should stay if she wished: she would get no harm in the warm room.

They went in to dinner. Not Clara; what little solid food she could take yet was eaten in the middle of the day. There was a fowl on the table; and Mr. Lake, leaving his own dinner to get cold, prepared to carry a piece of it to his wife.

"It will be of no use," said Mrs. Chester to him, in rather a cross tone, as if she thought the morsel was going to be wasted; but he quitted the room, paying no attention.

He found his wife in a perfect paroxysm of tears, sobbing wildly. Left alone, her long pent-up feelings had given way. Putting the plate on the table, he bent over her—

"My dearest, this will never do. Why do you grieve so? What is the matter?"

"Oh, you know! you know!" she answered.

There was a dead pause. She employed it in smothering and choking down her sobs; he in any reflection that might be agreeable to him.

"I want to go home."

"The very instant that you may go with safety, you shall go," he readily assented. "If the doctor says you may go tomorrow, Clara, why we will. I must not have my dear little wife grieve like this."

No response. She seemed quite exhausted.

"I have brought you a bit of fowl, Clara; try and eat it."

She waved it away, briefly saying she could not touch it: she could not eat. She waved him away, telling him to go to his dinner. Mr. Lake simply put the plate down again, and stood near her.

"I must go home. I shall die if I stay here."

"Clara, I promise that you shall go. What more can I say? The house is sufficiently habitable now; there's nothing to detain us. Settle it yourself with the doctor. If he says you may travel tomorrow, so be it."

She closed her eyes—a sign that the contest was over. Mr. Lake carried the plate of fowl back to the dining-room, not feeling altogether upon the best terms with himself. For the first time he was realizing the fact that his wife's full recovery might be a more precarious affair than he had suspected.

"I knew she'd not touch it," said Mrs. Chester; "though I think she might eat it if she would."

"Surely she is not sulky!" spoke Lady Ellis, in an undertone, to Mr. Lake, turning her brilliant and fascinating eyes upon him, as he sat down in his place beside her.

He was not quite bad. He cared for his wife probably as much as he had ever done, although he had become enthralled by another, according to his light and unsteady nature. A haughty flush darkened his brow, and he pointedly turned from Lady Ellis without answering.

"It is the breast of the fowl wasted," cried thrifty Mrs. Chester, in her vexation.

It was not wasted. Mr. Lake took it upon his own plate, and made his dinner off it, never speaking a word all the while to anybody.

What of that? With her wiles and her sweet glances, my lady won him round again to good-humour; and before the meal was over he was as much her own as ever. But when the dessert was put on the table— consisting of a dish of apples and another of nuts—Mr. Lake left them to it, and went back to his wife.

She lay on the sofa all the evening. Mrs. Chester grumbled at the imprudence; but Clara said it was a change for the better: she was so tired of her bedroom. Her husband waited upon her at tea—a willing slave; and Clara really said a few cheerful words. Lady Ellis challenged him to chess again afterwards. Mrs. Chester and Anna sat by Clara.

"Very shortly," said the doctor, the following morning, in answer to the appeal which Mr. Lake himself made. "Yearning for home, is she? I fancied there was something of the sort. Not today: perhaps not tomorrow; but I think you may venture to take her the following one, provided the wind's fair."

"All right," was the answer. "Tell her so yourself, will you, my good sir?"

Clara was told accordingly. And on the third day, sure enough, the wind being fair and soft for November, Mr. and Mrs. Lake terminated their long sojourn at Guild, and returned to Katterley.

Home at last! In her exhilaration of spirit, it seemed just as though she had taken a renewed lease of happy life.

CHAPTER IX

Colour Blindness

The difference of opinion touching the lights at the railway station on the night of the fatal accident, continued to create no small sensation. The jury turned nearly rampant; vowing they'd not attend the everlastingly adjourned inquest, and wanting every time to return no verdict at all, say they could not, and have done with it. The coroner told them that was impossible; though he avowed that he did not see his way clearly out of it. But for being the responsible party, he would have willingly pitched the whole affair into the sea.

Over and over again did the public recount the circumstances one with another. When anybody could get hold of a stranger, hitherto in happy ignorance, he thought himself in luck, and went gushingly into all the details. It was a stock-in-trade for the local newspapers; and two of them entered on a sharp weekly controversy in regard to it. In truth, the matter, that is the conflict in the evidence, was most remarkable. That one party should stand to it the lights were red, and that the other should maintain they were green, was astonishing from the simple fact that both sides were worthy of credit. In the earlier stage of the enquiry the coroner had significantly remarked upon the "hard swearing somewhere:" it seemed more of a mystery than ever on which side that reproach could attach to. The jury could arrive at no decision, and thus the inquest had been adjourned time after time, and now the county was getting tired of it. Cooper, meanwhile suspended from employment, stood a chance of being reduced to straits if it lasted much longer. The colonel and Oliver Jupp, who had become intimate, made rather merry over it when they met, each accusing the other of having "seen double;" but neither would give way an inch. The lawyers were confounded, and knew not which side to believe; neither of the two gentlemen had the slightest personal interest in the matter; they spoke to further the ends of justice alone, and the one and the other were alike worthy of credit.

Affairs were in this unsatisfactory state, when a gentleman arrived in the neighbourhood on a short sojourn, a Dr. Macpherson, LL.D., F.R.S., and so on; about seventeen letters in all he could put after his name if he chose to do it. He was a man great in science, had devoted the most part of his life to it, no branch came amiss to him; he had travelled much and was renowned in the world. Amidst other acquirements he had phrenology at his fingers' ends, being as much at home in it as we poor unlearned mortals are in reading a newspaper; or as Mr. Lake was in making himself agreeable to a pretty woman.

They were staying at the "Rose Inn," at Guild, this learned gentleman and his wife. Professor Macpherson (as he was frequently called) had come down on some mission connected with geology. He was a very wire of a man, tall and thin as a lamp-post, exceedingly near-sighted, even in his silver-rimmed spectacles that he constantly wore; a meek, gentle, simple-minded man, whose coats and hats were threadbare, a very child in the ways of the world; as these excessively abstruse spirits are apt to be.

Mrs. Macpherson was in all respects his opposite: stout in figure, fine in dress, loud in speech; and keen in the affairs of common life. Good-hearted enough at the main, but sadly wanting in refinement, Mrs. Macpherson rarely pleased at first; in short, not to mince the matter, she was undeniably vulgar. Mrs. Macpherson's education had not been equal to her merits; her early associations were not of the silver-fork school. She was a very pretty girl when Caleb Macpherson (not the great man he was now) married her; habit reconciles us to most things, and he had discovered no fault in her yet. That she made him a good wife was certain, and a very capable one.

This was the second visit Professor Macpherson had made to Guild. The first took place about half a dozen years ago, when he had come on a question of "pneumatics." He had then become acquainted with the Reverend Mr. Chester, not himself unlearned in science, and had spent several hours of three separate days at the rectory. James Chester had gone now where science probably avails not; Mrs. Chester had quitted the rectory; and it might have chanced that the acquaintanceship would never have been renewed but for an accidental meeting.

Mrs. Chester was walking quickly into Guild on an errand when she met him. He would have passed her; her style of dress was altered—and for the matter of that he always went (as his wife put it) mooning on, his head in the skies and looking at nobody. But Mrs. Chester stopped him. Except that he looked taller and thinner, and his coat a little more threadbare than of old, and his spectacles staring out straighter up at the clouds or at the far-off horizon, he was not altered.

"Have you forgotten me, Dr. Macpherson?"

It took the doctor some few minutes to bring himself and his thoughts down to the level of passing life. Mrs. Chester had to tell him who she was, and that she was now alone in the world. He took both her hands in his then, and spoke a few words of genuine sympathy, with the sorrowful look in his kind eyes, and the tone of true pity coming from his ever-open heart.

"You will come and call on me, will you not?" she asked, after telling him where she lived.

"I'll come this evening," he said, "and bring my wife. She's with me this time."

So Mrs. Chester went home and told Lady Ellis of the promised visit. That lady, who had been fit to die of weariness since the departure of Mr. Lake, welcomed it eagerly; on the principle that even an old professor with seventeen letters beyond his name was of the man species, and consequently better than nobody.

"I don't know his wife," spoke Mrs. Chester. "She is rather exclusive, most likely. The wife of a man who has made so much noise in the world may look down upon us."

Lady Ellis raised her black eyebrows and had a great mind to tell Mrs. Chester to speak for herself; she was not accustomed to be looked down upon.

"Does the wife wear a threadbare gown?" she asked, having heard the description of the professor's coats.

"Very likely," said Mrs. Chester. "She need not, you know; they are rich."

"Rich, are they?"

"Very rich—now. In early life they had to pinch and screw, and live without a servant. Dr. Macpherson told us about it."

"He is not above confessing it, then?"

"He!" Mrs. Chester laughed. The simple professor, being "above" confessing anything of that sort, was a ludicrous idea. She attempted to describe him as he was.

"My dear Lady Ellis, you can have no notion of his simplicity—his utter unworldliness. In all that relates to learning and that sort of thing he is of the very keenest intellect; sharp; but in social life he is just a child. He would respect a woman who has to wash up her dishes herself just as much as he would if she kept ten servants to do it for her. I don't believe he can distinguish any difference."

"Oh!" concluded Lady Ellis, casting a gesture of contempt on the absent and unconscious professor.

Dr. Macpherson meanwhile, immediately after parting with Mrs. Chester, put his hand in his pocket for his case of gradients—or whatever the name might be—and found he had not got it. To go geologizing or botanizing without it would have been so much waste of time, and he turned back to the "Rose." It was well for the evening visit that he did so; but for telling his wife at once while it was fresh in his head, they had never paid it; for the professor would have forgotten all about it in half an hour.

Mrs. Macpherson sat fanning herself at the window. She was a stout woman, comely, red-faced, and jolly; and the fire was large, throwing out a great heat. Her face and that of her pale thin husband's presented a very contrast. She wore a bright green silk gown, garnished with scarlet, and scarlet bows in her rich lace cap.

"I forgot my case, Betsy," said he, on entering.

"'Twouldn't be you, professor, if you didn't forget some'at," returned she, equably. "For a man who has had his head filled with learning, you be the greatest oaf I know."

Accustomed to these compliments from his wife—meekly receiving them as his due—Dr. Macpherson took up his case, a thick pocket-book apparently, the size of a small milestone. He then mentioned his meeting with Mrs. Chester, and the promised evening visit, which was received favourably.

"It'll be a godsend," said Mrs. Macpherson. "With you over them writings of yours, and me a-nodding asleep, the evenings here is fearful dull. Is the invite for tea and supper?"

Rather a puzzling question. Tea and supper were so little thought of by the professor, that but for his wife he might never have partaken of either; and he had to consider for some moments before he could hit upon any answer.

"I don't think it is, Betsy; I only said I'd call."

"Oh!" returned Mrs. Macpherson, ungraciously, for she liked good cheer,—"It'll hardly be worth going for. It's not a party, then?"

The professor supposed not. On these matters of social intercourse his ideas were always misty. He remembered that Mrs. Chester said she had a Lady Ellis visiting her, and mentioned the fact.

Mrs. Macpherson brightened up. "A Lady Ellis! Are you sure?"

"Yes; I think I'm sure."

"Well now, Caleb, you look here. We must go properly," said Mrs. Macpherson. "I never was brought into contract with a real live lady in my life; I haven't never had the chance of saying 'your ladyship,' except in sport. We'll have out a chaise and pair, and, drive up in it."

Had she proposed to drive up in a chaise and eight, it would have been all one to the professor. Conscious of his own deficiency on the score of sociality (not sociability) and fashion, he had been content this many a year to leave these things to her.

They arrived at Mrs. Chester's about seven. The chaise and pair rattled up to the gate; but as it was dark night, the pomp of the arrival could not be seen from within, and the gilt was taken off the gingerbread. It happened that Mr. Lake had come over that afternoon—a rather frequent occurrence—and Mrs. Chester had asked him to stay and see the strangers. He and Lady Ellis were at their usual game, chess, and Mrs. Chester was at work close by, when the visitors were announced by Nanny, the names having been given her by the lady—

"Professor and Mrs. Macpherson."

He came in first—the long, thin, absorbed, self-denying man, in his threadbare frock-coat. Mrs. Macpherson had left off fighting against these coats long ago. She ordered him in new ones in vain. As soon as one came home, he would put it on unconsciously, utterly unable to distinguish between that and his old one, and go to his work in it: "his chemical tests, and his proofs, and all that rubbish," as she was in the habit of saying. Somehow he had a knack of wearing his coats out incredibly quick, or else the poisons and the fires did it for him. In a week the new one would be as bad as the rest—shabby and threadbare. Mrs. Macpherson grew tired at last. "After all, it don't much matter," was her final conclusion, in pardonable pride. "Good coat or bad coat, he's Professor Macpherson." His scanty dark hair was brushed smoothly across his head, his brown eyes, shining through his spectacles, went kindly out in search of Mrs. Chester, who advanced to receive him.

"My wife, ma'am; Mrs. Macpherson."

Mrs. Macpherson came in—a ship in full sail. She had dressed herself to go into the presence of a real live lady. She did not travel without her attire, if he did. The forgetful man was apt to start on a journey with nothing but what he stood up in; she took travelling trunks.

An amber satin gown with white brocade flowers on it, white lace shawl, and small bonnet with nodding bird-of-paradise feather, white gloves, flaxen hair. Lady Ellis simply stared while the introductions were gone through and seats were taken. Mrs. Macpherson was free and unreserved in her conversation with strangers, concealing nothing.

"I was as glad as anything when the prefessor said we were coming here for a call this evening," she remarked to Mrs. Chester. "Not knowing a soul in the place, it's naturally dull for me; and we shall have to stop a week at it, I b'lieve."

"You were not with Dr. Macpherson last time, when I and my late husband had the pleasure of making his acquaintance," observed Mrs. Chester, surreptitiously regarding the bird-of-paradise.

"Not I," answered Mrs. Macpherson. "If I went about always with him, I should have a life of it. What with his geographies, and his botanies, and his astronomies, and his chemistries, and his social sciences, and the meetings he has to attend in all parts of the globe, and the country excursions the societies make in a body, he is not much at home."

"This is only the second visit he has paid to Guild, I think?"

"That's all. It's geology this time; last time it was—Prefessor, what's the name of the thing you were down here for last?" broke off Mrs. Macpherson.

"Pneumatics," he answered, looking lovingly at the child, Fanny Chester, and a bit of heath she was showing him.

"Eumatics," repeated Mrs. Macpherson. "Not that I can ever understand what it means. The name's hard enough, let alone the thing itself."

Perhaps the other ladies were in the same blissful ignorance. Mr. Lake checkmated his adversary, left her to put up the men, and went over to the professor.

Before tea came in they were out in the garden peering about by starlight, the remains of an old Roman wall there, that Mr. Lake happened to mention, keenly exciting the interest of the professor. Mrs. Macpherson was invited to take off her things, and she threw the handsome white shawl aside; but having brought no cap, the bird-of-paradise retained its place. This much might be said for her, that though addicted to very gay clothes, they were always rich and good. Mrs. Macpherson would have worn nothing poor or tawdry.

"How fond they are of these miserable bits of things—pieces of an old wall, strata of earth, wild plants, and such rubbish!" exclaimed Lady Ellis, with acrimony, inwardly vexed that Mr. Lake should have gone out a-roving.

"Rubbish it is—your ladyship's right," spoke Mrs. Macpherson. "Leastways, so it seems to us: but when folks have gifted minds, as the professor has, why perhaps they can see beauties in 'em that's hid to us others."

Not very complimentary on the whole; but Lady Ellis did not choose to see it.

"Of course," she said, "your husband is wonderfully clever; he has a world-wide fame. I heard of him in India."

"Clever on one side, a gander on t'other," said Mrs. Macpherson.

"A gander?"

"Well, you'd not say a goose, I suppose. In his sciences and his ologies, and his chemicals and his other learnings, why he's uncommon; there's hardly his equal, the public says. But take him in the useful things of life, your ladyship, and see what he's good for. Law bless me!"

"Not for much, I suppose," laughed Mrs. Chester.

"I'd be bound that any child of seven would have more sense. But for me helping him to it, he'd never have a meal; no, I don't believe, as I'm an honest woman, that he'd recollect to sit down to one. When he's away from me, he, as I tell him, goes in for trying to live upon air."

"Do you mean that he really tries to see if he can live upon it?"

"Bless you, no. He must know he couldn't. What I mean is, that he neglects his food—either forgets it out and out, or does not find time to sit down to it. And then his clothes! Look at the coat he has got on now."

Neither of the two ladies having particularly noticed the coat, they could not make much answering comment. Mrs. Macpherson, fond of talking, did not wait for any.

"I wonder sometimes what would become of him, and how long he would wear a coat, but for being looked after. Why, till it dropped off his back. I have to put every earthly thing ready for him—even to a pocket-handkercher—and then he can't see them. I used to let him have a chest of drawers to himself, handkerchers in one, gloves and collars in another, shirts in a third, and so on. He'd want, let's say, a necktie. Every individual thing would be taken out of every drawer, nicked over, thrown on the floor, and he in quite a state of agitation. Up I'd go, and show it to him. There it would be, staring him in the face, right under his very eyes."

"And he not seeing it?"

"Never. I soon left off letting him have the control of his own drawers. I give him one now, and lock up the rest, so that he has to call me when he wants things. He'll have his spectacles on his nose and be looking after them; his hand might be touching the ink, and he'd not see it. Ah! One might wonder why such useless mortals were born."

"But the professor is so kind and good," observed Mrs. Chester.

"I didn't say he wasn't; I'm not complaining of him," returned the professor's lady, giving a nod to the bird-of-paradise. "One tells these things as one would tell stories of a child that's not responsible for its actions. His brains are too clever, you know, for ordinary life. Thank ye, ma'am; I like it pretty sweet. There again, in the small matter of sugar: put the cup half full, or put in none at all, and it's all one to the preffesor; he'd never notice the difference."

"I once knew a very clever but very absent man who went to a wedding in his slippers," said Lady Ellis, leaning back in her armchair and speaking languidly for the benefit of the lady opposite. "He had forgotten to put his boots on."

"That's nothing; your ladyship should live for a month with Preffesor Macpherson. I've quaked in fear before now of seeing him go out without—worse things than boots."

Mrs. Chester laughed; and what further revelations might have been made were put an end to by the entrance of the professor himself and Mr. Lake. They came in talking eagerly, not of the Roman wall, but of the late fatal railway accident. Mr. Lake was giving him the details, and especially those relating to the conflicting nature of the evidence. As soon as Dr. Macpherson had mastered the particulars, he gave it as his opinion that it must be a case of colour-blindness.

"Of colour-blindness?' echoed Mr. Lake.

"Rely upon it, it is a case of colour-blindness on one s de or the other," continued the professor, who was now showing himself in his element, the keen man of science, the sensible, sound-judging reasoner. And so well did he proceed to argue the matter, so aptly and clearly did he lay the case before them, that Mr. Lake was half converted; and it was decided that the theory should be followed up.

On the next day the professor was brought into contact with Colonel West and Oliver Jupp, Mr. Lake having arranged a meeting at his own house. One or two friends were also present. The subject was entered upon, and the professor's opinion given. Oliver Jupp believed he might be right; the colonel was simply astonished at the assertion.

"Not know colours!" cried he. "Not able to tell white from black! Why, what have our eyes been about all our lives, Mr. Professor? My sight is keen and clear; I can answer for that; and I've not heard that there's anything amiss with Mr. Oliver Jupp's."

"It has nothing whatever to do with a keen sight—in the way you are thinking of," returned Dr. Macpherson. "Nay, it frequently happens that those who are afflicted with colour-blindness possess a remarkably good and clear sight. The defect is not in the vision: it lies in the absence of the organ of colour."

"That's logic," laughed the colonel, who had never heard of such a theory, and did not believe many others had.

"Look here," said the professor, endeavouring to put the case in an understandable light "You will allow that men are differently endowed. One man will have the gift of calculation in an eminent degree; he will go through a whcle ledger swimmingly, while his friend by his side is labouring at a single column of it: another will possess the organ of music so largely that he will probably make you a second Mozart; but his own brother can't tell one tune from another, and could not learn to play if his very life depended on it: this man will draw you, untaught, plans and buildings of wondrous and beautiful design; that one, who has served his stupid apprenticeship to the art, cannot accomplish a pigsty fit for a civilized pig to live in—and so I might go on, illustrating examples all. Am I right or wrong?" he concluded, turning his spectacles full on his attentive listeners.

"Right," they all said, including Colonel West.

"Very well," resumed the professor. "Then I would ask you, gentlemen, why should colour be an exception? I mean the capability of perceiving it; the faculty of distinguishing one shade from another?"

There was no immediate answer. The professor wert on.

"This brain is totally deficient in the organ of tune; that one is deficient in some other faculty; a third in something else: why should not the organ of colour sometimes fail?"

"I thought everybody possessed the organ of colour." observed Mr. Lake.

"The greater portion of people do possess it; but there are many who do not."

Colonel West, unconvinced, was rather amused than otherwise. "And you think, sir, that I and Mr. Oliver Jupp do not possess it," he said, laughing.

"Pardon me," replied the professor, laughing also, "I never said you both did not. Had that been the case, you probably would not have been in opposition to each other. But I have been using my own eyes since we stood here, and I see which of you has the defect. One of you possesses the organ of colour (as we call it) in a full degree; the other does not possess it at all. It lies here."

Dr. Macpherson raised his fingers to his eyebrow, and pointed out a spot near its middle. The colonel and Oliver Jupp immediately passed their fingers over their eyebrows, somewhat after the manner of a curious child. Oliver's eyebrows were prominent; the colonel's remarkably flat.

"You can testify by experiment whether I am right or wrong, Colonel West; but I give it as my opinion that you are not able to distinguish colours."

For some moments the colonel could not find his tongue. "I never heard of such a thing in all my life!" cried he. "Do you mean to say that I can see the blue sky" (turning his face upwards), "and not know it's blue?"

"You know it is blue, and call it blue, because you have heard it so called all your life," returned the undaunted professor. "But, if half the sky were blue and half green, you would not be able to say which was the green half and which the blue."

"That caps everything," retorted the colonel, in high good-humour. "It's a pity my wife can't hear this; she'd shake hands with you at once. She has, you must know, a couple of garden parasols: one green, the other blue. If she sends me indoors for the green, she says I bring her the blue; and if for the blue, I bring the green. She sets it down to inattention, and lectures me accordingly."

"You could not have given us a better confirmation that my opinion is correct," said Professor Macpherson, glancing at the group around. "Your wife has set this down to inattention, you say, colonel. May I ask what you have set it down to?"

"I? Not to anything. I never troubled myself to think about it."

The learned gentleman rubbed his hands with satisfaction. "What you acknowledge is so true to nature, colonel! Those who, like you, are affected with colour-blindness, can rarely be brought to believe in their own defect. It is a fact that the greater portion of them are not conscious of it; they really don't know that they cannot distinguish colours. Some few have perhaps a dim idea that they are not so quick in that particular as others, but they never think of questioning the cause. To use your own expression, it does not trouble them. I understand you maintain that on the night of the accident the usual light was up—green?"

"Yes," said the colonel. "They exhibit the green light always at Coombe Dalton station, to enforce caution, on account of the nasty turning just after passing it. I maintain, as you say, that the customary green light was shown that night."

"Now I will tell you how to account for that belief;" said the professor. "It was not so much that you could be sure the green light was up, as that you could not distinguish any difference between the one you saw, and the one you were accustomed to see. You could not discern the difference, I say, and therefore you maintained it to be, as you believed, the same one—the green."

"This seems plausible enough, as you state it," acknowledged Colonel West, at length. "But pray why should it not be my young friend, Jupp, who was mistaken—and not I?"

The professor shook his head. "I am quite sure that this gentleman"—indicating Oliver Jupp—"can never be mistaken in colours or in their shades, so long as he retains his eyesight to see anything: he has the organ very largely developed. I am right, colonel," he added, nodding.

"But what do you say to Cooper, the driver?" returned the colonel. "He says the light was green: and everybody agrees that he would only assert what was true."

"What he thought was true," corrected Dr. Macpherson. "There is little doubt, in my mind, that Cooper's case will turn out to be like your own—a fact of colour-blindness. He could not distinguish the difference in the light from the ordinary light, and therefore believed it to be the same."

"Both of us blind!" exclaimed the colonel, with wide-open eyes. "That would be too good, Mr. Professor."

"I said only colour-blind," corrected the professor. "There is not the least doubt that it will turn out to be so."

And he carried the opinions of nearly all present with him. It seemed, indeed, to be the only feasible solution of the difficulty; and so the gentlemen said to each other as they dispersed.

"I promised to take you in to see my wife," whispered Mr. Lake to the man of science, arresting him as he was departing.

Clara was sitting in an easy-chair, a shawl on her shoulders; but she looked up brightly when the professor entered. If the old feeling of secure happiness had not come back again, a portion of it had; and she said to everybody that she was getting well. Mary Jupp was with her. They had felt half scared at the thought of encountering familiarly so renowned a man. He turned out to be a very shy and simple one—in manners, at least; and Miss Jupp, in the revulsion of relieved feeling, nearly talked him deaf.

"She's a pretty thing, that young man's wife," observed the professor to Mrs. Macpherson, when he had got back to Guild. "But I'd not like to take an insurance on her life."

"I never knew you had turned doctor, professor."

"It does not require a doctor's eye to see when a blossom's delicate, Betsy. And those delicate blossoms want a vast deal of care."

The strange opinion avowed by Dr. Macpherson, that the matter which had been puzzling the world so long, would turn out to be a case of colour-blindness, excited the wonder of the simple country people.

In these rural districts men are content to live without science, and cannot well understand it when it is brought home to them. This opinion, nevertheless, coming from so great an authority, obtained weight with all, causing some commotion; and it was resolved to test the sight of the unfortunate driver, Cooper. Colonel West proposed, half jokingly, half seriously, that his own eyes should also be tested. It would set the matter at rest in his mind, he said. Mrs. West devoutly wished she could be present, and see the solution of what had been hitherto inexplicable. "I'd used to tell that husband of mine he couldn't see colours," she exclaimed to a select audience, "but I didn't really suppose it was so; I thought he was careless and stupid."

On the evening fixed for the test, those concerned in it assembled at the station of Coombe Dalton. Matthew Cooper came from Katterley in obedience to the summons sent for him. Colonel West, Mr. Lake, Oliver Jupp, the coroner, and some of the jury were present: and others also with whom we have had nothing to do.

The instant that Professor Macpherson cast his eyes on Cooper's face, he found his anticipation verified. The man laboured under the defect of colour-blindness, in even a greater degree than Colonel West.

They proceeded to the trial. Lamps of various colours were in readiness, and the Professor was constituted master of the ceremonies. He commenced his task by running up a light to the signal-post. Colonel West and Cooper stood a little forward; the coroner and other interested people, official and otherwise, behind; the mob behind them; all at a convenient distance from the lights.

"What light is that?" asked Dr. Macpherson of the two who were on trial, amidst breathless silence.

A momentary pause. Colonel West and Cooper turned their eyes up to the raised lamp; the crowd turned theirs.

"It's green," said the colonel.

"It's red," said Cooper.

And there arose a general laugh. For the lamp was blue.

Two lamps were next run up.

"What are they?" was the demand

A dead silence ensued. Neither Cooper nor the colonel could tell.

"I ask what are the colours of these two lamps?" repeated the professor.

"I think they are green and white," hazarded Cooper, at length.

"And I say they are red and blue," cried the colonel.

They were white and blue.

Then the four lamps were exhibited, green, red, white, and blue, and the mistakes made by both essayists kept the platform in a roar. The colonel did tell which was the white—but it was probably more of a guess than a certainty. They could distinguish a "difference," they said, between two or more colours when exhibited at once, but were unable to state what that difference was. Both of them were honestly anxious that the test should be fully carried out, and answered to the utmost of their ability. Various colours were exhibited, sometimes two of nearly the same shade: it all came to the same. Long before the experiment came to an end, the fact had been fully established that both Colonel West and Matthew Cooper laboured under the defect of colour-blindness.

"Cooper," said Oliver Jupp, in a good-natured tone, "they must never make an engine-driver of you again."

"Well, I don't know, sir," returned Cooper, who seemed very chapfallen, "if it's true what this strange gentleman says, why—I suppose it is true. But I hope they'll make something else of me; I know I am keen enough at most things. If a man is deficient in one line, he may be all the quicker in another."

"Now you have given utterance to a truism, without perhaps knowing it," interposed the professor, cheerily. "Be assured that where a defect does exist, it is amply made up for by the largeness of some other gift. Never fear that an intelligent man, like you, will want employment, because you are found not suited to the one they placed you on."

"About the worst they could have given him, as it turns out," remarked Oliver Jupp, as he stood aside with the professor out of the hearing of others. "An engine-driver ought, of all men, to be able to distinguish colours."

"There are some of our engine-drivers who do not, though," was the reply, as the professor cautiously lowered his voice. "Several of our worst accidents have occurred from this very fact."

"Do you think so?"

"I know it. It is a more frequent defect than would be thought, this absence of the organ of colour, but it is one to which little attention has been hitherto given; a subject that with some excites ridicule. A company engaging an engine-driver would as soon think of testing his capacity for eating a good dinner, as that of being able to distinguish signal lights. Most essentially necessary is it, though, that drivers, present or future, should undergo the examination."

"It seems so to me," said Oliver. "And always will seem so—after this night's experiment."

"And until such examination is made general, I should change the form of the signal lamps," remarked Dr. Macpherson. "Let the safety signal be of one uniform shape, and small; let the red, or danger signal, be of as different a shape as can be made, and large; so different that it could never fail to catch the eye. For, look you, a head deficient in the organ of colour will usually have that of form very much developed: and if a driver could not see the light, he might the form: and so save his train."

"Quite right," said. Oliver.

"In many of the railway calamities we read of, you find that a difference of testimony exists as to the colour of the signal exhibited. One side or the other is supposed to swear falsely; just as it has been in this case. But for the testimony of Colonel West, the jury would have returned a verdict against Cooper at once, and convicted him of falsehood. But rely upon it, the cause, generally speaking, of these conflicting and painful cases lies not in false swearing, but in colour-blindness."

So concluded the professor. And so was concluded the long-adjourned puzzle that had set Coombe Dalton together by the ears. Once more the inquest was called for the last time; and the jury returned a verdict of "Accidental death." In the face of the proved defect in Cooper's capacity for distinguishing the different signals, how could they with justice punish him? He was sent forth, a free man so far, but discharged from his employment to begin the world again.

Now, my friendly readers, the above is a bit of honest truth; a fact from the past. It may be that you will not believe it; may feel inclined to cavil at it. But search cases out and mark for yourselves. Blindness to colour is a far more common defect than the world suspects: it has existed—and does exist—in some of the railway-engine guards and drivers.

CHAPTER X

Mary Jupp's Explosion

A frosty day in December. Time had gone on, winter had come in: the seasons go their round, whatever the world may be doing.

How grew Clara Lake? Better? Well, she did not seem to grow much better; at any rate, she was not well, and the old doctor at Katterley, who had known her constitution from infancy, appeared puzzled. She dressed, as in her days of health, and went about the house: on fine days would go out for a walk in the sunshine: but she remained weak and debilitated, and could not get rid of her cough.

Compared to the dangerous attack she had at Guild, of course her present state seemed to be a vast improvement. On first coming home, the change for the better appeared to be marvellous; and Mr. Lake, never seeing anything but the bright side of things, congratulated himself that she was well again. The improvement did not go on as it ought to have gone; but the falling off was so gradual, the increasing degrees of weakness were so imperceptible, that he neither saw nor suspected either. Had any one told him his wife was in a bad way, he had simply stared in amazement. Latterly the inertness, the seeming debility had certainly made itself apparent to him, but only as a dim idea; so little importance did he attach to it, that he set it all down to apathy on his wife's part, and chided her for not "rousing herself." He did not mean to be unkind; never think that of him; for his wife he would have gone through fire and water, as the saying runs; but he was light, unobservant by nature, and careless.

He was enjoying himself immensely. Chiefly dividing his leisure time between Katterley and Guild. To-day he would be at home with his wife, tomorrow with Lady Ellis; the affectionate husband to the one, saying soft nothings (it must be supposed) to the other. Of course he never went for the sake of seeing my lady; certainly not; there was an excuse ever ready. Mrs. Chester had given him this commission, and he must go and report to her; or Mrs. Chester had given him the other; or she wanted to consult him on her affairs, which were going downwards; or he went over to escort some of the Jupps; or he had business with his tailor; for he had fallen into a freak to employ one who lived at Guild. On one plea or another, a plausible excuse for taking him to Guild never failed.

The fault of this lay partially with Mrs. Chester. Nearly at her wits' end lest Lady Ellis, wearied with the monotony of the house, should leave her; plainly seeing that Mr. Lake's visits were the sole attraction that kept her, Mrs. Chester invented demands upon him to draw him over to Guild. That the confidential footing on which he and Lady Ellis continued was scarcely seemly for a married man, Mrs. Chester completely ignored. She shut her eyes to it; just as she had shut them in the days when Clara was at Guild. I am telling the simple truth of the woman, and things took place exactly as I am relating them. What mattered it to Mrs. Chester whether the wife's feelings were pained, outraged, so long as her own ends were served? Clara was at a safe distance, seeing nothing; and, after all, it was but a bit of passing nonsense between them—there was no real wrong, reasoned Mrs. Chester in her sophistry. "What the eye does not see the heart cannot rue."

"But Mr. Lake ought not to have given way to her," remonstrates the upright reader. Of course he ought not, everybody knows that; but he liked the pastime. Lady Ellis made herself uncommonly attractive to him, and it never occurred to him to see that she ought not to have done so. She was exacting now; saying to him "You must come tomorrow," or "You must come the next day." They rode together and walked together as before; not so much, because it was winter weather; and they strolled out in the wide gardens in the dim afternoons, and sat alone very much in the drawing-room by twilight.

Unfortunately these pleasant arrangements were not kept from Clara. If she had partially forgotten her jealousy upon returning home, her husband's constant visits to Guild, and the whispers reaching her from thence, brought it back in all its unhappy force. She was not told purposely. Of the Jupps, the only one whose eyes were open to the flirtation going on—that is, to a suspicion that it was deeper than it ought to be, considering that Mr. Lake had a wife—was the eldest of them, Mary. She held her tongue. But the others, after a day spent at Guild, would jokingly allude in Clara's hearing to the soft hours spent together by him and Lady Ellis, and tell her she ought to keep her husband in better order. They meant nothing. Had Clara been there she might have thought far less of it than she was doing; incertitude always increases suspicion, just as jealousy makes the food it feeds on. So Mrs. Lake sat at home with her cough, and her increasing weakness, and her miserable torture; conscious of little save one great fact, that her husband was perpetually at Guild. Had he gone more openly, as it were, without framing (as he invariably did) some plausible plea for the journey, she had thought less. What could Clara do? Could she descend to say to him, you shall not go there? No; she suffered in silence; but it was killing her.

A bright December morning, clear and frosty, Mrs. Lake was seated at the window in their comfortable room, making tiny little flannel petticoats. There was a good deal of distress in Katterley, and she was intending to give warm garments to sundry poor half-naked children. Stooping over the work, her cheeks had acquired their hectic tinge, seen frequently now, otherwise the face was pale and thin; the fingers were attenuated. Mr. Lake, who had been looking at the newspaper, reading occasional scraps of news from it to his wife, rose from his chair by the fire and stretched himself.

"How busy you are, little wife! Who on earth are all those small things for?"

"The poor children in the cottages by the brick-fields. They are so badly off, Robert," she added, glancing up, with a pleading look. "I could not help doing something for them."

"All right, my dear; do whatever you like. Only, don't over-work yourself."

"There's no fear of that. Elizabeth will do part of them; and Mary Jupp is coming to help me."

"What a lovely day it is for December!" he added, looking at the sparkling sunlight.

"Very. It almost tempts me to go out."

"I will take you tomorrow, Clara; I must go to Guild today."

Mrs. Lake resumed her work with trembling fingers. "Penelope's watch is at Van Buren's. I promised faithfully to take it to her today."

"Are there no watchmakers at Guild, that Mrs. Chester should send her watch to Katterley?"

"I don't know. I brought it to him at her request a fortnight ago. Van Buren has a great name in his trade, you know."

As he spoke he looked at his own watch; it was time to depart.

"Shall you be home to dinner, Robert?"

"No. But I shall to tea. I shall be in by the seven train. Good-bye, Clary."

She raised her face with its crimson hectic colour, the result of emotion, to receive his farewell kiss. Its loveliness could but strike him.

"How well you are getting to look, my darling," he said, tenderly.

And it would no doubt have astonished Mr. Lake excessively could he have glanced back at his wife through the garden and the walls of the house as he went off, gaily whistling. Dropping her work on the floor, she fell into a storm of sobs in her utter self-abandonment. Miss Jupp came in, and so found her.

"Clara! Clara!"

Up she got: but to affect indifference was an impossibility. Mary Jupp, greatly shocked, took the sorrowful face in her sheltering arms.

"Tell me what it is, Clara. Open your poor little heart to me, my dear. I am older than you by many years, and have had trouble myself. Where's your husband?"

"Gone to Guild."

"Oh," said Miss Jupp, shortly, who had her private opinion on many things. "Well, dear, he has got a nice day for it."

Clara dried her eyes and stifled her sobs, and sat down to work again.

"I am so stupid," she said, in a tone of apology. "Since my illness I don't feel strong; it makes me cry sometimes."

Mary Jupp said no more, perhaps wisely. She took her things off and remained the day. And Mr. Lake got home, not by seven at night, but by the last train.

Christmas approached, and Mrs. Lake got thinner and weaker. Still her husband suspected nothing amiss. She rose in the morning, went through her duties, such as they were, and had a bright colour. How was he, an unobservant man by nature and habit, to detect that it was all wrong? Had he suspected the truth, none would have been more anxiously troubled than he.

It was in Clara Lake's nature to conceal what was amiss. With these reticent temperaments, a great grief touching the heart, a grief unto death, never can be spoken of. At the last, perhaps, when hours are numbered, but not always then. He saw no signs of it: the low spirits, the nervous weakness were given way to when alone: never before him. Except that she had grown strangely still and quiet, he saw no alteration. She tried to be cheerful, and succeeded often.

So the days, as I have said, glided on, bringing the end nearer and nearer. Mr. Lake went on his heedless way, and she sat at home and did silent battle with the anguish that was killing her. Her history is drawing to a close. The world, going round in its hard, matter-of-fact reality, is apt to laugh at such stories; but they are taking place, for all that, in some of its nooks and corners.

One day, when it wanted but three or four to Christmas, Mr. Lake tempted his wife into the greenhouse to see his winter plants. She was more cheerful than customary—talked more; an artificial renovation had brought back some of the passing strength.

"Clary, I have promised to spend Christmas-day with Penelope."

A sudden rush of colour to her wasted cheeks, a pause, and a response that came forth faintly.

"Have you?"

"She said how dull it would be for us at home, and would not take a denial. You will be able to go?"

"I go!" She glanced at him in surprise, and shook her head.

"Why not?"

"I am too ill."

Mr. Lake felt annoyed. The proposed expedition had been presenting itself to his mind in a very agreeable light: for his wife to set her face against it, whether on the plea of ill-health or any other plea, would be especially provoking.

"My dear, I tell you what it is," he said in a voice that betrayed his temper, "you will fancy yourself ill and lie-by and stay at home, until it ends in your being ill."

"Do you think I am well?"

"You are not strong; but if you would rouse yourself, and go more out, and shake off fancies, you would soon become so. An illness, such as yours was in the autumn, leaves its weakening effects behind it as a matter of course; but there's no sense in giving way to them."

"I go out sometimes."

"Just for a walk or so; that does little good. What you want is cheerful society; change. You have not been once to Guild since we came home."

"You make up for it, then; you are there often enough."

She could not help the retort; it seemed to slip from her tongue unguided. Mr. Lake kicked out at a broken pot.

"Something or other is always happening to take me there. Mrs. Chester loads me with commissions, and I don't like to refuse to execute them."

They went in. Mr. Lake returned to the charge.

"You will go on Christmas-day, Clary, won't you? Penelope is preparing for us."

"No; I am not well enough. And if I were, I should prefer to be at home. Say no more," she added almost passionately interrupting what he was about to urge. "You ought not to wish me to go there."

A long silence. "I shall go. I must. I can't get off it."

She did not speak.

"What is to be done, Clara? It will never do for me to spend Christmas-day there, and you to spend it at home." And he finished the clause by breaking out, half-singing, half muttering, with the lines of a popular ditty that our childhood was familiar with—

"To-morrow is our wedding-day, and all the world would stare
If wife should dine at Edmonton, and I should dine at Ware."

She sat with her hands folded before her, and did not immediately answer. If he could not tell what was to be done, or what ought to be done, she would not. Mr. Lake looked at her and waited.

"You must do as you think right," she said, laying a slight stress upon the word. "I am too unwell to be anywhere but at home on Christmas-day."

Mr. Lake left the room, whistling to hide his anger. Had he possessed the worst wife in the world he had never reproached or quarrelled with her. Some men cannot be actively unkind to women, and he was one. He thought her very obstinate, unreasonably so, and said to himself that he would go to Guild. If Clara did not come to her senses beforehand and accompany him, his going without her would bring her to them after. Not another word was said between them; each seemed to avoid the subject.

Christmas-day dawned, cloudy but tolerably fine. Mr. Lake was going to Guild. Not doing exactly as he thought right, for his conscience was giving him a sharp twinge or two, but following the bias of his inclination, which urged him into the sunshine of my Lady Ellis's smiles. Clara felt worse that morning, dreadfully weak and languid, but she put on her things to attend church. Mr. Lake went with her, and they sat out the service together. At its termination he rose to quit the church; she remained.

"Shall you not be too tired with the long service, Clara?" he whispered. "You had better leave it until another opportunity."

"Please don't! let me stay."

There was something in the pleading words—in the pleading up-turned glance of the wan face, that struck upon him as being strange, leaving a momentarily unpleasant impression. He never stayed the sacrament himself, and went out.

She gathered herself into the corner of their high, broad, old-fashioned pew, and knelt down, leaning her arms and head on the seat. An intense weariness was upon her frame and spirit; she did not feel things as keenly as she used—it was as if the world were drifting away from her. Her soul was longing for the comfort of the approaching rite—for its comfort. Ah, my friends, we kneel periodically at the altar, and take the bread and wine, and hope that we return comforted and refreshed. Believe me, it is but those from whom the comfort of this world has utterly departed who can indeed realize what that other comfort is, and how great our need of it. Only when earth and its interests fail us, when the silver cord is loosed, the golden bowl broken—in that hour do we desire the rest from travail, as a yearning longing. That hour had come for Clara Lake: she knelt there, feeling that earth had no longer a place for her,—the home above was ready for her,—the Redeemer at hand to welcome her, and take her to God.

She walked home quietly, a dim consciousness upon her that it might be the last time she should partake of the sacrament here. It was not far off two o'clock, and Mr. Lake was walking about, all impatience, for his train started at five minutes past. She had thought he would be gone.

"I waited for you, Clary. Won't you come with me?"

"Indeed I cannot."

"Then it's a case of Johnny Gilpin."

With a farewell to his wife, full of paraded affection, Mr. Lake took himself off to the station, telling his wife to be sure and eat a good dinner and drink everybody's health in champagne, including his and her own.

In spite of the inward peace that was hers, she was feeling terribly dispirited. A fond thought had delusively whispered that, after all, perhaps he might not go. She remembered the epoch of her dream; how he had stayed at home then in tender consideration of her wishes. Things were altered now.

At three o'clock she sat down to dinner, cutting herself a small slice from the turkey placed before her. When the sauces were brought round she simply shook her head. She had no appetite: an oppressive feeling of bitter grief sat on her spirit; the tears dropped on her plate silently, and she could not control them.

Presently she laid down her knife and fork, the little bit of meat only half eaten. Elizabeth ventured to remonstrate.

"I can't swallow it; it is like dry chips in my throat."

"And no wonder, ma'am: the meat's dry by itself. And such delicious bread-sauce and gravy that's here."

Sauce or no sauce, gravy or no gravy, Mrs. Lake could not eat. They brought in the pudding. She cut it, eat a mouthful, and, sent it away again.

Leaving her to her solitary dessert—for her a mere matter of form—the servants sat down to their own dinner. Some short time had elapsed, when Elizabeth thought she heard a noise in the dining-parlour, and went in to see if her mistress wanted anything. A cry of alarm burst from the girl as she opened the door: Mrs. Lake was lying on the carpet.

Whether she had fainted—whether she had been crossing the room and fell over anything—could not then be ascertained. As the servants raised her, a thin stream of blood issued from her mouth. Nearly beside themselves with terror, they laid her on the sofa, and Elizabeth ran for the doctor. She had to pass Mr. Jupp's house, and on her return it occurred to Elizabeth to call and ask to see Miss Jupp. That young lady came out to her from the dining-room, her mouth full of turkey.

"Good gracious!" she exclaimed, half petrified at the news. "Burst a blood-vessel! Dying! Is any one with her besides Mr. Lake?"

"He is not with her—there's nobody with her," answered Elizabeth. "That's why I made bold to disturb you, miss. He is gone off to dine at Mrs. Chester's."

Catching up a garden hat and woollen shawl that hung close at hand, Mary Jupp flung them on without a moment's pause for consideration, and started at a gallop down the street. The worthy shopkeepers, standing at their sitting-room windows, saw the transit with amazement, and thought the eldest Miss Jupp had gone suddenly mad. She was in the house before Dr. Marlow: his old steps were slow at the best—hers fleet. Mrs. Lake had broken a vessel on the chest or lungs.

"There is no immediate danger, as I hope," said the old doctor in Miss Jupp's ear; "but her husband ought to be here." Mary looked at her watch, and found that she had just time to catch a train.

But that Mary Ann Jupp was a strong-minded female, she might not have cared to go a journey on Christmas-day in the guise she presented. It may be questioned if she as much as gave a thought to her attire, except to remember that there was no time to go home and change it. In addition to being strong-minded, she was also an exceedingly upright-minded, right-feeling young woman, and had for a long while past greatly condemned what was going on—the absurd intimacy between Mr. Lake and Lady Ellis, and his consequent neglect of his wife. Her eyes had been open to it if nobody else's had; and Mary Jupp, in her impulsive way, had threatened herself that she should "one day have it out with the lot." That day had come.

Very considerably astonished was Mr. Lake to find himself burst in upon by Mary Jupp. Mrs. Chester and Lady Ellis looked up in amaze. They had dined together, a family party, and Mrs. Chester's children, with

Anna and the two Clapperton girls, who were guests that day, had retired to another room to make what noise they pleased, leaving the trio round the comfortable fire, wine and good things on the table behind them. Miss Jupp walked in without notice or ceremony. Her old red woollen shawl had jagged ends and a slit; her brown hat, white once, was vastly disreputable, and had a notch in the brim. Excited and out of breath, having run all the way from Guild station, she walked straight up to Mr. Lake and spoke. "Would you see your wife before she dies?"

He had risen and stood in consternation. Mrs. Chester rose. She sat still, calmly equable, listening and looking. Mr. Lake's lips turned white as he asked Miss Jupp for an explanation.

It was given in a sharp, ringing tone. Mrs. Lake had been found on the floor in her solitary dining-room, and when they lifted her up blood issued from her mouth. A vessel of some sort had given way. Dr. Marlow was with her, and said that Mr. Lake ought to be found. "Will you go to her?" asked the young lady as she finished her recital; "or shall I go back and take word that you will not?"

"Why do you say that to me?" he asked with emotion.

"My dear Miss Jupp!" struck in Mrs. Chester, in a voice of remonstrance.

"Why do I say it to you?" retorted Mary Jupp, in her storm of angry indignation. "It is time some one said it to you. You have been killing her by inches: yes, I speak to all of you," she added, turning about upon them. "You have been killing his wife by inches: you, Angeline Ellis, with your false and subtle snares; and you, Penelope Chester, with your complacent winking at sin. He is weak and foolish—look at him, as he stands there in his littleness!—but he would scarcely have been wicked, had not you drawn him to it. You wonder that I can thus speak out"—drowning some interrupted words of Mrs. Chester's—"is it right for me to be silent, a hypocritical glosser over of crime, when she is dying? I am an English gentlewoman, with a gentlewoman's principles about me, and I hope some Christian ones: it behoves such to speak out sometimes."

"You are mad," gasped Mrs. Chester.

"You have been mad, to allow this conduct in your house—folly, frivolity, much that is bad going on under your very eyes. Had your brother been a single man, it might have been deemed excusable by some: never by me: but he had a fair young wife, and you deliberately set to work to injure her. You did, Penelope Chester: you knew quite well what you were doing: and to encourage ill by winking at it, is the same thing as committing it. I say nothing more to you," she added, turning upon Lady Ellis with ineffable scorn. "You may remember certain words you said to me regarding Mr. Lake and his wife, the first afternoon you came here: I did not understand them then; I do now; and I know that, in that first hour of your meeting, you were laying your toils around him to gain his admiration and wean him from his wife. If you retain a spark of feeling, of conscience, the remembrance of Clara Lake, when the grave shall have closed on her, will be as a sharp iron, ever eating into it."

Lady Ellis rose, her jet-black eyes flashing. "Who are you, that you should dare thus insult me?"

Mary Jupp dropped her tone to one of calmness—mockingly calm it was, considering the scorn that mingled with it. "I have told you who I am: an English gentlewoman amidst gentlewomen: and with such I should think you will never henceforth presume to consort."

Mr. Lake had made no further retort, good or bad. While they were speaking, he took out his watch, saw that he had time, too much of it, to catch the next train, and quitted the room. Mary Jupp was following. Up started Mrs. Chester.

"If Clara is in the sad state you describe, Mary Jupp, I ought to go to her."

Mary Jupp turned short round and faced them. "I do not pretend to any right of control over your actions; but, were I you, I would at least allow my brother to be alone with his wife in her last hours. You have come between them enough, as it is, Mrs. Chester. The sight of you cannot be pleasant to her."

She quitted the room, condescending to give no farewell to either of those she left in it, and followed in the steps of Mr. Lake, who was already on his way to the station, buttoning his coat as he went, taking care not to catch him up. On the platform, as the train was dashing in, he spoke to her.

"Your accusations have been harsh, Mary."

"What has your conduct been?" she sharply retorted. "I loved your wife, and I feel her unhappy fate as keenly as though it had fallen on one of my own sisters. The world may spare you; it may flatter and caress you, for it is wonderfully tender to these venial sins of conduct; but you cannot recall to life her whom you vowed before God to love and to cherish."

"Step in. The train is going."

"Not into that carriage—with you. Others are in it, and I might be saying things that they would stare at. My temper is up, today."

"First class, miss?" cried an impatient porter "There's only that there one first-class carriage on."

And Mary Jupp walked away; opened the door of another, which was a third-class, and took her seat in it.

Thus they reached Katterley. Mr. Lake came to the carriage to assist her out, but she simply put his arm away. Her face looked awfully severe as the gaslights fell upon it.

"One moment," he said, arresting her as she was passing. "I do not know what turn your suspicions can have taken; a very free one, as it seems to me. Let me assure you that you are mistaken. On my word of honour as a man there has been nothing; nothing wrong. In justice to Lady Ellis I am bound to say this."

"Justice to Lady Ellis! Don't talk to me about justice to Lady Ellis," was the young lady's retort. Her temper, as she said, was up, that day. "Think of justice to your wife, rather. You are either a fool or a knave, sir."

"Thank you, Miss Jupp."

"Nothing wrong!" she repeated, returning to the charge. "I don't know what you mean. What do you call wrong? You have been tied to that woman's skirts these five months; lavishing your money and your time upon her; and leaving your wife alone to die. If that's not wrong, I should like to know what is."

He made no reply; almost too confounded to do it.

"I don't blame you, Robert Lake, as much as I blame them," she took occasion to say as they were parting. "You are a vain, thoughtless, empty-headed fellow, made so, I believe, by your enforced idleness; and they, those two women, are old and crafty. Mrs. Chester was serving her self-interest; the other her unjustifiable woman's vanity. You yielded yourself a willing prisoner to the birdlime spread under your feet, and now your folly has come home with interest. I saw your wife was dying of the pain, if you did not."

Without another word, whether of adieu or apology, she brushed past him up the street; and Mr. Lake turned to his home, something like a beaten dog that dare not lift its tail from between its legs.

CHAPTER XI

The Dream worked out

Mrs. Lake was better. The bleeding was stopped, the doctor gone, and she seemed comfortable. There was less danger than Miss Jupp had supposed, for the blood-vessel which had broken proved to be only a small one on the chest—not the lungs. To her husband it appeared incomprehensible that she should be in any danger at all: his mind had never admitted the possibility of it.

He was all alive to it now. As long as she lay in bed he scarcely left her chamber. To talk with her much was not allowed, but he sat there, holding her hand, looking into her eyes with the old love in his. What his reflections were, or how great his self-reproaches, was best known to himself. When these men, essentially kind and tender by nature, have to indulge in such remorse, be assured it is not very light. He could not bring himself to believe that any conduct of his had contributed to his wife's illness; still less that he had caused it. That was a flight of fancy not easy to him to understand; but he saw now how ill she must have been all along, and bitterly regretted that he had left her so much alone. Rather than have wilfully ill-treated her, he would have forfeited his life. His love had come back to him, now that it was too late—it may be more appropriate to say his senses had come back to him.

In a day or two she grew so much better that she was allowed to leave her bed for a small sitting-room on the same floor, carried into it by him. Late in the afternoon, he left her comfortably lying back in the easy chair, and inclined to sleep. Taking his hat, he walked out.

His errand was to the doctor. His wife seemed to assume that she should not recover; Miss Jupp and the servants the same; for all he saw, she might be well in a week or two: and he went to put the question. Dr. Marlow had said nothing particular to him of her state, one way or the other, and he could not question him before his wife.

Dr. Marlow was at home, and came to him at once. The two families had been very intimate; on familiar terms one with the other. Mr. Lake plunged into the matter at once, speaking of the danger other people seemed to apprehend, and of his own inability to see it.

"Is she, or is she not, in peril?" he asked. "Tell me the plain truth."

The old man laid his hand upon the speaker's shoulder. "What if the truth should be painful? Will you hear it—the whole of it?"

"I am come to hear it."

"Then I can only tell you that she is in danger; and I fear that a little time will see the end."

Very rapidly beat his pulses as he listened. Repentant pulses. A whole lifetime of repentance seemed, in that moment, to be in every one of them.

"But what is killing her? What is it?"

"The primary cause is of course that cold she caught at Guild. It laid hold of her system. Still, I think she might have rallied: many a time, since she came home, I have deemed her all but well again. You ought to know best, Master Robert, but to me it appears as though she had some grievance on her mind, and that it has been working mischief. I hope you have been a good husband to her, as Joan says to Hodge," added the doctor, turning from Mr. Lake to take a pinch of snuff. "Your wife has possessed one of those high y sensitive, rarely-refined temperaments, that, when joined to a fragile body, an unkind blow would shatter. I once told you this."

He made no comment; he was battling with his pain. Dr. Marlow continued.

"The body was a healthy body; there was no inherent disease, as I have always believed, and I cannot see why it should not have recovered; but the mind seemed to pull it back; two powers, one working against the other. Between them they have conquered, and will lay her low."

"Do you call it consumption?" Mr. Lake jerked out. And really the words were jerked out, rather than fairly spoken.

"Decidedly not. More of a decline: a waste of the system."

"Those declines are cured sometimes."

"Not often: when they fairly set in."

"Oh, doctor," he cried, clasping the old man's hand, and giving vent to some of the anguish that was rending him, "try and save her! Save her for my sake! You don't know the cause I have to ask it."

"I wish I could—for both your sakes. She is beyond earthly aid."

They stood looking at each other. Dr. Marlow, willing if possible to soothe in a degree the blow, resumed.

"I suppose I must, after all, have been mistaken in her constitution. When consumption showed itself in her brother, and he died of it, I watched her all the closer. But I could detect nothing wrong: though she was always one of those blossoms that a sharp wind would blow away. The disease was there, we must assume, and I failed to detect it."

"You say—you said but now—that it is not consumption," returned Mr. Lake, speaking sharply in his pain.

"Neither is it. But when unsoundness is inherent in the constitution it does not always show itself in the same form. Sometimes it comes out in one shape, sometimes in another."

There was no more to be said; nothing further to be learnt. Mr. Lake returned home with his burden of knowledge, wondering how much of this dread fiat Clara suspected, how much not. The shades of evening were on the room when he entered it, imparting to it a semi-gloom, but the rays of the fire-light fell on his wife's wasted face. Stirring the coals into a bright blaze, he sat down by her chair, and took her hand. Her wasted fingers entwined themselves fondly with his.

"I know where you have been, Robert. And I guess for what purpose."

"Ah. You are wise, my little wife. I went out to get a breath of fresh air."

"You have been to Dr. Marlow's. Margaret Jupp called, and she said she saw you turn into his house. You went to ask him whether I should get well. He told you No: for he knows I shall not. Was it not so?"

She leaned a little forward to look at him. He suddenly clasped her to his breast with a gush of passionate tenderness, and his hot tears fell upon her face.

"Oh, my darling! my darling!"

"It must be," she softly whispered. "There is no appeal against it now."

"Clara, if we are indeed to part, at least let perfect confidence be restored between us," he resumed, controlling his emotion with an effort. "What is the trouble that has been upon you?"

"The trouble?"

"Some of them are hinting at such a thing," he said, thinking of the doctor and of Miss Jupp: "I must know from you what it is."

"Need you ask?"

"Yes. For I cannot comprehend it. My darling, you must tell me."

"If she had never come between us, I do not think I should have been ill now."

"I cannot understand it," he repeated, a wailing sound in his emphasized words. "I have been foolish, thoughtless, wrong: though not to the extent you may possibly have imagined. But surely, taking it at its worst, that was not cause sufficient to bring you to death."

"Your love left me for another. It seemed to me—it seemed to me—more than I could bear."

Partly from the agitation the topic called up, partly that she was in hesitation how to frame her words, the pauses came. It was as if she would fain have said more.

"My love? oh no. It was but a passing—" the word at his tongue's end was "fancy," but he substituted another—"folly. Clara! do not give me more than my share of blame; that will be heavy enough, Heaven knows. The old man says that the violent cold you caught at Guild, was the primary cause of decay: surely that cannot be charged upon me."

She was silent a few moments—but, as he had said, there ought to be full confidence between them now—and she had been longing to tell him the whole unreserved truth; a longing that had grown into a sick yearning.

"I will tell you now how I caught that cold. Do you remember the night?"

"Not particularly." He was of a forgetful nature, and the events of the night had only been those of many another.

"Don't you remember it? When you were walking with—her—in the shrubbery in the raw twilight.—"

Mr. Lake slightly shook his head in the pause she made. Twilight shrubbery walks were lying in numbers on his conscience.

"She complained of cold, and you went to get her shawl out of the summer-house, leaving her seated on the bench in front of the green alcove. She sang a song to herself: I think I could repeat its words now. You brought the shawl and folded it lovingly around her, and kissed her afterwards, and called her—"

In great astonishment he raised his wife's face to gaze into it. Where had she learnt that little episode? Had she dreamt it? He did not ask: he only stared at her.

She bent down her head again to its resting-place, and folded her arm round him in token of forgiveness. "And called her 'My dearest.' I was standing there, Robert, behind the bench. I saw and heard all."

Not a word spoke he. He hardly dared to accept the loving sign of pardon, or to press her to him. Had she glanced up she would have seen his face in a hot glow. These little private episodes may be very gratifying in the passing, but it is uncommonly disagreeable to find out that your wife has made a third at them.

"It was very thoughtless of me to run out from the heated room on that cold damp night without anything on," she resumed hastily, as if conscious of the feeling and wishing to cover it "But oh! I was so unhappy—scarcely, I think, in my senses. I thought you had not returned from Guild: Fanny came in and said you had been home a long while and were with her. An impulse took me that I would go and see: I never did such a thing in my life; never, never, before or since: and I opened the glass doors and went out. I was half way down the shrubbery when I heard you coming into it from a cross walk, and I darted into the green alcove, and stood back to hide myself; not to spy upon you."

She paused, but was not interrupted. Mrs. Lake began to hurry over her tale.

"So you see that, in a measure, she was the cause of the cold which struck to me. And then I was laid up; and many a time when you deemed I should fancy you were out shooting, or had gone to Guild, or something or other, you were with her. I knew it all. And since we came home, you have been ever restless to go to her—leaving me alone—even on Christmas-day."

Ay: even on Christmas-day. He almost gnashed his teeth, in his self-condemnation. She, with her impassioned and entire love for him, with her rare and peculiar temperament that, as the doctor had observed, a rude blow would destroy! The misery of mind reacting upon a wasted frame! He no longer wondered why she was dying.

"Why could you not speak out and tell me this?"

"But that the world seems to have nearly passed away from me, and that earthly passions—pride, self-reticence, shame, I mean the shame of betraying one's dearest feelings, are over—I could not tell you now."

"But don't you see the bed of remorse you have made for me? Had I suspected the one quarter of what you tell me you felt, the woman might have gone to the uttermost ends of the earth, for me. I wish you had spoken."

"It might not have prevented it. My belief is that it would not. It was to be."

Mr. Lake looked at her.

"You remember the dream: how it shadowed forth that I was to meet, in some way, my death through going to Mrs. Chester's."

"Child! Can you still dwell upon that dream?"

"Yes. And so will you when the hearse comes here to take me away. Never was a dream more completely worked out. Not quite yet: it will be shortly. I have something else to tell you; about it and her."

Mr. Lake passed his hand across his brow. It seemed to him that he had heard enough already.

"The very first moment, when I met Lady Ellis at your sister's, her eyes puzzled me: those strange, jet-black eyes. I could not think where I had seen them. They seemed to be familiar to my memory, and I thought and thought in vain, even when the weeks went on. On this same night that we are speaking of, I alarmed you by my looks. Mrs. Chester happened to look at me as I sat by the fire; she called out; and you, who were at chess with—with her, came up. You all came round me. I was shaking, and my cheeks were scarlet, somebody exclaimed: I believe you thought I was seized with an ague-fit. Robert, I was shaking with fear, with undefined dread: for an instant before, as I sat looking at her eyes, it flashed into my mind whose eyes they were."

"Well, whose?" he asked, for she paused.

"They were those of the man who drove the hearse in my dream," she whispered in an awestruck tone. "The very same. You must recollect my describing them to you when I awoke: 'strangely black eyes, the blackest eyes I ever saw,' though of his face I retained no impression. It was singular it should have struck upon me then, when I had been for weeks trying unsuccessfully to get the thread of the mystery."

"Oh Clara, my darling, these superstitious feelings are very sad!" he remonstrated. "You ought not to indulge them."

"Will you tell me how I could have avoided them? It was not my fault that the dream came to me: or that the eyes of the driver were her eyes: or that my death had been induced through going to Mrs. Chester's. Both you and Mrs. Chester seemed to help me on to it in my dream: and as surely as the man appeared to drive me to the grave in the hearse, so has she driven me to it in reality. I wrote out the dream in full at the time, and you will find the paper in my desk. Read it over when I am gone, and reflect how completely it has been fulfilled."

He was silent. A nasty feeling of superstition was beginning to creep over himself.

"Will you let me ask you something?" she whispered, presently.

He bent his tearful face down upon hers. "Ask me anything."

"When—I—am—no longer here, shall you marry her?"

Robert Lake darted up with a tremendous word, almost flinging his wife's face from him. His anger bubbled over for a few moments: not at his wife's question, but at the idea it suggested. For remorse was very strong upon him then; the image of Lady Ellis in consequence distasteful.

"Mary her! Her! I would rather take a pistol, and shoot myself through the heart—and—sin that it implies—I assert it before my Maker."

Clara gave utterance to a faint sigh of relief, and unclasped her arms. "Then you do not love her as you have loved me?"

He flung himself on his knees before her, and sobbed aloud in his repentant anguish. She leaned over him endearingly, stroking his face and his hair.

"I only wanted to know that. The misery is over now, darling. For the little while we have to be together, let us be as happy as we used to be."

Emotion shook him to the very centre as he listened. Scarcely twice in a lifetime can a man give way to such. For the little while they had to be together! Ay. As Mary Jupp had said, he could not recall her back to life: he could not keep her here to make reparation.

Mrs. Lake lay back in her chair exhausted. Her husband stood by the mantelpiece gazing at her with his yearning eyes, hot and feverish after their tears. Silence had succeeded to the interview of agitation: these strong emotional storms always bring their reaction.

A knock at the room door, followed by the entrance of Elizabeth. She came to say that Mrs. Chester was below, asking if she might come up. A moment's pause, and Mrs. Lake answered "yes." The impulse to deny it had been upon her, but she wished to be at peace with all the world. Mr. Lake, less forgiving than his wife, did not care to meet Mrs. Chester, and quitted the room to avoid her. In his propensity to blame somebody else for the past as well as himself, he felt very much inclined to curse Mrs. Chester.

But she had been very quick, and encountered him outside the door, inquiring after his wife in a whisper. Mr. Lake muttered some unintelligible answer, and passed on.

"There's a friend in the drawing-room waiting to see you, Robert," she called after him.

Now, strange though it may seem, the thought of who the "friend" really was, did not occur to Mr. Lake. After the explosion of Christmas-day, brought about by Miss Jupp, he had never supposed that Lady Ellis would show herself at his house. He went downstairs mechanically, expecting to see nobody in particular; some acquaintance might have called. In another moment he stood face to face with her—Angeline Ellis. The exceeding unfitness of her visit, the bad taste which it displayed after that public explosion, struck him with dismay. Perhaps the recent explanation with his wife, their reconciliation, and his own bitter repentance helped the feeling. He bit his angry lips.

She extended to him her delicately-gloved hand, lavender, sewn with black, and melted into her sweetest smile. But the smiles had lost their power. He glanced at her coal-black eyes, as they flashed in the rays of the lamp, remembered the eyes of his wife's dream, and—shuddered.

"You have become a stranger to Guild," she said. "Has that mad woman, Mary Jupp, persuaded you that you will be poisoned if you come?"

He did not choose to see her proffered hand "I can no longer spare time from my wife, Lady Ellis: I have spared too much from her."

The resentful tone struck her with wonder; the cold manner chilled her unpleasantly: but she smiled yet.

"Is it really true that your wife is so very ill?" she asked. "The maid says so. We had news that she was better, recovering fast; and of course treated Miss Jupp's assertion for what it was worth—as we did the rest she said."

Had he been covered with quills like a porcupine every one of them would have bristled up on end in defence of his wife. Surely her ladyship should have exercised better judgment an' she wished to win him back to her.

Never again! Never again!

"She is dying," he hoarsely answered; "dying through our folly. I beg your pardon, my lady," he added, speaking the two last words in, as it struck her, the refinement of mockery, "it had been better perhaps that I had said my folly."

"Folly? Oh!"

"It has been a folly that will entail upon me a lifetime of repentance. Were my whole days to be spent in striving to work it off, as we work off a debt, they could not make atonement. There are follies that leave their results behind them—a heavy burthen to be borne afterwards throughout life. Take a seat, I beg, while you wait for Mrs. Chester."

He quitted the room; and she compressed her thin lips, which had turned white, for she fully understood him to imply that he had quitted herself and the "folly" for ever. Rarely had her ears heard such truths spoken, and they set on to glow with resentment. She saw Mr. Lake walk out at the garden gate and up the road, all to avoid her. Why? She had committed no wrong—as she counted wrong, as the world counts it: never a woman less likely to commit that than Lady Ellis. She had but amused herself, and he the same; and she really could not understand why Mrs. Lake should make a fuss over it.

Mrs. Chester, meanwhile, seated with Clara, was in her most amiable mood. That the episode of Christmas-day had taken her aback far more than it had taken Lady Ellis, was indisputable; but she was one of those easy-going women who never retain unpleasant impressions long. Besides, she had her way to make in the world. Before Mr. Lake had left her house many minutes, Miss Jupp in his wake, she had recovered her equanimity, and was laughing over the matter with my lady, assuring her that Mary Jupp was taken with these fits sometimes, and tried to set the world to-rights—the result of bile. Anything rather than that Lady Ellis should quit her now, in the depth of winter. They had come over today, my lady fully understanding and tacitly falling into her plans, hoping to patch up a reconciliation. He was but a light-headed fellow at best—turned about any way, as the wind turns a feather, mentally argued Mrs. Chester; and he was safe not to have said anything to his wife.

"You are looking so very much better than I expected, dear Clara. All you want is complete rest, with good nursing; as I remarked to Anna Chester the day after Christmas-day, when she came over to inquire about you. I was glad you saw her. I couldn't come myself—I had one of my wretched sick-headaches."

She spoke quickly, running one sentence into another. Clara sat back in her chair, meek, quiet, calm, a smile of peace upon her face.

"I should not have asked your husband to dine with us that day without you," spoke Mrs. Chester, deliberating how to heal breaches—"we should never have cared to see him at any time unaccompanied by you, but that you were not able to come."

Mrs. Lake made no reply.

"Clara, I must speak out. There's poor Lady Ellis downstairs wanting to see you. She says she has talked and laughed with Mr. Lake, and is terribly afraid now that you might not have liked it. She meant nothing. He is ten years younger than she is. Goodness me, child! you could never have thought ill of it. Surely you will see her?"

"I could not talk with her about—about the past," murmured poor Clara, the hectic cheeks becoming crimson.

"Good gracious me! who said anything of talking about it with her?" exclaimed Mrs. Chester. "My dear Clara, she'd not speak of it for the world. She has not spoken of it to me; but I can see what she feels. She's so afraid you should reproach her in your heart; she would so like to be reconciled in spirit. Oh! my dear, there's nothing like peace."

With the peace on her own spirit; with the fresh love of her husband in her heart; with the consciousness that she should soon be with Him who has enjoined love and peace on earth if we would inherit Heaven, Clara did not hesitate. Lady Ellis could do her no harm with her husband now: and a sudden wish for at least a tacit proof of the full forgiveness she accorded, arose within her. But she did not speak immediately; and Mrs. Chester was impatient.

"You would not bear malice, Clara?"

"I will see Lady Ellis. As to bearing malice, if you only knew how different it is! All that kind of feeling has passed away from me. I wish you would note what I say now, Mrs. Chester, and—and repeat it, should you think it might be acceptable after I am dead. Should anybody in the world have injured me, intentionally or unintentionally, I give them my free and full forgiveness, as I hope to be myself forgiven. I trust we shall meet in Heaven; you, and I, and Lady Ellis, and all the world, and live together in happy bliss for ever. There's a great joy upon me when I say this."

The words were a little different from any anticipated by Mrs. Chester. She rubbed her face with her handkerchief and stared; and her tone, as she rejoined, partook in a degree of the solemnity of that other one.

"After you are dead, Clara! You are not surely going to die?"

Mrs. Lake did not answer in words. She looked full at Mrs. Chester with her clear brown eyes, and the wan face from which the hectic was fading.

"Good patience me!" thought that lady, "I hope I shan't dream of her as she looks now."

Elizabeth entered with a cup of tea on a waiter. "Here comes my tea," said Clara. "Would you like some?"

"Indeed I should: my mouth is quite parched. And poor Lady Ellis? You will let her drink one, too, here with us, Clara? It will be the seal of peace."

"Bring two cups of tea and some bread and butter," said Clara to the maid in a low tone. Certainly she had not intended to invite the lady downstairs to tea with her; but Mrs. Chester had put it in a point of view scarcely rejectable.

Now Mrs. Chester, crafty and clever, had been drawing largely upon her own active imagination. It had never occurred to Lady Ellis to wish for the kiss of peace, or for any token of reconciliation whatsoever. Therefore when Mrs. Chester brought her up and introduced her to the room, the two—her ladyship and the dying woman—were inwardly at cross purposes.

Nothing of which was betrayed, or likely to be. Lady Ellis's delicately-gloved hand met that attenuated one in a moment's greeting, and she sat down with calm composure. A few remarks passed upon indifferent topics between the three, and Elizabeth came in with the tea. The next moment another visitor appeared on the scene—Mary Jupp, shown in by Mr. Lake. To describe their faces of astonishment at seeing the ladies there, would take the pen of a great artist in words. Not seeing Lady Ellis downstairs, he thought they had left. Miss Jupp stood with a stony stare; and her companion bit his annoyed lips.

"Come in, Mary; come in."

Mrs. Lake's invitation bore a hurried pleading sound to Miss Jupp's ear, as if she had been uneasy in her company, and welcomed the relief. But for that, the strong-minded lady had turned away again without leaving behind her so much as a word. She came forward and sat down.

"Elizabeth shall bring you some tea."

"Tea for me!" cried Miss Jupp, bluntly. "I couldn't drink a drop. It would choke me."

"Is your throat bad, Mary Jupp?" asked Mrs. Chester.

"No; only my temper."

A frightened look in Clara's eyes, a pleading gaze that went right into Mary Jupp's. The young lady, doing violence to her inclinations, shut up her month resolutely, and folded her hands upon her lap, and spoke not another word, good, bad, or indifferent.

The curious meeting came to an end, brought to a summary close by Mrs. Chester. That lady, not altogether liking the aspect of affairs, and privately wishing Miss Jupp at the antipodes, thought it good to take herself away, and leave, so to say, well alone. Lady Ellis and Clara Lake shook hands for the last time in life.

"I wish you well," Clara whispered.

"Thanks," airily answered my lady.

Mr. Lake, in the very commonest politeness, went down with them. As they stood in the garden Mrs. Chester went back to get her muff, and they waited for her.

"Are you reconciled to me, Mr. Lake?" asked Lady Ellis.

"I wish to beg your pardon for aught I may have said that was unwarrantable," he rejoined. "I had no right to reproach you when the fault of the past was mine."

Mrs. Chester came forth, and he held the gate open for them. But my lady noticed that he did not choose to see her hand when she held it out.

My lady gave a little toss to her head. If this was to be the end of platonic friendships, keep her from them in future.

And Robert Lake, a whole world of self-condemning bitterness in his face, leaned on the gate, and looked after them.

CHAPTER XII

Coastdown

Rushing through the streets of London, as if he were rushing for his life, went a gentleman in deep mourning. It was Robert Hunter. Very soon after we last saw her, he had followed the hearse that conveyed his wife to her long home in Katterley churchyard.

Putting aside his grief, his regret, his bitter repentance, her death made every difference to him. Had there been a child, the house and income would have remained his; being none, it all went from him. Of his own money but little remained: he had been extravagant during the brief period when he was Lieutenant Hunter, had spent right and left. One does not do these things without having to pay for it. Mrs. Chester, going over to offer a condoling visit, heard this, and spoke out her opinion with her usual want of reserve. She looked upon him as a man lost. "No," said he, "I am saved! I shall go to work now." "Hoping to redeem fortune?" she rejoined. "Yes," he said, "and something else besides."

Heavily lay the shadow of the past upon Robert Hunter. The drooping form of his loving and neglected wife, bright with hope once, mouldering in her grave now, was in his mind always; the years that he had wasted in frivolity, the money he had recklessly spent. Oh, the simpleton he was—as he thought now, looking back in his repentance. When he had become master of a good profession, why did he abandon it because a little money was left him? To become a gentleman amongst gentlemen, forsooth; to put away the soiling of his hands; to live a life of vanity and indolence. Heaven had recompensed him in its own just way: whatsoever a man soweth, that shall he reap. His soldiership was gone; his wife was gone; money, the greater portion of it, was gone. Nothing left to him but remembrance, and the ever-present, bitter sense of his folly. He was beginning life anew: he must go back to the bottom of the tree of his engineering profession, lower than where he had left off: he would so begin it and take up his work daily, and untiringly persevere in it, so as—Heaven helping him—to atone for the past. Not all the past. The wasted years were gone for ever; the gentle wife, whom he had surely helped to send to the grave, could not be recalled to earth. Not so much on his wife were his musings bent as on the career of work lying before him. He had so grieved for her in the days before and immediately after her death, that it seemed as though the sorrow had, in a degree, spent itself, and reaction set in. If his handicraft's best skill, indifference to privation, unflagging industry, could redeem the past idleness, he would surely redeem that. Not in a pecuniary point of view, it was not of that he thought, but in the far graver one of wasted life. His eyes were opening a little; he saw how offensive on High must be a life of mere idle indulgence; a waste of that precious time, short at the best, bestowed upon him to use. This, this was what he had resolved to atone for: Heaven helping him, he once more aspired in the sad but resolute earnestness of his heart.

Making an end of his affairs at Katterley, he came to London, presented himself at the office of the firm where he was formerly employed, and said he had come to ask for work. They remembered the clever, active, industrious young man, and were glad to have him again. And Robert Hunter—dropping his easy life, just as he dropped the name he had borne in it—entered on his career of toil and usefulness.

The spring was growing late when his employers intimated to him that he was going to be sent to Spain, to superintend some work there. Anywhere, he answered; he was quite ready, let them send him where they would.

On this morning that we see him splashing through the mud of London improvised by the water carts, he was busy making his preparations for departure, and was on his way to call on Professor Macpherson. He wanted some information in regard to the locality for which he was bound, and thought the professor could supply it. The previous night, sitting alone in his lodgings, he had been surprised, and rather annoyed, by the appearance of Mrs. Chester. That lady was in town on her own business, and found him out. Incautiously he let slip that he was going on the morrow to Dr. Macpherson's. She seized upon the occasion to make a visit also.

At this very moment Mrs. Chester was en route also. Pushing her way along, inquiring her road perpetually, getting into all sorts of odd nooks and turnings, she at length emerged on the more open squares of Bloomsbury, and there she saw her brother, who had been calling at places on his way, in front of her.

"You might have waited for me, Robert, I think."

"I did wait twenty minutes. I came on then. My time is not my own, you know, Penelope."

"Have you seen anything of Lady Ellis since you came to London?" inquired Mrs. Chester, as they walked on together.

"No, I should not be likely to see her."

"She is staying in London; she came to it direct when she left me. At least, she was staying here, but in a letter I had from her she said she thought of going on a visit to Coastdown. Her plans—"

"Excuse me, Penelope, I don't care to hear of Lady Ellis's plans."

"You have grown quite a bear, Robert! That's what work's doing for you."

He laughed pleasantly. "I think it is hurry that is doing it for me this morning, I feel as if I had no time for anything. Number fifteen. Here we are!"

It was a commodious house, this one in Bloomsbury, steps leading up to the entrance. He sent in his card, "Mr. Robert Hunter," and they were admitted.

"Lawk a' mercy! Is it you?" exclaimed Mrs. Macpherson, looking first at the card and then at its owner, as they were shown into a handsome room, and the professor's lady, in sky-blue silk, and a scarlet Garibaldi body elaborately braided with black, advanced to receive them. She did not wear the bird-of-paradise feather, but she wore something equivalent to it: some people might call it a cap and some a turban, the front ornament of which, perching on the forehead, was an artificial bird, with shining wings of green and gold.

Mrs. Macpherson took a hand of each, shaking them heartily. "And so you have put away your name?" she said.

"Strictly speaking, it never was my name," he answered. "It was my wife's. I had to assume it with her property, but when the property left me again, I thought it time to drop the name."

The professor came forward in his threadbare coat, with (it must be owned) a great stream of some sticky red liquid down the front of it, for they had fetched him from his experimenting laboratory. But his smile was bright, his welcome genial. Mrs. Macpherson, whose first thoughts were always of hospitality, ordered luncheon to be got ready. Robert Hunter, sitting down between them, quietly told them he had become a working man again, and where he was going, and what to do. Mrs. Macpherson heard him with a world of sympathy.

"It's just one o' them crosses in life that come to a many of us," remarked she. "Play first and work afterwards! it's out o' the order of things. But take heart. You've got your youth yet, and you'll grow reconciled."

"If you only knew how glad I am to be at work again!" he said, a faint light of earnestness crossing his face. "My years of idleness follow me as a reproach—as a waste of life."

"But for steady attention to my work and studies, I should never have been able to contribute my poor mite to further the cause of science," said the professor, meekly, speaking it as an encouragement to Robert Hunter.

"If he hadn't stuck at it late and early—burning the candle at both ends, as 'twere—he'd not have had his ologies at his fingers' tips," pursued Mrs. Macpherson, who often deemed it necessary to explain more lucidly her husband's meaning.

"And so you are about to migrate to Spain?" said the professor. "You—"

"He says he's going off to it by rail," interposed Mrs. Macpherson. "What are the people there? Blacks?"

"No, no, Betsy; they are white, as we are."

"I knew a Spanish man once, professor, and he was olive brown."

"They are dark from the effects of the sun. I thought you alluded to the race. The radiation of heat there is excessive; and—"

"That is, it's burning hot in the place," corrected Mrs. Macpherson. "I wish you joy of it, Mr. Hunter. You'll catch it full, a-laying down of your lines of rail."

"I think you have been in Spain?" observed Mr. Hunter to the doctor.

"I once stayed some months there. What do you say?—that you want some information that you think I can supply? I hope I can. What is it? Please to step into my room."

The professor passed out of the door by which he entered, Mr. Hunter following him. A short passage, and then they were in the square back room consecrated to the professor and his pursuits. It was not a museum, it was not a laboratory, it was not a library, or an aviary of stuffed birds, or an astronomical observatory; but it was something of all. Specimens of earth, of rock, of flowers, of plants, of weeds, of antiquarian walls; of animals, birds, fish, insects; books in cases, owls in cages; and a vast many more odd things too numerous to mention. Mrs. Macpherson thought it well to follow them.

"Law!" said she to Mrs. Chester, "did living mortal ever see the like o' the place?"

"What a confused mass of things it is!" was the answer, as Mrs. Chester's eyes went roving around in curiosity.

"He says it isn't. He has the face to tell me everything is in its place, and he could find it in the dark. The great beast there with its round eyes, is a owl that some of 'em caught and killed when they went out moralizing into Herefordshire."

"Not moralizing, Betsy. One of the excursions of the Geological Society—"

"It's all the same," interrupted Mrs. Macpherson; and the professor meekly turned to Mr. Hunter and continued an explanation he was giving him, a sort of earthenware pipe in his hand. The ladies drew near.

"You perceive, Mr. Hunter, there is a small aperture for the passing in of the atmospheric air?"

"That is, there's a hole where the wind goes out," explained the professor's wife.

"By these means, taking the precautions I have previously shown you, the pressure on the valve may be increased to almost any given extent! As a natural consequence—"

"Oh, bother consequences!" cried Mrs. Macpherson; "I'm sure young Robert Hunter don't care to waste his time with that rubbish, when there's cold beef and pickled salmon waiting."

"Just two minutes, Betsy, and Mr. Hunter shall be with you. Perhaps you and Mrs. Chester will oblige us by going on."

"Not if I know it," said the lady, resolutely. "I've had experience of your 'two minutes' before today, prefessor, and seen 'em swell into two mortal hours. Come! finish what you've got to say to him, and we'll all go together."

Dr. Macpherson continued his explanations in a low voice, possibly to avoid more interruptions. Five minutes or so, and they moved from the table, the doctor still talking in answer to a question.

"Not yet. I grieve to say we have not any certain clue to it, and opinions are much divided among us. It needs these checks to remind us of our finite nature, Mr. Hunter. So far shalt thou go, but no farther. That is a law of the Divine Creator, and we cannot break it."

Robert Hunter smiled. "The strangest thing of all is to hear one of you learned men acknowledge as much. The philosopher's stone; perpetual motion; the advancing and receding tides—do you not live in expectation of making the secret of these marvels yours?"

Professor Macpherson shook his head. "If we were permitted: but we never shall be. If. That word has been the arresting point of man in the past ages, as it will be in the future. Archimedes said he could move the world, you know, if he had but an outward spot to rest the fulcrum of his lever on."

"It's a lucky thing for us that Archimy didn't," was the comment of Mrs. Macpherson. "It wouldn't be pleasant to be swayed about promiscous, the earth tossing like a ship at sea."

Robert Hunter declined the luncheon; he had many things to do still, and his time in England was growing very short; so he said adieu to them both then, and to his sister.

"Now remember, Robert Hunter," said Mrs. Macpherson, taking both his hands, "when you visit England temporay, and want a friendly bed to put yourself into, come to us. Me and the professor took to you when we first saw you at Guild. You remember that n ght," she added, turning to Mrs. Chester: "we come up in a carriage and pair; I wore my orange brocade and my bird-o'-paradise; and there was a Lady Somebody there, one o' those folks that put on airs and graces; which isn't pretty in a my lady, any more than it is in a missis. You took our fancies, Mr. Hunter—though it does seem odd to be calling you that, and not Lake—and we'll look upon it as a favour if you'll come to us sometimes. The prefessor knows we shall, but he's never cute at compliments. He was born without gumption."

The professor's lingering shake of the hand, the welcoming look in his kindly eyes, said at least as much as his wife's words; and Robert Hunter went forth, knowing that they wished to be his friends.

So they sat down to their luncheon and he departed; and the same night went forth on his travels.

Coastdown lay low in the light of the morning sun. The skies were clear, the rippling sea was gay with its fishing boats. Spring had been very late that year, but this was a day warm and bright. The birds were singing, the lambs were sporting in the fields, the hedges were bursting into buds of green.

Swinging through the gate of the Red Court Farm, having been making a call there to fetch a newspaper, came Captain Copp: a sailor with a wooden leg, a pea jacket, and a black glazed hat. Captain Copp had been a merchant captain of the better class, as his father was before him. After his misfortune—the loss of his leg in an encounter with pirates—he gave up the sea, and settled at Coastdown on his small but sufficient income.

The captain's womenkind—as he was in the habit of calling the inmates of his house—consisted of his wife and a maid servant. The former was meek, yielding, gentle as those gentle lambs in the field; the latter, Sarah Ford, worth her weight in gold for honest capability, liked to manage the captain and the world on occasions. There were encounters between them. He was apt to call her a she-pirate and other affectionate names. She openly avowed her disbelief in his marvellous reminiscences, especially one that was a standing story with him concerning a sea-serpent that he saw with his own eyes in the Pacific Ocean. He had also seen a mermaid. Like many another sailor, the captain was a simple-minded man in land affairs, only great at sea and its surroundings; with implicit faith in all its marvels.

On occasions the captain's mother honoured him with a visit; a resolute, well-to-do lady, who used to voyage with her husband, and had now settled in Liverpool. When she came she ruled the house and the captain, for she thought him (forty, now) and his wife little better than children yet. In solid sense, if you believed herself, nobody could approach her.

Captain Copp came forth from his call at the Red Court Farm, letting the gate swing behind him, and stumped along quickly, his stout stick and his wooden leg keeping time on the ground. The captain's face was beaming with satisfaction, for he had contrived to lay hold of young Cyril Thornycroft, and recount to him (for the fiftieth time) the whole story of the sea-serpent from beginning to end. He was a short, wiry man, with the broad round shoulders of a sailor. The road branched off before him two ways, like an old-fashioned fork; the way on the right led direct to the village and the common beach; the way on the left to his home.

The captain halted. Sociably inclined, he was rather fond of taking himself to the Mermaid; that noted-public house where the sailors and the coastguard men congregated to watch the omnibus come in from Jutpoint. It must be getting near to the time of its arrival, half-past eleven, and the captain's leg moved a step forward in the direction; on the other hand, he wanted to say a word to that she-serpent Sarah (with whom he had enjoyed an encounter before coming out) about the dinner. The striking of the clock decided him, and he bore on for home, past the churchyard. Crossing part of the heath, he came to the houses, red brick, detached, cheerful, his own being the third. At the window of the first sat an old lady. Captain Copp went through the little gate and put his face without ceremony against the pane, close to Mrs. Connaught's.

"How's the master this morning?" he called out through the glass.

She answered by drawing aside and pointing to the fire. An asthmatical old gentleman, just recovering from a fit of the gout, sat there in a white cotton nightcap and dressing-gown made of yellow flannel.

"He's come down for the first time, Captain Copp. He looks brave this morning," was Mrs. Connaught's answer.

"Glad to see ye, comrade; I'll come in later," cried the captain through the window, flourishing his stick in token of congratulation. And old Mr. Connaught, who had not heard a word, nodded the tassel of the white cap by way of answer.

In the parlour at home, when Captain Copp entered it, sat his wife at work, a faded lady with a thin and fair face. Taking out the newspaper he had brought, he began to open it.

"Did you see the justice, Sam?" asked his wife in her gentle, loving tones.

"No, he was out. I only saw Cyril. There'll be a fine row when he comes home. Mary Anne has run away."

Mrs. Copp dropped her work. "Run away! oh, Sam! Run away from where?"

"From where?—why, from school," said the choleric captain, who was just as hot as his wife was calm. "She came bursting in upon them this morning at breakfast, having run home all the eight miles. And she says she won't go back."

Mrs. Samuel Copp, who had never in her life presumed to take a walk without express permission given for it, lifted her hands in dismay. "I feared she would never stay at school; I feared she would not."

"Old Connaught is downstairs today, Amy," observed the captain to her after a long interval of silence, as he turned his paper.

"I am glad of that. He suffers sadly, poor man."

"Well, he's getting old, you see; and he's one that has coddled himself all his life, which doesn't answer. I say! who's this?"

A vision of something bright had flashed in at the little garden gate, on its way to the door. Mrs. Copp started up, saying that it was Mary Anne Thornycroft.

"Not a bit of it," said the captain. "Mary Anne Thornycroft would come right in and not stand knocking at the door like a simpleton."

The knocking was very load and decisive, such as, one is apt to fancy in a simple country place, must herald the approach of a visitor of consequence. Sarah appeared showing in the stranger.

"Lady Ellis, ma'am," she said to her mistress.

A dress of rich black s lk, a handsome India shawl, a girlish straw bonnet, with a great deal of bright mauve ribbon about it, a white veil, and delicate lavender gloves. My lady had got up herself well for her journey; stylish, but not too fine to travel. She had discarded her mourning, but it was convenient to wear her black silks. The captain and his wife rose.

Yes, it was Lady Ellis. But she had mistaken the direction given her, and had come to Captain Copp's instead of Mrs. Connaught's. When the explanation came, the gallant captain offered to take her in.

"Old Connaught is better today," observed he, volunteering the information. "He's downstairs in a nightcap and flannel gown."

Another minute, and Lady Ellis had the opportunity cf making acquaintance with the articles of attire mentioned, and the old gentleman they adorned. Captain Copp, with his nautical disregard to ceremony, went into his neighbour's house as usual, without knocking, opened the sitting-room door, and sent the visitor in. Mrs. Connaught was not there, and he went to the kitchen in search of her. They were primitive-mannered, these worthy people of Coastdown, entering each others' kitchens or parlours at will.

Mr. Connaught, very excessively taken aback at the unexpected apparition, did nothing but look up with a stolid stare, as unable mentally to comprehend what the lady did there, and who she might be, as he was physically to rise and receive her. Lady Ellis lost her ready suavity for a moment, struck out of it by the curious old figure before her.

Mrs. Connaught was preparing some dainty little dish for her husband; sick people have fancies, and he liked her cooking better than the cook's. She heard the wooden leg coming along the passage.

"Here!" said the captain, "some lady wants you. Came by the omnibus from Jutpoint, I gather; got a white figure-head."

He stumped out the back way as he spoke, and Mrs. Connaught entered the parlour. When Lady Ellis was a girl of fifteen, twenty years before, and she an unmarried woman getting on for forty, they had seen a good deal of each other. Not having met since, each had some little difficulty in making the recognition of the other; but it dawned at last.

"I could not stay any longer from coming to see you," said Lady Ellis. "You seem to be the only link left of my early home and my dear parents. Forgive me for intruding on you today; had I waited longer I might not have been able to come at all."

She sat down and untied her bonnet, and laid hold of Mrs. Connaught's hand and kept it, letting fall some tears. Old Connaught stared more than ever; Mrs. Connaught, not a demonstrative woman, but simple and kindly, answered in kind.

"How long it seems ago! And you must have grown grand since then, Lady Ellis! But I never knew your people very much, you know."

"Ah, you forget! I grand!"—she went on, with a cheery laugh; "you will soon see how different I am from that. I came home to find nearly all those I cared for dead; you only are left, and I thought I must come down and find you out. Dear Mrs. Connaught, dear old friend, the longing for it got irrepressible."

Lady Ellis, it may be remembered, had pencilled down Mrs. Connaught's address at Mrs. Chester's, as supplied by Mr. Thornycroft. It might prove useful, she thought, on some future occasion. And the occasion had come.

The world, as she thought, had not dealt bountifully with her; quite the opposite. Not to mince the matter, she had to scheme to live, just as much as Mrs. Chester had, only in a different way. She liked good clothes, she liked ease and good living. Never, save for those few short days of her Indian marriage, had she known what it was to be free from care. Her father had liked play better than work; he and her mother, both, had a propensity to live beyond their income, to get into society that was above them, for they were not altogether gentlepeople. Extravagance, struggles, debts, pinching; all sorts of contrivances and care, outside show, meanness at home—such had been the experience of Angeline Finch, until some lucky chance took her to India as companion to a lady, and a still luckier introduced her to Sir George Ellis, an old man in his dotage. Two years of her reign as my lady—two blessed years; show, ease, life. Looking back upon them now, they seemed like a very haven. But Sir George died; it came to an end; and she home to Europe again, where she found herself a little embarrassed how to get along in the world.

Whether she had lost sight of her European acquaintances during her stay in India, or whether she had originally not possessed many, certain it was they seemed scarce now.

The vision, coming and going almost like a flash of lightning, of Mr. Thornycroft and his daughter, the gentleman's evident admiration of her, the tales she heard (perhaps exaggerated) of the style of living and the wealth at the Red Court, had set her mind a-longing. She thought often how desirable would be a visit there: what might it not lead to? The determination to effect it grew into a settled hope. It might almost have been called a prevision, as you will find from what came of it. Of all the ills that can possibly befal this life, Lady Ellis, perhaps from the circumstances of her early experience, regarded poverty as the most fatal. She had grown to dread it awfully. After that short interval of ease and luxury, the thought of having to relapse back to contrivances, debts, duns, difficulties, turned her sick. Ah, what a difference it is!—what a wide gap between!—a shoulder of mutton for dinner one day, cold the next, hashed the third, beer limited, a gown turned and turned again, shabby at the best; and a good dinner of three courses and wines, and the toilette of Madame Elise!

And so, Lady Ellis, working out her own plans, had come swooping down today on Coastdown and Mrs. Connaught.

She went up to Mr. Connaught and took his hand; she looked admiringly at him, as if a yellow flannel gown and cotton nightcap were the most charming articles of attire that fashion could produce; she expressed her sorrow for his ailments with a gentle voice. Certainly she did her best to win his heart and his wife's, and went three-parts of the way towards doing it.

Meanwhile things were in a commotion at the Red Court Farm. On the departure of Miss Derode at Christmas the justice had put his daughter to school, an eligible place eight miles only away. She had gone rebelliously; stayed rebelliously; and now finished up by running home again.

As the justice found when he got home. Mary Anne flatly refused to go back. She refused altogether to leave home.

Mr. Thornycroft, privately not knowing in the least what to do with his self-willed daughter, sat in his magisterial chair, the young lady carpeted before him. All he could say, and he said a great deal, did not move her in the least; back to school she would not go. It seemed that she had resumed at once old habits; had fed her birds, sang her songs to the grand piano, danced gleefully in and out amid the servants, and finally put on a most charming silk dress of delicate colour, that she would never have been permitted to wear at school, and was too good to have been taken there.

"I shall drive you back in an hour, Mary Anne."

"I will not go, papa."

"What's that, girl? Do you mean to tell me to my face you will not go when I say you shall? That's something new."

"Of course if you make me get into the carriage and drive me there yourself, I cannot help it; but I should ran away again tomorrow."

"It is enough disgrace to you to have run away once."

Mary Anne stood, half in contrition, half in defiance. Nearly seventeen now, tall and fair, very handsome, she scarcely looked one to be coerced to this step. Her clear blue eyes met those of her father; the very self-same eyes as his, the self-same will in them.

"As to disgrace, papa, I did nothing more than come straight home. It was the same thing as a morning walk, and I have often gone out for that."

"What do you suppose is to become of you?" questioned Mr. Thornycroft, the conviction seating itself within him that she would not be forced from home again. He ran away from school himself, and his father had never been able to get him back to it. Mary Anne had inherited his self-will.

"I can learn at home. Oh, papa, I will be very good and obedient if you let me stay."

"You are too old now to be at home alone. And you would not obey mademoiselle, you know."

"If you had wanted to place me at school, you should have done it when I was young, papa. I am too old to be sent there now, for the first time."

Inwardly the justice acknowledged the truth of this. He began thinking that he must keep her, and engage some strict governess. But he did not want to do this; he objected to having governesses at the Red Court Farm.

"You don't believe me perhaps, papa. Indeed, I will be good and obedient; but you must not send me away!"

He supposed it must be so. He did not see his way clearly out of the dilemma; she had been indulged always, she must be indulged still. Some signs of relenting in the blue eyes—handsome still as his daughter's—Mary Anne saw it, and flew into his arms with a shower of tears.

What an opportunity for Lady Ellis! She stayed on at Mrs. Connaught's, and went daily to the Red Court, and read with Mary Anne and saw to her studies; and was her charming companion and indulgent governess. Excursions abroad in plenty! Going to Jutpoint in Mr. Thornycroft's high carriage; sailing to sea in Tomlett's boat; here, there, everywhere! The young men happened to be away at this period, and Lady Ellis had the field open.

There were some weeks of it. My lady had made a private arrangement with Mrs. Connaught, insisting upon paying for herself while she stayed. The sea air was doing her so much good, she said. The sea air! My lady would have taken up her permanent abode in old Betts's boat rather than have removed herself to a distance from that desirable pile of buildings, the Red Court Farm. Looking at it from her little chamber window, that is, at its chimneys, and imagining the charming life underneath, it appeared to her as a very haven of refuge.

And Justice Thornycroft was becoming fascinated. He began to think there was not such another woman in the world.

Perhaps there was not. Let Harry Thornycroft be assured of one thing—that when these clever women set their minds to lay hold of a man, to bend him to their will, in nine cases out of ten they will carry it out, surrounding circumstances aiding and abetting.

One day when she was dining at the Red Court Farm, she suggested to Mr. Thornycroft that he should take a dame de compagnie for Mary Anne. She always appeared to have that young lady's best interest on her mind and heart and tongue. Mary Anne, accustomed to do what she liked, went out with the cheese.

"It is the only thing, as you will not have a governess. Believe me, my dear sir, it is the only thing for that dear child," she urged, her dark eyes going straight out to the honest blue ones of Harry Thornycroft.

He made no reply. He was thinking that a dame de compagnie might be more troublesome at the Red Court than even a governess.

"Mary Anne wants now some one who will train her mind and form her manners, Mr. Thornycroft. It is essential that it should be done. Wanting a mother, wanting a stepmother, I see only one alternative—a gentlewoman, who will be friend, governess, and companion in one. It is a pity, for her sake, that you did not marry again."

Mr. Thornycroft put out a glass of wine with a sudden movement, and drank it. Lady Ellis resumed, piteously.

"Ah, forgive me! I know I ought not to be so free; to say these things. I was but thinking of that dear child. You will forgive me?"

"There's nothing to forgive," said the justice. "I am exceedingly obliged for the interest you take in her, and for any suggestion you may make. The consideration is—what to do for the best? I don't see my way clear."

He sat with his fine head a little bent, the light of the wax chandelier falling on his fair, and still luxuriant, hair; his blue eyes went out to the opposite wall, seeing nothing; his fingers played with the wine glass on the table. Evidently there were considerations to be regarded of which Lady Ellis knew nothing.

"It has been partly out of love to my daughter that I have never given her a stepmother," said he, coming out of his reverie. "Second wives are apt to make the home unhappy for the first children; you often see it."

She smiled sweetly on him. "Dear Mr. Thornycroft! Make the home unhappy! Ah, then, yes, perhaps so! Women with a hard selfish nature. Still I do not see how even they could help loving Mary Anne. She is so—"

What she was, Mr. Thornycroft lost the pleasure of hearing. Sinnett the housekeeper came in at this juncture, and said the landlord of the Mermaid, John Pettipher, had come up, asking to see the justice. "Tomlett has been quarrelling with him, he says, sir," added Sinnett, "and he wants to have the law of him."

"Tomlett's a fool!" burst impulsively from the lips of Mr. Thornycroft. "Show him into the justice room, Sinnett."

He went out with a brief word of apology, and he never came back again. My lady sat and waited, and looked and hoped, but he did not return to gladden her with his presence. At length Sinnett came in with some tea.

"Is Mr. Thornycroft gone out?" she asked.

"Yes, my lady. He went out with John Pettipher."

She almost crushed the fragile cup of Sèvres china in her passionate fingers. Had Mr. John Pettipher heard the good wishes lavished upon him that evening, he might have stared considerably.

CHAPTER XIII

What was the Fear?

The early buds had gone, the flowers of May were springing. Richard and Isaac Thornycroft were at home again, and the old profuse, irregular mode of life reigned at the Red Court Farm.

The skies are grey this afternoon; there is a chillness in the early summer air. Mr. Thornycroft, leaning lightly on the slender railings, that separate his grounds from the plateau, looks up to see whether rain will be falling.

There was trouble at home with Mary Anne. Uncontrolled as she was just now, no female friend to watch over her, she went her own way. Not any very bad way; only a little inexpedient. Masters came from the nearest town for her studies, taking up an hour or two each day; the rest of it she exercised her own will. The fear of school had subsided by this time, and she was growing wilful again—careering about on the heath; calling in at Captain Copp's and other houses; seated on some old timber on the beach, talking to the fishermen; riding off alone on her pony; jolting away (she had done it twice) in the omnibus to Jutpoint, without saying a word to anybody. Only on the previous day she had gone out in old Betts's tub of a boat, with the old man and his little son, got benighted, and frightened them at home. Clearly this was a state of things that could not be allowed to continue; and Mr. Thornycroft, leaning there on the railings, was revolving a question: should he ask Lady Ellis to come to the Red Court as dame de compagnie?—or as his wife?

"Of the two, a wife would be less dangerous than a companion," thought Justice Thornycroft, giving the light railings a shake with his strong hand "I'm not dying for either; but then—there's Mary Anne."

Almost as if she had heard the word, his daughter came out of the house and ran up to him. The justice put his hand on hers.

"What are you doing here, papa?"

"Thinking about you."

"About me?"

"Yes, about you. You are getting on for seventeen, Mary Anne; you have as much common sense as most people; therefore—listen, I want to speak to yon seriously."

She had turned her head at the ringing of the bell of the outer gate. But the injunction brought it round again.

"Therefore you must be quite well aware, without my having to reiterate it to you, that this kind of thing cannot be allowed to go on."

"I do no harm," said Mary Anne, knowing well to what the words tended.

"Harm or no harm, it cannot go on; it shall not. Now, which will you do—go to school again, or have a governess?"

"I don't want either," she answered, with a pout of her decisive lips.

"Or would you like—it is the one other alternative—a lady to come here as your friend and companion?"

"Frankly speaking, papa, I don't see what the difference would be between a companion and a governess. Of course, of the two I'd rather have a companion. To school I will not go. Lady Ellis was talking to me of this. I think she was fishing to be the companion herself."

"Fishing!" echoed the justice.

"Well, I do."

"Would you like her?"

"Not at all, papa."

"Who is it that you would like?" asked the justice, tartly.

"I should like nobody in that capacity. I might put up with it; but that is very different from liking."

"For my own part, if we decide upon a companion, there's no one I would so soon have as Lady Ellis," remarked Mr. Thornycroft. "Would you?"

"La la, la la!" sang Mary Anne, her eyes following a passing bird.

"Answer me without further trifling," sternly resumed Mr. Thornycroft, putting his hand on her shoulder.

The tone sobered her. "Of course, papa; if some one must come, why, let it be Lady Ellis."

Heaving a sort of relieved sigh, he released her, and she went away singing to herself a scrap of a pretty little French song, the refrain of which was, rendered in English—"If you come today, madam, you go tomorrow."

The misapprehension that arises in this world! None of us are perfectly open one with the other. Between the husband and the wife, the parents and the children, the brothers and the sisters, involuntary deceit reigns. Mr. Thornycroft assumed that Lady Ellis would be more acceptable to his daughter as a resident at the Red Court than any one else that could be found: had Miss Thornycroft spoken the truth boldly, she would have said that my Lady Ellis was her bête noire; the person she most disliked of all others on earth.

But the chief question was not solved yet in the mind of Justice Thornycroft. Should it be wife, or should it be only companion? He was quite sufficiently taken with my lady's fascinations to render the first alternative sufficiently agreeable in prospective; he deemed her a soft-hearted, yielding gentlewoman; he repeated over again to himself the mysterious words, "As a wife she would be less dangerous than a companion." But still, there were considerations against it that made him hesitate. And with good cause.

He went strolling towards the village, turning down the waste land, a right of way that was his own, past the plateau. The first house, at the corner of the street, was the Mermaid. He passed the end of it, and struck across to a low commodious cottage on the cliffs, whose rooms were all on the ground-floor. Tomlett lived in it; he was called the fishing-boat master, and was also employed occasionally on the farm of Mr. Thornycroft, as he had leisure. Mrs. Tomlett, a little woman with a red face and shrill voice, was hanging out linen on the lines to dry.

"Where's Tomlett today?" asked the justice. "He has not been to the farm."

Mrs. Tomlett turned sharply round, for she had not heard the approach, and dropped a curtsey to the justice. "He have gone to Dartfield, sir," she answered, lowering her voice to the key people use when talking secrets. "Mr. Richard he come in the first thing this morning and sent him."

Mr. Thornycroft nodded, and went away, muttering to himself exclusively something to the effect that Richard might have mentioned it. Passing round by the Mermaid again, he went towards home.

And he was charmingly rewarded. Standing on the waste land near the plateau, in her pretty and becoming bonnet of delicate primrose and white, her Indian shawl folded gracefully round her, her dress looped, was Lady Ellis.

"Do you know, Mr. Thornycroft," she said, as he took her hand, "I have never been on the plateau. Will you take me?"

Mr. Thornycroft hesitated visibly. "It is not a place for a lady to go to," he said, after a pause.

"But why not? Mary Anne told me one day you objected to her going on it."

"I do. The real objection is the danger. The cliff has a treacherous edge just there, and you might be over before you were aware. A sharp gust of wind, a footing too near or not quite secure, and the evil is done. Some accidents have occurred there; one, the last of them, was attended by very sad circumstances, and I then had these railings put round."

"You said the real objection was the danger; is there any other objection?" resumed Lady Ellis, who never lost a word or its emphasis.

"There are certain superstitious fancies connected with the plateau," answered Mr. Thornycroft, and very much to her surprise his face took a solemn look, his voice a subdued tone, just as if he himself believed in them: "a less tangible fear than the danger, but one that effectually scares visitors away, at night especially."

They were walking round towards the Red Court now, to which he had turned, and Mr. Thornycroft changed the subject. She could not fail to see that he wished it dropped. At the gates of the farm she wished him good afternoon, and took the road to the heath.

Justice Thornycroft did not enter the gates, but went round to the back entrance. Passing by the various outbuildings, he gained the yard, just as a man was driving out with a waggon and team.

"Where are you going?" asked the justice.

"After the oats, sir. Mr. Richard told me."

"Is Mr. Richard about?"

"He be close to his own stables, sir."

Mr. Thornycroft went on across the yard, not to the house but to the stables at its end. This portion of the stables (as may be remembered) was detached from the rest, and had formed part of the old ruins. It was shut in by a wall. The horses of the two elder sons were kept there, and their dog-cart. It was their whim and pleasure that Hyde, the man-servant (who could turn his hand to anything indoors or out), should attend to this dog-cart and the horses used in it, and not the groom. Richard was sitting on the frame of the well just on this side the wall, doing something to the collar of his dog.

"Dicky," said the justice, without any sort of circumlocution, "I think I shall give the Red Court a mistress."

Richard lifted his dark stern face to see whether—as he verily thought—his father was joking. "Give it a what?" he asked.

"A mistress. I shall take a wife, I think."

"Are you mad, sir?" asked Richard, after a pause.

"Softly, softly, Dick."

Richard lifted his towering form to its full height. Every feeling within him, every sense of reason rebelled against the notion of the measure. A few sharp words ensued, and Richard went into a swearing fit.

"I knew it would be so; he was always hot and hasty," thought the justice to himself. "What behaviour do you call this?" he asked aloud. "Perhaps if you'll hear what I have to say you may cool down. Do you suppose I should be intending to marry for my own gratification?"

"I don't suppose you'd be marrying for that of anybody else," said the undaunted Richard.

"It is for the sake of Mary Anne. Some one must be here with her, and a wife will be less—less risk than a crafty, inquisitive governess."

"For the sake of Mary Anne!" ironically retorted Richard. "Send Mary Anne to school."

"I did send her; and she came back again."

"I'd keep her there with cords. I said so at the time."

"Unfortunately she won't be kept. She has a touch of the Thornycroft will, Dick."

"Hang the Thornycroft will!" was Dick's angry answer. Not but what it was a stronger word he said.

"When you have cooled down from your passion I'll talk further with you," said the justice, some irritation arising in his own tone. "You have no right to display this temper to me. I am master here, remember, Dick; though sometimes, if appearances may be trusted, you like to act as if you forgot that."

Richard bit his dark lip. "You must know how inexpedient the measure would be, sir. Give yourself a wife!—the house a mistress! Why, the place might no longer be our own."

"Do you suppose I have not weighed the subject on all sides? I have been weeks considering it, and I have come to the conclusion that of the two—a wife or a governess—the former will be the less risk."

"No," said Richard; "a governess may be got rid of in an hour; a wife, never."

"But a governess might go out in the world and talk; a wife would not."

Richard dashed the dog's collar on the ground which he had held all the while. "Mark me, father"—he said, his stern eyes and resolute lips presenting a picture of angry warning rarely equalled—"this step, if you enter on it, will lead to what you have so long lived in dread of,—to what we are ever scheming to guard against. Mary Anne! Before that girl's puny interests should lead me to—to a measure that may bring ruin in its wake, I'd send her off to the wilds of Africa."

He strode away, haughty, imperious, rigid in his sharp condemnation. Mr. Thornycroft, one of those men whom opposition only hardens, turned to the fields, thinking of his brother Richard; Dick was so like him. There he found Isaac, stretched idly on the ground with a book. The young man rose at once in his respect to his father. His handsome velveteen coat, light summer trousers and white linen, his tall form with its nameless grace, his fair features, clear blue eyes and waving light hair, presenting as fine a picture as man ever made.

"That's one way of being useful," remarked Mr. Thornycroft.

Isaac laughed. "I confess I am idle this afternoon: and there's nothing particular to do."

"Isaac—" Mr. Thornycroft came to a long pause, and then went on rapidly, imparting the news that he had to tell. And it was a somewhat curious fact, that an embarrassment pervaded his manner in making this communication to his second son, quite contrasting with the easy coolness shown to his eldest. A bright flush rose to Isaac's fair Saxon face as he listened.

"A wife, sir! Will it be well that you should introduce one to the Red Court?"

"Don't make me go over the ground again, Isaac. I repeat that I think it will be well. Some lady must be had here—a wife or a governess, and the former in my judgment will be the lesser evil."

"As you please, of course, sir," returned Isaac, who could not forget the perfect respect and courtesy due to his father, however he might deplore the news. "I have heard you say—"

"Well? Speak out, Ikey."

"That had the time to come over again you would not have married my mother. I think it killed her, sir."

"My marrying her?" asked the justice in a joke. Isaac smiled.

"No, sir. You know what I mean; the constant state of fear she lived in."

"She was one of those sensitive, timid women that fear works upon; Cyril is the only one of you like her," said the justice, his thoughts reverting with some sadness to his departed wife. "But the error committed there, Isaac, lay in my disclosing it to her. '

"In disclosing what, sir?" asked Isaac, rather at sea.

"The secret connected with the Red Court Farm," laconically answered Mr. Thornycroft.

There ensued a pause. Isaac put a straw in his lips and bit it like a man in pain. He had loved his mother with no common love; to hear that her place was to be occupied fell on him like a blow, putting aside other considerations against it.

"It is a great risk, sir."

"I don't see it, Isaac. But for an accident your mother would never have suspected. I then disclosed the truth to her, and I cursed myself for my folly afterwards. But for that she might have been with us now. As to risk, we run the same every day with Mary Anne. Ah me! your poor mother was too sensitive, and the fear killed her."

Isaac winced. He remembered how his mother had faded visibly, day by day; he could see, even now, the alarm in her soft eyes that the twilight often brought.

Mr. Thornycroft went away with the last words. Richard, who appeared to have been reconnoitring, came striding up to his brother, and let off a little of his superfluous anger, talking loud and fast.

"He is going out of his senses; you know it must be so, Isaac. Who is the woman? Did he tell you?"

"No," replied Isaac; "but I can give a pretty shrewd guess at her."

"Well?"

"Lady Ellis."

"Who?" roared Richard, as if too much surprised to hear the name distinctly.

"Lady Ellis. I have seen him walking with her two or three times lately."

"The devil take Lady Ellis!"

"So say I; rather than she should come into the Red Court."

"Lady Ellis!" repeated Richard, panic-stricken. "That beetle-browed, bold-eyed woman—with her soft, false words, and her stealthy step! 'Ware her, Isaac. Mark me, 'ware her, all of us, should she come home to the Red Court!"

The June roses were in bloom, and the nightingales sang in the green branches. Perfume was exhaled from the linden trees; butterflies floated in the air; insects hummed through the summer day. Out at sea the fishing-boats lay idly on the sparkling waves that gently rippled in the sun. And in this joyous time the new mistress came home to the Red Court Farm.

Lady Ellis had departed for London. Some three weeks afterwards Mr. Thornycroft went up one day, and was married the next, having said nothing at all at home. It came upon Mary Anne like a thunderbolt. She cried, she sobbed, she felt every feeling within her outraged.

"Isaac, I hate Lady Ellis!"

In that first moment, with the shock upon her, it was worse than useless to argue or persuade, and Isaac wisely left it. The mischief was done; and all that remained for them was to make the best of it. Mary Anne, with the independence of will that characterized her, wrote off a pressing mandate to France, which brought Mademoiselle Derode back again. In the girl's grief she instinctively turned to the little governess, her kind friend in the past years.

And now, after a fortnight's lapse, the mature bridegroom and bride were coming home. The Red Court had made its preparations to receive them. Mary Anne Thornycroft stood in the large drawing-room, in use this evening, wearing a pale blue silk of delicate brightness. Her hard opposition had yielded. Isaac persuaded, mademoiselle reasoned, Richard came down upon her with a short, stern command—and she stood ready, if not exactly to welcome, at least to receive civilly her father's wife. Richard appeared to have fallen in with Isaac's recommendation—that they should "make the best of it." At any rate he no longer showed anger; and he ordered his sister not to do it. So, apparently, all was smooth.

She stood there in her gleaming silk, with blue ribbons in her hair, and a deep flush in her fair face. Little Miss Derode, her dark brown eyes kindly and simple as ever, her small face browner, sat placidly working at a strip of embroidery. It was striking six, the hour for which Mr. Thornycroft had desired dinner to be ready.

Wheels were heard, the signal of the approach. They were pretty punctual, then. Isaac went out; it was evident that he at least intended to pay due respect to his father's wife. Presently Hyde, who had worn a long face ever since the wedding, threw open the drawing-room door.

"The justice and Lady Ellis."

The man had spoken her old name in his sore feeling, little thinking that she intended to retain it, in defiance of good taste. She approached Mary Anne, and kissed her. That ill-trained young lady submitted to it for an instant, and then burst into a passionate fit of angry sobs on her father's breast.

"Don't be a goose," whispered the justice, fondly kissing her. "Halloa! why, is it you, mademoiselle?" he cried out, his eyes falling on the governess. "When did you come over?"

"She came over because I sent for her, papa; and she has been here nine or ten days."

A few minutes and they went in to dinner. Richard's place was vacant.

"Where's your brother, Isaac?" asked the justice. "I believe he had to go out, sir."

Lady Ellis wondered a little at the profuseness of the dinner, but supposed it was in honour of herself, and felt gratified. It was, in fact, the usual style of dining at the Red Court, except at those quiet times (somewhat rare) when the two elder sons were away from home. But Lady Ellis did not suspect this.

Vastly agreeable did she make herself. Isaac, seated at her left elbow, was the most attractive man she had come in contact with since the advent of Mr. Lake, and Lady Ellis liked attractive men, even though they could be nothing more to her than step-sons. But she had come home to the Court really intending to be cordial with its inmates. And, as it has been already hinted, Richard and Isaac saw the policy of making the best of things.

If ever Mademoiselle Derode had been fascinated with a person at first sight, it was with Lady Ellis. The delicate attentions of that lady won her heart. When they crossed the hall to the drawing-room after dinner, and my lady linked her arm within that of her unwilling step-daughter, and extended the other to take the poor little withered hand of the Frenchwoman, mademoiselle's heart went out to her. Very far indeed was it from the intention of Lady Ellis to undertake the completion of Mary Anne's education, whatever might be the private expectation of Mr. Thornycroft: in the visit of the ex-governess she saw a solution of the difficulty—mademoiselle should remain and resume her situation. To bring this about by crafty means, her usual way of going to work, instead of open ones, my lady set out by being very charming with the governess. The very fact of mademoiselle's having been prejudiced by Miss Thornycroft against the stepmother who was coming home, served to augment within her the feeling of fascination. "A dark, ugly woman, poor and pretentious, who has not an iota of good feeling or of truth within her whole composition," spoke Miss Mary Anne, judging of her exactly as Richard did. Great was mademoiselle's surprise to see the handsome, fascinating, superbly dressed lady, who came in upon them with her soft smile and suave manners. She thought Miss Thornycroft had spoken in prejudice only, and almost resented it for the new lady's sake.

It was daylight still, and Lady Ellis stood for a minute at the window, open to the evening's loveliness. The sun had set, but some of its golden brightness lingered yet in the sky. Lady Ellis leaned from the window and plucked a rose from a tree within reach. Mademoiselle stood near; Mary Anne sat down on the music stool, her back to the room and her eyes busied with an uninteresting page of music, striking a bar of it now and again.

"Are you fond of flowers, miladi?" asked the simple little Frenchwoman. "I think there's nothing so good hardly in the world."

"You shall have this rose, then. Stay, let me place it in your waistband. There!—you will have the perfume now until it fades."

Mademoiselle caught the delicate hand and imprinted a kiss upon it. Single-minded, simple-hearted, possessing no discernment at the best of times, artless as a child, she took all the sweet looks and kind tones for real. Lady Ellis sat down on an ottoman in front of the window, and graciously drew mademoiselle beside her.

"Do you live in Paris?"

"I live in Paris now with my mother. We have a sweet little appartement near the Rue Montagne—one room and a cabinet de toilette and a very little kitchen, and we are happy. We go to the Champs Elysées with our work on fine days, to sit there and see the world:—the fine toilettes and the little ones at play. It was long to be separated from her, all the years that I was here."

"How many were they?"

"Seven. Yes, miladi, seven! But what will you? I had to gain. My mother she has a very small rente, and I came here. Mr. Thornycroft he was liberal to me—he is liberal to all,—and I saved enough to have on my side a little rente too. I went home when it was decided I should leave my pupil, and took my mother from the pension where she had stayed: and now we are happy together."

A thought crossed Lady Ellis that the charming apartment near the Rue Montague, and the mother in it, might prove some impediment to her scheme. Well—it would require the greater diplomacy.

"Is your mother old?"

"She will be sixty-five on the day of the All-Saints; and I was forty last month," added mademoiselle, with the candour as to age that is characteristic of a Frenchwoman. Suddenly, just as Lady Ellis was clasping the withered brown hand with a sweet smile, mademoiselle, without intending the least discourtesy, started up, her eyes fixed upon the plateau.

"Ah, bah," she said, sitting down again. "It is but the douanier—the preventive man."

Lady Ellis naturally looked out, and saw a man pacing along the border of the plateau. The superstition said to be connected with the place came into her mind, but did not stay there.

"You were here in the time of Mrs. Thornycroft, mademoiselle?"

"Ah, yes; she did not die for a long while after I came."

"She had years of ill health, I have heard. What was the matter with her?"

"It was but weakness, as we all thought," answered the Frenchwoman. "There was nothing to be told; no disease to be found.. She got thinner every week, and month, and year; like one who fades away. The doctor he came and came, and said the lungs were wrong; and so she died. Ah, she was so gentle, so patient; never murmuring, never complaining. Miladi, she was just an angel."

"What had she to complain of?" asked miladi.

"What to complain of? Why, her sickness; her waste of strength. Everything was done for her that could be, except one—and that was to go from home. It was urged upon her, but she would not listen; she used to shudder at the thought."

"But why?" wondered Lady Ellis.

"I never knew. My pupil, Miss Mary Anne, never knew. She would kneel at her mamma's feet, and beg her to go anywhere, and to take her; but the poor lady would shake her head, or say quietly, no; and that would end it."

Mademoiselle Virginie Derode was a capable woman in her vocation. She could do a vast many things useful, good, necessary to be done in the world. But there was one thing that she could not do, and that was—hold her tongue. Some people are born with the bump of reticence; my Lady Ellis was a case in point: some, it may be said, with the bump of communicativeness, though I don't know where it lies. Mademoiselle was an exemplification of the latter.

"There was some secret—some trouble on Madame Thornycroft's mind," said good mademoiselle in her open-heartedness. "Towards the last, when the weakness grew to worse and worse, she would—what do you call it?—wander a little; and I once heard her say that it had killed her. Mr. Isaac, he was in the room at the time, and he shook his mother—gently, you know, he loved her very much; and told her she was dreaming, and talking in her sleep. That aroused her; and she laid her head upon his shoulder, and thanked him for awaking her."

"And was she talking in her sleep?"

"Ah, no; she was not asleep. But I think Mr. Isaac said it because of me. I saw there was something, always from the time I first came; she used to start at shadows; if the window did but creak she would turn white, and stare at it; if the door but opened suddenly, she would turn all over in a cold sweat. It was like a great fear that never went away."

"But what fear was it?" reiterated Lady Ellis.

"I used to repeat to myself that same question—'What is it?' One day I said to Hyde, as I saw him watching his mistress, 'She has got some trouble upon her mind?' and he, that polite Hyde called me a French idiot to my face, saying she had no more trouble on her mind than he had on his. I never saw Hyde fierce but that one time. Ah, but yes; she certainly said it; that it had killed her."

"That what had killed her?" still questioned Lady Ellis, considerably at sea.

"I had to guess what; I knew it quite well as I listened; the secret trouble that had been upon her like a fright perpetual."

Lady Ellis threw her piercing eyes upon the soft and simple ones of the little Frenchwoman. All this was as food for her curious mind. "A perpetual fright!" she repeated musingly. "I never heard of such a thing. What was it connected with?"

"I don't know, unless it was connected with that horror of the plateau. Miladi, I used to think it might be."

Casting her thoughts back some few weeks, Lady Ellis remembered the little episode of her proposing to go on the plateau, and Mr. Thornycroft's words as he opposed it. She turned this to use now with mademoiselle in her clever way.

"Mr. Thornycroft was speaking to me about this—this mystery connected with the plateau, but we were interrupted, and I did not gather much. It is a mystery, is it not, mademoiselle?"

"But, yes; it might be called a mystery," was the answer.

"Will you recite it to me?"

Mademoiselle knew very little to recite; but that little she remembered with as much distinctness as though it had happened yesterday. One light evening in the bygone years, shortly after she came to the Red Court, she went out in the garden and strolled on to the plateau. There were no preventive railings round it then. It was fresh and pleasant there; the sea was calm, the moonbeams fell across the waves; and a vessel far away, lying apparently at anchor, showed its cheery white light. Mademoiselle strolled back towards the house, and was about to take another turn, when she saw a figure on the edge of the plateau, seemingly standing to look at the sea. To her sight it either wore some white garment, or else the rays of the moon caused it to appear so. At that moment Richard Thornycroft came up. In turning to speak to him mademoiselle lost sight of the plateau, and when she looked again, the figure was gone. "Was it a shadowy sort of figure?" Richard asked her, in a low voice, when she expressed her surprise at the disappearance; and mademoiselle answered after a moment's consideration that she thought it was shadowy. Mr. Richard looked up at the sky, and then down at her, and then far away; his countenance (it seemed to mademoiselle that she could see it now) wearing a curious expression of care and awe. "It must have been the ghost," he said; "it is apt to show itself when strangers appear at night on the plateau." The words nearly startled mademoiselle out of her seven senses; "ghosts" had been her one dread through life. She put her poor trembling fingers on Richard's coat sleeve, and humbly begged him to walk back with her as far as the house. Richard did so; giving her scraps of information on the way. He had never seen the figure himself, perhaps because he had specially looked for it, but many at Coastdown had seen it; nay, some even then living at the Red Court. Why did the ghost come there? Well, it was said that a murder had been committed on that very spot, the edge of the plateau, and the murderer, stung with remorse, killed himself within a few hours, and could not rest in his grave. Mademoiselle was too scared to hear all he said; she heard quite enough for her own peace; and she went into the presence of Mrs. Thornycroft, bursting into tears. When that lady heard what the matter was, she chided Richard in her gentle manner. "Was there need to have told her this?" she whispered to him with a strange sorrow, a great reproach, in her sad brown eyes. "I am sorry to have said it if it has alarmed mademoiselle," was Richard's answer. "It need not trouble her; let her keep off the plateau at night; it never comes in the day." That Richard believed in it himself appeared all too evident, and she remarked it to Mrs. Thornycroft as she left the room. That good lady poured a glass of wine out for her with her own hand, and begged her, in accents so imploring as to take a tone of wildness, never again to go on the plateau after dusk had fallen. No need of the injunction; mademoiselle had scuttered onwards ever since with her head down, if obliged to go abroad at night in attendance on Miss Thornycroft.

To hear her tell this in a low earnest whisper, her brown hands clasped, her scared eyes strained on the opposite plateau, whose edge stood out defined and clear against the line of sea beyond and the sky above, was the strangest of all to Lady Ellis.

"If there is one thing that I have feared in life it is a revenant," confessed mademoiselle. "Were I to see one, knowing it was one, I think I should die. There was a revenant in the convent where they put me when I was a little child; a white-faced nun who had died unshriven; and we used to hear her in the upper corridors on a windy night. Ah, me! I was sick with fear when I listened; I was but a poor little weak thing then, and the dread of revenants has always rested with me."

Lady Ellis suppressed her inclination to smile, and pressed the trembling brown fingers in her calm ones. With the matter-of-fact plateau lying there before her, with her own matter-of-fact mind so hard and real, the ghost story sounded like what it must be, simple delusion. But that something strange was connected with the plateau, she had little doubt.

"And what more did you hear of it?" she asked.

"Nothing—nothing more after that night. In a day or two, when my courage came to me, and I would have asked details, Mr. Thornycroft, who happened to be in the room, went into great anger. He told me to hold my tongue; never to speak or think of the subject again, or he should send me back to France. I obeyed him; I did not speak of it; even when there was talk in the village because of the accident, and he had the railings put up, I kept myself silent. I could not obey him in the other thing— not to think of it. I tried not; and I got dear Mrs. Thornycroft to put my bed in a back room, so that I did not see the plateau from my window. Well, to go back, miladi: I think it must have been this cause, or something connected with it, that brought the fear in which she lived to Mrs. Thornycroft."

Lady Ellis was silent. She could not think anything of the sort. Unless, indeed, the late Mrs. Thornycroft was of a kindred nature to mademoiselle; timorous and weak-minded.

"The preventive men pace there, do they not?"

"By day, yes; they walk on to it from their beat below, but not much at night. Ah, no! not since the accident; they do not like the ghost."

Mademoiselle rose; she was going to Mrs. Wilkinson's, on the heath, for the rest of her stay in Coastdown. Saying good night to my lady, she went in search of Mary Anne, and could not find her.

Mary Anne was with her brother Isaac. She had flown to him after quitting the presence of her stepmother, having had much ado to repress all the feelings that went well-nigh to choke her. With a crimson face and heaving bosom, with wild sobs, no longer checked, she threw herself on his neck.

"Now, Mary Anne!"

"It has been my place ever since mamma died. It is not right that she should take it."

He found she was speaking of the seat at table. Every little incident of this kind, that must inevitably occur when a second wife is brought home, did but add to the feeling of bitter grief, of wrong. Not for the place in itself did she care, but because a stranger had usurped what had been their mother's.

Letting the burst of grief spend itself, Isaac Thornycroft then sat down, put her in a chair near him, and gave her some wise counsel. It would be so much happier for her—for all of them—for papa—that they should unite in making the best of the new wife come amidst them; of her, and for her.

All he said was of little use. Anger, pain, bitter, bitter self-reproach sat passionately this night on the heart of Mary Anne Thornycroft.

"Don't talk, Isaac. I hope I shall not die of it."

"Die of it?"

"The fault is mine. I can see it well. Had I been obedient to Miss Derode; had I only stayed quietly at school, it never would have happened. Papa would not have brought her home, or thought of bringing her home, but for me."

That was very true. Mary Anne Thornycroft, in her strong good sense, saw the past in its right light. She could blame herself just as much as she could others when the cause of blame rested with her. Isaac strove to still her emotion; to speak comfort to her; but she only broke out again with the words that seemed to come from a bursting heart.

"I hope I shall not die of it!"

CHAPTER XIV

Superstitious Tales

With the morning Lady Ellis assumed her position as mistress of the Red Court. She took her breakfast in bed—a habit she favoured—but came down before ten, in a beautiful challi dress, delicate roses on a white ground, with some white net lace and pink ribbons in her hair. The usual breakfast hour was eight o'clock, at least it was always laid for that hour; and Mr. Thornycroft and his sons went out afterwards on their land.

Looking into the different rooms, my lady found no one, and found her way to the servants' offices.

The kitchen, a large square apartment, fitted up with every known apparatus for cooking, was the first room she came to. Its two sash windows looked on the side of the house towards the church. It had been built out, comparatively of late years, beyond the back of the dining-room, a sort of added wing, or projecting corner. But altogether the back of the house was irregular; a nook here, a projection there; rooms in angles; casements large or small as might happen. The sash windows of the kitchen alone were good and modern, but you could not see them from the back. Whatever the irregularity of the architecture, the premises were spacious; affording every accommodation necessary for a large household. A room near the kitchen was called the housekeeper's room; it was carpeted, and the servants sat in it when they pleased; but they were by no means fashionable servants, going in for style and ceremony, and as a rule preferred the kitchen. There were seven servants indoors; Sinnett being the housekeeper.

My lady—as she was to be called in the house—was gracious. The cook showed her the larder, the dairy, and anything else she chose to see, and then received the orders for dinner—a plain one—fish, a joint, pudding, and cream.

It was the intention of my lady to feel her way, rather than assume authority hurriedly. She saw, with some little surprise, that no remnant was left of the last day's dinner; at least none was to be seen. Not that day would she inquire after it, but keep a watchful eye on what went from table for the future. To say that her rule in the house was to have one guiding principle—economy—would be only stating the fact. There had been no marriage settlements, and my lady meant to line her pocket by dint of saving.

The rooms were still deserted when she returned to them. My lady stood a moment in the hall, wondering if everybody was out. The door at the end, shutting off the portion of the house used by the young men, caught her eye, and she resolved to go on an exploration tour. Opening the door softly, she saw Richard Thornycroft in the passage talking to Hyde. He raised his hat, as in courtesy bound; but his dark stern face never relaxed a muscle; and somehow it rather daunted her.

"My father's wife, I believe," said Richard. "To what am I indebted for the honour of this visit?"

Just as if the rooms at this end of the house were his! But my lady made the best of it.

"It is Mr. Richard, I am sure! Let us be friends." She held out her hand, and he touched the tips of her fingers.

"Certainly. If we are not friends the fault will lie on your side," he pointedly said. "I interfere with no one in the house. I expect no one to interfere with me. Let us observe this rule to each other, and I dare say we shall get on very well."

She gently slid her hand within his, encased in its rough coat. Hyde, recovering from his trance of amazement, touched his hat, and went out at the outer door.

"I have not been in this portion of the house. Will you show it to me?"

"I will show it to you with pleasure: what little there is of it to see," replied Richard. "But—once seen, I must request you to understand that these rooms are for gentlemen only. Ladies are out of place in them."

She had a great mind to ask why; but did not. Very poor rooms, as Richard said—one on either side the passage. Small and plain in comparison with the rest of the house. A strip of thick cocoa-nut matting ran along the passage to the outer door. It was open, and my lady advanced to it.

Looking at the most confined prospect she ever saw; in fact, at no prospect at all. A wall, in which there was a small door of egress, shut out all view of the sea and the plateau. Another wall, with wide gates of wood, hid the courtyard and the buildings beyond. Opposite, in almost close proximity, leaving just space for the dog-cart or other vehicles to come in and turn, was the room used as a coach-house, formerly part of the stables when the house was a castle. My lady walked across the gravel, and entered it. A half-smile crossed Richard's face.

"There's not much to see here," he said.

Certainly not much. The dog-cart stood in one corner; in another were some trusses of straw, and a dilapidated cart turned upside down. Adjoining was a stable for the two horses alternately used in the dog-cart. My lady stepped back to the house door, and took a deliberate survey of the whole.

"It strikes me as being the dreariest-looking spot possible," she said. "A dead wall on each side, and a shut-in coach-house opposite!"

"Yes. Those who planned it had not much regard to prospect," answered Richard. "But, then, prospect is not wanted here."

She turned into the rooms; the windows of both looking on this confined yard. In the one room, crowded with guns, fishing-rods, dog-collars, boxing gloves, and other implements used by the young men, she stood a minute, scanning it curiously. In the other, on the opposite side the passage, was a closed desk-table, a telescope and weather-glass, some armchairs, pipes, and tobacco.

"This is the room I have heard Mr. Thornycroft call his den," said she, quickly.

"It is. The other one is mine and my brother's."

A narrow twisting staircase led to the two rooms above. My lady, twisting up it, turned into one of the two—Richard's bed-chamber. The window looked to the dreary line of coast stretching forward in the distance.

"Who sleeps in the other room?" she asked.

"Hyde. This part of the house is lonely, and I choose to have him within call."

In her amazement to hear him say this—the brave strong man, whom no physical fear could daunt—a thought arose that the superstition obtaining at the Red Court, whatever it might be, was connected with these shut-in-rooms; shut in from within and without. Somehow the feeling was not pleasant to her, and she turned to descend the stairs.

"But, Mr. Richard, why do you sleep here yourself?"

"I would not change my room for another; I am used to it. At one time no one slept here, but my mother grew to think it was not safe at night. She was nervous at the last."

He held the passage-door open, and raised his hat, which he had worn all the while, as she went through it, then shut it with a loud, decisive click.

"A sort of intimation that I am not wanted there," thought she. "He need not fear; there's nothing so pleasant to go for, rather the contrary."

In the afternoon, tired of being alone, she put on her things to go out, and met Mr. Thornycroft. She began a shower of questions. Where had he been? What doing? Where were all of them—Isaac—Mary Anne? Not a soul had she seen the whole day, except Richard. Mr. Thornycroft lifted his finger to command attention, as he answered her.

It would be better that they should at once begin as they were to go on; and she, his lady wife, must not expect to get a categorical account of daily movements. He never presumed to ask his sons how their days were spent. Farmers—farming a large tract of land—had to be in fifty places at least in the course of the day; here, and there, and everywhere. This applied to himself as well as to his sons. When Cyril came home he could attend upon her; he had nothing to do with the out-door work, and never would have.

"Hyde said you rode out this morning."

"I had business at Dartfield: have just got home."

"Dartfield! where's that?"

"A place five or six miles away: with a dreary road to it, too," added the justice.

"Won't you walk with me?" she pleaded, in the soft manner that had, so attracted him before marriage.

"If you like. Let us go for a stroll on the heath."

"Where is Mary Anne?" she inquired, as they went on.

"Mary Anne is your concern now, not mine. Has she not been with you?"

"I have not seen her at all today. When I got down—it was before ten—all the world seemed flown. I found Richard. He took me over the rooms at the end of the passage; to your bureau (he called the room that, as the French do), and to his chamber and Hyde's, and to the place filled with their guns and things."

The justice gave a sort of grin. "That's quite a come-out for Dick. Showing you his chamber! You must have won his heart."

My lady's private opinion was that she had not won it; but she did not say so. Gracefully twitching up her expensive robe, lest it should gather harm in its contact with the common, she tripped on, and they reached the heath. Mr. Thornycroft proposed to make calls at the different houses in succession, beginning with Captain Copp's. She heard him with a little shriek of dismay. "It was not etiquette."

"Etiquette?" responded the justice.

"I am but just married. It is their place to call on me first."

Mr. Thornycroft laughed. Etiquette was about as much understood as Greek at Coastdown. "Come along!" cried he, heartily. "There's the sailor and his wooden leg opening the door to welcome us."

The sailor was doing it in a sailorly fashion,—flourishing his wooden leg, waving his glazed hat round and round, cheering and beckoning. The bride made a merit of necessity, and went in. Here they had news of Mary Anne. Mrs. Copp, Mademoiselle Derode, and Miss Thornycroft had gone to Jutpoint by omnibus under Isaac's convoy.

"And the women are coming back here to a tea-fight," said the plain sea-captain; "cold mackerel and shrimps and hot cakes; that she-pirate of ours is baking the cakes in the oven; so you need not expect your daughter home, justice."

Mr. Thornycroft nodded in answer. His daughter was welcome to stay.

The dinner-party at the Red Court that evening consisted of five. Its master and mistress, the two sons, and a stranger named Hopley from Dartfield, whom Richard brought in. He was not much of a gentleman, and none of them had dressed. My lady thought she was going in for a prosy sort of life— not exactly the one she had anticipated.

Very much to her surprise she found the dinner-courses much augmented; quite a different dinner altogether from that which she had ordered. Boiled fowls, roast ducklings, tarts, ice-creams, macaroni— all sorts of additions. My lady compressed her lips, and came to the conclusion that her orders had been misunderstood. There is more to be said yet about the dinners at the Red Court Farm; not for the especial benefit of the reader, he is requested to take notice, but because they bear upon the story.

At its conclusion she left the gentlemen and sat alone at the open window of the drawing-room;—sat there until the shades of evening darkened; the flowers on the lawn sent up their perfume, the evening star came twinkling out, the beautiful sea beyond the plateau lay calm and still. She supposed they had all gone out, or else were smoking in the dining-room. When Sinnett brought her a cup of tea, presenting it on a silver waiter, she said, in answer to an inquiry, that the gentlemen as a rule had not taken tea since the late Mrs. Thornycroft's time. Miss Thornycroft and her governess had it served for themselves, with Mr. Cyril when he was at home from his tutor's.

"That is it," muttered my lady to herself, as Sinnett left the room. "Since their mother's death there has been no one to enforce order in the house, and they have had the run like wild animals. It's not likely they would care to be with the girl and that soft French governess."

It was dull, sitting there alone, and she wound an Indian shawl round her shoulders, went out across the lawn, and crossed the railings to the banned plateau.

It was very dreary. Not a soul was in sight; the landscape lay still and grey, the sea dull and silent. A mist seemed to have come on. This plateau, bare in places, was a small weary waste. Standing as near to the dangerous edge as she dared, my lady stretched her neck and saw the outline of the Half-moon underneath, surrounded by its waters, for the tide was nearly at its height. The projecting rocks right and left seemed to clip nearly round it, hiding it from the sea beyond. The cliff, as she looked over, was almost perpendicular, its surface jagged, altogether dangerous to look upon, and she drew back with a slight shudder—drew back to find Richard Thornycroft gazing at her from the plateau's railings, on which he leaned. They met halfway.

"Were you watching me, Mr. Richard?"

"I was," he gravely answered. "And not daring to advance or make the least sound, lest I should startle you."

"It is a dangerous spot. Mr. Thornycroft was saying so to me one day. But I had never been here, and I thought I would have a look at it; it was lonely indoors. So I came. Braving the ghost," she added, with a slight laugh.

Richard looked at her, as much as to ask what she knew, but did not speak.

"Last evening, when we were sitting in the drawing-room, the plateau in view, your sister's governess plunged into the superstitious, telling me of a 'revenant' that appears. I had heard somewhat of it before. She thinks you believe in it."

Richard Thornycroft extended his hand to help her over the railings. "Revenant, or no revenant, I would very strongly advise you not to frequent the plateau at night," he said, as they walked on to the house. "Do not be tempted to risk the danger."

"Are you advising me against the ghostly danger or the tangible?"

"The tangible."

"What is the other tale? What gave rise to this superstition?"

Richard Thornycroft did not answer. He piloted her indoors as far as the drawing-room, all in silence. The room was so dusk now that she could scarcely see the outline of the furniture.

"Will you not tell it me, Mr. Richard? Mademoiselle's was but a lame tale."

"What was mademoiselle's tale?"

"That she saw a shadowy figure on the plateau, which disappeared almost as she looked at it. You gave her some explanation about a murderer that came again as a revenant, and she had lived in dread of seeing it ever since."

If my lady had expected Richard Thornycroft to laugh in answer to her laugh, she was entirely mistaken; his face remained stern, sad, solemn.

"I cannot tell you anything, Lady Ellis, that you might not hear from any soul at Coastdown," he said presently. "People, however, don't much care to talk of this."

"Why don't they?"

Richard lifted his dark eyebrows. "I scarcely know: a feeling undoubtedly exists against doing so. What is it you wish to hear?"

"All the story, from beginning to end. Was there a murder?"

"Yes; it took place on the plateau. I can give you no particulars, I was but a little fellow at the time, except that the man who committed the deed hung himself before the night was out. The superstition obtaining is, that he does not rest quietly in his unconsecrated grave, and comes abroad at times to haunt the plateau, especially the spot where the deed was done."

"And that spot?"

Richard extended his hand and pointed to the edge as nearly as possible in a line with the window.

"It was there; just above the place they call the Half-moon. The figure appears on the brink, and stands there looking out over the sea. I should have said is reported to appear," he corrected himself.

"Did you ever see it yourself?"

"I cannot tell you."

"Not tell me!"

"I have undoubtedly seen a figure hovering there; but whether ghostly or human it has never given me time to ascertain. Before I could well cross the railings even, it has gone."

"Gone where?"

"I never could detect where. And to tell you the truth, I have thought it strange."

"Have you seen it many times?"

"Three or four."

He was standing close against the side of the window as he spoke, his profile stern as ever, distinct in the nearly faded light. My lady sat and watched him.

"The superstition has caused an accident or two," he resumed. "A poor coastguard-man was on his beat there one moonlight night and discerned a figure coming towards him walking on the brink of the cliff, as he was. What he saw to induce him to take it for the apparition, or to impart fear, was never explained. With a wild cry he either leaped from the cliff in his fright, or fell from it."

"Was he killed on the spot?"

"So to say. He lived but a few minutes after help came: the tide was up, and they had to get to him in boats: just long enough to say some nearly incoherent words, to the effect of what I have told you. A night or two after that a man, living in the village, went on the plateau looking for the ghost, as was supposed, and he managed to miss his footing, fell over, and was killed. It was then that my father had the railings put; almost a superfluous caution, as it turned out, for the impression made on the neighbourhood by these two accidents was so great, and the plateau became so associated in men's minds with so much horror, that I think nobody would go on it at night unless compelled."

"Lest they should see three ghosts instead of one," interrupted a light, careless voice at the back of the room. My lady started, Richard turned.

It came from Isaac Thornycroft. He had come in unheard, the door was but half closed, and gathered the sense of what was passing.

"Quite an appropriate atmosphere for ghostly stories," he said; "you are all in the dark here. Shall I ring for lights?"

"Not yet," interposed my lady, hastily; "I want to hear more."

"There's no more to hear," said Richard.

"Yes there is. You cannot think how this interests me, Mr. Richard; but I want to know—I want to know what was the cause of the murder. Can't you tell me?"

Isaac Thornycroft had perched himself on the music-stool, his fair, gay, open face a very contrast just now to his brother's grave one. In the uncertain light he fancied that my lady looked to him with the last question, as if in appeal, and he answered it.

"Richard can tell it if he likes."

But it seemed that Richard aid not like. He had said the neighbourhood cared not to speak of this; most certainly he did not. It was remembered afterwards, when years had passed; and the strange fact was regarded as some subtle instinct lying far beyond the ken of man. But there was my lady casting her exacting looks towards him.

"They were two brothers, the disputants, and the cause was said to be jealousy. Both loved the same woman, and she played them off one on the other. Hence the murder. Had I been the Nemesis I should have slain the woman after them."

"Brothers!" repeated Lady Ellis. "It was a dreadful thing."

Richard, quitting his place by the window, left the room. Isaac, who had been softly humming a tune to himself, brought it to a close. A broad smile sat on his face: it appeared evident to my lady that the superstition was regarded by him as fun rather than otherwise. She fell into thought.

"You do not believe in the ghost, Mr. Isaac?"

"I don't say that. I do not fear it."

"Did you ever see it?"

"Never so much as its shadow; but it is currently believed, you know, that some people are born without the gift of seeing ghosts."

He laughed a merry laugh. My lady resumed in a low tone.

"Is it not thought that your mother feared it? That it—it helped to kill her?"

As if by magic, changed the mood of Isaac Thornycroft. He rose from the stool, and stood for a moment at the window in the faint rays of the light; his face was little less dark than his brother's, his voice as stern.

"By your leave, madam, we will not bring my mother's name up in connexion with this subject."

"I beg your pardon; but—there is one thing I should like to ask you. Do not look upon me as a stranger, but as one of yourselves from henceforth; come here, I hope, to make life pleasanter to all of us," she continued, in her sweetest tone. "Those rooms at the end of the house, with the high walls on either side—is there any superstition connected with them?"

Isaac Thornycroft simply stared at her.

"I cannot tell why I fancy it. To-day when Mr. Richard was showing me those rooms, the thought struck me that the superstition said to obtain at the Red Court Farm must be connected with them."

"Who says that superstition obtains at the Red Court Farm?" questioned Isaac sharply.

"I seem to have gathered that impression from one or another."

"Then I should think, for your own peace of mind, you had better ungather it—if you will allow me to coin a word," he answered. "The superstition of the plateau does not extend to the Red Court."

She gave a slight sniff. "Those rooms looked dull enough for it. And your brother—your strong, stern, resolute brother—confessed to feeling so lonely in them that he had Hyde to sleep in the chamber near him. There's not so much space between them and the plateau."

Isaac turned from the window and faced her; voice, eye, face resolute as Richard's.

"Mrs. Thornycroft—or Lady Ellis, whichever it may please you to be called—let me say a word of advice to you in all kindness. Forget these things; do not allow yourself to recur to them. For your own sake I would warn you never to go on the plateau after daylight; the edge is more treacherous than you imagine; and your roving there could not be meet or pleasant. As to the rooms you speak of, there is no superstition attaching to them that I am aware of; but there may be other reasons to render it inexpedient for ladies to enter them. They belong to me and my brother; to my father also, when he chooses to enter; and we like to know that they are private to us. Shall I ring for lights now?" he concluded, as he turned to quit the room.

"Yes, please. I wonder where Mr. Thornycroft can be?"

"Probably at the Mermaid," he stayed to say.

"At the Mermaid? Do you mean the public-house?"

"Yes. A smoking bout takes place in its best parlour occasionally. My father, Mr. Southall, Captain Copp, Dangerfield the superintendent of the coastguard, old Connaught, and a few other gentlemen, meet there."

"Oh!" she answered. "Where are you going?"

"To fetch my sister from Mrs. Copp's."

In the short interval that elapsed before the appearance of the lights, my lady took a rapid survey of matters in her mind. The conclusion she arrived at was, that there were some items of the recent conversation altogether curious; that a certain mysterious atmosphere enveloped the present as well as the past; not the least of which was Richard Thornycroft's manner and his too evident faith in mystery. Take it for all in all, the most incomprehensible place she had ever come in contact with was the Red Court Farm.

CHAPTER XV

The New Mistress of the Red Court

My lady was up betimes in the morning. Remembering the previous day's dinner, she went to seek the cook, intending to come down upon her with a reprimand. The servants were only just rising from breakfast, which afforded my lady an opportunity of seeing the style of that meal as served in the kitchen of the Red Court Farm.

Tea and coffee; part of a ham, cold; toasted bacon, hot; eggs boiled; watercress and radishes; a raised pie; cold beef; shrimps; hot rolls; toast and butter. The sight of all this so completely took Lady Ellis aback, that she could only stare and wonder.

"Is this your usual breakfast table?" she asked of the cook when the rest had left the kitchen.

"Yes, my lady."

"By whose permission?"

"By—I don't understand," said the cook, a stolid sort of woman in ordinary, with a placid face, though very great in her own department.

"Who is it that allows all this?"

Still the woman did not quite comprehend. The scale of living at the Red Court Farm was so profuse, that the servants in point of fact could eat what they pleased.

"Sometimes the eatables is varied, my lady."

"But—does Mr. Thornycroft know of this extravagance going on? Is he aware that you sit down to such a breakfast?"

Cook could not say. He did not trouble himself about the matter. Yes, now she remembered, the justice had come in when they were at breakfast and other meals.

"Who has been the manager here?—who has had the ordering of things?" inquired my lady, in a suppressed passion.

"Sinnett, chiefly. Once in a way the justice would give the orders for dinner; a'most never," was the reply.

Compressing her lips, determining to suppress all this ere many days should be over, my lady quitted the subject for the one she had chiefly come to speak upon.

"And now, cook, what did you mean by flying in the face of my orders yesterday?"

"Did I fly in the face of 'em?" asked the cook, simply.

"Did you! I ordered a plain dinner—fish, a joint, and pudding. You sent up—I know not what in addition to it."

"Oh, it's them extra dishes you mean. Yes, my lady, Sinnett ordered 'em."

"Sinnett!" echoed my lady. "Did you tell her I had desired the dinner should be plain—that I had fixed on it?" she asked after a pause.

"Sinnett said that sort of dinner wouldn't do for the justice, and I was to send up a better one."

My lady bit her thin lips. "Call Sinnett here if you please."

Sinnett, about her work upstairs, came in obedience to the summons. She was a little, pale-faced, dark woman, of about thirty-five, given to wear smart caps. My lady attacked her quietly enough, but with a manner authoritative.

"I beg you to understand at once that I am mistress here, Sinnett, and must be obeyed. When I give my orders, whether for dinner or for anything else, they are not to be improved upon."

"My lady, in regard to adding to the dinner yesterday, I did it for the best; not to act in opposition to you," replied Sinnett, respectfully. "A good dinner has to be sent in always: those are the general orders. The young gentlemen are so much in the habit of bringing in chance guests, that the contingency has to be provided for. I have known a party of eight or ten brought in before now, and we servants quite unaware of it until about to lay the cloth."

"Yes," said my lady, hastily, "that might be all very well when there was no controlling mistress here. Mr. Thornycroft's sons appear to have been allowed great license in the house; of course it will be different now. Remember one thing, if you please, Sinnett, that you do not interfere with my orders for dinner today."

"Very well, my lady."

Catching up her dress—a beautiful muslin that shone like gold—my lady turned to the larder, telling the cook to follow her. She had expected to see on its shelves the dishes that left the table yesterday; but she saw very little.

"What has become of the ducks, cook? They were scarcely touched at table."

"We had 'em for our suppers, my lady."

My lady had a wrathful word on the tip of her tongue; she did not speak it.

"Ducks for supper in the kitchen! Are you in the habit of taking your supper indiscriminately from the dinner dishes that come down?"

"Yes, my lady. Such is master's orders."

"It appears to me that a vast quantity of provisions must be consumed," remarked my lady.

"Pretty well," was the cook's answer. "It's a tolerable large family; and Mr. Thornycroft has a good deal given away."

"Provisions?"

"He do; he's a downright good man, my lady. Not a morning passes, but some poor family or other from the village comes up and carries home what's not wanted here."

"I wonder you don't have them up at night as well," said my lady, in sarcasm.

The cook took it literally.

"That's one of the few things not allowed at the Red Court Farm. Mr. Thornycroft won't have people coming here at night: and for the matter of that," added the woman, "they'd not care to come by the plateau after dark.—About today's dinner, my lady?"

Yes; about today's dinner. As if in aggravation of the powers that had been, my lady ordered soles, a piece of roast beef, the tart that had not been cut yesterday, and the remainder of the lemon cream.

As she went sailing away, the cook returned into the kitchen to Sinnett. The woman was really perplexed.

"I say, Sinnett, here's a start! A piece of ribs of beef, and nothing else. What's to be done?"

"Send it up," quietly replied Sinnett.

"But what on earth will the justice and the young masters say?"

"We shall see. I wash my hands of interfering. Exactly what she has ordered, cook, and no more, mind: she and the master must settle it between them."

Mary Anne Thornycroft had hoped she "should not die of it." Of that there was little chance; but that the girl had received a great blow, there was no disputing. Mr. Thornycroft had said a word to her that morning after breakfast in his authoritative manner, to remind her that she was not to run wild, now there was some one at home to be her friend, mother, companion. Smarting under the sense of wrongs that in her limited experience, her ignorance of the woes of the world, she believed had never fallen on anybody's head before, Mary Anne when left alone burst into a flood of tears; and Isaac surprised her in them. Half in vexation, half in pride, she dried them hastily. Isaac drew her before him, and stood holding her hands in his, looking down gravely into her face.

"What did you promise me, Mary Anne?"

No answer.

"That you would, for a time at least, make the best of things. That you would try the new rule before rebelling against it."

"But I can't. It is too hard, Isaac. Papa's beginning to interfere now."

"Interfere! Is that the right word to use?"

She looked down, pouting her pretty lips. It was a good sign, as Isaac knew.

"There was no harm in my walking to Mrs. Copp's after breakfast yesterday; or in my staying there; or in my going with you to Jutpoint."

"Did papa say there was harm?"

"He told me I was not to run wild now. He told me that I had a"—the poor chest heaved piteously—"a mother. A mother to control me!"

"Well!" said Isaac.

"She is not my mother—I will never call her so. Oh, Isaac! why can't the old days come back again, when mademoiselle was here?"

"Hush! don't cry. Richard or she may be coming in. There; be your own calm self, while I say a word to you. Listen. This calamity has been—"

"There!" she interrupted. "You say yourself it is a calamity."

"I have never thought it anything else; but it cannot be averted now, and therefore nothing remains but to try and lighten it. It has been brought about by you; by you alone, Mary Anne; and if I revert to that fact for a moment, my dear, it is not to pain you, but to draw an inference from it for the future. Do not rebel at first to the control of my lady. It would be unjust, ungracious, altogether wrong; it might lead to further trouble for you; we know not of what sort. Promise me," he added, kissing her lips, "that you will not be the one to make first mischief. It is for your own good that I urge it."

Her better judgment came to her, and she gave Isaac a little nod in answer.

My lady reaped the benefit of this lecture. Coming in from her somewhat unsatisfactory visit to the cook, she found the young lady dutifully practising the Moonlight sonata. My lady looked about the room, as if by good luck she might find something to avert weariness. Miss Thornycroft had hoped she should not die of her; my lady was beginning to hope she should not die of ennui.

"Do you never have any books here? Novels?"

"Sometimes," replied Mary Anne, turning round to speak. "We get them from the library at Jutpoint. There are some books upstairs in the book-case that used to be mamma's—Walter Scott's, and Dickens's, and others."

The Moonlight sonata went on again. My lady, who had no soul for music, thought it the most wofully dull piece she had ever listened to. She sat inert on the sofa. Life—this life at the Red Court Farm—was already looking indescribably dreary. And she had pictured it as a second Utopia! It is ever so; when anticipation becomes lost in possession, romance and desire are alike gone.

"How long has Sinnett lived here?" she suddenly asked, again interrupting Miss Thornycroft.

"Ever so long," was the young lady's reply. "She came just before mamma died."

"What are her precise functions here?—What does she call herself?"

"We don't call her anything in particular. She is a sort of general servant, overlooking everything. She is housekeeper and manager."

"Ah! she has taken a great deal of authority on herself, I can see."

"Has she?" replied Mary Anne. "I have heard papa say she is one of the best servants we ever had; thoroughly capable."

My lady gave her head a little defiant nod: and relapsed into silence and ennui.

Somehow the morning was got through. In the afternoon they set out to walk to the heath; it was rather late, for my lady, lying on the sofa in her bedroom, dropped off to sleep after luncheon. The dinner hour had been postponed to eight in the evening in consequence of a message from Mr. Thornycroft.

Winding round the churchyard, Mary Anne stood a moment and looked over the dwarf quickset hedge, on that side not much higher than her knee. My lady observed that her hands were clasped for a moment, that her lips moved.

"What are you doing, Mary Anne?"

"I never like to go by mamma's grave without staying a moment to look at it, and to say a word or two of prayer," was the simple answer.

My lady laughed, not kindly. "That comes of having a Roman Catholic governess."

"Does it!" answered the girl quietly, indignant at the augh. "Mademoiselle happens to be a Protestant. I did not learn it from her, or from any one; it comes from my heart."

Turning abruptly on to the heath, Mary Anne saw Mademoiselle Derode coming towards them, and sprung off to meet her with a glad step.

Disappointment was in store for my lady's private dream of keeping Miss Derode as governess. Mademoiselle was then on her way to the Red Court to tell them she was leaving for France in two days.

"You cannot go," said Mary Anne, with the decisively authoritative manner peculiar to the Thornycrofts. "You must come and spend some weeks with me at the Red Court."

Mademoiselle shook her little brown head. It was not possible, she said; happy as she could be at the Red Court; much as she would have liked to stay again with her dear Miss Mary Anne. Her mother wanted her, and she must go.

Turning about and about, they paced the heath while she repeated the substance of her mother's letter. Madame, said she, was suffering from a cold, from the separation, from loneliness, and had written for her. The Champs Elysées had no charms without her dear daughter; the toilettes were miserable; the playing children hustled her, their bonnes were not polite. Virginie must return the very first hour it would be convenient to do so. The pot-au-feu got burnt, the appartement smoked; madame had been so long en pension that she had forgotten how to manage things; never clever at household affairs, the craft of her hand appeared to have gone from her utterly. She had not had a dinner, so to say, since Virginie left; she had not slept one whole night. While Monsieur and Madame—her pupil's parents—had been away on their wedding tour, she had said nothing of this, but now that they were home again she would no longer keep silence. Virginie must come; and her best prayers would be upon her on the journey.

A sort of mocking smile, covered on the instant by a sweet word, crossed my lady's lips.

"It was all very well," she said, "just what a good mother would write; but mademoiselle must write back, and explain that she was wanted yet for some weeks at the Red Court Farm."

"I cannot," said mademoiselle; "I wish I could. Miladi is very good to invite me; but my mother is my mother."

"You left your mother for seven years; she did well then."

"But, yes; that was different. Miladi can picture it. We have our ménage now."

"I have set my heart upon your coming to us, mademoiselle," was miladi's rejoinder, showing for a moment her white teeth.

"I should not need the pressing, if I could come," was the simple answer. "It is a holiday to me now to be at the Red Court Farm; but some things are practicable and others are not practicable, as miladi knows."

And the poor little governess in the cause of her mother was hard as adamant. They walked about until my lady's legs were tired, and then prepared to return.

"Of course you will come back with us, and dine for the last time?" said Mary Anne.

On any other occasion my lady might have interposed with an intimation that Mary Anne Thornycroft had no longer licence to invite whom she pleased to the table of the Red Court Farm. Without waiting for her to second the invitation, mademoiselle at once accepted it.

"For the last time," she repeated; "I shall be making my baggage tomorrow."

My lady did not change her dress for dinner. The odds and ends of what we are pleased to call full dinner-dress did not seem to be appreciated at the Red Court. Yesterday Richard and Isaac had sat down in their velveteen clothes. A moment before dinner Mr. Thornycroft came into the drawing-room, and said his sons had brought in two or three friends. My lady, meeting them in the hall, stared at their appearance and number.

"What is it? who are they?" she whispered to Mary Anne.

"Oh, it is only one of their impromptu dinner parties," carelessly replied Mary Anne. "I guessed they were thinking of it by their delaying the dinner. They have supper parties instead sometimes."

My lady thought she had never seen so rough a dinner party in her life, in the matter of dress. Richard and Isaac wore thin light clothes, loose and easy; the strangers' costume was, to say the least of it, varied. Old Connaught, temporarily abroad again, was wrapped in a suit of grey flannel; the superintendent of the coastguard wore brown; and Captain Copp had arrived in a pea-jacket. Mary Anne shook hands with them all; Miss Derode chattered; and Mr. Thornycroft introduced the superintendent by name to his wife—Mr. Dangerfield.

"Only six today," whispered Mary Anne to her stepmother. "Sometimes they have a dozen."

Quite enough for the fare provided. Before Mr. Thornycroft began to help the soles, he looked everywhere for a second dish—on the table, on the sideboard, on the dumb waiter. "There's more fish than this, Sinnett?" he exclaimed, hastily.

"No, sir. That's all."

Mr. Thornycroft stared his servants severally in the face, as if the fault were theirs. Three of them were in waiting: Sinnett, a maid, and Hyde. He then applied himself to the helping of the fish, and, by dint of contrivance, managed to make it go round.

Well and good. Some ribs of beef came on next, fortunately a large piece. Mr. Thornycroft let it get cold before him; he could not imagine what the hindrance meant. Presently it struck him that the three servants stood in their places waiting for the meat to be served. The guests waited.

"Where are the other things, Hyde?"

"There's only that, sir."

The justice looked up the table and down the table; never in his whole life had he felt ashamed of his hospitality until now. But by this time the curious aspect of affairs had penetrated to Richard.

"Is this all you have to give us for dinner?" he asked of Sinnett, in his deep, stern tones; and he did not think it necessary to lower his voice.

"Yes, sir."

"This! That piece of beef?"

"There's nothing else, sir."

"By whose management?—by whose fault? Speak, woman."

"My lady gave the orders, sir."

Richard turned his dark face on my lady, as if demanding whether Sinnett was not telling a lie; and Mr. Thornycroft began to cut the beef as fast as he could cut it.

'I did not anticipate that we should have friends with us," murmured the new mistress. She felt truly uncomfortable, really sorry for the contretemps; all eyes were turned upon her, following the dark condemning ones of Richard.

"We must make the best of our beef; there are worse misfortunes at sea," said Isaac, his good-natured voice breaking the silence. "You will judge of our appetites better when you get more used to us," he added to my lady with a kind smile.

"I should think there is worse misfortunes at sea," observed Captain Copp, forgetting his grammar in his wish to smooth the unpleasantness. "Bless and save my wooden leg! if us sailors had such a glorious piece of beef to sit down to of a day on the long voyages, we should not hear quite so much of hardships. I remember once—it was the very voyage before the one when I saw that sea-serpent in the Pacific—our tins of preserved meat turned bad, and an awful gale we met washed away our live stock. Ah, you should have been with us then, Mr. Richard; you'd never despise a piece of prime beef again."

Richard vouchsafed no answer: he had been thoroughly vexed. Captain Copp, seated at my lady's right hand, asked her to take wine with him, and then took it with the table generally.

My lady got away as soon as she could: hardly knowing whether to resent the advent of the visitors, the free and easy hospitality that appeared to prevail at the Red Court, or her own mistake in not having provided better. With that dark resolute face of power in her mind—Richard's—instinct whispered her that it would not answer to draw the reins too tight. At any rate, she felt uncomfortable at the table, and quitted it.

Leaving Miss Thornycroft and mademoiselle to go where they pleased, she went up at once to her chamber: a roomy apartment facing the sea. By its side was a small dressing-room, or boudoir; with a pleasant window to sit at on a summer's day. It was night now, but my lady threw up the window, and remained at it. A mist was arising out at sea: not much as yet. She was musing on the state of affairs. Had she made a mistake in coming to the Red Court for life? Early days as yet to think so, but a doubt of it lay upon her spirit.

The subdued tones of the piano underneath were echoing to the beautiful touch of Mademoiselle Derode; the soft, light touch that she had not been able to impart to her pupil. Mary Anne Thornycroft's playing, though clear, brilliant, and good, was, like herself, firm and decisive. You never heard the low melodious music from her that charms the heart to sweet sadness, rather than wins the ear and the admiration.

Suddenly, as my lady stood listening and musing, a figure, very dim and shadowy, appeared on the edge of the plateau, and she strained her eyes on it with a start.

Not of fear; she had no superstition in her hard composition, and all she felt was curiosity—surprise. Mademoiselle Derode might have given utterance to a faint scream, and scuttered away where she could not see the plateau, in dread belief that the ghost was walking. My lady had the good sense to know that a figure, shadowy by this light, might be very substantial by daylight. All in a moment she lost sight of it. It appeared to be standing still on the plateau's edge, whether looking this way or over the sea, her far sight, remarkably keen, could not tell her, but as she looked the figure disappeared. It was gone, so, far as she could see; certainly it did not walk either to the right or the left. For a brief instant my lady wondered whether it had fallen over the cliff—as the poor coastguard-man had once done.

Footsteps underneath. Some one was crossing the garden, apparently having come from the direction of the plateau, and making for the solitary door in the dead wall at the unused end of the house; the end that she had been warned could not welcome ladies. TO her intense surprise she recognised her husband, but dressed differently from what he had been at dinner. The black frock coat (his usual attire) was replaced by one of common velveteen, the gaiters were buttoned over the pantaloons, the customary hat by a disreputable wide-awake. Where could he have been?—when she had thought him busy with his guests!

The mist was extending to the land very rapidly; my lady shut down the window in haste and descended the stairs. The drawing-room windows were open, and she rang the bell for them to be closed. In those few moments the mist had increased so greatly that she could not see halfway across the garden. It was almost like an instantaneous cloud of blight.

"Mr. Thornycroft has left the dining-room," she observed to Hyde, as he was shutting the windows. "Have the people gone?"

"No, my lady. I have just taken in the pipes and spirits. '

"Pipes and spirits! Do they smoke at these impromptu dinner gatherings—and drink spirits?"

"Generally," answered Hyde.

"But Mr. Thornycroft is not with them? I saw him out of doors."

Hyde, his windows and shutters closed, turned round to face her, and spoke with emphasis.

"The justice is in the dining-room, my lady. He does not quit it when he has friends with him."

Believing the man told her a lie, for her own sight was perfectly reliable sight—at least it had been so hitherto—she determined to satisfy herself. Waiting until he had gone, she crossed the hall, opened the dining-room door an inch and peeped in. Hyde was right. There sat Mr. Thornycroft in his place at the foot of the table, almost close to her, in the same dress he had worn at dinner, a long churchwarden's pipe in his mouth, and a steaming glass of something hot before him.

"What will you allow me for housekeeping, Mr. Thornycroft?" she asked in the morning.

"Nothing."

"Nothing?"

"Nothing," repeated the justice in his firmest tone, decisive as Richard's. She was taking her breakfast languidly in her room. It was eleven o'clock, but she had a headache, she said: the truth being that my lady liked to lie in bed. Mr. Thornycroft, coming in, condoled with her in his hearty manner, never believing but the plea was genuine—the straightforward country gentleman would as soon have believed Captain Copp's wooden leg to be a real one, as a headache false. He entered on the matter he came to speak of, the dinner of yesterday. Kindly enough, but very emphatically, he warned her that such a thing must not occur a second time. It had been altogether a mistake.

"Any money you may wish for yourself, for your own purposes, is yours heartily," he resumed; "but in the housekeeping you must not interfere. The cost is my care, and Sinnett sees to it: she has been in the house so long as to know perfectly well how to provide. I would have given ten pounds out of my pocket rather than have had that happen last night," added the justice, giving a flick to his trousers' right-hand pocket in momentary irritation at the recollection.

"But to provide such dinners is most unreasonable," she remonstrated. "It is only for the servants to eat. I don't think you can have an idea of the extravagance that goes on in the kitchen."

'Pooh! Extravagance! I can afford it. The servants only eat what goes down from our table; and what they can't eat is given away to those who want food. It was my father's plan before me, and it is mine."

"It is sinful waste," retorted my lady. "If you choose to sit down to an outrageously profuse table yourself, the servants ought not to follow suit."

"What would you have done with the superfluous victuals?" demanded the justice. "Put up for auction of a morning and sold?"

'As you ask me what I would have done, I will answer—do not provide them. The housekeeping is altogether on too liberal a scale."

Mr. Thornycroft, who had been looking from the window over the sea, lying hot and clear and beautiful this morning, turned and stood before her; his fair, handsome face grave, his towering form raised to its full height, his voice, as he spoke, impressive in its calm decision.

"Lady Ellis, understand one thing—that this is a matter you must not interfere in. The housekeeping at the Red Court Farm that you are pleased to find cause of fault with—is an established rule; so to say, an institution. It cannot be changed. Sinnett will conduct it as hitherto without trouble to or interference from yourself. Whenever it does not please you to sit down to table, there are other rooms in which you can order your dinner served."

"And suppose I say that I must exert my right of authority—my privilege of controlling the dinners?" she rejoined, her voice getting just a little harsh with the opposition.

"You cannot say it. I am master of my own house and my own table."

"You have made me the mistress!"

"Just so; but not to alter the established usages."

Lady Ellis tapped her foot on the soft carpet. "Do you consider that there is any reason in keeping so large a table?"

"There may or may not be. My pleasure is that it shall be kept. My sons have been brought up to it; they would not have it curtailed."

"I think your sons have been brought up to a great deal that is unfitting. One would think they were lords."

"Handsome, noble fellows!" aspirated the justice, with perhaps a little spice of aggravation. "There are not many lords that can match them."

My lady bit her thin lips, a sure sign of rising temper. 'It seems to me to be my duty, Mr. Thornycroft, exercising the authority you have vested in me by making me your wife, to control the extravagance hitherto running riot. Opposition, ill-feeling, in the house will not be seemly."

"Neither will I have it," put in the justice.

"I do not see that it can be avoided. I give certain orders. Sinnett, acting under you, opposes them. What can the result be but unseemly contention? How would you avoid it, I ask?"

"By going to live in one of the cottages on the heath, and leaving Isaac—I mean Richard—master of the Red Court Farm."

He spoke promptly—like a man whose mind is fully made up. The prospect of living in a cottage on the heath nearly took my lady's breath away.

"Mr. Thornycroft!" she passionately exclaimed, and then her tone changed to one of peevish remonstrance: "why do you bring up impossibilities? A cottage on the heath!"

Mr. Thornycroft brought down his hand, not in anger but emphasis, on the small breakfast table.

"Were the order of the Red Court upset by unnecessary interference on your part—were I to find that I could be no longer master of it without being subjected to continual opposition, I should surely quit it. If a cottage on the heath were distasteful to you I would take lodgings at Jutpoint."

Lady Ellis sipped her coffee. It did not appear safe to say more. A cottage on the heath, or lodgings at Jutpoint!

"I only wished to put a stop to unnecessary extravagance," she said, in a tone of conciliation.

"No doubt. I give you credit for good motives, of course; but these things must be left to me. The same gentlemen who dined here yesterday evening are coming to supper this. I have made out the bill of fare myself, and given it to Sinnett."

"Coming again to-night!" she could not help exclaiming.

"To atone for the shortcomings of yesterday's dinner," spoke the justice. "I never had occasion to feel ashamed of my table before."

"I cannot think what possible pleasure you can find in the society of such men," she said, after a pause. "Look at them, coming out to dinner in those rough coats!"

Mr. Thornycroft laughed. "We don't go in often for evening dress at Coastdown. As to the pleasure, they have been in the habit of sitting at my table for some years now, madam, and I enjoy the companionship."

"I fancied you left them early; I thought I saw you cross the garden, as if coming from the plateau," she said, resolving to speak of the matter which had so puzzled her.

"We did not leave the dining-room until eleven o'clock."

"Well—it was very strange. I was standing at this window, and certainly saw some one exactly like you; the same figure, the same face; but not in the same dress. He seemed to have on gaiters and a velveteen coat, and a low broad-brimmed hat, very ugly. What should you say it could have been?"

"I should say that you were dreaming."

"I was wide awake. It was just before that mist came on," she added.

"Ah, the fault must have lain in the mist. I have known it come as a mirage occasionally, bringing deception and confusion."

Did he really mean it? It seemed so, for there was seriousness on his face as he spoke. Quitting the room, he descended the stairs, and made his way to the fields. In the four-acre mead—as it was called in common parlance on the farm—he came upon Richard watching the hay-makers. Richard wished him good morning; abroad early, it was the first time he had seen his father that day.

"What was the failure, Dick?" asked the justice. "Fog," shortly answered Richard. "Couldn't see the light."

Mr. Thornycroft nodded.

"Are we to have a repetition, sir, of yesterday's dinner table?" resumed Richard. "If so, I think the sooner your wife is requested to take up her residence somewhere else, the better."

"You will not have it again. Sinnett holds my orders, and my wife has been made aware she does. There's no need for you to put yourself out."

With the injunction, spoken rather testily, Mr. Thornycroft left him. But a little later, when he met Isaac, he voluntarily entered on the subject; hinting his vexation at the past, promising that it would never again occur, almost as if he were tendering an apology for the accident.

"I'm afraid I made a mistake, Ikey; I'm afraid I made a mistake; but I meant it for the best."

It was ever thus. To his second son Mr. Thornycroft's behaviour was somewhat different from what it was to his eldest. It could not be said that he paid him more deference: but it was to Isaac he generally spoke of business, when speaking was needed; if an opinion was required, Isaac's was sought in preference to Richard's. It was just as though Isaac had been the eldest son. That Richard had brought this on himself, by his assumption of authority, was quite probable: and the little preference seemed to spring from the justice involuntarily.

The evening supper took place, and the guests were consoled by the ample table for the scantiness of the previous dinner. My lady was not invited to join it; nothing appeared further from Mr. Thornycroft's thoughts than to have ladies at table. She spent a solitary sort of evening; Mary Anne was at Mrs. Wilkinson's, taking leave of Miss Derode.

Was it, she asked herself, to go on like this always and always? Had she become the wife of Justice Thornycroft only to die of the dreary life at the Red Court Farm? Let us give her her due. When she married him she did intend to do her duty as an honest woman, and send ridiculous flirtations, such as that carried on with Robert Lake, to the winds. But she did not expect to be done to death of ennui.

A short while went on. Nearly open warfare set in between Mary Anne and her stepmother. To-day my lady would be harsh, exacting, almost cruel in her rule: tomorrow the girl would be wholly neglected—suffered to run wild. Mr. Thornycroft saw that things could not continue thus, and the refrain of the words he had spoken to Isaac beat ever on his brain, day by day bringing greater force to them: "I fear I made a mistake; I fear I made a mistake."

One morning Mary Anne astonished the justice by appearing before him in his bureau, in what she was pleased to call the uncivilized rooms. He sat there with Mr. Hopley, of Dartfield, some account books before them. Her dress, a beautiful muslin with a raised blue spot, was torn out at the gathers and trailed behind her. My lady had done it in a passion.

"Holloa! what do you do here?" cried the justice, emphatically; and Mr. Hopley went out whistling, with his hands in his pockets, and crossed over to stare at the idle dog-cart in the coach-house, as if to give privacy for the explanation.

She had come with one of her tales of woe. She had come to beg and pray to be sent to school. What a change! Mr. Thornycroft was nearly at his wits' end.

Ere the day was over, his wife brought a complaint to him on her own score: not altogether of Mary Anne. She simply said, incidentally, that ill-trained young lady was getting quite beyond her control, and therefore she must wash her hands of her. The complaint was of her own health; it appeared to be failing her in a rather remarkable manner, certainly a sudden one. This was true. She had concluded that the air of Coastdown was inimical to her, she wished it might be managed for her to live away—say Cheltenham, or some other healthy place.

How eagerly Mr. Thornycroft caught at the suggestion, he felt afterwards half ashamed to think of. In matters involving money he was always liberal, and he at once named a handsome sum per month that she might enjoy, at Cheltenham, or anywhere else that pleased her.

VOLUME II

CHAPTER I

Two years have gone by, and it is June again.

A good, substantial house in one of the western suburbs of the metropolis—Kensington. By the well-rubbed brass plate on the iron gate of the garden, and the lady's name on it—"Miss Jupp"—it may be taken for a boarding-school. In fact, it is one: a small select school (as so many schools proclaim themselves now; but this really is such); and, kept by Miss Jupp, once of Katterley. That is, by Miss Jupp and two of her sisters, but she wisely calls it by her own name singly, avoiding the ugly style of the plural 'Miss Jupp's establishment."

Fortune changes with a great many of us; every day, every hour of our lives, some are going up, others down. When death removed old Mr. Jupp (an event that occurred almost close upon poor Mrs. Lake's), then his daughters found that they had not enough to get along in the world. Wisely taking time and circumstances by the forelock, the three elder ones, Mary, Margaret, and Emma, removed to London, took a good house at Kensington, and by the help of influential friends very soon had pupils in it. Dorothy and Rose were married; Louisa remained at Katterley with her widowed mother. They professed to take ten pupils only: once or twice the number had been increased to twelve; the terms were high, but the teaching was good, and the arrangements were really first-class. It was with the Miss Jupps that Mary Anne Thornycroft had been placed. And she did not run away from them.

Quite the contrary. The summer holidays have just set in, and she is to go home for them; as she did the previous midsummer; but she is expressing a half wish, now as she stands before Miss Margaret Jupp, that she could spend them where she is, in London. Long and long ago has she grown reconciled to the regularity of a school life, and to regard Miss Jupp's as a second and happy home. She spent the first Christmas holidays with them; the second Christmas (last) at Cheltenham with her stepmother; she and her brother Cyril.

Lady Ellis (retaining still the name) is in very ill health now. Almost simultaneously with quitting the Red Court after her marriage, a grave inward disorder manifested itself. Symptoms of it indeed had been upon her for some time, even before leaving India; but—as is the case with many other symptoms—they had been entirely disregarded, their grave nature unsuspected. Instead of leading a gay life at the gay inland watering-place, flaunting her charms and her fashion in the eyes of other sojourners, Lady Ellis found herself compelled to live a very quiet one. She has a small villa, an establishment of two servants only; and she does not wish for more. In heart, in nature, she is growing altered, and the refining, holy influence that very often—God be praised!—changes the whole heart and spirit with a change which is not of this world, is coming over her. Two visits only has she paid to the Red Court Farm, staying about six weeks each time, and Mr. Thornycroft goes to Cheltenham two or three times a year. Miss Thornycroft and her stepmother are civil to each other now, not to say friendly; and when she invited the young lady and her brother Cyril for the holidays last Christmas, they went. The previous midsummer they had spent together at Coastdown, it having been one of the periods of my lady's two visits. Fortune had contrived well for Lady Ellis, and her marriage with the wealthy master of the Red Court Farm enabled her to enjoy every substantial comfort in her hour of need.

Two other young ladies connected in a degree with this history are at Miss Jupp's this evening; the rest of the pupils have left. One of the two we have met before, one not. They are in the room now, and you may look at them. All three, including Miss Thornycroft, are about the same age—between eighteen and nineteen. She, Mary Anne, is the same tall, stately, fair, handsome, and (it must be owned) haughty girl that you knew before; the fine face is resolute as ever, the cold blue eyes as honest and uncompromising. She had been allowed to dress as expensively at Miss Jupp's as her inclination leads: to-day she wears a rich pale-blue silk; blue ribbons are falling from her fair hair. She is standing doing nothing: but sitting in a chair by her side, toying with a bit of fancy-work, is a plain, dark, merry-looking girl in a good useful nut-brown silk, Susan Hunter. She is the sister of Robert Hunter, several years his junior, and has been sent up from Yorkshire by her aunt, with whom she lives, to have two years of "finish" at a London school. Accident—not their having once known something of her brother—led to the school fixed on being Miss Jupp's. And now for the last.

In a grey alpaca dress, trimmed with a little ribbon velvet of the same hue, her head bent patiently over a pile of drawings that she is touching up, sits the third. A very different footing in the school, hers, from that of the other two; they pay the high, full terms; she pays nothing, but works out her board with industry. Have you forgotten that pale, gentle face, one of the sweetest both in feature and expression ever looked upon, with the fine silky chestnut hair modestly braided round it, and the soft brown eyes that take all the best feelings of a genuine heart by storm? The weary look telling of incessant industry, the pile of work that she does not look up from, the cheap holiday-dress (her best) costing little, all proclaim sufficiently her dependent position in the house—a slight, graceful girl of middle height, with a sort of drooping look in her figure, as if she were, and had been all her life, in the habit of being pushed into the background?

It is Anna Chester. Her life since we saw her has been like that of a dray horse. Mrs. Chester placed her at an inferior school as pupil-teacher, where she had many kinds of things to do, and the mistress's own children to take care of in the holidays. For a year and a half she stayed at it, doing her best patiently, and then the Miss Jupps took her. She has to work very much still, and her health is failing. Captain and Mrs. Copp have invited her to Coastdown for a change, and she goes down to-morrow with Miss Thornycroft. Miss Hunter spends the holidays at school.

Mrs. Chester? Mrs. Chester quitted Guild, to set up a fashionable boarding-house in London. It did not answer; the mass of people remained cruelly indifferent to its advertisements; and the few who tried it ran away and never paid her. She then removed to Paris, where (as some friends assured her) a good English boarding-house was much wanted; and, if her own reports are to be trusted, she is likely to do pretty well at it.

There remains only one more person to mention of those we formerly knew; and that is Robert Hunter. Putting his shoulder to the wheel in earnest, as only a resolute and capable man can put it; I had almost said as one only who has some expiation to work out; his days are spent in hard industry. He is the practical energetic man of business; never spending a moment in waste, never willingly allowing himself recreation. The past folly, the past idleness of that time, not so very long gone by, recurs to his memory less frequently than it used, but ever with the feeling of a nightmare. He is still with the same firm, earning a liberal salary. Since a day or two only has he been in London, but there's some talk of his remaining in it now. Nothing seems to be further from his thoughts than any sort of pleasure: it would seem that he has one vocation alone in life—work.

These three young ladies were going out this afternoon. To a grand house, too: Mrs. Macpherson's. The professor, good simple man, had been content, socially speaking, with a shed on the top of Aldgate pump: not so madam. As the professor rose more and more into distinction, she rose; and the residence in Bloomsbury was exchanged for a place at Kensington. Possibly the calling occasionally on the Miss

Jupps, had put it into her head. A house as grand as its name in the matter of decoration; but not of undue size: Mrs. Macpherson had good common sense, and generally exercised it. A dazzling white front with a pillared portico and much ornamentation outside and in—"Majestic Villa." The professor had wanted to change the name, but madam preferred to retain it. It was not very far from Miss Jupp's, and these young ladies were going there to spend the evening.

In all the glory of her large room, with its decorations of white and gold, its mirrors, its glittering cabinets, its soft luxurious carpet, its chairs of delicate green velvet, sat Mrs. Macpherson, waiting for these young guests. In all her own glory of dress, it may be said, for that was not less conspicuous than of yore, and that of to-day looked just as if it were chosen to accord with the hangings—a green satin robe with gold leaves for trimmings, and a cap that could not be seen for sprays and spangles. In her sense of politeness—and she possessed an old-fashioned stock of it—Mrs. Macpherson had dressed herself betimes, not to leave the young ladies alone after they came. Thus, when they arrived, under the convoy of Miss Emma Jupp, who left them at the door, Mrs. Macpherson was ready to receive them.

It was the first time they had been there for many weeks; for the professor had been abroad on a tour in connexion with some of the ologies, as his wife expressed it, in which she had accompanied him. The result of this was, that Mrs. Macpherson had no end of Parisian novelties, in the shape of dress, to display to them in her chamber.

"I know what girls like," she said, in her hearty manner, "and that is, to look at new bonnets and mantles, and try 'em on."

But Mary Anne Thornycroft—perhaps because she could indulge in such articles at will—cared not a jot for these attractions, and said she should go down to see the professor.

He had some rooms at the back of the house, where his collection of scientific curiosities—to call things by a polite name—had been stowed. And here the professor, when not out, spent his time. Mary Anne quite loved the man, so simple-minded and yet great-minded at one and the same time, and never failed to penetrate to his rooms when occasion offered. Quickly wending her way through the passages, she opened the door softly.

It was not very easy to distinguish clearly at first, what with the crowd of things darkening the windows, and the mass of objects generally. At a few yards' distance, slightly bending over a sort of upright desk, as if writing something, stood a gentleman; but certainly not the professor. His back was towards her; he had evidently not heard her enter, and a faint flush of surprise dawned on Mary Anne's face, for in that first moment she thought it was her brother Cyril. It was the same youthful, supple, slender figure; the same waving hair, of a dark auburn, clustering round the head above the collar of the coat. Altogether, seen in this way, there was a certain resemblance; and that was the first primary link in the chain that attracted Mary Anne to him. The door, which she had left open, closed with a slight bang, and the gentleman spoke, without lifting his head.

"I have worked it out at last. You were right about its being less than the other."

"Is Dr. Macpherson not here?"

He turned sharply at the words, a pencil in his hand, surprise on his face. A good face; for its old gay careless look had departed for ever, and the dark blue eyes—darker even than of yore—wore a serious gravity that never left them, a gravity born of remorse. The face was older than the figure, and not in the least like Cyril Thornycroft's; it looked fully its seven-and-twenty years—nay, looked nearer thirty; but all its expression was merged in surprise. No wonder; to see a beautiful girl in blue silk, with blue ribbons in her fair hair, standing there; when he had only expected the professor, in his old threadbare coat and spectacles. It was Robert Hunter.

"I beg your pardon," he said, coming forward. "Can I do anything for you?"

"I thought Dr. Macpherson was here. I came to see him."

Never losing her calm self-possession on any occasion, as so many young ladies do on no occasion at all, Miss Thornycroft stepped up to the side glass cases to examine the curiosities, talking as easily to him as though she had known him all her life. Without being in the least free, there was an openness of manner about her, an utter absence of tricks and affectation, a straightforward independence, rather remarkable in a young lady. For Robert Hunter it possessed a singular charm.

Before the professor came in, who had forgotten himself down in his cellar, where he had gone after a cherished specimen in the frog line; before Mr. Hunter had pointed out to her a quarter of the new acquisitions in the glass cases—animal, vegetable, and mineral—they knew all about each other: that he was Susan Hunter's brother, and that she was Miss Thornycroft of Coastdown. At mention of her name, a brief vision connected with the past floated across Robert Hunter's brain—of a certain summer evening when he was returning to Guild with his poor young wife, and saw the back of a high open carriage bowling away from his sister's gate, which he was told contained Mr. and Miss Thornycroft. Never since that had he heard the name or thought of the people.

"Do you know, when I came into the room just now, and you were standing with your back to me, I nearly took you for one of my brothers. At the back you are just like him."

Robert Hunter smiled slightly. "And not in the face?"

"Not at all—except, perhaps, a little in the forehead. Cyril has hazel eyes and small features. The hair is exactly like his, the same colour, and grows just as his does in front, leaving the forehead square. If you were to hide your face, showing only the top of the forehead and the hair, I should say you were Cyril."

The professor appeared, and they went into the more habitable part of the house. Robert had not seen his sister since she was a little girl; he had not seen Anna since they parted at Guild. It was altogether an acceptable meeting; but he looked at Anna's face somewhat anxiously.

"Have you been working very much, Anna?" he took occasion to ask, drawing her for a moment aside.

"I am always working very hard," she answered, with her sweet smile of patient endurance. "There is a great deal to be done in schools, you know; but I am well off at Miss Jupp's compared to what I was at the other place. They are very kind to me."

"You have a look upon you as if you felt tired always. It is a curious impression to draw though, perhaps, considering I have seen you but for ten minutes."

"I do feel tired nearly always," acknowledged Anna. "The Miss Jupps think London does not agree with me. I am going to Coastdown for a change for the holidays; I shall get better there."

He thought she would require a longer change than a few holiday weeks. Never in the old days had it struck him that Anna looked fragile; but she certainly did now.

"And now, Robert Hunter, you'll stay with us, as these young ladies are here?" said hospitable Mrs. Macpherson.

He hesitated before replying. Very much indeed would he have liked to remain, but he had made an appointment with a gentleman.

"Put it off," said Mrs. Macpherson.

"There's no time for that. Certainly—if I am not at the office when he comes, one of the partners would see him. But—"

"But what?" asked the professor. "Would not that be a solution of the difficulty?"

"A way out of the mess," put in the professor's wife.

Mr. Hunter laughed. "I was going to say that I have never put away any business for my own convenience since—since I took to it again."

The attraction, or whatever it might be, however, proved too strong for business this afternoon, and Robert Hunter remained at the professor's. When he and Miss Thornycroft parted at night, it seemed that they had known each other for years.

It was very singular; a thing of rare occurrence. We have heard of this sudden mutual liking, the nameless affinity that draws one soul to another; but believe me it is not of very frequent experience. The thought that crossed Robert Hunter's mind that evening more than once was—"I wish that girl was my sister." Any idea of another sort of attachment would be a very long while yet before it penetrated to him as even a possibility.

In the evening, when they got home, at an early hour—Miss Jupp had only given them until eight o'clock, for there was packing to do—Mary Anne Thornycroft went into a fever of indignation to think that no message had been left by or from any of her brothers.

"It is so fearfully careless of them! That is just like my brothers. Do they expect we are to travel alone?"

"My dear, do not put yourself out," said Miss Jupp. "Two young ladies can travel alone very well. You will get there quite safely."

"So far as that goes, ma'am, I could travel alone fearlessly to the end of the world," spoke Mary Anne. "But that is not the question; neither does it excuse their negligence. For all they know, I might have spent all my money, and have none to take me down."

Miss Emma Jupp laughed. "They would suppose that we should supply you."

"Yes, Miss Emma, no doubt. But they had no business to send me word that one of them would be in London to-day to take charge of me home, unless—"

The words were brought to a sudden standstill by the opening of the door. One of the maids appeared at it to announce a guest.

"Mr. Isaac Thornycroft."

There entered the same noble-looking young man, noble in his towering height and strength, that we knew two years ago at Coastdown; he came in with a smile on his bright face—on its fair features, in its blue eyes. Miss Emma Jupp's first thought was, what a likeness he bore to his sister; her second that she had never in her whole life seen any one half so good-looking. It happened that she had never seen him before. Mary Anne began to reproach him for carelessness. He received it all with the most ineffable good humour, the smile brightening on his sunny face.

"I know it is too late, quite wrong of me, but I missed the train at Jutpoint, and had to come by a later one. Which of these two young ladies is Miss Chester?" he added, turning to the two girls who stood together. "I have a—a trifle for her from Captain Copp. '

"You shall guess," interposed Mary Anne. "One of them is Anna Chester. Now guess."

It was not difficult. Miss Hunter met his glance fearlessly in a merry spirit; Anna blushed and let fall her eyes. Isaac Thornycroft smiled.

"This is Miss Chester."

"It is all through your stupid shyness, Anna," said Mary Anne in a cross tone. Which of course only increased her confusion. Isaac crossed the room, his eyes bent on the sweet blushing face, as he held out the "trifle" forwarded by Captain Copp.

"Will you accept it, Miss Chester? Captain Copp charged me to take particular care of it, and not to touch it myself."

It was a travelling wickered bottle, holding about a pint. Anna looked at it with curiosity, and Emma Jupp took it out of her hand.

"What can it be?"

"Take out the cork and smell it," suggested Mr. Isaac Thornycroft.

Miss Emma did so; giving a strong sniff. "Dear me! I think it is rum."

"Rum-and-water," corrected Isaac. "Captain Copp begged me to assure Miss Chester that it was only half-and-half, she being a young lady. It is for her refreshment as she goes down to-morrow."

"If that's not exactly like Sam Copp!" exclaimed Miss Jupp with some asperity, while the laugh against Anna went round. "He will never acquire an idea beyond his old sea notions; never. I remember what he was before his leg came off."

"He came all the way to Jutpoint in the omnibus after me when I had driven over, to make sure, I believe, that Mrs. Copp should not be privy to the transaction. It was through his injunctions as to the wicker bottle that I missed my train," concluded Isaac—his eyes, that were bent on Anna Chester, dancing with mirth. At which hers fell again.

If all of us estimated people alike, especially in regard to that subtle matter of "liking" or "disliking" on first impression, what a curious world it would be! Miss Emma Jupp considered Isaac Thornycroft the best-looking, the most attractive man she had ever seen. Mary Anne Thornycroft, on the contrary, was thinking the same of somebody else.

"I never saw anybody I liked half so much at first sight as Robert Hunter," she softly said to herself, as she laid her head on her pillow.

CHAPTER II

Captain Copp

Captain Copp was a true sailor, gifted with more good nature than common sense. On the rare occasion of receiving a young lady visitor under his roof, his hospitality and his heart alike ran riot. Anna Chester, the pretty, friendless girl whom he had heard of but never seen, was coming to him and his wife to be nursed into strength and health, and the captain anticipated the arrival as something to be made a fête of.

A feast too, by appearances. It was a bright summer morning, with a fresh breeze blowing from the sea; and the captain was abroad betimes with some flowing purple ribbons fastened round his glazed hat. Greatly to the grievance of Mrs. Copp: who had ventured to say that Anna was not a captured prize-ship, or a battle won, or even a wedding, that she should be rejoiced over to the extent of streamers. All of which Captain Copp was deaf to. He started by the ten o'clock omnibus for Jutpoint, having undertaken first of all to send home provisions for dinner. A pair of soles and two pounds of veal cutlet had been meekly suggested by Mrs. Copp.

The morning wore on. Sarah, the middle-aged, hard-featured, sensible-looking, thoroughly capable woman-servant, who was bold enough to dispute with her master, and not in the least to care at being likened to pirates and other disrespectful things, stood in the kitchen making a gooseberry pudding, when the butcher-boy came in without the ceremony of announcing himself; unless a knocking and pushing of his tray against the back-door posts, through awkwardness, could be called such.

"Some dishes, please," said he.

"Dishes!" retorted Sarah, who had one of the strongest tongues in Coastdown. "Dishes for what?"

"For this here meat. The captain have just been in and bought it, and master have sent it up."

He displayed some twelve or fifteen pounds of meat—beef, veal, lamb. Sarah's green eyes—good, honest, pleasant eyes in the main—glistened.

"Then your master's a fool. Didn't I tell him not to pay attention to the captain when he took these freaks in his head?" she demanded. "When he goes and buys up the whole shop—as he did one day last winter because he was expecting a old mate of his down—your master's not to notice him no more nor if he was a child. An uncommon soft you must be, to bring up all them joints! Did you think you was supplying the Red Court? Just you march back with 'em."

There was an interruption. While the boy stood staring at the meat, hardly knowing what to do, and rubbing his fingers amidst his shining black hair, Mrs. Copp entered the kitchen, and became acquainted with the state of affairs. She wore a pale muslin gown, as faded as her gentle self, with pale green ribbons.

"Dear me," she meekly cried, "all that meat! We could not get through the half of it while it was good? Do you think, James, your master would have any objection to take it back?"

"Objection! He'll take it back, ma'am, whether he has any objection or not," cried the positive Sarah. "Now then! who's this?"

Somebody seemed to be clattering up in clogs. A woman with the fish: three pairs of large soles and a score or two of herrings, which the captain had bought and paid for. Mrs. Copp, fearing what else might be coming, looked inclined to cry. The exasperated Sarah, more practical, took her hands out of the paste, wiped the flour off them on her check apron, and went darting across the heath without bonnet to the butcher's shop, the boy and his tray of rejected meat slowly following her. There she commenced a wordy war with the butcher, accusing him of being an idiot, with other disparaging epithets, and went marching home in triumph carrying two pounds of veal cutlet.

"And that's too much for us," she cried to her mistress, "with all that stock of fish and the pudding. What on earth is to be done with the fish, I don't know. If I fry a pair for dinner, and pickle the herrings, there'll be two pair left. They won't pickle. One had need to have poor folk coming here as they do at the Red Court. Master's gone off with purple streamers flying from his hat; I think he'd more need to put on bells."

Scarcely had she got her hands into the flour again, when another person arrived. A girl with a goose. It was in its feathers, just killed.

"If you please, ma'am," said she to Sarah, with a curtsey, "mother says she'll stick the other as soon as ever she can catch him; but he's runned away over the common. Mother sent me up with this for 'fraid you should be waiting to pluck him. The captain said they was to come up sharp."

Sarah could almost have found in her heart to "stick' her master. She was a faithful servant, and the waste of money vexed her. Mrs. Copp, quite unable to battle with the petty ills of life, left the strong-minded woman to fight against these, and ran away to her parlour.

The respected cause of all this, meanwhile, had reached Jutpoint, he and his streamers. There he had to wait a considerable time, but the train came in at last, and brought the travellers.

They occupied a first-class compartment in the middle of the train. There had been a little matter about the tickets at starting. Isaac Thornycroft procured them, and when they were seated, Anna took out her purse to repay him, and found she had not enough money in it. A little more that she possessed was in her box. Accustomed to travel second-class, even third, the cost of the ticket was more than she had thought for. Eighteenpence short!

"If you will please to take this, I will repay you the rest as soon as I can get to my box," she said, with painful embarrassment—an embarrassment that Isaac could not fail to notice and to wonder at. Reared as she had been, money wore to her an undue value; to want it in a time of need seemed little short of a crime. She turned the silver about in her hands, blushing painfully. Miss Thornycroft discerned somewhat of the case.

"Never mind, Anna. I dare say you thought to travel second-class. You can repay my brother later."

Isaac's quick brain took in the whole. This poor friendless girl, kept at the Miss Jupps' almost out of charity, had less money in a year for necessities than he would sometimes spend in an hour in frivolity. Anna held out the silver still, with the rose-coloured flush deepening on her delicate cheeks.

"What is it, Miss Chester?" he suddenly said. "Why do you offer me your money?"

"You took my ticket, did you not?"

"Certainly," he answered, showing the three little pieces of card in his waistcoat. "But I held the money for yours beforehand. Put up your purse."

"Did you," she answered, in great relief, but embarrassed still. "Did Mrs. Copp give it you?—or—Miss Jupp?—or—or the captain?" Isaac laughed.

"You had better not inquire into secrets, Miss Chester. All I can tell you is, I had the money for your ticket in my pocket. Where is that important article—the wicker bottle? Captain Copp will expect it returned to him—empty."

"It is empty now; Miss Jupp poured out the rum-and-water," she answered, laughing. "I have it all safe."

She put up her purse as she spoke, inquiring no further as to the donor in her spirit of implicit obedience, but concluded it must have been Miss Jupp. And she never knew the truth until—until it was too late to repay Isaac.

At the terminus, side by side with the captain and his streamers, stood Justice Thornycroft. Anna remembered him well; the tall, fine, genial-natured man whom she had seen three years before in the day's visit to Mrs. Chester. All thought of her had long ago passed from his memory, but he recognised the face—the pale, patient, gentle face, which, even then, had struck Mr. Thornycroft as being the sweetest he had ever looked upon. It so struck him now.

"Where have I seen you?" he asked. And Anna told him.

The carriage, very much to the displeasure of Mary Anne, had not come over for her. Mr. Thornycroft explained that one of the horses he generally drove in it was found to be lame that morning. They got into the omnibus, the captain preferring to place himself with his ribbons and his wooden leg flat on the roof amidst the luggage. On the outskirts of Jutpoint, in obedience to his signal, the driver came to a standstill before the door of the "White Cliff" public-house, and the captain's head appeared at the back window, in a hanging position, inquiring whether brandy or rum would be preferred; adding, with a somewhat fierce look at Mr. Thornycroft and Isaac, that he should stand glasses round this time. Very much to the captain's discomfiture, the young ladies and the gentlemen declined both; so the only order the crestfallen captain could give the White Cliff was for two glasses of rum, cold without; that were disposed of by himself and the driver.

"Mind, Anna! I feel three-parts of a stranger in this place, and have really not a friend of my own age and condition in it, so you must supply the place of one to me during these holidays," said Miss Thornycroft, as the omnibus reached its destination—the Mermaid. "Part of every day I shall expect you to spend at the Red Court."

"I beg to second that,' whispered Isaac, taking Anna's hand to help her out. And she blushed again that day for about the fiftieth time without knowing why or wherefore.

Not upon these summer holidays can we linger, because so much time must be spent on those of the next winter. On those of the next winter! If the inmates of the Red Court Farm could but have foreseen what those holidays were to bring forth for them! or Mary Anne Thornycroft dreamt of the consequences of indulging her own self-will! Just a few words more of the present, and then we go on.

Anna Chester's sojourn at Coastdown was passing swiftly, and she seemed as in a very Elysium. The days of toil, of servitude, of incessant care for others were over, temporarily at any rate, and she enjoyed comfort and rest. The hospitable, good-hearted sailor-captain, with his tales of the sea-serpent, the mermaid he had seen, and other marvels; the meek, gentle, ever-thoughtful Mrs. Copp, who caused Anna to address her as "aunt," and behaved more kindly to her than any aunt did yet; the most charming visits day by day to the Red Court Farm, and the constant society of Isaac Thornycroft. Ah, there it lay—the strange fascination that all things were beginning to possess around her—in the companionship of him. To say that Isaac Thornycroft, hitherto so mockingly heart-whole, had fallen in love with Anna the first evening he saw her at Miss Jupp's, would be going too far, but he was certainly three-parts in love before they reached Coastdown the following day. To watch her gentle face became like the sweetest music to Isaac Thornycroft. To see her ever-wakeful attentions to her entertainers, her gratitude for their kindness, her prompt help of Sarah when extra work was to be done, her loving care for the friendless and poor, was something new to Isaac, altogether out of his experience. Come weal, come woe, he resolved that this girl should be his wife. People, in their thoughtless gossip, had been wont to predict a high-born and wealthy bride for the attractive second son of Justice Thornycroft; this humble orphan, the poor daughter of the many years poor and humble curate, was the one he fixed upon, with all the world before him to choose from. How Fate changes plans! "L'homme propose, mais Dieu dispose," was one of the most solemn truisms ever penned. Long ere the six weeks of holidays had passed, Isaac Thornycroft and Anna Chester had become all in all to each other: and he, a man accustomed to act upon impulse, spoke out.

It was during an evening walk to the Red Court Farm. Anna was going to tea there; Isaac met her on the heath—no unusual thing—and turned to walk by her side. Both were silent after the first greeting: true love is rarely eloquent. With her soft cheeks blushing, her pale eyelids drooping, her heart wildly beating, Anna sought—at first in vain—to find some topic of conversation, and chose but a lame one.

"Has Mary Anne finished her screen?"

Isaac smiled. "As if I knew!"

"She has the other one to do; and we shall be going back in a week."

"Not in a week!"

"The holidays will be up a week to-morrow."

A vista of the miserable time after her departure, when all things would be dark and dreary, wanting her who had come to make his heart's sunshine, cast its foreshadowing across the brain of Isaac. He turned to her in his impulse, speaking passionately.

"Anna, I cannot lose you. Rather than that, I must—I must—"

"Must what?" she asked, innocently.

"Keep you here on a visit to myself—a visit that can never terminate."

Insensibly, she drew a little from him. Not that the words would have been unwelcome had circumstances justified them; how welcome, the sudden rush of inward joy, the wild coursing on of all her pulses, told her. But—loving him though she did; conscious or half-conscious of his love for her—it never occurred to the mind of Anna Chester that a union would be within the range of possibility. She—the poor humble slave—be wedded by a great and wealthy gentleman like Isaac Thornycroft!

"Would you object to the visit, Anna—though it were to be for life?"

"It could not be," she answered, in a low tone, not affecting to misunderstand him.

"Oh, couldn't it!" said Isaac, amused, and taking up rather the wrong view of the words. "But if you and I say it shall?"

"Halloa! Is it you, Isaac? How d'ye do, Miss Chester?"

Richard Thornycroft, coming suddenly into the path from a side crossing, halted as he spoke. Isaac, put out for once in his life, bit his lips.

"I want you, Isaac. I was looking for you. Here's some bother up."

"What bother?" testily rejoined Isaac.

"You had better come down and hear it. Tomlett—Come along."

Seeing plainly that his walk with Anna was over for the time, Isaac Thornycroft turned off with his brother, leaving Anna to go on alone to the gate, which was in sight.

"Good-day for the present, Anna," he said, with apparent carelessness. "Tell Mary Anne not to wait tea for me. I may not be in."

More forcibly than ever on this evening, when she sat n the spacious drawing-room surrounded by its many elegancies, did the contrast between the Red Court and her own poor home of the past strike on the senses of Anna Chester. Nothing that moderate wealth could purchase was here wanting. Several servants, spacious and handsome rooms, luxuries to please the eye and please the palate. Look at the tea-table laid out there! The delicately-made Worcester china, rich in hues of purple and gold; the chased silver tea and coffee service on their chased silver stands; small fringed damask napkins on the purple and gold plates. Shrimps large as prawns, potted meats, rolled bread-and-butter, muffins, rich cake, and marmalade, are there; for it is Justice Thornycroft's will that all meals, if laid, shall be laid well. Sometimes a cup of tea only came in for Miss Thornycroft, as it used to do for my lady when she was there. It almost seemed to Anna Chester as if she were enacting a deceit, a lie, in sitting at it, its honoured guest, for whom these things were spread, when she thought of the scrambling meals in her former home with Mrs. Chester's children. The odd teacups—for as one got broken it would be-replaced by another of any shape or pattern, provided it were cheap; saucers notched; cracked cups without handles; the stale loaf on the table; the scanty, untidy plate of salt butter, of which she had to cut perpetual slices, like Werther's Charlotte; the stained table without a cover, crumbs strewing it. Look on this picture and on that. Anna did, in deep dejection; and the thought which had faintly presented itself to her mind when Isaac Thornycroft spoke his momentous words, grew into grim and defined shape, and would not be scared away—that she could be no fit wife for Isaac. She resolved to tell him of these things, and of her own unfitness; how very poor she was, always had been, always (according to present prospects) would be; and beg him to think no more of her; and she did not doubt he would unsay his words of his own accord when he came to know of it. It is true she winced at the task: but her conscience told her it must be done, though her heart should faint at it. She could imagine no fate so bright in the wide world as that of becoming the wife of Isaac Thornycroft.

"What makes you so silent this evening?"

Anna started at Miss Thornycroft's words. That young lady was eyeing her with curiosity.

"I was only thinking," she answered, with a vivid blush. "Oh, and I forgot: your brother wished me to ask you not to wait tea for him."

"My brother! Which of them?"

"Mr. Isaac."

"Very considerate, I'm sure! seeing that I never do wait, and that if I did he would probably not come in."

There was a mocking tone in her voice that Anna rather winced at as applied to Isaac. She went on explaining where she saw him; that he and Richard had walked away together—she fancied to Tomlett's.

"They are a great deal too intimate with Tomlett," spoke Miss Thornycroft, curling her lip. "He is no better than a boatman. My belief is, they go and drink gin-and-water with him. They ought to have more pride."

"Mr. Richard said there was some 'bother.'"

"Oh! of course; any excuse before you. I tell you, Anna, they are just a couple of loose young men."

The "loose young men" came in shortly; Richard to go away again, Isaac to remain. He had told Mrs. Copp he would see her home safely. "Let it be by daylight, if you please," answered that discreet lady.

Not by daylight, but under the stars of the sweet summer's night, they went out. There was no one to see; the way was lonely; and Isaac drew Anna's hand within his arm for the first time, and kept it a prisoner.

"I must take care of you, Anna, as you are to become my own property."

"But I—I am not to become that; I wish I could, but it is impossible," she stammered, setting about her task in hesitating perplexity.

"Anna, do you understand me? I am asking you to be my wife."

"Yes, I—I believe I understood; and I feel very grateful to you, all the same."

"All the same!" Isaac Thornycroft released her hand and turned to face her.

"Just tell me what you mean. Don't you care for me?"

Agitated, embarrassed, she burst into tears. Isaac took both her hands now, holding them before him. They had reached the churchyard, and its graves were distinct in the twilight; the stars looked down on them from the blue sky above; the sound of the surging sea came over with a faint murmur.

"I thought you loved me, Anna. Surely I cannot have been steering on a wrong tack?"

As the soft eyes glanced at him through their tears, he saw enough to know that she did love him. Reassured on that score, he turned and walked on again, her arm kept within his.

"Now, tell me what you mean," he said, quietly. "There can be no other bar."

"I do not know how to tell you," she answered. "I do not like to tell you."

"Nonsense, Anna. I shall keep you out here pacing the heath until you do tell, though it be until morning, which would certainly send Mrs. Copp into a fit."

Not very awkwardly when she had fairly entered upon it, Anna told her tale—her sense of the unfitness, nay, the impossibility of the union—of the wide social gulf that lay between them. Isaac met the communication with a laugh.

"Is that all! It is my turn now not to understand. You have been reared a gentlewoman, Anna."

"Papa was a clergyman. I have been reared, I think, to nothing but work. We were so very poor. My home—ah! if you could see, if you could imagine the contrast it presented to this of yours! As I sat in your drawing-room to-night I could not help feeling the difference forcibly."

If Isaac Thornycroft had not seen what she spoke of, he had seen something else—that never in his whole life had he met any one who gave him so entirely the idea of a gentlewoman—a refined, well-bred gentlewoman—as this girl now speaking with him, Anna Chester. He continued in evident amusement.

"Let us see how your objections can be refuted. You play and sing?"

"A little."

"You draw?"

"A little."

"You can dance?"

"Yes; I can dance."

"Why, then—not to enter on other desirable qualities—you are an accomplished young lady. What do you mean about unfitness?"

"I see you are laughing at me," she said, the tears struggling to her eyes again. "I am so very poor; I teach for the merest trifle: it barely finds me in the cheapest clothes. I only looked forward to a life of work. And you are rich—at least Mr. Thornycroft is."

"If we have a superfluity of riches, there's all the more cause for me to dispense with them in a wife. Besides, when I set up my tent, it will not be on the scale of my father's house. Anna, my darling!" he added, with a strange gravity in his eye and tone, "we are more on an equality than you may deem."

She made no reply, having enough to do to keep her tears from falling.

"I have sufficient for comfort—a sort of love-in-a-cottage establishment," went on Isaac; "and I am heartily sick of my bachelor's life. It leads me into all sorts of extravagances, and is unsatisfactory at the best. You must promise to be my wife, Anna."

"There are the lights in Captain Copp's parlour," said she, with singular irrelevance.

"Just so. But you do not go in until I have your promise."

"They were saying one day, some of them—I think it was Mrs. Connaught—that you would be sure to marry into one of the good county families," murmured Anna.

"Did they? I hope the disappointment won't be too much for them. I shall marry you, Anna, and none other."

"But what would your family say? Your father—your sister?"

"Just what they pleased. Anna, pardon me, I am only teasing you. Believe me, they will only be too glad to hear of it; glad that the wild, unsteady (as Mary Anne is pleased to call me on occasion) Isaac Thornycroft should make himself into a respectable man. Anna! can you not trust me?"

She had trusted all her life, yielded implicitly to the sway of those who held influence over her; little chance was there, then, that she could hold out now. Isaac Thornycroft received the promise his heart hungered for, and sealed it.

Her face gathered against his breast; her slight form shrinking in his strong arms; he kept her there a prisoner; his voice breathing soft love-vows; his blue eyes bent greedily on her blushing face; his kisses, the only honest kisses his life had known, pressed again and again upon her lips.

"Who on earth is that? Avast, thieves! Bea serpents! pirates!"

The gallant Captain Copp, his night-glass pushed out at the open window to an acute angle, had been contemplating these puzzling proceedings for some time. Fortunately he did not distinguish very clearly, and remained ignorant of the real matter. Ill-conditioned people, tipsy fishermen and else, their brains muddled with drink, found their way to the heath on occasion, and the captain considered it a duty to society to order them off. Sweeping the horizon and the nearer plain to-night, his glass had shown him some object not easy to make out. The longer Captain Copp waited for it to move, the longer it stayed stationary; the more he turned his glass, the less chance did it appear to give of revealing itself. Naturally, two people in close proximity, the head of the taller one bent over the other so as to leave no indication of the human form, would present a puzzling paradox when viewed through a night-glass: the captain came to the conclusion that it was the most extraordinary spectacle ever presented to his eyes since they had looked on that sea serpent in the Pacific; and he raised his voice to hail it when suspense was becoming quite unbearable.

Isaac Thornycroft, adroitly sheltering his companion, glided up the little opening by Mrs. Connaught's. In a few minutes, when the captain had drawn his head and glass in for a respite, he walked boldly up to the door by the side of Anna.

"Good evening, captain."

"Good evening," blithely responded the captain. "Sorry you should have the trouble of bringing her home. Come in, Anna. I say, did you meet any queer thing on the heath?"

"Queer thing?" responded Isaac.

"A man without a head, or anything of that light sort?"

"No. There's a strange horse browsing a bit lower down," added Isaac. "Some stray animal."

The captain considered, and came to the conclusion that it could not well have been the horse. What it really was he did not conjecture.

Meanwhile Anna Chester had gone upstairs to the pleasant little room she occupied, and took off her bonnet in a maze of rapture. The world had changed into a heavenly Elysium.

CHAPTER III

Isaac Thornycroft's Stratagem

A still evening in October. The red light in the west, following on a glorious sunset, threw its last rays athwart the sea; the evening star came out in its brightness; the fishing boats were bearing steadily for home.

Captain Copp's parlour was alight with a ruddy glow; not of the sun but of the fire. It shone brightly on the captain's face, at rest now. He had put down his pipe on the hearth, after carefully knocking the smouldering ashes out, and gone quietly to sleep, his wooden leg laid flat on an opposite chair, his other leg stretched over it. Mrs. Copp sat knitting a stocking by fire-light, her gentle face rather thoughtful; and, half-kneeling, half-sitting on the hearth-rug, reading, was Anna Chester.

She was here still. When Mary Anne Thornycroft returned to school after the summer holidays, Captain Copp had resolutely avowed Anna should stay with him. What was six weeks, he fiercely demanded, to get up a lady's health: let her stop six months, and then he'd see about it. Mrs. Copp hardly knew what to say, between her wish to keep Anna and her fear of putting the Miss Jupps to an inconvenience. "Inconvenience be shot!" politely rejoined the captain; and Mary Anne Thornycroft went back without her, bearing an explanatory and deprecatory letter.

It almost seemed to the girl that the delighted beating of her heart—at the consciousness of staying longer in the place that contained him—must be a guilty joy,—guilty because it was concealed. Certainly not from herself might come the first news of her engagement to Isaac Thornycroft: she was far too humble, too timid, to make the announcement. Truth to say, she only half believed in it: it seemed too blissful to be true. While Isaac did not proclaim it, she was quite content to let it rest a secret from the whole world. And so the months had gone on; Anna living in her paradise of happiness; Isaac making love to her privately in very fervent tenderness.

In saying to Anna Chester that his family would be only too glad to see him married, Isaac Thornycroft (and a doubt that it might prove so lay dimly in his mind when he said it) found that he had reckoned without his host. At the first intimation of his possible intention, Mr. Thornycroft and Richard rose up in arms against it. What they said was breathed in his ear alone, earnestly, forcibly; and Isaac, who saw how fruitless would be all pleading on his part, burst out laughing, and let them think the whole a joke. A hasty word spoken by Richard in his temper as he came striding out of the inner passage, caught the ear of Mary Anne.

"Isaac, what did he mean? Surely you are not going to be married?"

"They thought I was," answered Isaac, laughing. "I married! Would anybody have me, do you suppose, Mary Anne?"

"I think Miss Tindal would. There would be heaps of money and a good connexion, you know, Isaac."

Miss Tindal was a strong-minded lady in spectacles, who owned to thirty years and thirty thousand pounds. She quoted Latin, rode straight across country after the hounds, and was moreover a baronet's niece. A broad smile played over Isaac's lips.

"Miss Tindal's big enough to shake me. I think she would, too, on provocation. She can take her fences better than I can. That's not the kind of woman I'd marry. I should like a meek one."

"A meek one!" echoed Mary Anne, wondering whether he was speaking in derision. "What do you call a meek one?"

"A modest, gentle girl who would not shake me. Such a one as—let me see, where is there one?—as Anna Chester, say, for example."

All the scorn the words deserved seemed concentrated in Miss Thornycroft's haughty face.

"As good marry a beggar as her. Why, Isaac, she is only a working teacher—a half-boarder at school! She is not one of us."

He laughed off the alarm as he had done his father's and brother's a few minutes before, the line of conduct completely disarming all parties. She would not tolerate Miss Chester, they would not tolerate his marriage at all: that was plain. Isaac Thornycroft did not care openly to oppose his family, or be opposed by them: he let the subject drop out of remembrance, and left the future to the future. But he said not a word of this to Anna; she suspected nothing of it, and was just as contented as he to let things take their course in silence. To her there seemed but one possible calamity in the world; and that lay in being separated from him.

Sitting there on the hearth-rug, in the October evening, her eyes on the small print by the firelight, getting dim now, Anna's heart was a-glow within her, for that evening was to be spent with Isaac Thornycroft. A gentleman with his daughter was staying for a couple of days at the Red Court, and Anna had been asked to go there for the evening, and bear the young lady company.

"My dear," whispered Mrs. Copp, in the midst of her knitting, "is it not getting late? You will have the daylight quite gone."

Anna glanced up. It was getting late; but Isaac Thornycroft had said to her, "I shall fetch you." Still the habit of implicit obedience was, as ever, strong upon her, and she would fain have started there and then, in compliance with the suggestion.

"What a noise Sarah's making!"

"So she is," assented Mrs. Copp, as a noise like the bumping about of boxes, followed by talking, grew upon their ears. Another moment, and Sarah opened the door.

"A visitor," she announced, in an uncompromising voice, and the captain started up, prepared to explode a little at being aroused. Which fact Sarah was no doubt anticipating, and she spoke again.

"It is your mother, sir."

"Yes, it's me, Sam;" cried an upright wiry lady, very positive and abrupt in manner. Her face looked as if weather-beaten, and she wore large round tortoiseshell spectacles.

"Who's that?" she cried, sitting down on the large sofa, as Anna stood up in her pretty silk dress, with the pink ribbons in her hair. "Who? The daughter of the Reverend James Chester and his first wife! You are very like your father, child, but prettier. Where's my sea-chest to go, Sam?"

"I am truly glad to see you, dear mother," whispered Amy Copp, in her loving way. "The best bedroom is not in order, but—"

"And can't be put in order before to-morrow," interposed Sarah, who had no notion of being taken by storm in this way. "The luggage had better be put in the back kitchen for to-night."

"Is there much luggage?" asked the captain.

"Nothing to speak of," said Mrs. Copp; who, being used to the accommodation of a roomy ship, regarded quantity accordingly. Sarah coughed.

"My biggest sea-chest, four trunks, two bandboxes, and a few odd parcels," continued the traveller. "I am going to spend Christmas with some friends in London, but I thought I'd come to you first. As to the room not being in apple-pie order, that's nothing I'm an old sailor; I'm not particular."

"Put a pillow down here, if that's all," cried the captain, indicating the hearthrug. "Mother has slept in many a worse berth, haven't ye, mother?"

"Ay, lad, that I have. But now I shall want some of those boxes unpacked to-night. I have got a set of furs for you, Amy, somewhere; I don't know which box they were put in."

Amy was overpowered. "You are too good to me," she murmured, with tears in her eyes.

"And I have brought you a potato-steamer; that's in another," added Mrs. Copp. "I have taken to have mine steamed lately, Sam; you'd never eat them again boiled if you once tried it."

n the midst of this bustle Isaac Thornycroft walked in. Anna, in a flutter of heart-delight, but with a calm manner, went upstairs, and came down with her bonnet on, to find Isaac opening box after box in the back kitchen, under Mrs. Copp's direction, in search of the furs and the potato-steamer, the captain assisting, Amy standing by. The articles were found, and Isaac, laughing heartily in his gay good-humour, went off with Anna.

"What time am I to fetch you, Miss Anna?" inquired Sarah, as they went out.

' I will see Miss Chester home," answered Isaac: "you are busy to-night."

Mrs. Copp, gazing through her tortoiseshell spectacles at the potato-steamer, as she pointed out its beauties, suddenly turned to another subject, and brought her glasses to bear on her son and his wife.

"Which of the young Thornycrofts is that? I forget."

"Isaac; the second son."

"To be sure; Isaac, the best and handsomest of the bunch. You must take care," added Mrs. Copp, shrewdly.

"Take care of what?"

"They might be falling in love with each other. I don't know whether he's much here. He is as fine a fellow as you'd see in a day's march; and she's just the pretty gentle thing that fine men fancy."

Had it been anybody but his mother, Captain Copp would have shown his sense of the caution in strong language. "Moonshine and rubbish," cried he. "Isaac Thornycroft's not the one to entangle himself with a sweetheart; the young Thornycrofts are not marrying men; and if he were, he would look a little higher than poor Anna Chester."

"That's just it, the reason why you should be cautious, Sam," rejoined Mrs. Copp. "Not being suitable, there'd be no doubt a bother over it at the Red Court."

Amy, saying something about looking to the state of the spare room, left them in the parlour. Truth to say, the hint had scared her. Down deep in her mind, for some short while past, had a suspicion lain that they were rather more attached to each other than need be. She had only hoped it was not so. She did not by any means see her way clear to hinder it, and was content to let the half fear rest; but these words had roused it in all its force. They had somehow brought a conviction of the fact, and she saw trouble looming. What else could come of it? Anna was no match for Isaac Thornycroft.

"Sam," began Mrs. Copp, when she was alone with her son, "how does Amy continue to go on? Makes a good wife still?"

Captain Copp nodded complacently. "Never a better wife going. No tantrums—no blowings off: knits all my stockings and woollen jerseys."

"You must have a quiet house."

"Should, if 'twere not for Sarah. She fires off for herself and Amy too. I'm obliged to keep her under."

"Ah," said Mrs. Copp, rubbing her chin. "Then I expect you get up some breezes together. But she's not a bad servant, Sam."

"She's a clipper, mother—A 1; couldn't steer along without her."

What with the boxes, and what with the exactions of the spare bed-room to render it habitable for the night, for Mrs. Copp generally chose to put herself into everybody's business, and especially into her own, the two ladies had to leave Captain Copp very much to his own society. Solitude is the time for reflection, we are told, and it may have been the cause of the captain's recurring again and again to the hint his mother had dropped in regard to Isaac Thornycroft. That there was nothing in it yet he fully assumed, and it might be as well to take precautions that nothing should be in it for the future. Prevention was better than cure. Being a straightforward man, one who could not have gone in a roundabout or cautious way to work, it occurred to the captain to say a word to Mr. Isaac on the very first opportunity.

It was the first evening Anna had spent at the Red Court since Miss Thornycroft left it. The walk there, the sojourn, the walk home again by moonlight, all seemed to partake of heaven's own happiness—perfect, pure, peaceful. There had been plenty and plenty of opportunities for lingering together in the twilight on the heath in coming home from the seashore, but this was the first long legitimate walk they had taken; and considering that they were sixty minutes over it, when they might have done it in sixteen, it cannot be said they hurried themselves.

The captain was at the window, not looking on the broad expanse of heath before him, but at the faint light seen now and again from some fishing vessel cruising in the distance. It was his favourite look-out; and, except on a boisterous or rainy night, the shutters were rarely closed until ten o'clock.

"Come in and have a glass of grog with me," was his salutation to Isaac Thornycroft as he and Anna came to the gate. "'Twill be a charity," added the captain. "I'm all alone. Mother's gone up to bed tired, and Amy's looking after her."

Isaac came in and sat down, but wanted to decline the grog. Captain Copp was offended, so to pacify him he mixed some. As Anna held out her hand to the captain to say good night he noticed that her soft eyes were full of loving light; her generally delicate cheeks were a hot crimson.

"Hope it hasn't come of kissing," thought the shrewd and somewhat discomfited sailor.

"How well your mother wears!" observed Isaac.

"She was always tough," replied Captain Copp, in a thankful accent. "Hope she will be for many a year to come. Look here, Mr. Isaac, I meant to say a word to you. Don't you begin any sweethearting with that girl of ours, or talking nonsense of that sort. It wouldn't do, you know."

"Wouldn't it?" returned Isaac, carelessly.

"Wouldn't it! Why, bless and save my wooden leg, would it? A pretty uproar there'd be at the Red Court. I'd not have such a thing happen for the best three-decker that was ever launched. I'd rather quarrel with the whole of Coastdown than with your folks."

"Rather quarrel with me, captain, than with them, I suppose," returned Isaac, stirring his grog.

Captain Copp looked hard at him. "I should think so."

By intuition, rather than by outward signs, Isaac Thornycroft saw that the obstinate old sailor would be true to the backbone to what he deemed right; that he might as well ask for Amy Copp as for Anna Chester, unless he could produce credentials from his father. And so he could only temporize and disarm suspicion. Honourable by nature though he was, he considered the suppression of affairs justifiable, on the score, we must suppose that "All stratagems are fair in love and war."

"Good health, captain," said he, with a merry laugh—a laugh that somehow reassured Captain Copp. "And now tell me what wonderful event put you up to say this."

"It was mother," answered the simple-minded captain. "The thought struck her somehow—you were both of you good-looking, she said. I knew there was no danger; 'the young Thornycrofts are not marrying men,' I said to her. But now, look here, you and Anna had not better go out together again, lest other people should take up the same notions."

With these words Captain Copp believed he had settled the matter, and done all that was necessary in the way of warning. He said as much to Amy, confidentially. Whether it might have proved so, he had not the opportunity of judging. On the following morning that lady received a pressing summons to repair to London. One of her sisters, staying there temporarily, was seized with illness, and begged the captain's wife to come and nurse her. By the next train she had started, taking Anna.

"To be out of harm's way," she said to herself. "To help me take care of Maria," she said to the captain.

Mrs. Wortley was a widow without children. So many events have to be crowded in, and the story thickens so greatly, that nothing more need be said of her. The lodgings she had been temporarily occupying were near to old St. Pancras Church, and there Mrs. Sam Copp and Anna found her—two brave, skilful, tender nurses, ever ready to do their best.

Never before had Anna found illness wearisome; never before thought London the most dreary spot on earth. Ah, it was not in the locality; it was not in the illness that the ennui lay; but in the absence of Isaac Thornycroft. He called to see them once, rather to the chagrin of the captain's wife, and he met Anna the same day when she went for her walk. Mrs. Sam Copp did not suspect it.

They had been in London about a month, the invalid was better, and Mrs. Copp began to talk of returning home again; when one dark November morning, upon Anna's returning home from her walk—which Mrs. Copp, remembering her past weak condition, the result of work and confinement, insisted on her taking—Isaac Thornycroft came in with her. He put his hat down on the table, took Mrs. Copp's hands in his, and was entering upon some story, evidently a solemn one, when Anna nearly startled Mrs. Copp into fits by falling at her feet with a prayer for forgiveness, and bursting into tears.

"Oh, aunt, forgive, forgive me! Isaac over-persuaded me; he did indeed."

"Persuaded you to what?" asked Mrs. Copp.

"To become my wife," interposed Isaac. "We were married this morning."

The first thing Mrs. Copp did was to sink into a chair, her hair rising up on end; the next was to go into hysterics. Isaac, quiet, calm, gentlemanly as ever, sent Anna away while he told the tale.

"I thought it the best plan," he avowed. "When I met Anna out yesterday—by chance as she thought—I got a promise from her to meet me again this morning, no matter what the weather might be. It turned out a dense fog, but she came. Through the fog I got her into the church door, and took her to the clergyman, waiting at the altar for us, before she well knew what was going to be."

Mrs. Copp threw up her hands, and screamed, and cried, and for once in her life called another creature deceitful—meaning Anna. But Anna—as he hastened to explain—had not been deceitful; she had but yielded to his strong will in the agitation and surprise of the moment. Calculating upon this defect in her character—if it could be called a defect, brought up as she had been—Isaac Thornycroft had made the arrangements at St. Pancras church without saying a word to her; and, as it really may be said, surprised her into the marriage at the time of its taking place.

"There's the certificate," he said; "I asked the clergyman to give me one. Put it up carefully, dear Mrs. Copp."

"To be married in this way!" moaned poor Mrs. Copp. "My husband had liqueur glasses of rum served out in the vestry at our wedding, but that was not half as bad as this. Not a single witness on either side to countenance it!"

"Pardon me; my brother Cyril was present," answered Isaac. "I telegraphed for him last night, and he reached town this morning."

Isaac Thornycroft had sent for his brother out of pure kindness to Anna, that the ceremony might so far be countenanced. It had turned out to be the most crafty precaution he could have taken. Seeing Cyril, Anna never supposed but that the Thornycroft family knew of it; otherwise, yielding though she was in spirit, she might have withstood even Isaac. Cyril gave her away.

"And now," said Isaac, in an interval between the tears and moans, "I am going to take Anna away with me for a week."

Little by little Mrs. Copp succeeded in comprehending Mr. Isaac's programme. To all intents and purposes he intended this to be a perfectly secret marriage, and to remain so until the horizon before them should be clear of clouds. When Mrs. Copp went back home, Anna would return with her as Miss Chester, and they must be content with seeing each other occasionally as ordinary acquaintances.

Mrs. Copp could only stare and gasp. "Away with you for a week! and then home again with me as Miss Chester? Oh, Mr. Isaac! you do not consider. Suppose her good name should suffer?"

A slight frown contracted the capacious brow of Isaac Thornycroft. "Do you not see the precautions I have taken will prevent that? On the first breath of need my brother Cyril will come forward to testify to the marriage, and you hold the certificate of it. Believe me, I weighed all, and laid my plans accordingly. I chose to make Anna my wife. It is not expedient to proclaim it just yet to the world—to your friends or to mine; but I have done the best I could do under the circumstances. Cyril will be true to us and keep the secret; I know you will also."

Mrs. Sam Copp faintly protested that she should never get over the blow. Isaac, with his sunny smile, his persuasive voice, told her she would do so before the day was out, and saw her seal the certificate in a large envelope and lock it up.

Then he started with his bride to a small unfrequented fishing village in quite the opposite direction to Coastdown. And Anna had been married some days before she knew that her marriage was a secret from her husband's family, Cyril excepted, and to be kept one.

CHAPTER IV

In Love

Robert Hunter sat in his chambers—as it is the fashion to call offices now. They were in a good position in Westminster, and he was well established; he had set up for himself, and was doing fairly—not yet making gold by shovelfuls, as engineers are reputed to have done of late years, but at least earning his bread and cheese, with every prospect that the gold was coming.

Plans were scattered on the desk at which he sat; some intricate calculations lay immediately before him. He regarded neither. His eyes were looking straight out at the opposite wall, a big chart of some district being there, but he saw it not; nothing but vacancy. Very unusual indeed was it for Robert Hunter the practical to allow his thoughts to stray away in the midst of his work, as they had done now.

During the past few months a change had come over his heart. It was of a different nature from that which, some two or three years before, after the death of his wife, had changed himself—changed, as it seemed, his whole nature, and made a man of him. Even now he could not bear to look back upon the idle, simple folly in which his days had been passed; the circumstances that had brought this folly home to his mind, opened his eyes to it, as it were, had no doubt caused him to acquire a very exaggerated view of it; but this did no harm to others, and worked good for himself.

With the death of his wife, Robert Hunter had, so to say, put aside the pleasant phase, the ideal view of life, and entered on the hard, the stern, the practical—as he thought for ever. He had not calculated well in this. He forgot that he was still a young and attractive man (though his being attractive or the contrary was not at all to the purpose); he forgot that neither the feelings nor the heart can grow old at will. It might have been very different had his heart received its death-blow; but it was nothing but his conscience; for he had not loved his wife. But of that he was unconscious until lately.

Love—real love—the sweet heart's dream that can never but once visit either man or woman, had come stealing over Robert Hunter. Never but once. What says a modern poet?

"Few hearts have never loved; but fewer still
Have felt a second passion. None a third.
The first was living fire; the next, a thrill;
The weary heart can never more be stirred:
Rely on it, the song has left the bird."

Truer words were rarely said or sung. The one only glimpse of Paradise vouchsafed to us on earth—a transitory glimpse at the best—cannot be repeated a second time. When it flies away it flies for ever.

Ah, how different it was, this love, that was making a heaven of Robert Hunter's life, from that which had been given to his poor dead wife—the child-wife, who had been so passionately attached to him!

He understood her agony now—when she had believed him false to her; when he, her heart's idol, had apparently gone over to another's worship—he did not understand it then. When inclined to be very self-condemnatory, to bring his sins and mistakes palpably before him, he would ask himself, looking back, what satisfaction he had derived from my Lady Ellis's society, taking it at its best. A few soft glances; a daily repetition of some sweet words; a dozen kisses—they had not been more—snatched from her face; and some hand pressing when they met or parted. Literally this was all: there had been nothing, nothing more; and Mr. Hunter had not even the poor consolation of knowing now that any love whatever on his side, or hers, had entered into the matter from the beginning to the ending. It was for this his wife had died; it was for this he had laden his conscience with a weight that could never wholly leave it. He was not a heathen; and when, close upon the death, remorse had pressed sorely upon him, an intolerable burthen of sin grievous to be borne, he had, in very pity for his own miserable state, carried it where he had never before carried anything. Consolation came in time, a sense of mercy, of help, of pardon; but the recollection could never be blotted out, or the sense of too late repentance quit him.

He remembered still; he repented yet. Whenever the past occurred to him, it brought with it that terrible conviction—a debt of atonement owing to the dead, which can never be rendered—and Robert Hunter would feel the most humble man on the face of the earth. This sense of humiliation was no doubt good for him; it came upon him at odd times and seasons, even in the midst of the new passion that filled his heart.

"Shall I ever win her?" he was thinking to himself, seated at his for once neglected desk. "Nay, must I ever dare to tell her of my love? A flourishing engineer, with his name up in the world, and half a score important undertakings in progress, might be deemed a fitting match for her by her people at the Red Court; but what would they say to me? I am not to be called flourishing yet; my great works I must be content to wait for; they will come; I can foresee it; but before then some man with settlements and a rent-roll may have stepped in."

It was not a strictly comforting prospect certainly, put in this light; and Mr. Hunter gave an impatient twist to some papers. But he could not this morning settle down to work, and the meditations began again.

"I know she loves me; I can see it in every turn of her beautiful face, hear it in every tone of her voice. This evening I shall see her; this evening I shall see her! Oh, the—"

"Mr. Barty is here, sir."

The interruption came from a clerk; it served to recal his master to what he so rarely forgot, the business of every-day life. Mr. Barty was an eminent contractor, and Robert Hunter's hopes went up to fever-heat as he welcomed him. One great work entrusted to him from this great man, and the future might be all plain sailing.

He was not wholly disappointed. Mr. Barty had come to offer him business; or rather, to pave the way for it; for the offer was not positively entered on then, only the proposed work—a new line of rail—discussed. There was one drawback—it was a line abroad—and Robert Hunter did not much like this.

Mary Anne Thornycroft had not many friends in London, nearly all her holidays during the half-year had been passed at Mrs. Macpherson's. Susan Hunter invariably accompanied her; and what more natural than that Robert should (invited, or uninvited, as it might happen) drop in to meet his sister? There had lain the whole thing—the intercourse afforded by these rather frequent meetings—and nothing more need be said; they had fallen in love with one another.

Yes. The singular attraction each had seemed to possess for the other the first time they met, but increased with every subsequent interview. It had not needed many. Mary Anne Thornycroft, who had scarcely ever so much as read of the name of love, had lost her heart to this young man, the widower Robert Hunter, entirely and hopelessly. That he was—at any rate at present—no suitable match for her, she never so much as glanced twice at: the Thornycrofts were not wont to regard expediency when it interfered with inclination. Not a word had been spoken; not a hint given; but there is a language of the heart, and they had become versed in it. Clever Mrs. Macpherson, so keen-sighted generally in the affairs of men and women, never so much as gave a thought to what was passing under her very eyes; Miss Hunter, who had discernment too, was totally blind here. As to the professor, with his spectacled eyes up aloft in the sky or buried in the earth, it would have been far too much to suspect him of seeing it. A very delightful state of things for the lovers.

When Robert Hunter reached Mrs. Macpherson's that dark December evening, he saw nobody in the drawing-room. He had been invited to dinner; five o'clock sharp, Mrs. Macpherson told him; for the professor had an engagement at six which would keep him out, and she did not intend that he should depart dinnerless.

This was Miss Thornycroft's farewell visit; in two days she was going home for Christmas, not again to return to school. She had invited Susan Hunter (who would remain at school until March), to come down during the holidays and spend a week at the Red Court Farm; and her brother was to accompany her.

It wanted a quarter to five when Mr. Hunter entered. The drawing-room was not lighted, and at first he thought no one was in it. The large fire had burnt down to red embers; as he stood before it, his head and shoulders reflected in the pier-glass, he (perhaps unconsciously) ran his hand through his hair—hair that was darker than it used to be; the once deep auburn had become a reddish-brown, and—and—some grey threads mingled with it.

"How vain you are!"

He started round at the sound—it was the voice he loved so well. Half buried in a lounging chair in the darkest corner was she. She came forward, laughing.

"I did not see you," he said, taking her hand "You are here alone!"

A conscious blush tinged her cheeks; she knew that she had stayed in the room to wait for him.

"They have gone somewhere, Susan and Mrs. Macpherson—to see a new cat of the professor's, I think. I have seen so many of those stuffed animals."

"When do you go down home?"

"The day after to-morrow. Susan has fixed the second week in January for her visit. Will that time suit you?"

"The time might suit," he replied, with a slight stress on the word "time," as if there were something else that might not. "Unless, indeed—"

"Unless what?"

"Unless I should have left England, I was going to say. An offer has been made me to-day—or rather, to speak more correctly, an intimation that an offer is about to be made me—of some work abroad. If I accept it, it will take me away for a couple of years."

She glanced up, and their eyes met. A yearning look of love, of dire tribulation at the news, shone momentarily in hers. Then they were bent on the carpet, and Mr. Hunter looked at the fire—the safest place just then.

"Are you obliged to accept it?" she inquired.

"Of course not. But it would be very much to my advantage. It would pave the way for—for—" He hesitated.

"For what?"

"Wealth and honours. I mean such honours (all might not call them so), as are open to one of my profession."

A whole array of sentences crowded into her mind—begging him not to go; what would the days be without the sunshine of his presence? They should be far enough apart as things were; he in London, she at home; but the other separation hinted at would be like all that was good in life dying out. This and a great deal more, lay in her thoughts; what she said, however, was cold and quiet enough.

"In the event of your remaining at home, then, the second week in January would suit you? It is Susan who has fixed it."

Not immediately did he reply. Since the first intimation of this visit to Coastdown, a feeling of repugnance to it had lain within him; an instinct, whenever he thought of it, warning him against accepting it. Ah! believe me, these instinctive warnings come to us. They occur oftener than we, in our carelessness, think for. Perhaps not one in ten of them is ever noticed, still less heeded; we go blindly on in disregard; and, when ill follows, scarcely ever remember that the warning voice, if attended to, would have saved us.

Just as Robert Hunter disregarded this. But for his visit, destined to take place at the time proposed, the great tragedy connected with the Red Court Farm had never taken place.

Stronger than ever was the deterring warning on him this evening. He said to himself that his repugnance lay in the dislike to be a guest in any house that Lady Ellis was connected with; never so much as thinking of any other cause. He fully assumed there would be no chance of meeting herself: he knew she lived in Cheltenham. Miss Thornycroft had once or twice casually mentioned her stepmother's name in his presence, but he had not pursued the topic; and the young lady did not know that they had ever met.

"You do not reply to me, Mr. Hunter. Would the time be inconvenient for you?"

"It is not that," he answered, speaking rather dreamily. "But—I am a stranger to your father: would he like me to intrude, uninvited by himself?"

"It would be a strange thing if I could not invite a dear school friend, as Susan is, down for a week, and you to accompany her," returned Miss Thornycroft, rather hotly. "You need not fear; papa is the most hospitable man living. They keep almost open house at home."

"You have brothers," returned Mr. Hunter, seeking for some further confronting argument. At which suggestion a ray of anger came into Miss Thornycroft's haughty blue eyes.

"As if my brothers would concern themselves with me or my visitors! They go their way, and I intend to go mine."

"Your stepmother—"

"She is nobody," quickly interposed Miss Thornycroft, mistaking what he was about to say. "Lady Ellis lives in Cheltenham. She is ill, and Coastdown does not suit her."

"Why does she still call herself Lady Ellis?" he asked, the question having before occurred to him.

"It is her whim. What does it signify? She is one of the most pretentious women you can imagine, Mr. Hunter—quite a parvenu, as I have always felt—and 'my lady' is sweeter to her ears than 'madam.'"

"What is it that is the matter with her?"

"It is some inward complaint; I don't quite understand what. The last time I saw my brother Cyril, he told me she was growing worse; that there was not the least hope of her cure."

"She does not come to the Red Court?"

"No, thank fortune! She has not been there at all during this past year. I believe she is now too ill to come."

Mr. Hunter glanced at the speaker with a smile. "You do not seem to like her."

"Like her! Like Lady Ellis! I do not think I could pretend to like her if she were dead. You do not know her."

A flush of remembrance darkened the brow of Robert Hunter. Time had been when he knew enough of her.

"She is a crafty, wily, utterly selfish woman," pursued Miss Thornycroft, who very much enjoyed a fling at her stepmother. "How ever papa came to be taken in by her—but I don't care to talk of that."

She seized the poker and began to crack the fire into a blaze. Mr. Hunter took it from her, and he adroitly kept her hand in his.

"Had she been a different woman, good and kind, she might have won me over to love her. The Red Court wanted a mistress at that time, as papa thought; and, to confess it, so did I. A little self-willed, perverse girl I was, rebellious to my French governess, perpetually getting into scrapes, running wild indoors and out."

Entirely unconscious was Miss Thornycroft how mistaken was one of her assumptions—"papa thought the Red Court wanted a mistress." Mr. Thornycroft had been rather too conscious that it did not want one, looking at it from his point of view; though his daughter did.

"Ah, well; let bygones be bygones. You will promise to come, Mr. Hunter?"

"Yes," he answered, in teeth of the voice that seemed to haunt him. "If I have not gone away from England on this expedition, I will come."

"Thank you," she said, with a soft flush.

He turned and looked fully at her. Her hand was in his, for he had not relinquished it. Only about half a minute had he held it; it takes longer to tell these things than to act them. The poker was in his other hand, and he put it down with a clatter, which prevented their hearing the footsteps of Mrs. Macpherson on the soft carpet outside. That discreet matron, glancing through the partially open door, took the view of what she saw with her keen brain, and stood transfixed.

"My heart alive, is there anything between them?" ran her surprised thoughts. "Well, that would be a go! Robert Hunter ain't no match for her father's child. Hand in hand, be they! and his eyes dropped on her face as if he was a-hungering to eat it. Not in this house, my good gentleman."

With a cough and a shuffling, as if the carpet had got entangled with her feet, Mrs. Macpherson made her advent known. When she advanced into the room the position of the parties had changed: he was at one corner of the fire-place, she at the other, silent, demure, innocent-looking both of them as two doves.

Not a word said Mrs. Macpherson. Miss Hunter came in, the professor followed, the announcement of dinner followed him. And somehow there arose no further opportunity for as much as a hand-shake between the suspected pair. But on the next day Mrs. Macpherson drove round to Miss Jupp's, and made to that lady a communication.

"I don't say as it is so, Miss Jupp; mind that; their fingers might have got together accidental. I am bound to say that I never noticed nothing between 'em before. But I'm a straightforward body, liking to go to the root o' things at first with folks, and do as I'd be done by. And goodness only knows what might have become of us if I'd not been, with the professor's brain a-lodging up in the skies! I'll go to Miss Jupp, says I to myself last night; and here I am."

"I think—I hope that it is quite unlikely," said Miss Jupp; beginning, however, to feel uncomfortable.

"So do I. I've told you so. But it was my place to come and put you on your guard. I declare to goodness that never a thought of such a thing struck me, or you may be sure I'd not have had Robert Hunter to my house when she was there. 'When the steed's stole, one locks the stable door.'"

"Miss Hunter tells me that she and her brother are going to spend a week at Coastdown."

"And so much the better," said Mrs. Macpherson, emphatically. "If there is anything between 'em, her folks won't fail to see it, and they can act accordingly. And now that I've done my duty, and had my say, I'll be going."

"Thank you," said Miss Jupp. "Is the professor well?"

"As well as getting up at three o'clock on a winter's morning and starting off in the dark and cold'll let him be," was the response. "I told him last night he shouldn't go; there's no sense in such practices; but he wouldn't listen. It's astronomicals this time."

Watching her departure, remaining for a few minutes in undecisive thought, Miss Jupp at length made up her mind to speak, and sent for Mary Anne Thornycroft. No prevision was on the young lady's mind of the lecture in store; upright, elegant, beautiful, in she swept and stood calmly before her governess. Miss Jupp spoke considerately, making light of the matter, merely saying that Mrs. Macpherson thought she and Mr. Hunter were rather fond of "talking" together. "I thought it as well just to mention it to you, my dear; school-girls—and you are but one as yet, you know—should always be reticent."

Mary Anne Thornycroft's haughty blue eyes, raised in general so fearlessly, drooped before Miss Jupp's gaze, and her face turned to a glowing crimson. Only for a moment: the next she was looking up again, meeting the gaze and answering with straightforward candour.

"Nothing has ever passed between me and Mr. Hunter that Mrs. Macpherson might not have heard and seen. I like Mr. Hunter very much. I have frequently met him there; but why should Mrs. Macpherson seek to make mischief out of that?"

"My dear girl, she neither seeks to make mischief nor has she made any. All I would say to you—leaving the past—is a word of caution. At your age, with your good sense, you cannot fail to be aware that it is advisable young ladies should be circumspect in their choice of acquaintances. A mutual inclination is sometimes formed, which can never lead to fruition, only to unhappiness."

Mary Anne did not answer, and the eyes dropped again.

"I have a great mind to tell you a little episode of my life," resumed poor Miss Jupp, her cheeks faintly flushing. "Such an inclination as I speak of arose between me and one with whom, many years ago when out on a visit, I was brought into daily contact. We learnt to care for each other as much as it is possible for people to care in this world. So much so, that when it was all past and done with, and I received an excellent proposal of marriage, I could not accept it. That early attachment was the blight of my life, Mary Anne. Instead of being a poor school-mistress, worried with many anxieties—a despised old maid—I should now have been a good man's wife, the mistress of a prosperous home."

Miss Jupp kept her rising tears down; but Mary Anne Thornycroft's eyes were glistening.

"And that first one, dear Miss Jupp: could you not have married him?"

"No, my dear. Truth to tell, he never asked me. He dared not ask me; it would have been quite unsuitable. Believe me, many an unmarried woman could give you the same history nearly word for word. Hence you see how necessary it is to guard against an intimacy with unsuitable acquaintances."

"And you put Mr. Hunter into the catalogue?" returned Miss Thornycroft, affecting to speak lightly.

"Most emphatically—as considered in relation to you,' was Miss Jupp's answer. "Your family will expect you to marry well, and you owe it to them to do so. Mr. Hunter is in every respect unsuitable. Until recently he was only a clerk; he has his own way to carve yet in the world; he is much older than you; and—he has been already married."

"Of course I know all that," said Miss Thornycroft, with the deepest colour that had yet come over her. "But don't you think, ma'am, it would have been quite time to remind me of this when circumstances called for it?"

"Perhaps not. At any rate, my dear, the warning can do you no harm. If unrequired in regard to Mr. Hunter—as indeed I believe it to be—it may serve you n the future."

Miss Jupp said no more. "I have put it strong," she thought to herself, as the young lady curtsied and left the room. "It was well to do so."

"Engineers rise to honours, as he said, and I know he is going on for them," quoth Mary Anne Thornycroft, with characteristic obstinacy, slowly walking along the passage. "I should never care for anyone else in the world. As to money, I daresay I shall have plenty of that; so will he when he has become famous."

They travelled to Coastdown together—Isaac Thornycroft and his sister, Mrs. Copp and Anna Chester, as we must continue to call her—by a pleasant coincidence, as it was deemed by Miss Thornycroft. Mrs. Copp, living upon thorns—but that is a very faint figure of speech to express that timid lady's state of mind was ready some days before, but had to await the arrival of Anna. Isaac kept her out longer than the week, getting back just in time to take charge of his sister.

As they sat in the carriage together, what a momentous secret it was that three of them held, and had to conceal from the fourth! If Anna's eyes were bright with happiness, her cheeks looked pale with apprehension; and Mrs. Copp might well shiver, and lay it upon the frost. Not so Isaac. Easy, careless, gay, was he—"every inch a bridegroom." After all, there was not so very much for him to dread. It was expedient to keep his marriage secret, if it could be kept so; if' not, why he must face the explosion at home as he best could: the precautions he had taken would ward off reproach from his wife.

"Here's Jutpoint!" exclaimed Mary Anne Thornycroft. "How glad I am to come back!"

"How glad I should be if I were going away from it!" thought poor Mrs. Copp.

As they were getting out of the carriage, Isaac contrived to put his arm before Anna, an intimation that he wanted to detain her. The others were suffered to go on.

"What makes you look so pale?"

"Oh, Isaac! can you ask? Your father—my uncle—may be here waiting for us. I feel sick and faint at the thought of meeting them."

"But there's no reason in the world why you should. One minute after seeing them the feeling will wear off. Ce n'est quo le premier pas qui coute."

"If they should suspect!—if they should have heard! It seems to me people need only look in my face to learn all. I have never once met your sister's eyes freely in coming down."

He laughed lightly. "Reassure yourself, my darling. There's no fear that it will be known one hour before we choose it should be."

"I am remembering always that stories may get abroad about me."

"What you have to remember is that you are my honest wife," gravely returned Isaac. "I told Mrs. Copp—I have told you—that on the faintest breath of a whisper, I should avow the truth. You cannot doubt it, Anna; nothing in the world can be so precious to me as my wife's fair fame. They are looking back for us. God bless you, my darling, and farewell. For the present, you know—and that's the worst of the whole matter—you are not my wife, but Miss Chester."

CHAPTER V

Wilful Disobedience

Mary Ann Thornycroft sat in the large, luxurious, comfortable drawing-room of the Red Court Farm. The skies without were grey and wintry, the air was cold, the sea was of a dull leaden colour; but with that cheery fire blazing in the grate, the soft chairs and sofas scattered about, the fine pictures, the costly ornaments, things were decidedly bright within. Brighter a great deal than the young lady's face was; for something had just occurred to vex her. She was leaning back in her chair; her foot, peeping out from beneath the folds of her flowing dress, impatiently tapping the carpet: angry determination written on every line of her countenance. Between herself and Richard there had just occurred a passage at arms— as is apt to be the case with brother and sister, when each has a dominant and unyielding will.

At home for good, Miss Thornycroft had assumed her post as mistress of the house in a spirit of determination that said she meant to maintain it. The neighbours came flocking to see the handsome girl, a woman grown now. She had attained her nineteenth year. They found a lady-like, agreeable girl, with Cyril's love for reading, Isaac's fair skin and beautiful features, and Richard's resolute tone and lip. Very soon, within a week of her return, the servants whispered to each other that Miss Thornycroft and her brothers had already begun their quarrelling, for both sides wanted the mastery. They should have said her brother—very seldom indeed was it that Isaac interfered with her—Cyril never.

She had begun by attempting to set to rights matters that probably never would be set right; regularity in regard to the serving of the meals. They set all regularity at defiance, especially on the point of coming in to them. They might come, or they might not; they might sit down at the appointed hour, or they might appear an hour after it. Sometimes the dinners were simple, oftener elaborate; to-day they would be alone, to-morrow six or eight unexpected guests, invited on the spur of the moment, would sit down to table; just as it had been in the old days. Mr. Thornycroft's love of free-and-easy hospitality had not changed. To remedy this, Mary Anne did not attempt—it had grown into a usage; but she did wish to make Richard and Isaac pay more attention to decorum.

"They cannot be well-conducted, these two brothers of mine," soliloquized Miss Thornycroft, as she continued to tap her impatient foot. "And papa winks at it. I think they must have acquired a love for low companions. I hear of their going into the public-house, and, if not drinking themselves, standing treat for others. Last night they came in to dinner in their velveteen coats, and gaiters all mud—after keeping it waiting for five-and-forty minutes. I spoke about their clothes, and papa—papa took their part, saying it was not to be expected that young men engaged in agriculture could dress themselves up for dinner like a lord-in-waiting. It's a shame!"

Richard and Isaac did indeed appear to be rather loose young men in some things; but their conduct had not changed from what it used to be—the change lay in Miss Thornycroft. What as a girl she had not seen or noticed, she now, a young woman come home to exact propriety after the manner of well-conducted young ladies, saw at once, and put a black mark against. Their dog-cart, that ever-favourite vehicle, would be heard going out and coming in at all sorts of unseasonable hours; when Richard and Isaac lay abed till twelve (the case occasionally) Miss Thornycroft would contrive to gather that they had not gone to it until nearly daylight.

The grievance this morning, however, was not about any of these things: it concerned a more personal matter of Miss Thornycroft's. While she was reading a letter from Susan Hunter, fixing the day of the promised visit, Richard came in. He accused her of expecting visitors, and flatly ordered her to write and stop their coming. A few minutes of angry contention ensued, neither side giving way in the smallest degree: she said her friends should come, Richard said they should not. He strode away to find his father. The justice was in the four-acre paddock with his gun.

"This girl's turning the house upside down," began Richard. "We shall not be able to keep her at home."

"What girl? Do you mean Mary Anne?"

"There's nobody else I should mean," returned the young man, who was not more remarkable for courtesy of speech, even to his father, than he used to be. "I'd pretty soon shell out anybody else who came interfering. She has gone and invited some fellow and his sister down to stay for a week, she says. We can't have prying people here just now."

"Don't fly in a flurry, Dick. That's the worst of you."

"Well, sir, I think it should be stopped. For the next month, you know—"

"Yes, yes, I know," interposed the justice. "Of course."

"After that, it would not so much matter," continued Richard. "Not but that it would be an exceedingly bad precedent to allow it at all. If she begins to invite visitors here at will, there's no knowing what the upshot might be."

"I'll go and speak to her," said Mr. Thornycroft. "Here, take the gun, Dick."

Walking slowly, giving an eye to different matters as he passed, speaking a word here, giving an order there, the justice went on after the fashion of a man whose mind is at ease. It never occurred to him that his daughter would dispute his will.

"What is all this, Mary Anne?" he demanded, when he reached her. "Richard tells me you have been inviting some people to stay here."

Miss Thornycroft rose respectfully.

"So I have, papa. Susan Hunter was my great friend at school; she is remaining there for the holidays, which of course is very dull, and I asked her to come here for a week. Her brother will bring her."

"They cannot come," said Mr. Thornycroft.

"Not come!"

"No. You must understand one thing, Mary Anne—that you are not at liberty to invite people indiscriminately to the Red Court I cannot sanction it."

A hard look of resentment crossed her face; opposition never answered with the Thornycrofts, Cyril excepted: he was just as yielding as the rest were obstinate.

"I have invited them, papa. The time for the visit is fixed, the arrangements are made."

"I tell you, they cannot come."

"Not if Richard's whims are to be studied," returned Miss Thornycroft, angrily, for she had lost her temper. "Do you wish me to live on in this house for ever, papa, without a soul to speak to, save my brothers and the servants? And cordial companions they are," added the young lady, alluding to the former, "out, out, out, as they are, night after night! I should like to know where it is they go to. Perhaps I could find out if I tried."

A fanciful person might have thought that Mr. Thornycroft started. "Daughter!" he cried, in a hoarse whisper, hoarse with passion, "hold your peace about your brothers. What is it to you where they go or what they do? Is it seemly for you, a girl, to trouble yourself about the doings of young men? Are you going to turn out a firebrand amongst us? Take care that you don't set the Red Court alight."

The words might have struck her as strange, might indeed have imparted a sort of undefined fear, but that she was so filled with anger and resentment as to leave no room for other impressions. Nevertheless, there was that in her father's face and eye which warned her it would not do to oppose him now, and her rejoinder was spoken more civilly.

"Do you mean, papa, that you will never allow me to have a visitor?"

"I do not say that. But I must choose the times and seasons. This companion of yours may come a month later, if you wish it so very much. Not her brother. We have enough young men in the house of our own. And I suppose you don't care for him."

Miss Thornycroft would have liked to say that he was the one for whom she did care—not the sister—but that was inexpedient. A conscious flush dyed her face; which Mr. Thornycroft attributed to pain at her wish being opposed. He had not yet to learn how difficult it was to turn his daughter from any whim on which she had set her will.

"Write to-day and stop their coming. Tell Miss—what's the name?"

"Hunter," was the sullen answer.

"Tell Miss Hunter that it is not convenient to receive her at the time arranged, but that you hope to see her later. And—another word, Mary Anne," added Mr. Thornycroft, pausing in the act of leaving the room; "a word of caution; let your brothers alone; their movements are no business of yours, neither must you make it such. Shut your eyes and ears to all that does not concern you, if you want to live in peace under my roof."

"Shut my eyes and ears?" she repeated, looking after him, "that I never will. I can see how it is—papa has lived so long under the domineering of Richard that he yields to him as a habit. It is less trouble than opposing him. Richard is the most selfish man alive. He thinks if we had visitors staying at the court, he must be a little more civilized in dress and other matters, and he does not choose to be so. For no other reason has he set his face against their coming; there can be no other. But I will show him that I have a will as well as he, and as good a right to exercise it."

Even as Miss Thornycroft spoke, the assertion, "there can be no other," rose up again in her mind, and she paused to consider whether it was strictly in accordance with facts. But no; look on all sides as she would, there appeared to be no other reason whatever, or shadow of reason. It was just a whim of Richard's; who liked to act, in small things as in great, as though he were the master of the Red Court Farm—a whim which Miss Thornycroft was determined not to gratify.

And, flying in the face of the direct command of her father, she did not write to stop her guests.

The contest had not soothed her, and she put on her things to go out. The day was by no means inviting, the air was raw and chill, but Miss Thornycroft felt dissatisfied with home. Turning off by the plateau towards the village, the house inhabited by Tomlett met her view. It brought to her remembrance that the man was said to have received some slight accident, of which she had only heard a day or two ago. More as a diversion to her purposeless steps than anything else, she struck across to inquire after him. Mrs. Tomlett, an industrious little woman with a red face and shrill voice, as you may remember, stood at the kitchen table as Miss Thornycroft approached the open door, peeling potatoes. Down went the knife.

"Don't disturb yourself, Mrs. Tomlett. I hear your husband has met with some hurt. How was it done?"

For a woman of ordinary nerve and brain, Mrs. Tomlett decidedly showed herself wanting in self-possession at the question. It seemed to scare her. Looking here, looking there, looking everywhere like a frightened bird, she mumbled out some indistinct answer. Miss Thornycroft had seen her so on occasions before, and as a girl used to laugh at her.

"When did it happen, Mrs. Tomlett?"

"Last week, miss; that is, last month—last fortnight I meant to say," cried Mrs. Tomlett, hopelessly perplexed.

"What was the accident?" continued Miss Thornycroft. "Well, it was a—a—a pitching of himself down the stairs, miss."

"Down which stairs? This house has no stairs."

Mrs. Tomlett looked to the different points of the room as if to assist her remembrance that the house had none.

"No, miss, true; it wasn't stairs. He got hurted some way," added the woman, in a pang of desperation. "I never knowed clear how. When they brought him home—a carrying of him—his head up, as one might say, and his legs down, my senses was clean frightened out o' me: what they said and what they didn't say, I couldn't remember after no more nor nothing. May be 'twas out o' the tallet o' the Red Court stables he fell, miss: I think it was."

Miss Thornycroft thought not; she should have heard of that. "Where was he hurt?" she asked. "In the leg, was it not?"

"'Twas in the arm, miss," responded Mrs. Tomlett. "Leastways, in the ankle."

The young lady stared at her as a natural curiosity. "Was it in both, Mrs. Tomlett?"

Well, yes, Mrs. Tomlett thought it might be in both. His side also had got grazed. Her full opinion was, if she might venture to express it, that he had done it a climbing up into his boat. One blessed thing was—no bones was broke.

Miss Thornycroft laughed, and thought she might as well leave her to the peeling of the potatoes, the interruption to which essential duty had possibly driven her senses away.

"At any rate, whatever the hurt, I hope he will soon be about again," she kindly said, as she went out.

"Which he is a'most that a'ready," responded Mrs. Tomlett, standing on the threshold to curtsey to her guest.

No sooner was the door shut than Tomlett, a short, strong, dark man, with a seal-skin cap on, and his right arm bandaged up, came limping out of an inner room. The first thing he did was to glare at his wife; the second, to bring his left hand in loud contact with the small round table so effectually that the potatoes went flying off it.

"Now what do you think of yourself for a decent woman?"

Mrs. Tomlett sat down on a chair and began to cry. "It took to me, Ben, it did—it took to me awful," she said, deprecatingly, in the midst of her tears; "I never knowed as news of the hurt had got abroad."

"Do you suppose there ever was such a born fool afore as you?" again demanded Mr. Tomlett, in a slow, subdued, ironical, fearfully telling tone.

"When she come straight in with the query—what was Tomlett's hurt and how were it done?—my poor body set on a twittering, and my head went clean out o' me," pleaded Mrs. Tomlett.

"A pity but it had gone clean off ye," growled the strong-minded husband; "'tain't o' no good on."

"What were I to say, took at a pinch like that? I couldn t tell the truth; you know that, Tomlett."

"Yes, you could; you might ha' told enough on't to satisfy her:—'He was at work, and he fell and hurt hisself.' Warn't that enough for any reasonable woman to say? And if she'd asked where he fell, you might ha' said you didn't know. Not you! He 'throwed hisself down the stairs,' when there ain't no stairs to the place; he 'fell out o' the tallet;' he 'done it a climbing up into his boat!' Yah!"

"Don't be hard upon me, Tomlett, don't."

"'And the hurt,' she asked, 'was that in the leg?'" mercilessly continued Mr. Tomlett. "'No, it weren't in the leg, it were in the arm, leastways, in the ankle,' says you; and a fine bobbin o' contradiction that must ha' sounded to her. Yah again! Some women be born fools, and some makes theirselves into 'em."

"It were through knowing you'd get a listening, Tomlett. Nothing never scares the wits out o' me like that. When I see the door open a straw's breadth, I knew your ear was at it; and what with her afore me talking, and you ahind me listening, I didn't know the words I said no more nor if it wasn't me that spoke 'em. Do what I will, I'm blowed up."

"Blowed up!" amiably repeated Mr. Tomlett; "if you was the wife o' some persons, you'd get the blowing up and something atop of it. Go on with them taturs."

Leaving them to their domestic bliss and occupations—though from the above interlude Tomlett must not be judged: he made in general a good husband, only he had been so terribly put out—we will go after Miss Thornycroft. As she struck into the road again she saw Anna Chester talking to one of her two elder brothers, it was too far off to distinguish which; and indeed Richard and Isaac were so much alike in figure, that the one was often taken for the other. That it was the latter, Miss Thornycroft judged; there appeared to be a sort of intimacy—a friendship—between Isaac and Anna that she by no means approved of, and Isaac had taken to go rather often to Captain Copp's.

Anna came on alone; her gentle face beaming, her pretty lips breaking into smiles. But Miss Thornycroft was cold.

"Which of my brothers were you talking to?"

"It was Isaac," answered Anna, turning her face away, for the trick of colouring crimson at Isaac's name, acquired since her return, was all too visible.

"Ah, yes, I knew it must be Isaac. What good friends you seem to be growing!"

"Do you think so?" returned Anna, stooping to do something or other to her dainty little boot, and speaking as lightly as the circumstances permitted. "He stopped me to say that Captain Copp was going to dine at the Red Court this evening, and so asked if I would accompany him."

"Oh, it's to be one of their dinner gatherings this evening, is it?" replied Mary Anne, alluding to her brothers with her usual scant ceremony. "Well, I hope you will come, Anna; otherwise I shall not go in."

"Thank you. Yes."

"But look here. If you get telling Isaac things again that I tell you, you and I shall quarrel. What is he to you that you should do it?"

Not for a long while had Anna felt so miserably bewildered. She began ransacking her memory for all she had said. At these critical moments, discovery seemed very near.

"This morning, Richard chose to question me about Susan Hunter's coming down. He had heard of it from Isaac. Now I had not mentioned it to Isaac, or to any one else at home: time enough for that when the day was fixed; and Isaac could only have learnt it from you."

"I—I am not sure—I can't quite tell—it is possible I did mention it to him," stammered poor Anna. "I did not think to do harm."

"I dare say not. But it has done harm; it has caused no end of mischief and disturbance at home, and got me into what my brothers politely call a 'row.' Kindly keep my affairs to yourself for the future, Anna."

She turned away with the last words, and the poor young wife, in a sea of perplexity and distress, continued her way. The life she was leading was exceedingly unsatisfactory; never a moment, save in some chance and transitory meeting in the village or on the heath, did she obtain one private word with Isaac. Isaac was rather a frequent dropper-in now at Captain Copp's; but the cautious sailor, remembering the warning hint of his mother, took care to afford no scope for private talking; or, as he phrased it, sweethearting; and Mrs. Copp—her terror of discovery being always fresh upon her guarded Anna zealously. Could she have had her way, they would have passed each other with a formal nod whenever they met.

"Never again," murmured Anna. "I must never again speak to him about his home—unless it be of what the whole world knows. How I wish this dreadful state of things could terminate! I have heard of secrets—concealments—wearing the life away; I believe it now."

The former resident superintendent of the coastguard, Mr. Dangerfield, had left Coastdown, and been replaced by Mr. Kyne. Private opinion ran that Coastdown had not changed for the best; Mr. Supervisor Dangerfield (the official title awarded him by Coastdown) having been an easy, good-tempered, jolly kind of man, while Mr. Supervisor Kyne was turning out to be strict and fussy on the score of "duty." Justice Thornycroft, the great man of the place, had received him well, and the new officer evidently liked the good cheer he was made welcome to at the Red Court Farm.

On this same morning Mr. Thornycroft, strolling out from his home, saw the supervisor on the plateau, and crossed the rails to join him. Mr. Kyne, a spare man of middle age, with a greyish sort of face and hair cut close to his head, stood on the extreme edge of the plateau, attentively scanning the sea. He slowly turned as Mr. Thornycroft approached.

"Looking out for smugglers?" demanded the justice, jestingly. For this new superintendent had started the subject of smuggling soon after he came to Coastdown, avowing a suspicion that it was carried on; the justice had received it with a fit of laughter, and lost no opportunity since of throwing ridicule on it.

"Shall I tell him, or not?" mentally debated Mr. Kyne. "Better not, perhaps, until we can get hold of something more positive. He would never believe it; he would resent it as a libel on Coastdown."

The fact was, Mr. Kyne had received information some short while before, from what he considered a reliable source, that smuggling to a great extent was carried on at Coastdown, or on some part of the coast lying nearly contiguous to it. He was redoubling his own watchfulness and his preventive precautions: to find out such a thing would be a great feather in his cap.

"You won't ridicule me out of my conviction, sir."

"Not I," said the justice. "I don't want to."

"I shall put a man on this plateau at night."

Mr. Thornycroft opened his eyes. "What on earth for?"

"Well—I suspect that place below."

"Suspect that place below!" repeated the justice, advancing to the edge and looking down. "What is there on it to suspect?"

"Nothing—that's the truth. But if contraband things are landed, that's the most likely spot about. There is no other at all that I see where it could be done."

"And so you look at it on the negative principle," cried the justice, curling his lip. "Don't be afraid, Kyne. If the Half-moon had but a bale of smuggled goods on it, there it must be until you seized it. Is there a corner to hide it in, or facility for carrying it away?"

"That's what I say to myself," rejoined Mr. Kyne. "It's the only thing that makes me easy."

"Don't, for humanity's sake, leave your poor men here on a winter's night; it would be simply superfluous in the teeth of this impossibility! The cold on this bleak place might do for some of them before morning, or a false step in the dark send them over the cliff. Not to speak of the ghost," added the justice, with a grim smile.

The supervisor gave an impromptu grunt, as if the latter sentence had jarred on his nerves.

"That ghost tale is the worst part of it!" cried he. "Cold they are used to, danger they don't mind; but there's not one of them but shudders at the thought of seeing the ghost. I changed the men when I found how it was; sent the old ones away, and brought fresh ones here; well, will you believe me, justice, that in two days after they came they were as bad as the old ones? That fellow, Tomlett, with two or three more that congregate at the Mermaid, have told them the whole tale. I can hardly get 'em on here since, after nightfall—though it's only to walk along the plateau and back again."

Mr. Thornycroft looked straight out before him. The supervisor noticed the grave change that had come to his face; and remembered that this, or some other superstitious fear, was said to have killed the late Mrs. Thornycroft. What with this story, what with the other deaths spoken of, taking their rise remotely or unremotely in the ghost, what with the uncomfortable feeling altogether that these things left on the mind in dark and lonely moments, Mr. Supervisor Kyne might have confessed, had he been honest enough, to not caring to stay himself on the plateau at night. But for this fact, the place would have been better guarded, since his men, in spite of the ghost, must have remained on duty.

"Do you happen to know a little inlet of a spot lying near to Jutpoint?" asked Mr. Thornycroft. "They say that used to be famous for smuggling in the old days. If any is carried on still—a thing to be doubted—there's where you must look for it."

"Ay, I've heard before of that place," remarked the supervisor. "They say it's quiet enough now."

"I should have supposed most places were," said the justice, a mocking intonation again in his tone, which rather told on the ears it was meant for. "We revert to smuggling now as a thing of the past, not the present. What fortunes were made at it!"

"And lost," said the supervisor.

Mr. Thornycroft shrugged his shoulders. "Were they? Through bad management, then. Before that exposure of the custom-house frauds, both merchants and officers lined their pockets. And do still, no doubt."

They were slowly walking together, side by side on the brow of the plateau, as they talked. Mr. Thornycroft stole a glance at his companion. The supervisor's face was composed and cold; nothing to be gathered from it.

"It has its charms, no doubt, this cheating of the revenue," resumed the justice. "Were I a custom-house officer, and had the opportunity offered me, I might be tempted to embrace it. Look at the toil of these men—yours, for example—work, work, work and responsibility perpetually; and then look at the miserable pittance of pay. Why, a man may serve (and generally does) until he's fifty years of age, before he has enough salary doled out to him to keep his family in decent comfort."

"That's true," was the answer; "it keeps many of us from marrying. It has kept me."

"Just so. One can't wonder that illegitimate practices are considered justifiable. The world in its secret conscience exonerates you, I can tell you that, Mr. Supervisor."

Mr. Supervisor walked along, measuring his steps, as if in thought; but he did not answer.

"Why, how can it be otherwise?" continued the magistrate, warming with his subject and his sympathy. "Put the case before us for a moment as it used to be put. A merchant—Mr. Brown, let us say—has extensive dealings with continental countries, and imports largely. Every ship-load that comes for him must pay a duty of four hundred pounds, more or less, to the customs. Brown speaks to the examining officer' 'You wink at this ship-load, don't see it; and we'll divide the duty between us; you put two hundred in your pocket, and I'll put two.' Who is there among us that would not accede? Not many. It enables the poor, ill-paid gentleman to get a few comforts; and he does it."

"Yes; that is how many have been tempted."

"And I say we cannot blame them. No man with a spark of humanity within his breast could give blame. Answer for yourself, Kyne: were it possible that such a proposal could be made to you in these days, would you not fall in with it?"

"No," said the officer, in a low but decisive tone "I should not."

"No?" repeated Mr. Thornycroft, staring at him.

"It killed my father."

Mr. Thornycroft did not understand. The supervisor, looking straight before him as if he were seeing past events in the distance, explained, in a voice that was no louder than a whisper.

"He was tempted exactly as you have described; and yielded. When the exposures took place at the London Customs, he was one of the officers implicated, and made his escape abroad. There he died, yearning for the land to which he could not return. The French doctors said that unsatisfied yearning killed him; he had no other discoverable malady."

"What a curious thing!" exclaimed Mr. Thornycroft.

"There were some private, unhappy circumstances mixed with it. One was, that his wife would not share in his exile. I could not, I had already a place in the Customs. Just before he died I went over, and he extorted a solemn promise from me never to do as he had done. I never shall. No inducement possible to be offered would tempt me."

"It is a complete answer to the supposititious case propounded," said the justice, laughing pleasantly.

"Supposititious, indeed!" remarked Mr. Kyne. "It could not occur in these days."

"Certainly not. And therefore your theory of present smuggling must explode. I must be going. Will you come in to-night and dine with us, Kyne? Copp is coming, and a few more. We've got the finest turbot, the finest barrel of natives you ever tasted."

Inclination led Mr. Supervisor Kyne one way, duty another. He thought he ought not to accept it; the dinners at the Red Court were always prolonged until midnight at least, and his men would be safe to go off the watch. But—a prime turbot! and all the rest of it! Mr. Kyne's mouth watered.

"Thank you, sir; I'll come."

The evening dinner-gathering took place. Mr. Kyne and others, invited to attend it, assembled in the usual unceremonious fashion, and were very jolly to a late hour. Miss Thornycroft and Anna sat down to table, quitting the gentlemen as soon as dinner was over. Ladies, as a rule, were never invited to these feasts, but if Miss Thornycroft appeared at table, the justice had no objection to her asking a companion to join her. Generally speaking, however, her dinner on these occasions was served to her alone.

"My darling, I am unable to take you home tonight; I—I cannot leave my friends," whispered Isaac, finding himself by a happy chance alone with Anna. Going into the drawing-room for a minute, he found his sister had temporarily left it to get a book.

"Sarah is coming for me."

"Yes, I know."

His arms pressed jealously round her for the first time since they parted, his face laid on hers, he took from her lips a shower of impassioned kisses. Only for a moment. The sweeping trail of Miss Thornycroft's silk dress was even then heard. When she entered, Anna sat leaning her brow upon her raised fingers; Isaac was leaving the room, carelessly humming a scrap of a song. Yes, it was an unsatisfactory life at best—a wife and no wife; a heavy secret to guard; apprehension always.

The days went on. Miss Thornycroft, defiantly pursuing her own will, directly disobeying her father's command, did not write to stop the arrival of her guests; and yet an opportunity offered her of doing so. I fully believe that these opportunities of escape from the path of evil are nearly always afforded once at least in every fresh temptation, if we would but recognise and seize upon them.

It wanted but two days to that of the expected arrival, when a hasty note was received from Miss Hunter saying she was prevented coming; it concluded with these words: "My brother is undecided what to do; he thinks you will not want him without me. Please drop him just one line; or if he does not hear he will take it for granted that you expect him."

There was an opportunity!—"Just one line," and Mary Anne Thornycroft would have had the future comfort of knowing that she had (in substance at least) obeyed her father.

But she did not send it.

CHAPTER VI

The Half-moon Beach

Dodging about between the village and the Red Court Farm, went Miss Thornycroft. Her mind was not at rest. The day on which she had expected her guests—or rather, one of them—had passed. It was on Saturday; here was Monday passing, and nobody had come. Each time the omnibus had arrived from Jutpoint, the young lady had not been far off. It had not brought anybody in whom she was interested. Forty-five minutes past three now; ten minutes more, and it would be in again. She was beginning to feel sick with emotional suspense.

But, for all this dodging, Miss Thornycroft was a lady; and when the wheels of the omnibus were at length heard, and it drew up at the Mermaid, she was at a considerable distance, apparently taking a cold stroll in the wintry afternoon. One passenger only got out; she could see that; and—was it Robert Hunter?

If so, he must be habited in some curious attire. Looking at him from this distance, he seemed to be all white and black. But, before he had moved a step; while he was inquiring (as might be inferred) the way to the Red Court Farm; the wild beating of Mary Ann Thornycroft's heart told her who it was.

They met quietly enough, shaking hands calmly while he explained that he had been unable to get away on Saturday. Miss Thornycroft burst into a fit of laughter at the coat, partly genuine, partly put on to hide her tell-tale emotion. It was certainly a remarkable coat; made of a smooth sort of white cloth, exceedingly heavy, and trimmed with black fur. The collar, the facings, the wrists and the back pockets had all a broad strip. He turned himself about for her inspection, laughing too.

"I fear I shall astonish the natives. But I never had so warm a coat in my life. I got it from the professor."

"From the professor!"

Mr. Hunter laughed. "Some crafty acquaintance of his, hard up, persuaded him into the purchase of two, money down, saying they had just come over from Russia—latest fashion. Perhaps they had; perhaps they are. The professor does not go in for fashion, but he cannot refuse a request made to him on the plea of unmerited poverty, and all that. I happened to be at his house when he brought them home in a cab. You should have heard Mrs. Mac."

"I should have liked to," said Mary Anne.

"First of all she said she'd have the fellow taken up who had beguiled the professor into it; next she said she'd pledge them. It ended in the professor making me a present of one and keeping the other."

"And you are going to sport it here!"

"Better here than in London; as a beginning. I thought it a good opportunity to get reconciled to myself in it. I should like to see the professor there when he goes out in his."

"They must have taken you for somebody in the train."

"Yes," said Mr. Hunter. "I and an old lady and gentleman had the carriage to ourselves all the way. She evidently took me for a lord; her husband for a card-sharper. But I think I shall like the coat."

Opinions might differ upon it—as did those of the old couple in the train. It was decidedly a handsome coat in itself, and had probably cost as much as the professor gave for it; but, taken in conjunction with its oddity, some might not have elected to be seen wearing it. Mr. Hunter had brought no other; his last year's coat was much worn, and he had been about to get another when this came in his way.

"And what about Susan?" Miss Thornycroft asked.

"Susan is in Yorkshire. Her aunt—to whom she was left when my mother died—was taken ill, and sent for her. I do not suppose Susan will return to London."

"Not at all?"

Mr. Hunter thought not. 'It would be scarcely worth while; she was to have gone home in March."

Thus talking, they reached the Red Court Farm. When its inmates saw him arrive, his portmanteau carried behind by a porter, they were thunderstruck. Mr. Thornycroft scarcely knew which to stare at most, him or his coat. Mary Anne introduced him with characteristic equanimity. Richard vouchsafed no greeting in his stern displeasure, but the justice, a gentleman at heart, hospitably inclined always, could do no less than bid him welcome. Cyril, quiet and courteous, shook hands with him; and later, when Isaac came in, he grasped his hand warmly.

There is no doubt that the learning he was a connexion of Anna Chester's (it could not be called a relative) tended to smooth matters. As the days passed on, Mr. Hunter grew upon their liking; for his own sake he proved to be an agreeable companion; and even Richard fell into civility—an active, free, pleasant-mannered young fellow, as the justice called him, who made himself at home indoors and out.

Never, since the bygone days at Katterley, had Robert Hunter deserved the character; but in this brief holiday he could but give himself up to his perfect happiness. He made excursions to Jutpoint; he explored the cliffs; he went in at will to Captain Copp's and the other houses on the heath; he put out to sea with the fishermen in the boats; he talked to the wives in their huts: everybody soon knew Robert Hunter, and especially his coat, which had become the marvel of Coastdown; a few admiring it—a vast many abusing it.

Miss Thornycroft was his frequent companion, and they went out unrestrained. It never appeared to have crossed the mind of Mr. Thornycroft or his sons as being within the bounds of possibility that this struggling young engineer, who was not known to public repute as an engineer at all, could presume to be thinking of Mary Anne, still less that she could think of him; otherwise they had been more cautious. Anna Chester was out with them sometimes, Cyril on occasion; but they rambled about for the most part alone in the cold and frost, their spirits light as the rarefied air.

The plateau and its superstition had no terror for Mr. Hunter, rather amusement: but that he saw—and saw with surprise—it was a subject of gravity at the Red Court, he might have made fun of it. Mary Anne confessed to him that she did not understand the matter; her brothers were reticent even to discourtesy. That some mystery was at the bottom of it Mr. Hunter could not fail to detect, and was content to bury all allusion to the superstition.

He stood with Miss Thornycroft on the edge of the plateau one bright morning—the brightest they had had. It was the first time he had been so far, for Mary Anne had never gone beyond the railings. Not the slightest fear had she; for the matter of that, nobody else had in daylight; but she knew that her father did not like to see her there. In small things, when they did not cross her own will, the young lady could be obedient.

"I can see how dangerous it would be here on a dark night," observed Robert Hunter in answer to something she had been saying, as he drew a little back from the edge, over which he had been cautiously leaning to take his observations. "Mary Anne! I never in all my life saw a place so convenient for smuggling as that Half-moon below. I daresay it has seen plenty of it."

Before she could make any rejoinder Mr. Kyne came strolling up to them in a brown study, and they shook hands. Robert Hunter had dined with him at the Red Court.

"I was telling Miss Thornycroft that the place below looks as if it had been made for the convenience of smuggling," began Robert Hunter. "Have you much trouble here?"

"No; but I am in hopes of it," was the reply. And it so completely astonished Mr. Hunter, who had spoken in a careless manner, without real meaning, as we all do sometimes, that he turned sharply round and looked at the supervisor.

"I thought the days of smuggling were over."

"Not yet, here—so far as I believe," replied Mr. Kyne. "We have information that smuggling to an extent is carried on somewhere on this coast, and this is the most likely spot for it that I can discover. I heard of this suspicion soon after I was appointed to Coastdown, and so kept my eyes open; but never, in spite of my precautions, have I succeeded in dropping on the wretches. I don't speak of paltry packets of tobacco and sausage-skins of brandy, which the fishermen, boarding strange craft, contrive to stow about their ribs, but of more serious cargoes. I would almost stake my life that not a mile distant from this place there lies hidden a ton-load of lace, rich and costly as ever flourished at the Court of St. James."[2]

[Footnote 2: This was just before the late alteration in the Customs' import laws, when the duty on lace and other light articles was large: making the smuggling of them into England a clever and enormously profitable achievement, when it could be accomplished with impunity.]

Robert Hunter thought the story sounded about as likely as that of the ghost. The incredulous, amused light in his eye caused Mary Anne to laugh.

"Where can it be hidden?" she asked of the supervisor. "There's no place."

"I wish I could tell you where, Miss Thornycroft."

Anything but inclined to laugh did he appear himself. The fact was, Mr. Kyne was growing more fully confirmed in his opinion day by day, and had come out this morning determined to do something. Circumstances were occurring to baffle all his precautions, and he felt savage. His policy hitherto had been secrecy, henceforth he meant to speak of the matter openly, and see what that would do. It was very singular—noted hereafter—that Robert Hunter and this young lady should have been the first who fell in his way after the resolution to speak was taken. But no doubt the remark with which Mr. Hunter greeted him surprised him into it.

"But surely you do not think, Mr. Kyne, that boat-loads of lace are really run here!" exclaimed Robert Hunter.

"I do think it. If not in this precise spot,"—pointing with his finger to the Half-moon beach underneath— "somewhere close to it. There's only one thing staggers me—if they run their cargoes there, where can they stow it away? I have walked about there"—advancing to the edge cautiously and looking down— "from the time the tide went off the narrow path, leading to it round the rocks, until it came in again, puzzling over the problem, and peering with every eye I had."

"Peering?"

"Yes. We have heard of caves and other hiding-places being concealed in rocks," added the supervisor, doggedly; "why not in these? I cannot put it out of my head that there's something of the sort here; it's getting as bad to me as a haunting dream."

"It would be charming to find it!" exclaimed Mary Anne. "A cave in the rocks! Ah, Mr. Kyne, it is too good to be true. We shall never have so romantic a discovery at Coastdown."

"If such a thing were there, I should think you would have no difficulty in discovering it," said Mr. Hunter.

"I have found it difficult," returned Mr. Kyne, snappishly, as if certain remembrances connected with the non-finding did not soothe him. "There's only one thing keeps me from reporting the suspicions at head quarters."

"And that is—?"

"The doubt that it may turn out nothing after all."

"Oh, then, you are not so sure; you have no sufficient grounds to go upon," quickly rejoined Mr. Hunter, with a smile that nettled the other.

"Yes, I have grounds," he returned, somewhat incautiously perhaps, in his haste to vindicate himself. "We had information a short time back," he continued after a pause, as he dropped his voice to a low key "that a boat-load of something—my belief is, it's lace—was waiting to come in. Every night for a fortnight, in the dark age of the moon, did I haunt this naked plateau on the watch, one man with me, others being within call. A very agreeable task it was, lying perdu on its edge, with my cold face just extended beyond!"

"And what was the result?" eagerly asked Mr. Hunter, who was growing interested in the narrative.

"Nothing was the result. I never saw the ghost of a smuggler or a boat approach the place. And the very first night I was off the watch, I have reason to believe the job was done."

"Which night was that?" inquired Miss Thornycroft.

"This day week, when I was dining at the Red Court. I had told my men to be on the look-out; but I had certainly told them in a careless sort of way, for the moon was bright again, and who was to suspect that they would risk it on a light night? They are bold sinners."

The customs officer was so earnest, putting, as was evident, so much faith in his own suspicions, that Robert Hunter insensibly began to go over to his belief. Why should cargoes of lace, and other valuable articles, not be run? he asked himself. They bore enough duty to tempt the risk, as they had borne it in the days gone by.

"How was it your men were so negligent?" he inquired.

"There's the devil of it!" cried the supervisor. "I beg your pardon, young lady; wrong words slip out inadvertently when one's vexed. My careless orders made the men careless, and they sat boozing at the

Mermaid. Young Mr. Thornycroft, it seems, happened to go in, saw them sitting there with some of his farm-labourers, and, in a generous fit, ordered them to call for what drink they liked. They had red eyes and shaky hands the next morning."

"How stupid of my brother!" exclaimed Mary Anne. "Was it Richard or Isaac?"

"I don't know. But all your family are too liberal: their purse is longer than their discretion. It is not the first time, by many, they have treated my fellows. I wish they would not do so."

There was a slight pause. Mr. Kyne resumed in a sort of halting tone, as if the words came from him in spite of his better judgment.

"The greatest obstacle I have to contend with in keeping the men to their duty on the plateau here, is the superstition connected with it. When a fellow is got on at night, the slightest movement—a night-bird flying overhead—will send him off again. Ah! they don't want pressing to stay drinking at the Mermaid or anywhere else. The fact is, Coastdown has not been kept to its duty for a long while. My predecessor was good-hearted and easy, and the men did as they liked."

"How many men do you count here?"

"Only three or four, and they can't be available all together; they must have some rest, turn on, turn off. There's a longish strip of coast to pace, too; the plateau's but a fleabite of it."

"And your theory is that the smugglers run their boats below here?" continued Robert Hunter, indicating the Half-moon beach.

"I think they do—that is, if they run them anywhere," replied Mr. Kyne, who was in a state of miserable doubt, between his firm convictions and the improbabilities they involved. "You see, there is nowhere else that privateer boats can be run to. There's no possibility of such a thing higher up, beyond that point to the right, and it would be nearly as impossible for them to land a cargo of contraband goods beyond the left point, in the face of all the villagers."

There was a silence. All three were looking below at the scrap of beach over the sharp edges of the jutting rocks, Miss Thornycroft held safe by Mr. Hunter. She broke it.

"But, as you observe, Mr. Kyne, where could they stow a cargo there, allowing that they landed one? There is certainly no opening or place for concealment in those hard, bare rocks, or it would have been discovered long ago. Another thing—suppose for a moment that they do get a cargo stowed away somewhere in the rocks, how are they to get it out again? There would be equal danger of discovery."

"So there would," replied Mr. Kyne. "I have thought of all these things myself till my head is muddled."

"Did you ever read Cooper's novels, Mr. Kyne?" resumed Miss Thornycroft. "Some of them would give you a vast deal of insight into these sort of transactions."

"No," replied the officer, with an amused look. "I prefer to get my insight from practice. I am pretty sharp-sighted," he added with complacency.

Robert Hunter had been weighing possibilities in his mind, and woke up as from sudden thought, turning to the supervisor.

"I should like to go down there and have a look at these rocks. My profession has taken me much amidst such places: perhaps my experience could assist you."

"Let us walk there now!" exclaimed the supervisor, seizing at the idea—"if not taking you out of your way, Miss Thornycroft."

"Oh, I should be delighted," was the young lady's reply. "I call it quite an adventure. Some fine moonlight night I shall come and watch here myself, Mr. Kyne."

"They don't do their work on a moonlight night. At least," he hastened to correct himself; with a somewhat crestfallen expression, "not usually. But after what happened recently, I shall mistrust a light night as much as a dark one."

"Are you sure," she inquired, standing yet within them on the plateau, "that a cargo was really landed the night you speak of?"

"I am not sure; but I have cause to suspect it."

"It must be an adventurous life," she remarked, "bearing its charms, no doubt."

"They had better not get caught," was the officer's rejoinder, delivered with professional gusto; "they would not find it so charming then."

"I thought the days of smuggling were over," observed Mr. Hunter: "except the more legitimate way of doing it through the very eyes and nose of the custom-house. Did you know anything personally of the great custom-house frauds, as they were called, when so many officers and merchants were implicated, some years ago?"

"I did. I held a subordinate post in the London office then, and was in the thick of the discoveries."

"You were not one of the implicated?" jestingly demanded Mr. Hunter.

"Why, no—or you would not see me here now. I was not sufficiently high in the service for it."

"Or else you might have been?"

"That's a home question," laughed Mr. Kyne. "I really cannot answer for what might have been. My betters were tempted to be."

He spoke without a cloud on his face; a different man now, from the one who had betrayed his family's past trouble to Justice Thornycroft. Not to this rising young engineer, attired in his fantastic coat, which the supervisor always believed must be the very height of ton and fashion in London; not to this handsome, careless, light-hearted girl, would he suffer aught of that past to escape. He could joke with them of the custom-house frauds, which had driven so many into exile, and one—at least, as he believed—to death. On the whole, it was somewhat singular that the topic should have been again started. Miss Thornycroft took up the thread with a laugh.

"There, Mr. Kyne! You acknowledge that you custom-house gentlemen are not proof against temptation, and yet you boast of looking so sharply after these wretched fishermen!"

"If the game be carried on here as I suspect, Miss Thornycroft, it is not wretched fishermen who have to do with it; except, perhaps, as subordinates."

"Let us go and explore the Half-moon beach below," again said Robert Hunter. Mr. Kyne turned to it at once: he had been waiting to do so. The engineer's experience might be valuable. He had had somewhat to do with rocks and land.

It was a short walk as they made their way down to the village, and thence to the narrow path winding round the projection of rock. The tide was out, so they shelved round it with dry feet, and ascended to the Half-moon beach. They paced about from one end of the place to the other, looking and talking. Nothing was to be seen; nothing; no opening, or sign of opening. The engineer had an umbrella in his hand, and he struck the rocks repeatedly: in one part in particular, it was just the middle of the Half-moon, he struck and struck, and returned to strike again.

"What do you find?" inquired Mr. Kyne.

"Not much. Only it sounds hollow just here."

They looked again: they stooped down and looked; they stood upon a loose stone and raised themselves to look; they pushed and struck at the part with all their might and main. No, nothing came of it.

"Did you ever see a more convenient spot for working the game?" cried the supervisor. "Look at those embedded stones down there, rising from the lower beach: the very things to moor a boat to."

"Who do you suspect does this contraband business?" inquired Robert Hunter.

"My suspicions don't fall particularly upon any one. There are no parties in the neighbourhood whom one could suspect, except the boatmen, and if the trade is pushed in the extensive way I think, they are not the guilty men. A week ago (more or less) they ran, as I tell you, one cargo; I know they did; and may I be shot this moment, if they are not ready to ran another! That's a paying game, I hope."

Ready to run another! The pulses of Mr. Kyne's hearers ran riot with excitement. This spice of adventure was intensely charming.

"How do you know they are?" asked Robert Hunter.

"By two or three signs. One of them, which I have no objection to mention, is that a certain queer craft is fond of cruising about here. Whenever I catch sight of her ugly sides, I know it bodes no good for her Majesty's revenue. She carries plausible colours, the hussey, and has, I doubt not, a double bottom, false as her colours. I saw her stern, shooting off at daybreak this morning, and should like to have had the overhauling of her."

"Can you not?"

"No. She is apparently on legitimate business."

"I thought that her Majesty could search any vessel, legitimate or illegitimate."

Again Mr. Kyne looked slightly crestfallen. "I boarded her with my men the last time she was here, and nothing came of it. She happened by ill-luck to be really empty, or we were not clever enough to unearth the fox."

The reminiscence was not agreeable to Mr. Kyne. The empty vessel had staggered him professionally; the reception he met with insulted him personally. Until the search was over, the captain, a round, broad Dutchman, had been civil, affording every facility to the revenue officers; but the instant the work was done, he ordered them out of the ship in his bad English, and promised a different reception if they ever came on it again. That was not all. The mate, another Dutchman, was handling a loaded pistol the whole time on full cock, and staring at the superintendent in a very strange manner. Altogether the remembrance was unpleasant.

The tide was coming up, and they had to quit the strip of beach while the road was open. Mr. Kyne wished them good morning and departed on his own way. Robert Hunter turned towards the plateau again, which surprised Miss Thornycroft. "Just for a minute or two," he urged.

They ascended it, and stood on the brow as before, Robert Hunter in deep thought. His face, now turned to the sea, now to the land, wore a business-like expression.

"We are now standing exactly above the middle of the rocks on the Half-moon beach below," he remarked presently, "just where they had a hollow sound."

"Yes," she replied.

"And the Red Court, as you see, lies off in a straight line. It is a good thing your father lives there, Mary Anne."

"Why?"

"Because if suspicious persons inhabited it, I should say that house might have something to do with the mystery. If Kyne's conclusions are right—that smuggled goods are landed on the beach below, they must be stowed away in the rocks; although the ingress is hidden from the uninitiated. Should this be really the case, depend upon it there is some passage, some communication, in these rocks to an egress inland."

"But what has that to do with our house?" inquired Mary Anne, wonderingly.

"These old castles, lying contiguous to the coast, are sure to have subterranean passages underneath, leading to the sea. Many an escape has been made that way in time of war, and many an ill-fated prisoner has been so conducted to the waves, and put out of sight for ever. Were I your father, I would institute a search. He might come upon the hoarding-place of the smugglers."

"But the smugglers cannot get to their caverns and passages through our house!"

"Of course not. There must be some other opening. How I should like to drop upon the lads!"

Mr. Hunter spoke with animation. Such a discovery presented a tempting prospect, and he walked across the plateau as one who has got a new feather stuck in his cap. In passing the Round Tower, he turned aside to it, and stepped in through the opening. He found nothing there that could be converted into suspicion by the most lively imagination. The worn grass beneath the feet was all genuine; the circular wall, crumbling away, had stood for ages. Satisfied, so far, they crossed the railings on their way home.

Mr. Thornycroft was in the dining-room writing a note; Richard, who had apparently just stepped in to ask a question, held a gun; Cyril lay back in an easy-chair, reading. When Mary Anne and their gentleman guest burst in upon them with eager excitement, the one out-talking the other, it was rather startling.

"Such an adventure! Papa, did you know we probably have smugglers on the coast here?"

"Have you ever explored underneath your house, sir, under the old ruins of the castle? There may be a chain of subterranean passages and vaults conducting from here to the sea."

"Not common smugglers, papa, the poor tobacco-and-brandy sailors, but people in an extensive way. Boat-loads of lace they land."

"If it be as the man suspects, there may be often a rare booty there. There may be one at this very moment; I would lay any money there is," added Robert Hunter, improving upon the idea in his excitement. "Mr. Richard, will you bet a crown with me?"

The words had been poured forth so rapidly by both, that it would seem their hearers were powerless to interrupt. Yet the effect they produced was great. Cyril started upright, and let his book drop on his knees; Mr. Thornycroft pushed his glasses to the top of his brow, an angry paleness giving place to his healthy, rosy colour; while Richard, more demonstrative, dashed the gun on the carpet and broke into an ugly oath. The justice was the first to find his tongue.

"What absurd treason are you talking now? You are mad, Mary Anne."

"It is not treason at all, sir," replied Mr. Hunter, regarding Richard with surprise. "It is a pretty well ascertained fact that contraband goods are landed and housed in the rocks at the Half-moon. It will be loyalty, instead of treason, if we can contrive to lay a trap and catch the traitors."

Richard Thornycroft moved forward as if to strike the impetuous speaker. It would seem that one of the fits of passion he was liable to was coming on. Cyril, calm and cool, placed himself across his brother's path.

"Be quiet, Richard," he said, in a tone that savoured of authority; "stay you still. Where did you pick up this cock-and-bull story?" he demanded with light mockery of Robert Hunter.

"We had it from the supervisor. He has suspected ever since he came, he says, that this station was favoured by smugglers, and now he is sure of it. One cargo they landed a few days ago, and there's another dodging off the coast, waiting to come in. He intends to drop upon that."

"It is a made-up lie!" foamed Richard. "The fellow talks so to show his zeal. I'll tell him so. Smuggled goods landed here!"

"Well, lie or no lie, you need not fly in a passion over it," said Mary Anne. "It is not our affair."

"Then, if it is not our affair, what business have you interfering in it?" retorted Richard. "Interpose your authority, sir, and forbid her to concern herself with men's work," he added, turning sharply to his father. "No woman would do it who retains any sense of shame."

"Miss Thornycroft has done nothing unbecoming a lady," exclaimed Mr. Hunter, in a tone of wonder. "You forget that you are speaking to your sister, Mr. Richard. What can you mean?"

"Oh, he means nothing," said Mary Anne, "only he lets his temper get the better of his tongue. One would think, Richard, you had something to do with the smugglers, by your taking it up in this way," she pursued, in a spirit of aggravation. "And, indeed, it was partly your fault that they got their last cargo in."

"Explain yourself," said Cyril to his sister, pushing his arm before Richard's mouth.

"It was a night when we had a dinner party here," she pursued. "Mr. Kyne was here; the only night he had been off the watch for a fortnight, he says. But he left orders with his men to look out, and Richard got treating them to drink at the Mermaid, and they never looked. So the coast was clear, and the smugglers got their goods in."

Cyril burst into a pleasant laugh. "Ah, ha!" said he, "new brooms sweep clean. Mr. Superintendent Kyne is a fresh hand down here, so he thinks he must trumpet forth his fame as a keen officer—that he may be all the more negligent by-and-bye, you know. None but a stranger, as you are, Mr. Hunter, could have given ear to it."

"I have given both ear and belief," replied Robert Hunter, firmly; "and I have offered Mr. Kyne the benefit of my engineering experience to help him discover whether there is or is not a secret opening in the rocks."

"You have!" exclaimed Justice Thornycroft. He glared on Robert Hunter as he asked the question. From quite the first until now he had been bending over his note, leaving the discussion to them.

"To be sure I have, sir. I have been with him now, on the Half-moon, sounding them; but I had only an umbrella, and that was of little use. We are going to-morrow better prepared. It strikes me the mystery lies right in the middle. It sounds hollow there. I will do all I can to help him, that the fellows may be brought to punishment."

"Sir!" cried the old justice, in a voice of thunder, rising and sternly confronting Robert Hunter, "I forbid it. Do you understand? I forbid it. None under my roof shall take act or part in this."

"But justice demands it," replied Mr. Hunter, after a pause. "It behoves all loyal subjects of her Majesty to aid in discovering the offenders: especially you, sir, a sworn magistrate."

"It behoves me to protect the poor fishermen, who look to me for protection, who have looked to me for it for years; ay, and received it," was the warm reply, "better than it behoves you, sir, to presume to teach me my duty! Richard, leave me to speak. I tell you, sir, I do not believe this concocted story. I am the chief of the place, sir, and I will not believe it. The coast-guard and the fishermen are at variance; always have been; and I will not allow the poor fellows to be traduced and put upon, treated as if they were thieves and rogues. Neither I nor mine shall take part in it; no, nor any man who is under my roof eating the bread of friendliness. I hope you hear me, sir."

Robert Hunter stood confounded. All his golden visions of discoveries, that should make his name famous and put feathers in his cap, were vanishing into air. But the curious part was the justice's behaviour; that struck him as being very strange, not to say unreasonable.

"It is not the first time, sir, that the coast-guard have tried it on," pursued Mr. Thornycroft. "When the last superintendent was appointed, Dangerfield, he took something of the sort in his head, and came to me to assist him in an investigation. 'Investigate for yourself,' I said to him. 'I shall not aid you to tarnish the characters of the fishermen.' It may be presumed that his investigation did not come to much," was the ironical conclusion; "since I heard no more about the smugglers from him all the years he was stationed here."

"And you think, sir, that Mr. Kyne is also mistaken?" cried Robert Hunter, veering round.

"What I think, and what I do not think, you may gather from my words," was the haughty reply. "I tell you that no man living under my roof shall encourage by so much as a word, let alone an act, anything of the sort. Mr. Kyne can pursue his own business without us."

"If it were one of my own brothers who did so, I would shoot him dead," said Richard, with a meaning touch at his gun. "So I warn him."

"And commit murder?' echoed Robert Hunter, who did not admire this semi-threat of Richard's.

"It would not be murder, sir; it would be justifiable homicide," interposed the justice, rather to Robert Hunter's surprise. "When I was a young man, a guest abused my father's hospitality. My brother challenged him. They went out with their seconds, and my brother shot him. That was not murder."

"But, papa, that must have been a different thing altogether," said Mary Anne, who had stood transfixed at the turn the conversation was taking. "It—"

"To your room, Miss Thornycroft! To your room, I say!" cried the passionate justice, pushing her from him. "Would you beard my authority? Things are coming to a pretty pass."

It was a stormy ending to a stormy interview. Confused and terrified, Mary Anne Thornycroft hastened up and burst into tears in her chamber. Richard strode away with his gun; Cyril followed him; and the justice bent over his writing again quietly, as though nothing had happened.

As for Robert Hunter he felt entirely amazed. Of course, putting it as the justice had put it, he felt bound in honour not to interfere further, and would casually tell Mr. Kyne so on the first opportunity, giving no reason why. Pondering over the matter as he strolled out of doors uncomfortably, he came to the conclusion that Mr. Thornycroft must be self-arrogant, both as a magistrate and a man: one of the old-world sort, who jog on from year's end to year's end, seeing no abuses, and utterly refusing to reform them when seen.

CHAPTER VII

My Lady at the Red Court

At the end window of the corridor, looking towards the church and village, stood Mary Anne Thornycroft. Not yet had she recovered the recent stormy interview, and a resentful feeling in regard to it was rife within her. The conduct of her father and eldest brother appeared to have been so devoid of all reason in itself, and so gratuitously insulting to Robert Hunter, that Mary Anne, in the prejudice of her love for him, was wishing she could pay them off. It is the province of violent and unjust opposition to turn aside its own aim, just as it is the province of exaggeration to defeat itself; and Miss Thornycroft, conning over and over again in her mind the events of the day, wilfully persuaded herself that Mr. Kyne was right, her father wrong, and that smuggling of lace, or anything else that was valuable, was carried on under (as may be said) the very face and front of their supine house.

Cyril came up the stairs—his book in his hand—saw her standing there, and came to her side. The short winter's day was already verging towards twilight, and the house seemed intensely still.

"Is it not a shame?" exclaimed Mary Anne, as Cyril put his arm about her.

"Is what not a shame? That the brightness of the day is gone?"

"You know!" she passionately exclaimed. "Where's the use of attempting subterfuge with me, Cyril? Cyril, on my word I thought for the moment that papa and Richard must have gone suddenly mad."

In Cyril Thornycroft's soft brown eyes, thrown out to the far distance, there was a strange look of apprehension, as if they saw an unwelcome thing approaching. Something was approaching in fact, but not quite in sight yet. He had a mild, gentle face; his temper was of the calmest, his voice sweet and low. And yet Cyril seemed to have a great care ever upon him;—his mother, whom he so greatly resembled, used to have the same. He was the only one of her children who, as yet, had profited much by her counsel and monition. In the last few years of her life her earnest daily efforts had been directed to draw her children to God, and on Cyril they had borne fruit.

In the German schools, to which he had been sent, in the Oxford University life that succeeded, Cyril Thornycroft had walked unscathed amidst the surging sea of surrounding sins and perils. Whatever temptation might assail him, he seemed, in the language of one who watched his career, only to come out of them more fit for God. Self-denying, walking not to do his own will, remembering always that he had been bought with a price and had a Master to serve, Cyril Thornycroft's daily life was one of patient endurance of a great inward suffering, and of active kindness. Where he could do good he did it; when others were tempted to say a harsh word he said a kind one. He had been brought up to no profession;

his inclination led him to go into the Church; but some motive, of which he never spoke, seemed to hold him back. Meanwhile Mr. Thornycroft appeared quite content to let him stay on at the Red Court in idleness—idleness as the world called it. Save that he read a great deal, Cyril did no absolute work; but many in Coastdown blessed him. In sickness of body, in suffering of mind, there by the bed-side might be found Cyril Thornycroft, reading from the Book of Life—talking of good things in his low, earnest voice; and sometimes—if we may dare to write it—praying. Dare! For it is the fashion of the world to deride such things when spoken of—possibly to deride them also in reality.

And now that is all that will be said. It was well to say it for the satisfaction of the readers, as will be found presently, even though but one of those readers may be walking in a similar earnest path, the world lying on one hand, heaven on the other.

"Courtesy is certainly due to Mr. Hunter, and I am sorry that my father and Richard forgot it," resumed Cyril. "When does he leave?"

"On Saturday," she answered, sullenly.

"Then—endeavour to let things go on peaceably until that time. Do not excite him by any helping word on your part to oppose home prejudices. Believe me, Mary Anne, my advice is good. Another such scene as there was to-day, and I should be afraid of the ending."

"What ending?"

"That Richard might turn him out of the house."

Miss Thornycroft tossed her head. "Richard would be capable of it."

"Let us have peace for the rest of his sojourn here, forgetting this morning's episode. And—Mary Anne—do not ask him to prolong his visit beyond Saturday."

He looked with kindly earnestness into her eyes for a moment as if wishing to give impression to the concluding words, and then left her to digest them: which Miss Thornycroft was by no means inclined to do pleasantly. She was picking up the notion that she would be required to give way to her brothers on all occasions; here was even Cyril issuing his orders now! Not ask Robert Hunter to stay over Saturday!—when her whole heart had been set upon his doing it!

Playing with her neck-chain, tossing it hither and thither, she at length saw Robert Hunter come strolling home from the village, his air listless, his steps slow; just like a man who is finding time heavy on his hands.

"And not one of them to be with him!" came her passionate thought. "It is a shame. Bears! Why! who's this?"

The exclamation—cutting short the complimentary epithet on her brothers, though it could not apply with any sort of justice to Cyril, who had been prevented by his father from following Robert Hunter—related to a Jutpoint fly and pair. Driving in at the gates, it directly faced Mary Anne Thornycroft; she bent her eyes to peer into it, and started with surprise.

"Good gracious! What can bring her here?"

For she recognised Lady Ellis; with a maid beside her. And yet, in that pale, haggard, worn woman, who seemed scarcely able to sit upright, there was not much trace of the imperious face of her who had made for so brief a period the Red Court her home. Illness—long-continued illness, its termination of necessity fatal—changes both the looks and the spirit.

The chaise had passed Robert Hunter at right angles: had my lady recognised him?

But a moment must be given to Cyril. On descending the stairs, he saw Richard striding out at the front door, and hastened after him.

"Where are you going, Richard?"

"Where am I going?" retorted Richard. "To Tomlett's, if you must know. Something must be done."

Cyril laid his calm hand on his brother's restless one, and led him off towards the plateau.

"Do nothing, Richard. You are hasty and incautious. They cannot make any discovery."

"And that fellow talking of going to sound the rocks, with his boasted engineering experience?"

"Let him go. If the square sounds as hollow as his head, what then? They can make nothing else of it. No discovery can be made from the outside; you know it can not; and care must be taken that they don't get in."

"Perhaps you would not care if they did," spoke Richard in his unjust passion.

"You know better," said Cyril, sadly. "However I may have wished that certain circumstances did not exist, I would so far act with you now as to ward off discovery. I would give my life, Richard, to avert pain from you all, and disgrace from the Red Court's good name. Believe me, nothing bad will come of this, if you are only cautious. But your temper is enough to ruin all—to set Hunter's suspicions on you. You should have treated it derisively, jokingly, as I did."

Richard, never brooking interference, despising all advice, flung Cyril's arm aside, and turned off swearing, meeting Isaac, who was coming round by the plateau.

"Isaac, we are dropped upon."

"What?"

"We are dropped upon, I say."

"How? Who has done it?"

"That cursed fellow Mary Anne brought here—Hunter. He and Kyne have been putting their heads together; and, by all that's true, they have hit it hard. They had got up a suspicion of the rocks; been sounding the square rock, and found it hollow. Kyne has scented the cargo that's lying off now."

The corners of Isaac Thornycroft's mouth fell considerably. "We must get that in," he exclaimed. "It is double the usual value."

"I wish Hunter and the gauger were both hanging from the cliffs together!" was Richard's charitable conclusion, as he strode onwards. "It was a bad day's work for us when they moved Dangerfield. I'm on my way now to consult with Tomlett; will you come?"

Isaac turned with him. Bearing towards the plateau, but leaving it to the right—a road to the village rarely taken by any but the Thornycroft family, as indeed nobody else had a right to take it, the waste land belonging to Mr. Thornycroft—they went on to Tomlett's, meeting Mr. Kyne en route, with whom Isaac, sunny-mannered ever, exchanged a few gay words.

Cyril meanwhile strolled across the lawn as far as the railings, and watched them away. He was deep in thought; his eyes were sadder than usual, his high, square brow was troubled.

"If this incident could but turn out a blessing!" he half murmured. "Acted upon by the fear of discovery through Kyne's suspicions, if my father would but make it a plea for bringing things to a close, while quiet opportunity remains to him! But for Richard he would have done so, as I believe, long ago."

Turning round at the sound of wheels, Cyril saw the fly drive in. Reaching it as it drew up to the door, he recognised his stepmother. Mary Anne came out, and they helped her to alight. Hyde, every atom of surprise he possessed showing itself in his countenance, flung wide the great door. She leaned on Cyril's arm, and walked slowly. Her cheeks were hollow, her black eyes were no longer fierce, but dim; her gown sat about her thin form in folds.

"My dears, I thought your father would have had the carriage waiting for me at Jutpoint."

"My dears!" from the once cold and haughty Lady Ellis! It was spoken in a meek, loving tone, too. Mary Anne glanced at Cyril.

"I am sure my father knew nothing of your intended arrival," spoke Cyril; "otherwise some of us would certainly have been at Jutpoint."

"I wrote to tell him; he ought to have had the letter this morning. I have been a little better lately, Cyril; not really better, I know that, but more capable of exertion; and I thought I should like to have a look at you all once again. I stayed two days in London for rest, and wrote yesterday."

She passed the large drawing-rooms, and turned of her own accord into the small comfortable apartment that was formerly the school-room, and now the sitting-room of Mary Anne. Cyril drew an easy-chair to the fire, and she sat down in it, letting her travelling wraps fall from her. Sinnett, who had come in not less amazed than Hyde, picked them up.

"You are surprised to see me, Sinnett."

"Well—yes, I am, my lady," returned Sinnett, who did not add that she was shocked also. "I am sorry to see you looking so poorly."

"I have come for a few days to say good-bye to you all. You can take my bonnet as well."

Sinnett went out with the things. It was found afterwards that the letter, which ought to have announced her arrival, was delayed by some error on the part of the local carrier. It was delivered in the evening.

As she sat there facing the light, the ravages disease was making showed themselves all too plainly in her wasted countenance. In frame she was a very skeleton, her hands were painfully thin, her black silk gown hung in folds on her shrunken bosom. Mary Anne put a warm foot-stool under her feet, and wrapped a shawl about her shoulders; Cyril brought a glass of wine, which she drank.

"I have to take a great deal of it now, five or six glasses a day, and all kinds of strengthening nourishment," she said. "Thank you, Cyril. Sometimes I lie and think of those poor people whose case is similar to mine, and who cannot get it."

How strange the words sounded from her! Thinking for others! Miss Thornycroft, remembering her in the past, listened in a sort of amused incredulity, but a light as of some great gladness shone in the eyes of Cyril.

As he left the room to search for his father, who had gone out, Robert Hunter entered it. Seeing a stranger there, an apparent invalid, he was quitting it again hastily when Mary Anne arrested him.

"You need not go, Robert; it is my stepmother, Lady Ellis. Mr. Hunter."

At the first moment not a trace could he find of the handsome, haughty-faced woman who had beguiled him with her charms in the days gone by. Not a charm was left. She had left off using adjuncts, and her face was almost yellow; its roundness of contour had gone; the cheeks were hollow and wrinkled, the jaws angular. Only by the eyes, as they flashed for a moment into his with a sort of dismayed light, did he recognise her. Bowing coldly, he would have retreated, but she, recovering herself instantly, held out her hand.

"No wonder you have forgotten me; I am greatly changed."

Mary Anne Thornycroft looked on with astonishment. Had they ever met before?

"Yes," said Lady Ellis; "but he was mostly called Mr. Lake then."

A flush dyed Robert Hunter's brow. "I threw off the name years ago, when I threw off other things," he said.

"What other things did you throw off?" quickly asked Mary Anne.

"Oh, many," was the careless answer; "frivolity and idleness, amidst them."

Perhaps he remembered that his manner and words, in the view of that wasted face and form, were needlessly ungracious, for his tone changed; he sat down, and said he was sorry to see her looking ill.

"I have been ill now for a long while; I must have been ill when I knew you," she said; "that is, the disease was within me, but I did not suspect it. Had I taken heed of the symptoms, slight though they were and for that cause entirely unheeded, perhaps something might have been done for me; I don't know. As it is, I am slowly dying."

"I hope not," he said, n his humanity.

"You cannot hope it, Mr. Hunter. Look at me!"

Very true. Had she been all the world to him—had his whole happiness depended on his keeping her in life, he could not have hoped it. With her wan face, and eyes glistening with that peculiar glaze that tells of coming death; with her thin frame and deep, quick breath, that seemed to heave the body of her gown as though a furnace-bellows were underneath, there could be no thought of escape from the portals that were opening for her. As she sat before him leaning in the chair, the shawl thrown back from her chest, Robert Hunter looked at her and knew it.

There ensued a silence. He did not answer, and Mary Anne was much wondering at this suddenly-discovered past intimacy, never spoken of by either to her, and resenting it after the manner of women. The fire flickered its blaze aloft; the twilight deepened; but it was not yet so dark but that the plateau was distinct, and also the figure of the preventive man at the edge, pacing it. Lady Ellis suddenly broke the stillness.

"Do the people believe in the ghost still, Mary Anne?"

"I suppose so. There has been no change that I know of."

"I meant—has anything been discovered?"

Mary Anne Thornycroft lifted her eyes. "How do you mean, discovered? What is there to discover?"

"Not anything, I dare say," she said. "But it used to strike me as very singular—this superstitious belief in these enlightened times—and a feeling was always on my mind that something would occur to explain it away. Have you heard of it?" she asked, directing her eyes to Robert Hunter.

"Somewhat. There is a difficulty, I hear, in keeping the preventive men on the plateau after dusk. What it is they precisely fear, I do not know."

"Neither did I ever know," she observed, dreamily. "The curious part of it to me always was, that Mr. Thornycroft and his sons appeared to fear it."

Before Miss Thornycroft, who sat in silence, the subject was not pursued. Lady Ellis started a more open one, and inquired after Mrs. Chester.

"She is living in Paris," said Robert Hunter. "At least—she has been living there; but I am not sure that she is still. A few days ago I had a letter from her, in which she said she was about to change her residence to Brussels."

He did not add that the letter was one of Mrs. Chester's usual ones—complaining grievously of hard times, and the impossibility of "getting along." Somehow she seemed not to be able to do that anywhere. She had two hundred a year, and was always plunging into schemes to increase her income. They would turn out well at first, according to her report, promising nothing less than a speedy fortune; and then would come a downfall. In this recent letter, she had implored of Robert Hunter to "lend" her fifty pounds to set her going in Brussels, to which capital she was on the wing, with an excellent opportunity of establishing a first-class school. He sent the money, never expecting to see it again.

"Are her children with her?" questioned Lady Ellis.

"Only Fanny. The boys are at school in England. And Anna—you remember Anna?"

"I should think I do, poor girl. The slave of the whole house."

"Anna is here on a visit."

"Here!"

"I mean at Coastdown. She is staying with a Captain and Mrs. Copp, who are some slight relatives of hers."

"I have thought of Anna as teacher in a school. Mrs. Chester said she should place her in one."

"She is a teacher. This visit is only a temporary one, prolonged on account of Anna's health. She was with Miss Jupp."

With the last word, all the reminiscences, as connected with that lady's name and the past, rose up in the mind of Robert Hunter—of a certain Christmas-day, when Mary Jupp had brought some shame home to him: perhaps also to her of the faded face sitting opposite. It brought shame to him still; but, seeing that faded face, he was vexed to have inadvertently mentioned it.

"Mary Anne, I think I will go to my room. The fire must have burnt up now. No, don't come with me; I would be quiet for a little while."

As she got up from the chair, she staggered. Robert Hunter, who was crossing the room to open the door for her, stopped and offered his arm. He could do no less in common pity: but the time had been when he registered a mental vow that never again should the arm of that woman rest within his.

"Thank you: just to the foot of the stairs. I have but little strength left, and the journey to-day has temporarily taken away that. Are you getting on well in your profession, Mr. Hunter?"

"Oh, yes. My prospects are very fair."

Sinnett happened to be in the hall; her mistress called to her, took her arm, and quitted that of Robert Hunter. He returned to Mary Anne, who was rather sulky still. What with the scene in the afternoon, with the unexpected and not over-welcome appearance of her stepmother, and with this mysterious acquaintanceship, about which nothing had been said to her, the young lady was not in so amiable a mood as usual.

"When did you know Lady Ellis?" she abruptly began after an interval of silence. "And where?"

"Some years ago; she was staying, for a few months with my half-sister, Mrs. Chester, at Guild."

"At Guild; yes, I know; I saw her there when I went over with papa. But I was not aware that you were intimate there."

Robert Hunter had never spoken of that past time in any way to Mary Anne. It happened that Anna Chester had not.

"I went over to Guild sometimes. I was living at Katterley, seven miles off."

"Was that in your wife's time?"

"Yes."

"It is strange you never told me you knew my stepmother."

"It never occurred to me to tell you. Business matters have so entirely occupied my thoughts since, that those old days seem well-nigh blotted out of them."

"Were she and your wife great friends?"

"No. My wife did not like her."

Robert Hunter was standing at the window, looking out in the nearly faded twilight. He could not fail to perceive by the tone of her voice that Mary Anne was feeling displeased at something. But her better nature was returning to her, and she went and stood by him. He held out his arm, as he had done once or twice before when they were thus standing together: and she slipped her hand within it. The fire had burnt down to dulness, emitting scarcely any light: the preventive man could no longer be seen on the plateau.

"How dark it is getting, Robert!"

"Yes; but I think it will be a fine night. There's a star or two twinkling out."

Very, very conscious was each, as they stood there. In these silent moments, with the semi-darkness around, love, if it exists, must make itself felt. Love within, love around, love everywhere; the atmosphere teeming with it, the soul sick to trembling with its own bliss. It seemed to them that the beating of their own hearts was alone heard, and that too audibly. Thus they stood; how long it was hard to say. The room grew darker, the stars came out clearer. The softness of the hour was casting its spell on them both; never had love been so present and so powerful. In very desperation Mary Anne broke the silence, her tone sweet and low, her voice sunk to a half-whisper.

"Robert, how is it you have never spoken to me of your wife?"

"I did not know you would like it. And besides—"

"Besides what?"

"I have not cared to speak of her since her death. A feeling has been upon me that I never should speak of her again, except perhaps to one person."

"And that person?"

"My second wife. Should I be fortunate enough ever to marry one."

He turned involuntarily and looked at her. And then looked away again hastily. It might be dangerous just now. But that look, brief as it was, had shown him her glowing, downcast countenance.

"What was her name?"

"Clara. She was little more than a child—a gentle, loving child, unfit to encounter the blasts of the world. One, ruder than ordinary, struck her and carried her away."

"Did you love her very much?"

He paused, hesitated, and then turned to her again. "Am I to tell you, Mary Anne?"

"As you like," she whispered, the blushes deepening. "Of course not, if it be painful to you."

"I did not love her; taking the word in its truest extent. I thought I did, and it is only within a few months—yes, I may as well tell you all—that I have learnt my mistake."

Mary Anne Thornycroft glanced at him in surprise. "Only within a few months! How is that?"

"Because I have learnt to love another. To love—do you understand, Mary Anne?—to love. With my very heart and soul; with my best and entire being. Such love cannot come twice to any man, and it teaches him much. It has taught me, amidst other knowledge, that I liked my wife as one likes a dear child, but not otherwise."

Mary Anne Thornycroft's hand trembled as it lay upon his arm. In her bewilderment of feelings, in the tumultuous sensation born of this great love that was filling all her mind, she nearly lost command of her words, and spoke at random.

"But why should this be told only to your second wife?"

"Because I should wish to show her that my true love is hers; hers only in spite of my early marriage. The rest of the world it concerns not, and will never be spoken of to them."

"You assume confidently that you will feel this love for your second wife?"

"I shall if I marry her. That is by no means sure. Unless I marry her, the one to whom my love is given, I shall never marry at all."

Ah, where was the use of keeping up this farce? It was like children playing at bo-peep with the handkerchief over the face. The other is there, but we pretend to know it not. With their hearts wildly beating in unison—with her hand shaking visibly in its emotion—with the consciousness that concealment was no longer concealment but full and perfect knowledge, stood they. Mary Anne rejoined, her words more and more at random, her wits utterly gone a-woolgathering.

"And why should you not marry her?"

"I am not in a position to ask for her of her father."

It was all over in a moment. Save that he turned suddenly to look at her, and laid his hand on hers as if to still its trembling, Mary Anne Thornycroft doubted ever after if she had not made the first movement. Only a moment, and her head was lying on his breast, his clasped arms were holding her there, their pulses were tingling with rapture, their lips clinging together in a long and ardent kiss.

"Dare I speak to you, Mary Anne?" he asked, hoarsely.

"You know you may."

"Oh, my love—my love! It is you I would, if possible, make my wife. None other. But I may not ask for you of Mr. Thornycroft. He would not deem my position justified it."

"I will wait for you, Robert."

Only by bending his head could he catch the low words. His cheek lay on hers; he strained her closer, if that were possible, to his beating heart.

"It may be for years!"

"Let it be years and years. I ask no better than to wait for you."

The stars shone out brighter in the sky; the fire in the room went quite down; and nothing more could be heard from those living in their new and pure dream, but snatches of the sweet refrain—

"My love, my love!"

CHAPTER VIII

A Last Interview

The week went on to its close. Mary Anne Thornycroft, following out her own will and pleasure, despising her brother Cyril's warning, asked Robert Hunter to prolong his visit. He yielded so far as to defer his departure to the Sunday evening. Originally it had been fixed for the Saturday morning: business required his presence in London. Swayed by her, and by his own inclination—by his own love, he yielded to the tempting seduction of staying two further days. Alas, alas!

Peace had been established at the Red Court Farm; or, rather, the unpleasantness had been allowed to die away. Nothing further had come of the outbreak; it was not alluded to again in any way. Robert Hunter, meeting the superintendent, mentioned in a casual manner that he could not help him again in sounding the rocks, adding something about "want of time." It is probable that the surprise caused by the very unexpected arrival of Mr. Thornycroft's wife tended more than aught else to smooth matters. A stranger in our household keeps down angry tempers. Isaac and Cyril were courteous as ever; the justice was courteous also, though a little stiff; Richard sternly civil. Robert Hunter responded cordially, as if willing to do away with the impression left by his interference, and took things as he found them.

Not a word was said of the newly-avowed love. Any sort of concealment or dishonour was entirely against the nature of Mary Anne Thornycroft; but love was all-powerful. That Robert Hunter was not in a condition to propose for her yet, he knew; but if this project of going abroad were carried out, he thought he might speak before starting. And so they mutually decided to wait—at least, for a few weeks, or until that should be decided. But, though Mr. Thornycroft had not a suspicion of any attachment, the brothers were sharper sighted. They saw it clearly, and showed disapproval in accordance with their several dispositions. Richard resented it; Isaac told his sister she might do much better; Cyril said a word to her of concealment never bringing any good. It was rather singular that a dislike of Robert Hunter should exist in the breast of all three. Not one, save Richard, acknowledged it even to himself; not one could say whence or wherefore it arose, except perhaps that they had not taken cordially to him at first. And of course the outbreak did not tend to improve the feeling.

The arrival of Lady Ellis at the Red Court made no difference whatever to the routine of its daily life, since she was not well enough to come down and mix in it. The artificial excitement imparted by the journey was telling upon her now, and her available strength seemed to have gone. Not tracing this fact—the increased weakness—to its true source, she laid the blame on the atmosphere of Coastdown. It never had agreed with her, she said; she supposed it never would; and she already began to speak of getting back to Cheltenham. Not rising until nearly mid-day, she went afterwards into the dressing-room, or boudoir, adjoining her chamber—we saw her in it once in the old days—and there sat or lay for the rest of the day, watching the mysterious plateau and the sea beyond it, or reading between whiles. They went up and sat with her by turns—Mr. Thornycroft, Cyril, and Mary Anne; Isaac rarely, Richard never, except for a brief moment of civil inquiry. None of them remained with her long. It wearied her to converse, and she thought she was best with her maid, who was in part companion. Robert Hunter she neither saw nor asked after. And so the week came to an end.

Sunday—and the day of Mr. Hunter's departure. They attended church at St. Peter's in the morning, all except Mr. Thornycroft and Richard. The justice remained with his wife, and Richard was lax at the best of times in attendance on public worship. Mr. Richard spent the morning in a desultory manner at home, a short pipe in his mouth, and lounging about the stables with Hyde.

What Richard did with himself in the afternoon nobody knew; it was not usual to inquire into his movements; but the rest went over to Jutpoint to attend the church of St. Andrew's, where there was a famous afternoon preacher, whom they liked to hear. Anna Chester was with them. Captain Copp, confined to the house by a temporary indisposition, was indoors that day, and his wife remained in attendance on him; so that Anna appeared at church in the morning alone. The Red Court people took her home and kept her to luncheon; and she accompanied them afterwards to Jutpoint.

The omnibus conveyed them, and was to bring them home again. Never, when he could avoid it, did Mr. Thornycroft take out his own horses on Sunday: he chose that they and his servants should, so far, have rest. They had a large circle of acquaintances at Jutpoint, and on coming out of church the justice and Isaac laid hands on two and conveyed them back to dinner. The strangers liked these impromptu invitations—possibly laid themselves out to get them, and the omnibus had a merry freight back to Coastdown.

"If they are going to have one of their dinner-gatherings to-night, you must come home and sit down to it with me, Anna," spoke Miss Thornycroft, as they quitted the omnibus at the Mermaid.

Anna was nothing loth. She had sat in the omnibus by Isaac's side, her hand in his, under cover of the closely-packed company and the approaching darkness, happy for the time. Hastily answering that she would be glad to come, but must run on first of all to the heath and tell Mrs. Copp, she sped away fast. Isaac, having waited until the others should disperse before he followed, overtook her just as she was entering.

Captain Copp, up now, sat by the fire, groaning, and drinking some strong tea. The captain was occasionally afflicted with an intense sick-headache, never a worse than that he had to-day. He always laid the blame on the weather; it was the heat, or it was the cold; or it was the frost, or the rain. Mrs. Copp agreed with him, but Sarah in the kitchen thought the cause lay in rum-and-water. The groans were suspended when they went in, and Mrs. Copp, dutifully waiting on him, put down the cup and saucer.

"Aunt, may I dine at the Red Court?"

Mrs. Copp made no answer. Whenever she saw Isaac and Anna together, she was taken with a fit of inward shivering. Captain Copp spoke up: his opinion was that Anna had better not. Isaac laughed.

"She must," he said; "I am come to run away with her. Otherwise Mary Anne will not sit down to table with us."

"Is it a party?" cried the captain.

"Just two or three. My father has brought them over from Jutpoint; and I think Kyne is coming in. I was in hopes you could have come, captain."

Several dismal groans from Captain Copp. He said it was the pain in his head; in reality they sprung from pain at his heart. One of those glorious dinners at the Red Court, and he unable to be at it!

"Are you ready, Anna?" whispered Isaac.

She ran upstairs to get something she wanted in the shape of dress, and was down again in a minute, wishing them good evening. Captain Copp, who did not altogether approve of the proceeding, called out that he should send Sarah for her at eight o'clock.

Taking her arm within his, Isaac walked on in silence. At the close of the heath, instead of continuing his way down by the side of the churchyard, he turned into it by the small side gate.

"Just a minute, Anna," he said, sitting down on the narrow bench. "I want to say a word to you."

But before he began to say the word he enclosed her face in his loving arms, and took the kisses from it he had been longing for all the way from Jutpoint.

"What I want to say is this, Anna, that I do not think I can let the present state of things go on."

"No!'

"It is so unsatisfactory. My wife, and not my wife. I living at the Red Court, you secluded at Captain Copp's. Meeting once in a way in a formal manner, shaking hands and parting again, nothing more. Why, I have only twice I think had you for a moment to myself since we parted, now and that evening at the Red Court. And what was that?—what is this? I can't stand it, Anna."

"But what would you do?"

"I don't know," answered Isaac, looking straight forward at the gravestones, as if they could tell him what. "I would brave my father's anger in a minute if it were not for—for—if I were sure nothing would come of it. But it might."

"In what way?"

"I may tell you some time; not now. If Captain Copp would but be reasonable, so that I might entrust him with the secret, and—"

"He would go straight off with it to Mr. Thornycroft, Isaac."

"Precisely," said Isaac, answering her interruption; "and the time has hardly arrived for that. Besides, the information must come from myself. Do you think—"

"Hush, Isaac!"

The softly-breathed warning silenced him. On the other side the hedge was a sound of footsteps—slow steps passing towards the heath. Isaac held her to him in perfect silence until they were lost in the distance.

"Let us go, Isaac."

It certainly would not be expedient to be seen there, and Isaac rose, snatching as he did so his farewell kisses from her lips. Passing down the side path of the churchyard, they went out at its front entrance, and popped upon Mr. Kyne.

He was evidently coming from the heath. It might have been his footsteps they had heard going towards it. Mr. Kyne looked full at them, and Anna coloured in the night's darkness to the very roots of her hair. To be caught at that hour stealing out of the churchyard with Isaac Thornycroft!

"Is it you, Mr. Supervisor?" cried Isaac, gaily. "A fine evening! Take care, Miss Chester: you had better take my arm."

"It's very fine," answered the supervisor; "the weather seems to have cleared up. I've been taking a stroll before my tea. We shall have a frost to-night, Miss Chester."

"Safe to," rejoined Isaac, looking up at the clear sky.

"How is my lady?" asked Mr. Kyne; "I heard she had come."

"She has only come to go again. Coastdown never seems to suit her. She is very unwell indeed, and keeps her room."

The churchyard past, Mr. Kyne, without any warning whatever, turned off on the cross path towards his home, saying good-night. Isaac looked after him in a sort of surprise.

"Then Richard has left it to me," he said, half aloud.

"Isaac! Isaac! what will Mr. Kyne think of me?" murmured Anna.

Isaac laughed. "The most he can think is that we are sweethearts," he answered in his light manner.

"Oh, Isaac, have you considered? If scandal should arise!"

"My darling, I have told you why that cannot be. At the first breath of it I should avow the truth. Scandal! how is it possible, when we are living here but as common acquaintances?"

At the gate of the Red Court he let her enter alone, and ran back in search of Mr. Kyne. That functionary lodged at a cottage just beyond the village, and Isaac found him poking up his small fire to make the little tin kettle boil, preparatory to making his tea.

"I have come to carry you off to dinner," said Isaac. "We have got a friend or two dropped in from Jutpoint, and the parson's coming. There's a brave codfish and turkey."

Weak tea and bread-and-butter at home in his poor small room; and the handsome dinner table, the light, the warmth, the social friends at Justice Thornycroft's. It was a wide contrast, making Mr. Kyne's mouth water. He had dined at one o'clock off a mutton chop, and was hungry again. Codfish and turkey!

"I'll come with pleasure, Mr. Isaac. I must just say a word to Puffer first, if there's time."

"All right; I'll go with you," said Isaac.

Mr. Puffer, the coastguard-man for the night, was on the plateau, speculating upon how long it would be before daylight was quite gone, for a streak or two of yellow lingered yet in the west, when he was surprised by the sight of his superior, and began to pace the edge zealously, his eyes critically peering out to sea. The supervisor approached alone.

"Any news, Puffer?"

"None, sir," answered Mr. Puffer, saluting his master. "All's quiet."

"Very good. Keep a sharp look-out. I shall be up here again at seven or eight o'clock."

He had taken to say this to his men of late, by way of keeping them to their duty; he had also taken to pop upon them at all kinds of unpromised times: and, between the cold and the superstition, his men wished him at Hanover.

The party sat down to dinner at six. Richard came in with Mr. Hopley, from Dartfield, who was wont to come over to buy oats; the parson of the parish, Mr. Southall, was there; the gentlemen from Jutpoint, and Mr. Kyne. A jolly parson, Mr. Southall, who enjoyed the good cheer of the Red Court Farm on Sunday just as much as he did on week days, and made no scruple over it.

The only two in strict evening dress were Robert Hunter and Cyril Thornycroft; but they wore black neckties. The rest were dressed well, as befitted the day, even Richard, but they did not wear dress coats. Anna was in a gleaming blue silk. It had been bought for her by Isaac, as had a great many other things during their brief period of married life; and poor Mrs. Copp had to invent no end of stories to the captain on their return to Coastdown, saying they were presents from her sick sister. Altogether there were twelve at table.

The housekeeping at the Red Court proved itself just as well prepared for these impromptu guests as it ever had been, save in the one memorable instance marked by the interference of Lady Ellis. After-circumstances caused the items of the bill of fare to be discussed out of doors, and, indeed, every other detail, great and small, of the eventful night. Mock-turtle soup, a fine codfish, a round of beef boiled, a large roast turkey and tongue, side dishes, a plum pudding, sweets, and macaroni. All these were cooked and served in the best manner, with various vegetables, rich and plentiful sauces, strong ale, and the best of wines. Mr. Kyne thought of his solitary tea at home, and licked his lips.

On the withdrawal of the cloth, for Justice Thornycroft preserved that old-fashioned custom, and Mr. Southall had said grace, the young ladies retired. The gentlemen closed round the table to enjoy their wine. A merry party. By-and-by, spirits, cigars, and pipes were introduced—the usual practice on these occasions at the Red Court. The only one who did not touch them was Cyril Thornycroft.

It had been Mr. Kyne's intention to retire at eight o'clock precisely (he emphasised the word to himself), and go on the watch; or, at any rate, see that his subordinate was there. But the best of officers are but mortal; Mr. Kyne felt very jolly where he was; and, as common sense whispered him, the smuggling lads were safe not to attempt any bother on a Sunday night; they would be jollifying for themselves. So the officer sat on, paying his respects to the brandy-and-water, and getting rather dizzy about the eyes.

Another who stayed longer than he ought; at least, longer than he had intended; was Robert Hunter. Seduced into taking a cigar—and never were such cigars smoked as Justice Thornycroft's—he sat on, and let the time slip by unheeded. On ordinary evenings the omnibus left Coastdown at half-past nine o'clock to convey passengers to the last train, that passed through Jutpoint at midnight. On Sunday nights the omnibus left at half-past eight, some dim notion swaying the minds of the authorities that the earlier hour implied a sort of respect to the day. The convenience of the passengers went for nothing; they had to wait at Jutpoint where and how they could. It had been Robert Hunter's intention to go by this omnibus, and it was only by seeing Isaac Thornycroft look at his watch that he remembered time was flying. He pulled out his own.

"By Jove, I've missed the omnibus," he whispered to Cyril, who sat next him. "It is half-past eight now."

"What shall you do?"

"Walk it. I must be in London for to-morrow morning."

Rising as he spoke, he quietly said farewell to Mr. Thornycroft, Richard, Isaac and Mr. Kyne, and stole from the room, not to disturb the other guests, who were seated round the fire now in a cloud of tobacco smoke. Cyril went out with him. Miss Thornycroft and Anna were in the drawing-room drinking coffee. A cup was passed to Robert Hunter.

"What a sad thing—to have to walk to Jutpoint!" exclaimed Mary Anne.

He laughed at the words. "I shall enjoy it far more than I should the omnibus."

"Ah, I think you must have stayed on purpose, then. But what of the portmanteau?"

"It can come by train to-morrow, if one of your servants will take it to the Mermaid," was his answer. "My address is on it."

As he was speaking, Lady Ellis's maid came into the room and delivered him a small bit of twisted paper. Holding it to the light, he read the faintly-pencilled words:—

"I hear you are leaving. Will you come up for a minute, that I may wish you well?"

"What is it?" asked Mary Anne.

"Lady Ellis wishes to say farewell to me," he answered. "I will go to her now."

The maid led the way, and showed him up to the small sitting-room. Lady Ellis was leaning back in her easy-chair, but she sat upright when he entered. Even more than before was he struck with the white, hollow, skeleton look of the face, on which death had so unmistakably set his seal; but the disorder had arrived at that stage now when each day made a perceptible change. The black eyes, once glistening so fiercely with their vain passions, lighted up with a faint pleasure.

"I am glad you came up: so glad! I thought you did not intend to see me at all."

He answered that he did not know she was well enough to be seen, speaking cordially. With that dying face and form before him, three-parts of his cherished enmity to the woman died out. Not his dislike of her.

"I would bid you farewell, Mr. Hunter. I would wish you—an' you will permit me—God-speed. The next time we meet, both of us will have entered on a different world from this."

"Thank you," he said, in allusion to the wish, "but are you sure nothing can be done for your recovery?"

"Nothing whatever. And the end cannot be very far off now. Mr. Thornycroft is going back with me to Cheltenham, and I am glad of it. I should like him to see the last of me."

She was looking at the fire as she spoke. He, standing at the opposite side of the mantelpiece, looked at her. What a change from the vain, worldly, selfish woman of the past! Raising her eyes suddenly, she caught his gaze, perhaps divined somewhat of his thoughts.

"You cannot think me to be the same, can you?"

"Scarcely." He glanced at the timepiece. At best the interview was not pleasant to him, neither did he care to prolong it.

"You fear to lose the omnibus?"

"I have lost it. Your clock is slow. I am now about to start on foot to Jutpoint."

"Could they not send you in the dog-cart?"

"Thank you; I prefer to walk. The night is fine, and the road good. And I suppose I must be going."

She stood up as he moved, and held out her hand, her silk gown falling in folds from her shrunken form. He shook hands.

"God bless you; God prosper you here and hereafter!" she said with some emotion.

He hardly knew what to answer. To express a wish for her continued life was so palpable a fallacy, with those signs of decay before him: so he murmured a word of thanks, and gave the thin hand a friendly pressure as he released it.

But she did not release his. "It was not quite all I wished to say," she whispered, looking up to him with her sad eyes, in which stood a world of repentance. "I want to ask your forgiveness."

"My forgiveness?"

"For the past. For your lost wife. But for me she might not have died. My long illness has brought reflection home to me, and—and repentance: as I suppose hopeless illness does to most people: showing me things in their true light; showing me the awful mistakes and sins the best and the worst of us alike commit. Say that you forgive me."

"Lady Ellis," he said, his countenance assuming a solemn aspect as he looked straight at her, "I have far more need of forgiveness myself than any other can have: I saw that at the time; I see it always. My wife was mine; it was my duty to cherish her, and I failed; no one else owed obligation to her. The chief blame lay with me."

"Say you forgive me! I know she has, looking down from heaven."

"I do indeed. I forgive you with my whole heart, and I pray that we may, as you say, meet hereafter—all our mistakes and sins blotted out."

"I pray it always. Cyril knows I do. He was the first to lead me—ah, so kindly and imperceptibly!—to the remembrance that our sins needed blotting out. It was during a six weeks' visit he paid me with his sister. Few in this world are so good and pure and loving as Cyril Thornycroft. Fare you well, Robert Hunter! fare you well for ever."

"For ever on earth," he added. Another pressure of the poor weak hand, a warm, earnest look, a faint thought of the Heaven that might be attained to yet, and Robert Hunter turned away, and woke up to the world again.

His cold coffee stood in the drawing-room when he got back. He sat a short while with the two young ladies, very quiet and absorbed. Cyril was not there. Mary Anne inquired what was the matter with him.

"That poor woman upstairs," he briefly answered; "she seems so near to death, but I think she is prepared for it."

Mary Anne Thornycroft simply looked at him in reply; the manner and look were alike strange. Robert Hunter sipped the cold coffee by spoonfuls, evidently unconscious what it was he was doing.

"But I must be going!" he suddenly cried, starting up. "It would not do to miss the train as I have the omnibus. Good bye, Anna; you will be coming back to Miss Jupps's, I suppose, when school begins?"

The vivid blush went for nothing. She, Mrs. Isaac Thornycroft, a schoolteacher again! "Good-bye, Robert," she softly said. "I wish you safe to Jutpoint, but I should not like your walk. Give my love to the Miss Jupps if you see them, and to Mrs. Macpherson."

Mary Anne went out with him to the door. As they crossed the hall, sounds of talking came from the dining-room, and there was a sudden burst of laughter. Evidently the party were enjoying themselves. He took his remarkable coat from a peg and flung it over his arm.

"You must say good-bye to Cyril for me, Mary Anne."

"I will. But perhaps you will see him outside. Why don't you put your coat on?"

"Not yet; I am hot. By-and-by, when the air shall strike cool to me."

They stood just outside the door, in the shade of the walls, and he wound his arms round her for a last embrace. A last? "God bless you, Mary Anne!" he whispered; "the time will come, I trust, when we need not part."

She stood looking after him, the outline of his retreating form being very distinct in the bright night.

The stars were clear and the air was frosty. Mary Anne Thornycroft watched him pass through the gate, and then saw that instead of going straight on, he turned short off to the waste land skirting the side of the plateau.

She wondered. It was the farthest way to the village, and moreover the private way of Mr. Thornycroft. Another moment and she saw him running up the plateau, having crossed the railings.

"Why, what in the world!—he must be dreaming," she mentally concluded. "Perhaps he wants to take a farewell view of the sea. He would see enough of it between here and Jutpoint."

However, Miss Thornycroft found it cold standing there, and went indoors, meeting Sinnett in the hall.

"Sinnett, Mr. Hunter's portmanteau must go by the early omnibus. See that it is sent to the Mermaid in time."

"Very well, miss," replied Sinnett. And it may be here mentioned that she obeyed the order by sending it that night.

Very shortly after Robert Hunter had left the dining-room, Richard and Isaac Thornycroft also withdrew from it, one by one, and unperceived. That is, the guests and the justice were too agreeably engaged with their pipes and drink, their talk and laughter, to pay heed to it. One of the gentlemen from Jutpoint—a magistrate—was relating a story that convulsed the parson with laughter and sent the rest almost into fits. Altogether they were uncommonly jolly, and the lapse of one or two of the party counted for nothing. Mr. Kyne had nearly ceased to care whether his subordinate was on the watch, or off it.

As it happened, he was on it. With the promised visit of his superior before his eyes, Mr. Puffer had not dared to leave his post. He stood close to the bleak edge of the cold plateau, wishing himself anywhere else, and bemoaning the hard fate that had made him a coastguard-man. Unpleasant thoughts of ghosts, and such like visitants, intruded into his thoughts now and then: he entirely disbelieved Mr. Kyne's theory that there were smugglers; and the only cheering ray in his solitude, was the sight of the cheery lights in the Red Court Farm. Tomlett, the fishing-boat master, who had recovered his accident, suddenly hailed him.

"Cold work, my man," said he, sauntering up the plateau.

"It just is that!" was Mr. Puffer's surly answer.

"But it's a bright night: never saw a brighter when there was no moon: so you run no danger of making a false step in the dark and pitching over. There's consolation in that."

"Ugh!" grunted the shivering officer, as if the fact afforded little consolation to him.

"What on earth's the use of your airing yourself here?" went on Tomlett. "You coastguard fellows have got the biggest swallows! As if any smugglers would attempt the coast to-night! My belief is—and I am pretty well used to the place, and have got eyes on all sides of me—that this suspicion of Master Kyne's is all moonshine and empty herring-barrels. I could nearly take my oath of it."

"So could I," said the man.

"Let us go on to the Mermaid, and have a glass," continued Mr. Tomlett, persuasively. "I'll stand it. Johnson and Simms, and a lot more, are there."

"I wish I dare," cried the aggravated Puffer. "But Kyne will be up presently."

"No he won't. He is round old Thornycroft's fire, in a cloud of smoke and drink. There's a dinner-party at the Red Court, and Kyne and the rest are half-seas over."

"Are you sure of this?"

"I'll swear it if you wish me; I have just come from there. I went down to try and get speech of the justice about that boat loss: it comes on at Jutpoint to-morrow, and he is to be on the bench. But it was no go: they are all fixed in that dining-room; and will be there till twelve o'clock to-night, and then they'll reel off to bed with their boots on."

Tomlett was not in the habit of deceiving the men; he showed himself their friend on all occasions; and Mr. Puffer yielded to the seduction. Seeing him comfortably settled at the Mermaid, with what he liked best steaming before him, and some good fellows around, Tomlett withdrew, leaving him to enjoy himself.

From the Mermaid, Tomlett steered his course to the Red Court Farm, tearing over the intervening ground as if he had been flying from a mad bull. He took the liberty of crossing the lawn before the front windows (the shortest way), and went round by the unused path at the far end of the house, which led to the stables and to the young men's apartments. Carefully pushing open the small door in the dead wall, he encountered Richard Thornycroft.

"It is all right, sir," he panted, out of breath with running; "I have got the fellow in. We must lose no time."

"Very well," whispered Richard. "Find Hyde, and come down."

"I suppose he's safe, sir?" said Mr. Tomlett, jerking his head in the supposed direction of the dining-room.

"Couldn't be safer," responded Richard. "He had enough wine before he began at the brandy."

Isaac Thornycroft came up, a lighted lantern under his coat. Scarcely could either of the brothers be recognised for those who had so recently quitted the dining-room; they wore small caps; gaiters were buttoned over their legs; their dinner coats were replaced by coarse ones of fustian.

CHAPTER IX

The Crowd in the Early Morning

When Richard and Isaac Thornycroft left the dining-room, so unobtrusively as not to draw attention to the fact, they passed through the small door at the further end of the hall. Isaac, the last, silently locked it, thereby cutting off all communication with the busy part of the house. Swiftly ascending to Richard's chamber, they changed their clothes for others which were laid out in readiness. Hyde, his clothes also changed, was in waiting at the foot of the stairs when they came down, and he crossed with Isaac to the coach-house opposite, built, as must be remembered, on a portion of the old ruins. Richard undid the door in the wall looking to the front, and stayed there until joined by the breathless Tomlett—as above seen.

The dog-cart was in its place in the coach-house; the broken old cart and the bundles of straw were in the corner; all just as usual. Tomlett and Hyde removed the cart and the straw from their resting place (whence, by all appearance, they never were removed), and the brothers Thornycroft lifted a trap-door, invisible to the casual observer, that the straw had served to conceal. A flight of steps stood disclosed to view, which Isaac and Richard descended. The steps led to a subterranean passage; a long, long passage running straight under the plateau and terminating in a vault or cavern, its damp sides glistening as the light of the lantern flashed upon it. Traversing this passage to the end, Isaac put the lantern down: then they unwound a chain from its pulley, and a square portion of the rock, loose from the rest, was pulled in and turned aside by means of a pivot: thus affording an ingress for goods, smuggled or otherwise, to come in. No wonder Robert Hunter had thought the rock sounded hollow just there!

Ah, Mr. Kyne had scented the fox pretty keenly. But not the huntsmen who rode him to earth.

It took longer to do all this than it has to relate it. When Richard had helped Isaac to remove the rock, he returned along the passage on his way to the plateau. It was customary for one of the two brothers to stand on the plateau on the watch during these dangerous feats, with his descending signal of warning in case of alarm. Richard took that post to-night. Oh, that it had been Isaac! But it was marvellous how lucky they had hitherto been. Years had gone on, and years, and never a check had come. One great reason for this was that the late supervisor, Mr. Dangerfield—let us only whisper it!—had allowed himself to be bribed. What with that, and what with the horror the preventive men had of the plateau, the daring and profitable game had been carried on with impunity. Richard Thornycroft went on his way, little knowing the awful phantom that was pursuing him.

Midway in the passage he met Hyde and Tomlett, tried and true men, on their way to join Isaac. Mr. Tomlett's accident had occurred during one of these night exploits—hence his wife's terrified consternation at being questioned by Miss Thornycroft. A strange chance had led, some years ago, to Mrs. Tomlett's discovery of what her husband was engaged in at intervals: the woman kept the secret, but never was free from fear.

Isaac Thornycroft, left alone, proceeded with his necessary movements. By help of a long pole, thrust through the hole, he held forth a blazing flambeau, which for two minutes would light up the half-moon beach and the rocks behind it. It was the signal for the boats to put off from that especial vessel that was the object of the worthy supervisor's abhorrence. And so the night's secret work was fairly inaugurated. Isaac Thornycroft held his signal for the approach of the boats, laden with their heavy spoil; Richard was speeding back to assume his watch overhead; and it was just about this time that Mr. Hunter had taken his departure from the Red Court Farm.

It is quite useless to speculate, now, why Robert Hunter went on the plateau. Some power must have impelled him. These things, bearing great events in their train, do not occur by chance. Had he been questioned why, he probably could not have told. The most likely conjecture is, speaking according to human reason, that he intended to stand a few moments on its brow, and sniff the fresh breeze from the sea, so grateful to his heated senses. He had taken more wine than usual; certainly not to anything like intoxication, for he was by habit and principle a sober man. He had dined more freely; the hot room, the talking, all had contributed to heat him; and, following on it, came the interview with Lady Ellis. Whatever the cause, certain it is that, instead of pursuing the straight course of his road, like a sensible man, he turned off it and went on the plateau.

It was a remarkably light night—as already said—clear, still, frosty, very bright. The clouds, passing occasionally over the face of the clear sky, seemed to be moved by an upper current that did not stir the air below. The sea was like silver; no craft to be seen on it save one vessel that was hove-to close in-shore—a dark vessel, lying still and silent. Robert Hunter, at the very edge of the plateau, stood looking on all this: a peaceful scene; the broad expanse of sea stretching out, the half-moon beach lying cold and solitary below.

Suddenly a bright sheet of light shot out from underneath, illumining the half-moon, the rocks, and his own face, as he bent over to look. Was he dreaming?—was his brain treacherous, causing him to see things that were not? There, half-way down the rocks, shone a great flame, a flickering, flaring, blazing flame, as of a torch; and Robert Hunter rubbed his eyes, and slapped his chest, and pinched his arms, to make sure he was not in a dream of wine.

He stood staring at it, his eyes and mouth open; stared at it until, by some mysterious process, it steadily lowered itself, and disappeared inside the rocks. Light—not of the torch—flashed upon him.

"The smugglers!" he burst forth: and the clear night air carried the words over the sea. "The smugglers are abroad to-night! That must be their signal for the booty to approach. Then there is an opening in the rocks! I'll hasten and give word to Kyne."

Flying back straight towards the Red Court, he had leaped the railings when he encountered Richard Thornycroft, who seemed to be flying along with equal speed towards the plateau. Hunter seized his arm.

"Richard Thornycroft! Mr. Richard! the smugglers are at work! I have dropped upon them. Their signal has been hoisted beyond the rocks underneath."

"What?" roared Richard.

"It is true as that we are breathing here," continued Hunter. "I went on the plateau, and I saw their light—a flaming torch as big as your head. They are preparing to run the goods. It struck me there must be an opening there. I am going to fetch Kyne. Mr. Thornycroft, if he will come out, may be convinced now."

He would have resumed his way with the last words, but Richard caught him. The slight form of Robert Hunter was whirled round in his powerful grasp.

"Do you see this?" he hoarsely raved, his face wearing an awfully livid expression, born of anger, in the starlight. "It is well loaded."

Robert Hunter did see it. It was the bright end of a pistol barrel, pointed close to his head. He recoiled, as far as he could, but the grasp was tight upon him.

"What, in Heaven's name, do you mean?"

"You talk of Heaven, you treacherous cur!" panted Richard. "Down upon your knees—down, I say! You shall talk of it to some purpose."

By his superior strength, he forced the younger and slighter man to his knees on the waste ground as he would a child. The fur coat fell from Robert Hunter's arm, and lay beside him, a white heap streaked with black, in the starlight.

"Now, then! Swear, by all your hopes of Heaven, that what you have detected shall never pass your lips; shall be as if you had not seen it."

"I swear," answered Robert Hunter. "I believe I guess how it is. I will be silent; I swear it."

"Now and hereafter?"

"Now and hereafter."

"Get up, then, and go your way. But, another word, first of all," interrupted Richard, as if a thought struck him. "This must be kept secret from my sister."

"I swear that it shall be, for me."

Holding Robert Hunter still in his fierce grasp, he dictated to him yet another oath, as if not satisfied with the last one. In cooler moments neither of them might have acted as they were doing: Richard had been less imperative, the other less blindly yielding. Robert Hunter was no coward, but circumstances and Richard's fury momentarily over-mastered him.

He swore a solemn oath—Richard dictating it—not to hold further communication with Mary Anne at present, either by word or letter; not to do it until Richard should of his own will voluntarily give permission for it. He swore not again to put foot within the Red Court Farm; he swore not to write to any one of its inmates, failing this permission. The determination not to be pestered with letters perhaps caused Richard to insist on this. Any way, the oaths were taken, and were to hold force for six months.

"Now, then, go your way," said Richard. "Your path for departure lies there," and he pointed to the open highway leading from the entrance gates of the Red Court. "But first hear me swear an oath that I shall surely keep: If you do not go straight away; if you linger on this spot unnecessarily by so much as a few minutes; if you, having once started, return to it again I will put this bullet through your body. Cyril! See him off; he was turning traitor."

Cyril Thornycroft had come strolling towards them, somewhat at a distance yet; he did not catch the sense of his brother's concluding words, but he saw that some explosion of anger had occurred. Picking up the coat, Hunter put it on as he walked to join Cyril; while Richard, as if under the pressure of some urgent errand, flew off across the lawn and flower-beds towards the coach-house ruins and the secret passage leading from it.

"What is all this? What does Richard mean?" inquired Cyril as they commenced their walk along the high road. "He said something about a traitor."

"I was not a traitor; your brother lies. Would I turn traitor to a house whose hospitality I have been accepting? I saw, accidentally, a light exhibited from the Half-moon rocks, and I guessed what it meant. I guess more now than I will repeat, but the secret shall be safe with me."

"Safe now, and after your departure?"

"Safe always. I have sworn it."

"I am sorry this should have happened," said Cyril, after a pause.

"And so am I," returned Robert Hunter. "Circumstances, not my own will, led to it. It is a pity I missed the omnibus."

"Yes," said Cyril, speaking abstractedly, as if his thoughts were far away. "But if you step out well you may be at Jutpoint by half-past ten."

"Scarcely so," thought Robert Hunter. Cyril, perhaps, did not know the hour now.

"What! Have you missed the omnibus, sir?"

The question came from a woman who met them, Captain Copp's servant Sarah. She was coming along without her bonnet in the frosty night.

"Yes, I have; and must walk it for my pains," answered Mr. Hunter.

"Are you going to the Red Court, Sarah?" asked Cyril.

"I am, sir; I'm going there to fetch Miss Chester," returned Sarah in her hardest tone. "And a fine tantrum master's in over it, roaring out that I ought to have come a good hour ago. Why didn't they tell me, then?"

Saying good night to the woman, who wished Mr. Hunter a pleasant journey, they continued their way, striking into the village; a silent village to-night. In the windows of the Mermaid above, lights were no doubt gleaming, but they were not near enough to that hospitable hostelry to see. Everybody else seemed abed and asleep, as was generally the case at Coastdown by nine o'clock on a Sunday night.

Cyril had fallen into thought. Should he offer Hunter any apology or excuse for these practices of his house, so inopportunely discovered, and which had always been so distasteful to him? Better not, perhaps. What excusing plea could he justly offer? And besides, he knew not how far the discovery went, or what Richard had said. A feeling of resentment against Robert Hunter rose up in his heart, in his anxiety to ward off ill from his father and brothers, in his jealous care for the fair fame of the Red Court Farm. Good though he was, striving ever to follow in his Master's footsteps of love and peace, Cyril Thornycroft was but human, with a human heart disposed by its original nature to passion and sin.

"Let me advise you, at any rate for the present, not to hold communication with our house or its inmates," he said, gently breaking the silence. "In this I include my sister."

"I have promised all that. Your brother was not satisfied with exacting a simple promise; he made me swear it. I was to have written to Mary Anne on my arrival in town. Will you explain to her the reason why I do not?"

"I thought you and my sister did not correspond," interrupted Cyril.

"Neither do we. It was only to notify my safe arrival."

"I will explain sufficient to satisfy her. I suppose I must not ask you to give her up?"

"My intention is to win her if I can," avowed Robert Hunter. "She would share my fortunes tomorrow, but for the fear that my position would not be acceptable to Mr. Thornycroft."

"I see; it is decided. Well, in your own interest, I would advise you to break off all present relations with our house. What has occurred to-night will not tend to increase Richard's favour to you, and his opinion very greatly sways my father. Your visit here, taking it on the whole, has not been pleasant, or productive of pleasant results. Give us time to forget it and you for the present. Give Richard time to forget the name and sojourn of Robert Hunter."

"You say you suggest this in my own interest?"

"I do indeed," answered Cyril, his good, calm face turning on the speaker with a kindly light. "In yours and my sister's jointly. She will be true to you, I make no doubt; and things may come about after a short while. If you have decided to take each other, if your best affections are involved, why should I seek to part you? But I know what Richard is; you must give him time to get over this."

"True," answered Robert Hunter, his heart responding to the evident kindness. "At any rate, there can be no question of my holding communication with the Red Court Farm for six months, even by letter. It was a rash oath, no doubt; I was not quite myself when I took it; but I have undertaken not to write to any one of you until Richard shall give me leave. At the end of the six months I suppose I shall hear from him; if not, I shall consider myself at liberty to write—or to come."

"You will surely hear from him if he has implied that you shall. Richard never breaks a promise. And now that I have seen you thus far on your way, I'll wish you well, and turn back again."

"They had reached the end of the village, and he grasped Robert Hunter's hand with a warm and friendly pressure. The other was loth to part with him so soon.

"You may as well go with me as far as the Wherry."

Robert Hunter spoke not of a boat or of any landing for one, but of a lone and dismantled public-house, standing about a couple of hundred yards farther. Its sign swung on it still, and rattled in the wind. Cyril acquiesced, and they went down into the bit of lonely road leading to it.

We must go back for a moment to Richard Thornycroft. He gained the ruins, and lifted the trap-door with, as it seemed, almost superhuman strength, for it took of right two to do it. Completely upset by what had occurred, Richard was like a man half mad. He went thundering down the steps to the subterranean passage, his errand being to give' warning to Isaac, and assist in hoisting two lights, which those on board the vessel would understand as the signal not to advance. He had reached the cavern at the end, when his alarm began to subside, to give place to reason; and his steps came to a sudden standstill.

"Why stop the boats?" he demanded of himself. "If Hunter has cleared himself off—of which there can be no doubt—where is the danger?"

Where, indeed? He thought—Richard Thornycroft did think—that Hunter was not one to play false after undertaking to be true. So, after a little more deliberation, somewhat further of counsel with himself, he resolved to let things go on, and turned back again without warning Isaac.

What mattered it that the contraband cargo was safely run? What reeked the guilty parties concerned in it of the miserable deed of evil it involved, while the valuable and double valuable booty got stowed away in silence and safety? One was lying outside the Half-moon, while they housed it, with his battered face turned up to the sky—one whose departed soul had been worth all the cargoes in the world. The body was bruised, and crushed, and murdered—the body of Robert Hunter!

How did it come there?

Coastdown woke lazily up from its slumbers with the dawn—not very early in January—and only got roused into life and activity by the startling piece of news that a shocking murder had been committed in the night. Hastening down to its alleged scene, the Half-moon beach, as many as heard it, shopkeepers, fishermen, and inhabitants generally, they found it to be too true. The poor man lay in the extreme corner of the strip of beach, right against the rocks, and was recognised for the late guest at the Red Court Farm, Robert Hunter.

Not by his face; for that was disfigured beyond possibility of recognition; but by the clothes, hair, and appearance generally. He had been shot in the face, and, in falling from the heights above, the jagged edges of the rocks had also disfigured that poor face until not a trace of its humanity remained.

The tide was low; it present the passage to the beach was passable, and stragglers were flocking up. The frosty air was crisp, the sea sparkled in the early morning sun. Amidst others came Justice Thornycroft, upright, portly, a smile on his handsome face. He did not believe the report; as was evident by his greeting words.

"What's all this hullabaloo about a murder?" began he, as he shelved round the narrow ledge and put his foot upon the beach. "How d'ye do, Kyne?—How d'ye do, Copp—How d'ye do, all? When Martha brought up my shaving-water just now, she burst into my room, her hair and mouth all awry with a story of a man having been murdered in the night at the Half-moon. Some poor drowned fellow, I suppose, cast on the banks by the tide. What brings him so high up?"

"I wish it was drowning, and nothing worse, for that's not such an uncivilized death, if it's your fate to meet it," returned Captain Copp, who was brisk this morning after his headache, and had stumped down on the first alarm. "It's a horrible land murder; nothing less; and upon a friend of yours, justice."

"A friend of mine!" was the somewhat incredulous remark of Mr. Thornycroft. "Why, good Heaven!" he added, in an accent of horror, as the crowd parted and he caught sight of the body, "it is my late guest, Robert Hunter!"

"It is indeed," murmured the crowd; and the justice stood gazing at it with horror as he took in the different points of recognition. The face was gone—that is the best term for one so utterly unrecognisable—but the appearance and dress were not to be mistaken.

"He's buttoned close up in his fur coat, sir," one of the crowd remarked.

Just so. He was buttoned up in his remarkable fur coat—as the village wrongly called it, for the coat was of white cloth, as we know, and its facings only of fur. It had stains on it now, neither white nor black, and one of its sleeves was torn, no doubt by the rocks. The hat was nowhere to be found: it never was found: but the natural supposition was, that in the fall it had rolled down to the lower beach, and been carried away by the tide.

Mr. Thornycroft stooped, and touched one of the cold hands, stooped to hide the tears which filled his eyes, very unusual visitors to the eyes of the justice.

"Poor, poor fellow! how could it have happened? How could he have come here?"

"He must have been shot on the heights, and the shot hurled him over, there's no doubt of that," said Captain Copp. "Must have been standing at the edge of the plateau."

"But what should bring him on the plateau at night?" cried Tomlett, who made one of the spectators.

"What indeed!" returned the captain. "I don't know. A bare, bleak place even in daylight, with as good as no expanse of sea-view."

"I cannot understand this," said Justice Thornycroft, lifting his face with a puzzled expression on it. "Young Hunter took leave of us last night, and left for London. He missed the omnibus to Jutpoint and set off to walk. One of my sons saw him part of the way. What brought him back on the plateau?"

"Yes, he contrived to lose the omnibus," interrupted Supervisor Kyne; who, however, what with the wine and the brandy he had consumed, had a very confused and imperfect recollection of the events of the previous evening, but did not choose to let people know that, and chose to put in his testimony. "Mr. Hunter shook hands with me in the dining-room at the Red Court, and I wished him a pleasant journey. That must have been—what time, Mr. Justice?"

"Getting on for nine. And one of my boys saw him go."

"It's odd what could have spirited him back again," exclaimed Captain Copp. "Which of them steered him off?"

"I forget which," returned the justice. "I heard Isaac say that one of them did. To tell you the truth, captain, I sat late in the dining-room last night, and my head's none of the clearest this morning. How do you find yours, Kyne?"

"Oh, mine's all right, sir," answered the supervisor hastily. "A man in office is obliged to be cautious in what he takes."

"Ah, there's no coming over you," cried the justice, with a side wink to Captain Copp.

"There's Mr. Isaac hisself, a coming round the point now," exclaimed one of the fishermen.

The crowd turned and saw him. Isaac Thornycroft was approaching with a rapid step.

"They say Hunter is murdered!" he called out. "It cannot be."

"He is lying here, stiff and cold, Isaac, with a bullet in his head," was the sad reply of the justice. "Shot down from the heights above."

Isaac stooped in silence. His fair complexion and fine colour, heightened by the morning air, were something bright to look upon. But, as he gazed at that sadly disfigured form, yesterday so animate with life and health, a paleness as of the grave overspread his face; a shudder, which shook him from head to foot, passed through his frame.

"What brought him here—or on the plateau?" he asked. Almost the same words his father had used.

"What indeed!" repeated Mr. Thornycroft. "Did you tell me you saw him off, Isaac? Or was it Richard?"

"It was Cyril. I did not see him at all after he wished us good-bye on leaving the dining-room. But Richard, when he joined me later in the evening, said he had been—had been," repeated Isaac, having rather hesitated at these words, "saying a parting word to Hunter, and that Cyril was walking part of the way with him."

Throwing a pocket handkerchief lightly over the disfigured face, Isaac Thornycroft turned from it towards the sea. The justice spoke.

"I wonder where Cyril left him?"

To wonder it was only natural, but Mr. Thornycroft's remembrances of the matter, as to what he had heard, were altogether hazy. Shut up so long in the dining-room with his guests—for they had not parted until past midnight—doing his part as host at the pipes and grog, though not very extensively, for it was rare indeed that Mr. Thornycroft took too much, he was in a tired, sleepy state when Isaac had come to him after their departure to say that the work was done, the cargo safely in. Isaac had added that he understood from Richard there had been some trouble with Hunter; who had seen the torch-light exhibited on the Half-moon beach, and Richard had been obliged to swear him to secrecy, and had sent Cyril to see him safe away. Of all this, the justice retained an indistinct remembrance.

"Yes," he said slowly, "I recollect now; it was Cyril that you said, Isaac. We must go and find Cyril, and ascertain where he parted with Hunter."

"Why!" suddenly exclaimed a young fisherman of the name of East, "I saw them both together last night; the gentleman and Mr. Cyril. I'd been down at my old mother's and was coming out to go home, when they passed, a walking in the middle of the road. I'd never have noticed 'em, may be, but for the fur coat, for they'd got some way ahead. I see them stop and stand together like, and shake hands as if they was about to part; and then they went on again."

"Both of them went on again?" questioned Isaac. "Yes, sir, both. They went on into the hollow, and I came away."

This young man's mother lived in a solitary hut at the end of the village: in fact, just where Cyril had proposed to leave Hunter, and East must have come out at the same moment.

"We'll go at once and see what Cyril says," resumed the justice, moving away. "Hunter must have come back with him."

"What is to be done with Mr. Hunter, sir?" questioned Tomlett, who had some sort of authority in the place. It did seem like a mockery to call that poor mass of death lying there "Mr. Hunter."

He must be taken to the Mermaid, was the reply of Justice Thornycroft, as he left the beach with his son and three or four friends. "You had better come up and see Pettipher: he'll know what's right to be done. Don't be all the morning about it, Tomlett, or you will have the tide over the path."

Anything for more excitement in a moment like the present! Tomlett, following closely on the steps of Justice Thornycroft, went away with a fleet foot on his errand to the Mermaid, and the whole lot of hearers went racing after him: leaving Captain Copp, who could not race, and Mr. Supervisor Kyne to keep guard over the dead. Her Majesty's officer might have gone with the rest, but that he was in a brown study.

"There's more in this than meets the eye, captain," he began, rousing himself "If this has not been the work of smugglers, my name's not John Kyne."

"Smugglers be shivered!" returned Captain Copp, who it was pretty well suspected in the village obtained his spirits and tobacco without any trouble to her majesty's revenue: as did others. "There are no smugglers here, Mr. Officer. And if there were, what should they want with murdering Robert Hunter?"

"I have been on the work and watch for weeks, captain, and I know there is smuggling carried on; and to a deuced pretty extent."

"We are rich enough to buy our own brandy and pay duty on it, Mr. Supervisor," wrathfully retorted the offended captain.

"Oh, psha! I am not looking after the paltry dabs of brandy they bring ashore," returned the customs' officer. "One may as well try to wash a blackamoor white as to stop that. I look after booty of more consequence. There are cargoes of dry goods run here; foreign lace at a guinea a yard."

"My eye!" ejaculated Captain Copp in amazement, who was willing enough to hear the suspicions, now he found they did not point to anything likely to affect his comfort. "Where do they run them to?"

"They run them here, as I believe; here on the Half-moon; and I suspect they must have a hiding-place somewhere in these rocks."

To describe the intense wonder depicted on the face of the ex-merchant captain would be impossible. It ended in a laugh of incredulity, anything but flattering to his hearer.

"I could swear it," persisted the supervisor. "There! Only a few days ago, I was telling my suspicions to this poor fellow"—glancing over his shoulder—"and he offered to help me ferret out the matter. He came down with me here, examined the rocks, sounded them (he was an engineer, as perhaps you know), and appointed a further hunt for the next day. I never saw a man more interested, or more eager to pounce on the offenders. But before the next day arrived I happened to meet him, and he said he must apologize for not keeping his promise, but he preferred not to interfere further. When I pressed him for his reason he only hemmed and ha-ed, and said that, being a stranger, the neighbourhood might deem his doing so an impertinence. Which of course was sheer rubbish."

Captain Copp, rather slow at taking in ideas, began considering what his own opinion was. The supervisor went on, his tone impressive.

"Now, captain, it is my firm belief that this sudden change and Mr. Hunter's constrained manner, were caused by his having received some private hint from the smugglers themselves not to aid me in my search; and that it is nobody but they who have put it out of his power to do so."

"Whew!" whistled the staggered captain. "I could make more of a sinking ship than of what you say. Who are the smugglers? How did they find out he was going to interfere—unless he or you sent 'em word?"

"I don't know how they found it out. The affair is a mystery from beginning to end. Nobody was present at the conversation except Miss Thornycroft. And she cannot be suspected of holding communication with smugglers."

"This young fellow was a sweetheart of hers—eh?" cried the shrewd captain.

"I don't know anything about that. They seemed intimate. I could almost swear Old Nick has to do with this smuggling business," added the supervisor, earnestly. "A fortnight ago there was a dinner at the Red Court—you were there, by-the-way."

"A jolly spread the old justice gave us! Prime drink and cigars," chimed in the salt tar.

"Well—I was there: and one can't be in two places at once. That very evening they managed to run their cargo; ran it on, as I suspect, to this identical spot, sir," cried the disconcerted officer, warming with his grievance. "Vexed enough I was, and never once have I been off the watch since. Every night have I took up my station on that cursed damp plateau overhead, my stomach stretched on the ground, to keep myself dark, and just half an eye cocked out over the cliff—and all to no purpose. Last night, Sunday, I went in again to dine with the hospitable justice, and I'll be—I'll be shivered, sir, as you sometimes say, if they did not take advantage of it, and run another cargo!"

Never, since the memorable time of his encounter with the pirates which resulted in the disabling him for life, had Captain Copp been so struck—dumb, as it were. Nothing was left of him but amazement.

"Bless and save my wooden leg!" he exclaimed, when his tongue was found—"it is unbelievable. How do you know it?"

"I know it, and that's enough," replied Mr. Kyne, too much annoyed to stand upon politeness, or to explain that his boasted knowledge was assumed; not proved. "But, here's the devil of the thing," he continued—"how did the smugglers know I was off the watch those two particular nights? If it got wind the first night that I should be engaged at the Red Court—though I don't believe it did, for I can keep my own counsel, and did then—it could not have got wind the second. Five minutes before I went there last night, I had no notion whatever of going. Mr. Isaac looked into my rooms just before six, and would walk me off with him. I had had my chop at one o'clock, and was going to think about tea. Now how could the wretches have known last night that I was not on duty?"

"It's no good appealing to me, how," returned the captain. "I never was 'cute at breaking up marvels. Once, in the Pacific, there was a great big thing haunted the ship, bigger than the biggest sea-serpent, and—"

"Depend upon it we have traitors in the camp," unceremoniously interrupted the supervisor; for he knew by experience that when once Captain Copp was fairly launched upon that old marvel of the Pacific ocean, there was no stopping him. "Traitors round about us, at our very elbows and hearths, if we only knew in which direction to look for them."

"Well, I am not one," said the captain, "so you need not look after me. A pretty figure my wooden standard would cut, running smuggled goods! Why didn't you tell all this to Justice Thornycroft? He's the proper person. He's a magistrate."

"I know he is. But if I introduce a word about smugglers he throws cold water on it directly, and ridicules all I say. Once he quite rose up against me, all his bristles on end, in defence of the poor fishermen. Upon that, I hinted that I was not alluding to poor fishermen, but to people and transactions of far greater importance. It stirred up his anger beyond everything; he was barely civil, and turned away telling me to find the people and catch 'em, if I could find 'em; but not to apply to him."

"Well, that's reasonable," said Captain Copp. "Why don't you find 'em?"

"Because I can't find 'em," deplored the miserable officer. "There's the aggravation. I don't know in what quarter to look for them. The thing is like magic; it's altogether shrouded in mystery. I don't choose to speak of it publicly, or I might defeat the chance of discovery; the only time I did speak of it, was to Mr. Hunter, and got sympathy and aid offered and returned to me. You see what has come of that."

It was only too evident what he thought had come of it. And perhaps he was not far wrong. But for that recent morning's unlucky conversation between him and Robert Hunter, no dead man might have been lying on the Half-moon beach, with Isaac Thornycroft's handkerchief covering his face.

"Yes, that's the difficulty—where to look for them," resumed the mortified supervisor. "I cannot suspect any of the superior people in the neighbourhood. It's true I do not know much of those Connaughts. But they don't seem like smugglers either."

"The Connaughts!" roared out the captain, taking up their cause as a personal offence. "Why don't you say it's me? Why don't you say it's yourself? The Connaughts! Who next, Mr. Supervisor? Why, old Connaught is bedridden half his time, and the son has got his eyes strained on books all day, learning to be a parson."

"That's true," grumbled the officer, in his miserable incertitude. "All I know is, I can't fathom the affair, worry over it as I will."

"Here comes the plank," interrupted the captain. "I shan't stop to see that moved: so good morning to you, sir."

He stumped off, mortally offended; and met Tomlett and the landlord of the Mermaid inn, with the long queue of curious idlers behind them.

CHAPTER X

Shot down from the Heights

In the breakfast-room at the Red Court Farm, seated at its well-laid morning-table, was Richard Thornycroft. Seated at it only: not eating: his plate was unsupplied, his coffee stood cold before him. He seemed to be in some unpleasant meditation, every line of his dark face speaking of perplexity.

To be broken in upon by the irruption of numerous visitors, evidently astonished him not a little. The attendants on Mr. Thornycroft had gathered on the way from the Half-moon beach, just as some balls gather in rolling, and six or seven friends followed in or the tail of the master of the Red Court Farm. Isaac, on the contrary, seemed to have fallen away from it, for he did not enter with the rest. Richard rose to welcome them, with scant courtesy.

"Where's Cyril?" began the justice. "Is he down yet?"

"I don't know," answered Richard, taking out his watch and glancing at it. "I have not seen him. It is early yet."

"And Cyril never is very early," added the justice, quickly assuming that his youngest son was in his bed still. "Have you heard the news, Richard?"

"Yes," was Richard's laconic answer.

"What do you think of it? How do you suppose it could have happened?"

"I don't think about it," returned Richard. "I conclude that if he did not shoot himself, he must have got into some quarrelling fray. He drank enough wine last evening to heat his brain, and we had proof that he was fond of meddling in what did not concern him. The extraordinary part of the business is, what brought him back on the plateau, after he had once started on his journey."

"I'll go up and arouse Cyril, and know where he left Hunter. Gentlemen, if you will sit down and take some breakfast, we shall be glad of your company. There's a capital round of beef. Hallo you girls!" called out the justice, striding away in the direction of the kitchen, "some of you come in here and attend. Sinnett, let some more ham and eggs be sent in. '

Nothing loath, the gentlemen responded at once to the invitation: most of them had not breakfasted. The Rev. Mr. Southall made one. The round of beef was capital, as its master said; the game pies looked tempting, the cold ham, the hot rolls, the fresh eggs, the toasted bacon, all were excellent. Apparently, the Red Court Farm kept itself prepared for an impromptu public breakfast, just as well as it did for an impromptu dinner.

Mr. Thornycroft ascended the stairs, and presently his voice was heard on the landing, calling to Cyril. But it died away in the echoes of the large house, and there was no answer; unless the opening of the door of his wife's room by her maid could be called such.

"Did you want anything, sir?" she asked, looking out.

"Nothing particular. How is your lady this morning?"

"Much the same, sir, thank you."

The maid shut the door again, and Mr. Thornycroft went on to Cyril's chamber. He found it empty. It was so unusual for Cyril to be up and out early, that he felt a sort of surprise. That he had not gone far, however, was evident, as his watch and purse lay on the chest of drawers. The justice crossed the corridor and knocked at his daughter's room.

"Are you up, Mary Anne?"

"Yes," responded a faint and hurried voice within. "What do you want, papa?"

"I want you. Open the door."

But Miss Thornycroft did not obey. The justice, never remarkable for patience, when his behests were disregarded, laid hold of the handle and shook it with his strong hand.

"Open the door, I say, Mary Anne. What, girl! are you afraid of me?"

Miss Thornycroft slowly opened the door, and presented herself. She was in a handsome grey silk dress, but it looked tumbled, as if she had lain down in it, and her hair was rough and disarranged. It was the gown she had worn the previous evening, and it would almost seem as if she had done nothing to herself since going upstairs to bed. The signs caught her father's eye, and he spoke in astonishment.

"Why—what in the world, girl? You have never undressed yourself! Surely, you did not pay too much respect to the wine, as some of the men did!"

"You know better than that, sir. I was very tired, and threw myself on the bed when I came up: I suppose sleep overtook me. Do not allude to it, papa, downstairs. I will soon change my dress."

"Sleeping in your clothes does not seem to agree with you, Mary Anne: you look as white as if you had swallowed a doctor's shop. Do you know anything of Cyril?—that's what I wanted to ask you."

"No," she replied, "I have neither seen nor heard him."

Mr. Thornycroft came to the conclusion that Cyril had heard of the calamity, and gone out to see about it in his curiosity. He returned to the breakfast-room and said this. Sinnett, who was there, turned round and spoke.

"Mr. Cyril did not sleep at home last night, sir."

"Nonsense," responded the justice.

"He did not, sir," persisted Sinnett, in as positive a tone as she dared to use.

"Not sleep at home!" cried Mr. Thornycroft, ironically. "You must be mistaken, Sinnett. Cyril is not a night-bird," he continued, turning his fine and rather free blue eyes on the company: "he leaves late hours to his brothers.'

"When Martha took up his hot water just now, and knocked, there was no reply," returned Sinnett, quietly. "So she went in, fearing he might be ill, and found the bed had not been slept in."

For Cyril, who had never willingly been guilty of loose conduct in his whole life, to sleep out from home secretly, was as remarkable a fact as the going regularly to bed at ten o'clock would have been for his brothers. Mr. Thornycroft not only felt amazement, but showed it.

"I cannot understand this at all. Richard, do you know where he can be?"

"Not in the least. I was waiting for him to come down that I might question him where he parted with Hunter."

"When did you see him last?"

"When he was going off last night with Hunter. I have not seen him since. He will turn up by-and-by," continued Richard, carelessly. "If a fellow never has stopped out to make a night of it, that's no reason why he never may. Perhaps he came to an anchor at the Mermaid."

Clearly there was reason in this. Cyril Thornycroft might have remained out from some cause or other, though he never had before, and the gentlemen fell to their breakfast again. But for the strange and unhappy fact of Hunter's having come back to Coastdown, Mr. Thornycroft had concluded that Cyril must have walked with him to Jutpoint, and taken a bed there.

"Go up to Miss Thornycroft, Sinnett," said the justice. "She does not seem well. Perhaps she would like some tea."

Giving a look round the table first to see that nothing more was wanted (for the housekeeper liked to execute orders at her own time and will), she proceeded to Miss Thornycroft's room. The young lady then had her hair down and her dress off, apparently in the legitimate process of dressing.

"My goodness me, Miss Mary Anne, how white you look!" was the involuntary exclamation of the servant. "It is a dreadful thing, miss, but you must not take it too much to heart. It is worse for poor Mr. Hunter himself than it is for you."

Mary Anne Thornycroft, who had made a vain effort to hide her emotion and her ghastly face from the servant, opened her lips to speak, and closed them again, unable to utter a syllable.

"What a gaby the justice must have been to make such haste to tell her!" thought the woman. For it never occurred to Sinnett that Miss Thornycroft could have gained the information from any other source; or, rather, it may be more correct to say that she knew it could not have been gained from any other. Sinnett, standing in the hall underneath at the moment, had heard her master's knock for admission at his daughter's door, and the colloquy that ensued—not the words, only the sound of the voices.

"The whole village is up in arms," continued Sinnett. "It is an awful murder. Hyde—"

"Don't talk of it," came the interrupting wail; "I cannot bear it yet. Is he found?"

"Poor wretch, yes! with no look of a human face about him, they say," was Sinnett's answer.

"Shot down on to the Half-moon?" shuddered Miss Thornycroft, evidently speaking more to herself than to Sinnett.

"In the fur corner of it. I'll go and bring you a cup of tea, miss. You are shaking all over."

Mary Anne put out her hand to arrest her, but she was weak, feeble, suffering, and Sinnett went on, totally regardless. In the woman's opinion there was no panacea for ills, whether mental or bodily, like a cup of strong tea, and she hastened to bring one for her young lady. The shortest way of doing this was to get it from the breakfast-room, and in went Sinnett. She was not disposed to stand on too much ceremony at the best of times, especially when put out. Occupying her position for many years as mistress of the internal economy of the Red Court Farm, she felt her sway in it, and she was warmly condemning her master for having spoken. For Sinnett was one who liked on occasion to set those about her to rights. The large silver teapot was before the justice. Sinnett, a breakfast cup in her hand, went up and asked him to fill it.

"What a pity it is, sir, that you told Miss Thornycroft so soon; before she was well out of her bed!" began Sinnett in an undertone, as she stood waiting. "Time enough for her to have heard such a horrid thing, sir, when she had taken a bit of breakfast. There she is, shaking like a child, not able to dress herself."

"I did not tell her," returned. Mr. Thornycroft aloud. "What are you talking of?"

"Yes, you did, sir."

"I did not, I tell you."

"You must have told her, sir," persisted Sinnett. "The first thing she asked me was, whether the body was found on the Half-moon, and said it was shot down on to it. Nobody else has been to the room but yourself."

"Take up the tea to your mistress, and don't stand cavilling here," interposed Richard, in a tone of stern command.

Justice Thornycroft brooked not contradiction from a servant. Moreover, he began to think that his daughter must have got her information from Cyril. He rose from table and strode upstairs after Sinnett, following her into his daughter's room.

"Mary Anne"—in a sharp tone—"did you tell that woman I disclosed to you what had happened to Hunter?"

"No," was the reply.

"Did I tell you that anything had happened to him?"

"No, papa, you did not."

"Do you hear what Miss Thornycroft says?" continued the magistrate, turning to the servant. "I advise you not to presume to contradict me again. If the house were in less excitement, you should come in before them all, and beg my pardon."

A ghastly look of fear had started to the features of Miss Thornycroft. "I—I heard them talking of it outside," she murmured, looking at Sinnett.

"Outside!" exclaimed Sinnett.

"Underneath, in the herb-garden," faintly added Miss Thornycroft, whose very lips were white as ashes.

"Then you did not hear of it from Cyril, Mary Anne?"

"No, papa, I have not seen Cyril at all."

Justice Thornycroft strode downstairs again. Sinnett, who did not like to be rebuked—and, in truth, rarely gave occasion for it—looked rather sullen as she put down the cup and saucer.

"Nobody has been in the side garden since I got up," cried Sinnett.

"Oh, it was before that," too hastily affirmed Miss Thornycroft. "They were strange voices," she hurriedly added, as if afraid of more questions.

Sinnett shut the door on Miss Thornycroft, and went away ruminating. Something like fear had arisen to the woman's own face.

"What does it all mean?" she asked herself, unconsciously resting the small silver waiter on the window-seat, as she stood looking out. "She could not have heard anything outside in the herb-garden, for nobody has had the key of it this morning; and as to people having been up here talking of it before I was up, the poor man had not then been found."

That some dreadful mystery existed, something that would not bear the light of day, and in which Miss Thornycroft was in some way mixed up, Sinnett felt certain. And, woman-like, she spoke out her thoughts too freely: not in ill-nature; not to do harm to Miss Thornycroft or anyone else; but in the love of talking, in the wish to get her own curiosity satisfied. How had she learnt the news? Sinnett wondered again and again. What was it that had put her into this unnatural state of alarm and fear? Regret she might feel for Robert Hunter; horror at his dreadful fate—but whence arose the fear? Shrewd Sinnett finally descended, her brain in full work.

When the party in the breakfast-room had concluded their meal, which they did not spare, in spite of the sight their eyes had that morning looked on, they departed in a body, each one privately hoping he should be the first to alight on Mr. Cyril. In the present stage of the affair, Cyril Thornycroft was regarded as the one only person who could throw light upon it. It did not clearly appear where he could be. Richard's suggestion of the Mermaid was an exceedingly improbable one. He was not there; he seemed not to be anywhere else; nobody appeared to have seen him since the previous night, when he was starting to walk a little way with Robert Hunter.

Mr. Thornycroft sat down in the justice room to write to the coroner, and was interrupted by his eldest son. He looked up in expectation.

"Has Cyril turned up, Richard?"

"No, sir. Cyril's not gone far. His porte-monnaie and watch are in his room."

"Yes, I caught a sight of them myself. It is strange where he can be. I am rather uneasy."

"There's no occasion for that," returned Richard. "He must have gone on to Jutpoint. There's not a doubt of it."

"Well, I suppose it is so. The curious part is, what brought Hunter back again when he was once fairly on the road? They have been suggesting at the breakfast-table that he might have forgotten something; and I suppose it was so. But what took him to the plateau?"

Richard had his theory on that point. "Curiosity, unjustifiable curiosity; possibly a wicked, dishonourable resolution to betray us, after all," were the words rising so persistently in his mind that he had some difficulty not to speak them. He did not, however; he wished to spare unpleasantness to his father so far as might be. The only one to whom he gave the history of what took place on the previous night before parting with Hunter, was Isaac; and Isaac, as we know, had repeated just a word to his father. Mr. Thornycroft recurred to it now.

"What was it Isaac said about you and Hunter, Richard? I almost forget. That Hunter went on the plateau and saw the signal-light?"

"Hunter saw it. When he first quitted the house some devil's instinct took him to the plateau. I met him as he was running down, made him promise to hold his tongue, and sent him off with Cyril. I could have staked my life—yes, my life," added Richard, firmly—"that he would not have come back again."

"Was that all that passed?"

"Oh yes, that was all," carelessly returned Richard, who thought it well not to give the details of the unpleasant interview. "He and Cyril walked away together, and I fully assumed we had seen the colour of his ugly face for the last time."

"And East saw them down at the Hollow, so they must have gone that far. Well, it's very odd; but I suppose Cyril will clear it up."

Mr. Thornycroft drew down his spectacles before his eyes—they had been lifted while he talked—and went on with his note to the coroner. Again Richard broke in, speaking abruptly.

"Sir, this affair of Hunter's must be kept dark."

"Kept dark!" echoed the justice. "When a man's found murdered, one can't keep it dark. What do you mean, Dick?"

"I mean, kept as dark as the legal proceedings will allow. Don't make more stir in it, sir, than is absolutely necessary. It would have been well to keep secret his having gone on the plateau at all; but it's known already, and can't be helped now. Hush it up as much as you can."

"But why?"

"Hush it up," impressively repeated Richard, his dark face working with some inward agitation. "I shall know what to say in regard to his having gone on the plateau before departure; you and Isaac had better be silent. Hush it up—hush it up! You will be at the coroner's right hand, and can sway him imperceptibly. It is essential advice, father."

"What the deuce!" burst forth the magistrate, staring at his son; "you do not fear Cyril was the murderer of Hunter?"

"No, thank God!" fervently answered Richard. "Cyril would be the last in the world to speak an unkind word, let alone shoot a man. But, don't you see, sir—too minute enquiries may set them on the track of something else that was done on the Half-moon last night, and it would not do. That confounded Kyne has got his eyes and ears open enough, as it is."

"By George! there's something in that," deliberated the justice. "My sympathy for Hunter put that out of my mind. All right, Dicky, now I have the cue."

Mr. Thornycroft sealed his note to the coroner, despatched it, and went upstairs to Lady Ellis's room. She was up, and sitting on the sofa. He shook hands and enquired how she had rested. For a long while, in fact since the beginning of her illness, their relations with each other had been but those of common acquaintance. He was wondering whether it would be well to tell her of the catastrophe; but she had already heard of it, and sat, paler than usual, gazing at the idlers who were crowding the edge of the plateau, leaning over it in their curiosity. That unusual sight would alone have told her something was the matter.

"Is it possible that this can be true?" she asked, in a low tone of distress. "Is Robert Hunter really murdered?"

"It is too true, unfortunately," he answered; "at least, that he is dead. Whether murdered—as everybody has been in haste to say and assume or whether accidentally shot, remains to be proved."

"And what are the particulars? What is known?"

But here Mr. Thornycroft would not satisfy her, or could not stay to do it. His carriage was at the door to take him to Jutpoint, where he had magisterial business that could not be postponed. Mentioning just a fact or two, he quitted the room, and found Isaac talking rather sharply to Sinnett in the hall below.

Sinnett had not allowed her doubts or her tongue to slumber. First of all she had talked to Hyde—of Miss Thornycroft's curious demeanour, of her incautious avowal, of her remarkable state of alarm and of fear; and Hyde replied by telling her to "hold her peace if she couldn't talk sense." She next, as it chanced, mentioned it to Tomlett, and he retorted that Sinnett was a fool. Sinnett felt wrathful; and in some way or other the matter penetrated to the ears of Isaac. He did not believe it; he felt sure that his sister knew nothing, and was taking Sinnett to task when Mr. Thornycroft descended.

A few hasty words from the three, and Mr. Thornycroft opened the door of his daughter's parlour, where he understood she now was. Rather to his surprise, Richard was shut in with her. It was an unusual thing for him to be indoors in the day-time. She wore a morning dress now, and looked much as usual, except that her face was pale and her hands trembled. Richard went out as they entered.

"Now, then," said the justice, "we will have this cleared up. Where and from whom did you hear of this matter, Mary Anne?"

She answered briefly, leaning her forehead on her hand, that she had heard people talking of it early in the morning below her window. Sinnett, anxious to justify herself, and very vexed that this should have come to the ears of her masters, said this could not be; the key of the herb-garden was in her pocket, and nobody could have got into it.

The plot of ground on the side of the house, under Miss Thornycroft's window, where the herbs were grown, was enclosed. A small glass shed (it was not half large enough to be called a green-house) was at one corner of it, in which Sinnett had some plants. Three or four of these had been stolen one night, and since then Sinnett had kept the gate locked.

Miss Thornycroft, her hand held up still as if to hide her face, persisted. She had heard voices underneath in the early morning, strange voices; it was so unusual that she quietly opened her window to listen. They spoke of Mr. Hunter, and she caught distinctly the words "murder," and "shot down from the heights to the Half-moon." "It was as if one man was telling another," faintly concluded Miss Thornycroft. "I could only hope it was not true; it frightened me terribly. As to how they could have been in the herb-garden, I suppose they must have got over the palisades."

"Nothing more likely, that they might talk at leisure without interruption," cried the justice, turning angrily on his housekeeper. "Let the subject be dropped: do you hear, Sinnett? How dare you attempt to raise a cabal! What's the matter with you to-day? One would think you shot him down."

Striding across the hall, the justice went out to his restive horses, prancing and pawing the ground in their impatience. Isaac followed him.

"If you will allow me, sir, I should like to accompany you."

"All right, Isaac; get up."

The justice drove away, his son by his side his groom sitting behind, as he had once, years ago, driven away from the gate of Mrs. Chester; but his daughter was with him then. Isaac's errand to Jutpoint, unavowed, was to look after Cyril. Why it should have been so he could not have told, then or later, but an uneasy prevision lay on his mind that something or other was wrong, more than met the eye.

Sinnett, nettled beyond everything at her master's concluding reproach, spoken though it was in irony, and at the turn of affairs altogether, flounced off to her kitchen, leaving Miss Thornycroft alone. She—Mary Anne Thornycroft—had made her explanation almost glibly, after the manner of one who has learnt a part by heart, and recites it. That some most awful dread was upon her—apart from the natural grief and horror arising from the murder, if it was murder—was indisputable, and Sinnett felt sure of it still.

Her face buried in her hands; her body swaying backwards and forwards in her chair; her whole aspect evincing dire agony now she was alone, sat Mary Anne Thornycroft. In that one past night she seemed to have aged years. The knock of a visitor aroused her; some curious gossip come to inquire and chatter and comment; and she escaped upstairs, crossing Hyde in the hall.

"I cannot see anyone, Hyde; my head aches too much."

The door of her step-mother's room was open, and Lady Ellis called to her. One single moment of rebellion, of wish to escape, and then she remembered that she had not been in at all that morning, and also that it was well to avoid observation just now. Lady Ellis sat as Mr. Thornycroft had left her; her dark hair drawn simply from her wasted face, her purple morning-gown tied at the waist with a cord and tassel, its lace ruffles falling over her thin white hand.

"I was just going to ring and ask you to come up, Mary Anne. I must hear the particulars of this dreadful mystery; I cannot rest until they are told. Look at them!"

She pointed to the heights. Dotting the plateau, peeping in at the round tower, holding hands and waists for security as they bent forward over the edge to look at the scene of the tragedy below, were the idlers. Mary Anne sat down near the table, her elbow on it, her head leaning on her hand, her eyes bent on the carpet, and told the particulars that the world knew. Lady Ellis heard them to the end without comment.

"But why should he have gone on the plateau at all?" she questioned.

"I don't know. He did go. As I stood at the door watching him off, he turned from the road to the plateau. I saw him. I saw him cross the railings."

"And your brother Richard saw him?"

"Yes, as he was coming off. They stood talking for a minute or two, Richard says. Cyril came up then, and he started to walk a little way with Robert Hunter."

"But what does Cyril say? Where is he?"

"He has not been home since. They suppose he went on to Jutpoint and slept there. Nothing more except this is known."

"But Mr. Hunter must have come back again?"

"Of course he must. It is his coining back that is so unaccountable."

"And why—why should Cyril walk to Jutpoint, unless he walked with Mr. Hunter?" resumed Lady Ellis after a pause.

Miss Thornycroft shook her head. It was in truth so much involved in doubt and mystery from beginning to end, that she felt unable to cope with it, even by conjecture, she said faintly. "The terrible point in it all seems to be in his having come back again."

"Nay, the terrible point is the attack upon him," dissented her step-mother. "It might have been an accidental shot, after all. At what hour was it supposed to take place?"

Miss Thornycroft could not say. "Of course—yes—it might have been only accidental," she assented with whitening lips.

"Mary Ann, how ill you look!"

"Do I? It frightened me, you see. And I have a dreadful headache," she added, rising to escape those eyes bent on her with so much curiosity. "I must go and lie down on the bed, if you will spare me."

"Lie on my sofa," said Lady Ellis.

"No, thank you. Shut in by myself, I may get to sleep."

"Tell me one thing," and Lady Ellis laid her hand on her step-daughter's arm. "Is any one suspected?"

"No; oh no."

"I suppose, Mary Ann, it is quite sure that he is dead?"

A faint cry at the mockery of the almost suggested hope escaped Mary Anne's lips. When the surgeon saw him at eight o'clock that morning, he thought he must have been dead about ten hours.

Lady Ellis leaned back in her chair when she was left alone, her eyes closed, her wan hands clasped meekly on her bosom.

"Ah! was he fit to go? was he fit to go?" she murmured, the thought having lain on her as a great dream of agony. "Had it been Cyril Thornycroft, there could be no doubt. But he—? Perhaps he was changed, as I am," she resumed after a long pause. "Oh! yes, yes, it might have been so; Robert Hunter might have been READY. Thank God that he gave me his forgiveness last night!"

CHAPTER XI

The Coroner's Inquest

The coroner's inquest was held on the Wednesday. Nothing could exceed the state of ferment that Coastdown was in: not altogether from the fact of the murder itself—for murder it was universally assumed to be, and was—but also from one or two strange adjuncts that surrounded it. The first of these was the prolonged and unaccountable absence of Cyril Thornycroft; the second arose from sundry rumours rife in the town. It was whispered on the Tuesday that two or three witnesses had been present when the deed was committed; that they had seen it done; and the names of these, scarcely breathed at first, but gathering strength as the day wore on, were at length spoken freely: Miss Thornycroft, Miss Chester, and Captain Copp's maidservant, Sarah Ford.

Whether the reports arose, in the first place, in consequence of Sinnett's talking; whether Sarah Ford had spoken a hasty word on the Monday morning, in her surprise and shock at what she heard; or whether the facts had gone about through those strange instincts of suspicion that do sometimes arise in the most extraordinary manner, nobody can tell how or whence, was not yet known. But the rumours reached the ear of the summoning officer, and at ten o'clock on the Tuesday night that functionary delivered his mandates—one at the Red Court Farm, two at Captain Copp's, for these witnesses to attend the inquest. Speaking afterwards at the Mermaid of what he had done, the excitement knew no bounds.

Speculation was rife in regard to the most strange absence of Cyril Thornycroft. But not quite at first— not, in fact, until the Wednesday morning—was any unpleasant feeling connected with it. It might have been in men's minds—who could say it had not?—but on the Wednesday it began to be spoken. Was Cyril the guilty man? Had he, in a scuffle or else, fired the shot that killed Hunter?

The taint was carried in a whisper to the Red Court Farm. It staggered Mr. Thornycroft; it drove Isaac speechless; but Richard, in his usual fashion, went into a white heat of indignation. Cyril, who was one of the best men on the face of the earth!—who lived, as everybody knew, a gentle and blameless life, striving to follow, so far as might be, the example his Master set when He came on earth!—who would not hurt a fly, who was ever seeking to soothe others battling with the world's troubles, and help them on the road to Heaven!—he kill Robert Hunter! Richard's emotion overwhelmed him, and his lips turned white as he spoke it.

All very true: if ever a man strove to walk near to God, it was certainly Cyril Thornycroft; and Richard's hearers acknowledged it. But—and this they did not say—good men had been overtaken by temptation, by crime, before now; and, after all, this might have been a pure accident. If Cyril Thornycroft were innocent, argued Coastdown, why did he run away? Of course, his prolonged absence, if voluntary, was the great proof against him: even unprejudiced people admitted that. Mr. Thornycroft and his sons had another theory, and were not uneasy. It was not convenient to speak of it to the world; but they fully believed Cyril would return home in a week or two, safe and sound; and they also, one and all, implicitly believed that he was not only guiltless of the death of Robert Hunter, but ignorant of its having taken place. The fact of his having no money with him went for nothing—it has been mentioned that his purse was left in his room,—if Cyril had gone where they suspected, he could have what money he pleased for the asking.

In this state of excitement and uncertainty, Wednesday morning dawned. As the hour for the coroner's inquest drew near, all the world assembled round the Mermaid: to see the coroner and jury go in would be something. Captain Copp stumped about in a condition of wrath that promised momentary explosion, arising from the fact that his "women-kind" should be subp[oe]naed to give evidence on a land murder. What they might have to say about it, or what they had not to say, the captain was unable to get at; his questioning had been in vain: Sarah was silent and sullen; Anna Chester white and shivering, as if some great blow had fallen on her: and this unsatisfactory state of things did not tend to increase the captain's equanimity. He had been originally summoned to serve on the inquest, but when the officer came to the house at ten on the Tuesday night, he told him he had perhaps better not serve. All this was as bitter aloes to the merchant captain.

The inquest took place in the club-room of the Mermaid, the coroner taking his seat at the head of its long table covered with green baize, while the jury ranged themselves round it. Justice Thornycroft was seated at the right hand of the coroner. They had viewed the body, which lay in an adjoining room, just as it had been brought up.

The first witness called was Mr. Supervisor Kyne, he having been the first to discover the calamity. With break of day on the Monday morning he went on the plateau. Happening to look over as far as he could stretch, he saw what he thought to be Mr. Hunter asleep: the face was hidden from him as he stood above, but he knew him by his coat. Going round to the Half-moon beach, having been joined on his way by one or two fishermen, they discovered that the poor gentleman was not asleep, but dead: in fact that he had been killed, and in a most frightful manner.

The surgeon who had been called to examine the body spoke next. The cause of death was a shot, he said. The bullet had entered the face, gone through the brain, and passed out at the crown of the head. Death must have been instantaneous, he thought: and the face had also been very much defaced by the jagged points of the rock in falling. In answer to the coroner, the surgeon said he should think it had been many hours dead when he was called to see it at half-past seven in the morning: nine or ten at least.

The next witness was Mr. Thornycroft, who stood up to give his evidence. He spoke to the fact of the young man's having been his guest for a short while at the Red Court: that he had intended to leave on the Sunday night by the half-past eight omnibus for Jutpoint, to catch the train; but had missed it. He then said he would walk it, wished them good-bye, and left with that intention. He knew no more.

Mr. Thornycroft sat down again, and Richard was called. He confirmed his father's evidence, and gave some in addition. On the Sunday night he quitted the dining-room soon after the deceased, and went outside for a stroll. There he saw Hunter, who appeared to have been on the plateau. They stood together a few moments talking, and just as they were parting Cyril came up. He, Cyril, said he would walk a little way with Hunter, and they turned away together.

"To walk to Jutpoint?" interposed the coroner.

"Yes: speaking of Hunter. Of course I supposed my brother would turn back almost immediately."

"Were they upon angry terms one with the other?"

"Certainly not."

"And you never saw either of them afterwards?"

"No," replied Richard, in a low tone—which the room set down to uneasiness on the score of Cyril's absence. "I went indoors then."

"You are sure that the deceased was then starting, positively starting, on his walk to Jutpoint?"

"I am quite certain. There is no doubt of it whatever."

"What, then, caused him to come back again?"

"I am quite unable to conjecture. It is to me one of the strangest points connected with this strange business."

Cause, indeed, had Richard Thornycroft to say so! He, of all others, he alone, knew of the oath taken by Hunter not to come back; of the danger Hunter knew he would run in attempting it. To the very end of Richard's life—as it seemed, to him now—would the thing be a mystery to his mind: unless Cyril should be able to throw light upon it.

Richard Thornycroft had no further testimony to offer, and Isaac was next examined. He could say no more than his father had said; not having seen Hunter at all since the latter quitted the dining-room. Of the subsequent events of the night, he said he knew personally nothing: he was not out of doors. The fisherman, East, next appeared, and testified to having seen Cyril Thornycroft and Mr. Hunter together, as before stated.

"Were you looking out for them?" asked a sapient juryman.

"Looking out for 'em?" repeated East. "Lawk love ye, I warn't a-looking out for nobody. I'd not have noticed 'em, maybe, but for Mr. Hunter's white coat that he'd got buttoned on him. One couldn't be off seeing that."

"Call Cyril Thornycroft," said the coroner.

The calling of Cyril Thornycroft was a mere form, as the coroner was aware. He had learnt all the unpleasant rumours and suspicions attaching to Cyril's absence; had no doubt formed his own opinion on the point. But he was careful not to avow that opinion; perhaps also not to press for any evidence that might tend to confirm it, out of regard to his old friend, Justice Thornycroft.

"Have you any suggestion to offer as to your son's absence?" he asked in a considerate tone of the magistrate.

Mr. Thornycroft stood up to answer. His countenance was clear and open, his fine upright form raised to its full height: evidently he attached no suspicion to his son's non-return.

"I think it will be found that he has only gone to see some friends who live at a distance, and that a few days will bring him home again. My reasons for this belief are good, though I would rather not state them publicly; they are conclusive to my own mind, and to the minds of my two elder sons. And I beg to say that I affirm this in all honour, as a magistrate and a gentleman."

Again the coroner paused. "Do you consider, Mr. Thornycroft, that your son premeditated this visit?"

"No; or he would have spoken of it. I think that circumstances must have caused him to depart on it suddenly."

Mr. Thornycroft was thinking of one class of "circumstances," the coroner and jury of another. They could only connect any circumstances, causing sudden departure, with the tragedy of the night, with a sense of guilt. Mr. Thornycroft knew of another outlet.

"Is it usual for him to leave his watch and purse on the drawers, sir?" asked a juror.

"It is not unusual. He does so sometimes when changing his coat and waistcoat for dinner: not intentionally, but from forgetfulness. He is absentminded at the best of times: not at all practical as his brothers are."

"But what would he do without money on a journey?" persisted the gentleman.

Mr. Thornycroft paused for a moment, considering his answer. It was exceedingly unfortunate that he could not speak out freely: Cyril's reputation had suffered less.

"The fact of his having left his purse at home does not prove he has no money with him," said the justice. "In fact, I believe he keeps his porte-monnaie in his pocket from habit more than anything else, and carries his money loose. Most men, so far as I know, like to do so. I examined the porte-monnaie this morning, and found it empty."

There was a slight laugh at this, hushed immediately. Mr. Thornycroft, finding nothing farther was asked him, sat down again.

"Call Sarah Ford," said the coroner.

Sarah Ford came in, and Captain Copp, who made one of the few spectators, struck his wooden leg irascibly on the floor of the room: a respectable, intelligent-looking woman, quietly attired in a straw bonnet, a brown shawl with flowered border, with a white handkerchief in her gloved hands. She did not appear to be in the least put out at having to appear before the coroner and jury, and gave her evidence with the most perfect independence.

The coroner looked at his notes; not of the evidence already given, which his clerk was taking down, but of some he had brought to refresh his memory.

"Do you recollect last Sunday evening, witness?" he asked, when a few preliminary questions had been gone through.

"What should hinder me?" returned the witness, ever ready with her tongue. "It's not so long ago."

"Where did you go to that evening?"

"I went nowhere but to Justice Thornycroft's."

"For what purpose did you go there?"

"To fetch Miss Chester. She was to have been sent for at eight o'clock, but master and mistress forgot it. When it was on the stroke of nine they told me to go for her."

"Which you did?"

"Which I did, and without stopping to put anything on."

"Did you meet anybody as you went?"

"Yes; nearly close to the Red Court gates I met Mr. Hunter and young Cyril Thornycroft."

"Walking together towards the village?" interposed the coroner.

"Walking on that way. Mr. Hunter was buttoning himself up tight in that blessed fine coat of his."

"Did they seem angry with each other?"

"No, sir; they were talking pleasantly. Mr. Cyril was saying to the other that if he stepped out he would be at Jutpoint by half-past ten. That was before they came close, but the air was clear and brought out the sound of their voices."

"Did they speak to you?"

"I spoke to them. I asked Mr. Hunter if he had lost the omnibus, for, you must understand, Miss Chester had said in the afternoon that he was going by it, and he said 'Yes, he had, and had got to walk it.' So I wished him a good journey."

"Was that all?"

"All that he said. Mr. Cyril asked me was I going to the Court, and I said 'Yes, I was, to fetch Miss Chester,' and that 'master was in a tantrum at its being so late.' (An irascible word from Captain Copp.) With that they went their way and I went mine."

"After that, you reached the Red Court?"

"Of course I reached it."

"Well, what happened there? Relate it in full."

"Nothing particular happened that I know of, except that the servants gave me some mulled wine."

"While you were waiting?"

"Yes, while I was waiting; and a fine time Miss Chester kept me, although I told her about the anger at home. She—"

"Stay a moment, witness. How long do you think it was?"

"A quarter of an hour or twenty minutes. Quite that."

"And now go on. We know the details, witness," added the coroner, significantly. "I tell you this, that you may relate them without being questioned at every sentence; it will save time."

Sarah looked at him. That he was speaking the truth was self-evident; and she prepared to tell her story consecutively, without any suppression. The coroner was impatient.

"Speak up, witness. Miss Thornycroft went out with you. What induced her to go?"

"I suppose it was a freak she took," replied the witness. "When they said Miss Chester was ready I went into the hall, and Miss Thornycroft, in a sort of joke (I didn't think she meant it) said she would come out with her. Miss Chester asked her how she would get back again, and she answered, laughing, that she'd run back, to be sure, nobody was about to see her. Well, she put on her garden-bonnet, which hung there, and a shawl, and we came away, all three of us. In going out at the gates they both turned on the waste land, towards the plateau. I saw 'em stop and stare up on it, as if they saw something; and I wished they'd just stare at our way home instead, for I was not over warm, lagging there. Presently one of them said to me—for I had followed—'Sarah, do look, is not that Robert Hunter walking about there?' 'My eyes is to chilled to see so far, young ladies,' says I; 'what should bring Robert Hunter there, when I met him as I came along, speeding on his journey to Jutpoint?' 'I can see that it is Robert Hunter,' returned Miss Thornycroft; 'I can see him quite distinct on that high ground against the sky.' And with that they told me to wait there, and they'd just run up and frighten him. Precious cross I was, and I took off my black stuff apron and threw it over my head, shawl fashion, thinking what a fool I was to come out on a cold frosty night without—"

"Confine yourself to the evidence," sternly interrupted the coroner.

"Well," proceeded Sarah, who remained as cool and equable before the coroner and jury as she would have been in her own kitchen, "I doubled my apron over my head, and down I sat on that red stone which rises out of the ground there like a low milestone. In a minute or two somebody comes running on to the plateau, as if following the young ladies—"

"From what direction, witness?"

"I think from that of the Red Court Farm. It might have been from that of the village, but I think it was the other; I am not sure either way. You see, I had got my apron right over me, and my head bent down on my knees, afeard of catching the face-ache, and I never heard anything till he was on the plateau. When I saw him he was near the Round Tower, going straight up to it, as it were; so he might have come from either way."

"Did you recognise him?"

"No; I didn't try to. I saw it was a man, through the slit I had left in my apron. He was going fast, but stealthily, hardly letting his shoes touch the ground, as if he was up to no good. And I was not sorry to see him go there, for thinks I, he'll hurry back my young ladies."

"Witness—pay attention—were there no signs by which you could recognise that man? How was he dressed? As a gentleman?—as a sailor?—as a—"

"As a gentleman, for all I saw to the contrary," replied the witness, unceremoniously interrupting the coroner's question. "If I had known he was going on to the plateau to murder Mr. Hunter, you may be sure I'd have looked at him sharp enough."

"For all you saw to the contrary," repeated the coroner, taking up the words; "what do you mean by that?"

"Well, what I mean is. I suppose, that he might have been a gentleman or he might not. The fact is, I never noticed his dress at all. I think the clothes were dark, and I think he had leggings on—which are worn by common people and gentlemen alike down here. The stars was rather under a cloud at the time, and so was my temper."

"Honestly acknowledged," said the coroner. "What sized man was he?—tall or short?"

"Very tall."

"Taller than—Mr. Cyril Thornycroft, for instance?"

"A great deal taller."

"You are sure of this?"

"I am sure and certain. Why else should I say so?"

"Go on with your evidence."

"A minute or so afterwards, as I sat with my back to the plateau and my head in my lap, I heard a gun go off behind me."

"Did that startle you?" asked an interrupting juryman.

"No, I am not nervous. If I had known it was let off on the plateau it might have startled me, on account of the young ladies being there; but I thought it was only from some passing vessel."

"It is singular you should have thought so lightly of it. t is not common to hear a gun fired on a Sunday night."

"You'd find it common enough if you lived here, sir. What with rabbit and other game shooters, and signals from boats, it is nothing in this neighbourhood to hear a gun go off, and it's what nobody pays any attention to."

"Therefore you did not?"

"Therefore I did not. And the apron I had got muffled over my ears made the sound appear further off than it really was. But close upon the noise came an awful cry; and that was followed by a shrill scream, as if from a woman. That startled me, if you like, and I jumped up, and threw off my apron, and looked on to the plateau. I could not see anything; neither the man nor the young ladies; so I thought it time to go and search after them. I had got nearly up to the Round Tower, that ruined wall, breast high, which is on the plateau—"

"You need not explain," said the coroner, "we know the place."

"When a man darted out from the shade of it," continued the witness. "He cut across to the side of the plateau next the village, and disappeared down that dangerous steep path in the cliffs, which nobody afore, I guess, ever ventured down but in broad daylight."

"Was it the same man you saw just before running on to the plateau?"

"Of course it was."

"By what marks did you know him again?"

"By no marks at all. I should not know the man from Adam. My own senses told me it was the same, because there was no other man on the plateau."

"Your own senses will not do to speak from. Remember, witness, you are on your oath."

"Whether I am on my oath or off it, I should speak the truth," was the response of the imperturbable witness.

"What next?"

"I stood looking at the man; that is, at where he had disappeared; expecting he was pitching down head foremost and getting half killed, at the pace he was going, when Miss Thornycroft laid hold of me, shaking and crying, almost beside herself with terror. Then I found that Miss Chester had fainted away, and was lying like one dead on the frosty grass inside the Round Tower."

"What account did they give of this?"

"They gave none to me. Miss Chester, when she came to herself, was too much shook to do it, and Miss Thornycroft was no better. I thought they had been startled by the man; I never thought worse; and I did not hear of the murder till the next morning. They told me not to say anything about it at home, or it would be known they had been on the plateau. So Miss Thornycroft ran back to the Red Court, and I went home with Miss Chester."

"What else do you know about the matter?"

"I don't know any more myself. I have heard plenty."

The witness's "hearing" was dispensed with, and Captain Copp was requested to stand up and answer a question. The captain's face, as he listened to the foregoing evidence, was something ludicrous to look upon.

"What account did Miss Chester and your servant give you of this transaction?" demanded the coroner.

"What account did they give me?" spluttered Captain Copp, to whom the question sounded as the most intense aggravation. "They gave me none. This is the first time my ears have heard it. I only wish I had been behind them with a cat-o'-nine-tails"—shaking his stick in a menacing manner—"I'd have taught them to go gampusing on to the plateau at night, after sweethearts! I'll send my niece back to whence she came; her father was a clergyman, Mr. Coroner, a rector of a parish. And that vile bumboat-woman, Sarah, with her apron over her head, shall file out of my quarters this day; a she-pirate, a—"

The coroner interposed. But what with Captain Copp's irascibility and his real ignorance of the whole transaction, nothing satisfactory could be obtained from him, and the next witness called was Miss Chester. A lady-like, interesting girl, thought those of the spectators who had not previously seen her. She gave her evidence in a sad, low tone, trembling the whole of the time with inward terror. To a sensitive mind, as hers was, the very fact of having to give her name as Anna Chester when it was Anna Thornycroft, would have been enough alarm. But there was worse than that.

Her account of their going on to the plateau was the same as Sarah's. It was "done in the impulse of the moment," to "frighten," or "speak to," Robert Hunter, who was at its edge. (A groan from Captain Copp.) That they halted for a moment at the Round Tower, and then found that a man was following them on to the plateau, so they ran inside to hide themselves.

"Who was that man?" asked the coroner.

"I don't know," was the faint reply. "I am nearsighted."

"Did you look at him?"

"We peeped out, round the wall. At least, Miss Thornycroft did. I only looked for a moment."

"Proceed, witness, if you please."

"He had come quite close when I looked, and—then—"

"Then what?" said the coroner, looking searchingly at the witness, who seemed unable to continue. "You must speak up, young lady."

"Then I saw him with a pistol—and he fired it off—and I was so terrified that I fainted, and remembered no more. It all passed in a moment."

"A good thing if he had shot off your two figureheads!" burst forth Captain Copp, who was immediately silenced.

"Was he tall or short, this man?"

"Tall."

"Did you know him?" proceeded the coroner.

"Oh no, no," was Anna's answer, putting up her hands, as if to ward off the approach of some terror, and she burst into a fit of hysterical crying.

She was conducted from the room. Isaac Thornycroft advanced to give her his arm, but she turned from him and took that of the doctor, who was standing by. An impression was left on the mind of one or two of the listeners that Miss Chester could have told more.

With the subsiding of the hubbub, the coroner resumed his business.

"Call Mary Anne Thornycroft."

Miss Thornycroft appeared, led in by her brother Richard. She wore a rich black silk dress, a velvet mantle, and small bonnet with blue flowers. Her face was of a deadly white, her lips were compressed; but she delivered her evidence with composure (unlike Miss Chester), in a low, deliberate, thoughtful tone. Her account of their going on to the plateau, and running inside the Round Tower at the approach of some man, who appeared to be following them, was the same as that given by the last witness. The coroner inquired if she had recognised Robert Hunter.

"Yes," was the reply. "I saw the outline of his face and figure distinctly, and knew him. I recognised him first by the coat he had on; it was quite conspicuous in the star-light. He was standing on the brink, apparently looking out over the sea.

"That was before you saw the man who came running on to the plateau?"

"Yes."

"Who was that man?"

Mary Anne Thornycroft laid her hand upon her heart, as if pressing down its emotion, before she answered.

"I cannot tell."

"Did you not know him?"

"No."

"Upon your oath?"

Miss Thornycroft again pressed her hands, both hands, upon her bosom, and a convulsive twitching was perceptible in her throat; but she replied, in a low tone, "Upon my oath."

"Then, he was a stranger?"

She bowed her rigid face in reply, for the white strained lips refused to answer. Motions are no answers for coroners, and this one spoke again.

"I ask you whether he was a stranger?"

"Yes."

"From what direction did he come?"

"I do not know. He was near the Round Tower before I saw him."

"You saw him draw the pistol and fire?"

"Yes."

"Now, young lady, I am going to ask you a painful question, but the ends of justice demand that you should answer it. Was that man your brother, Cyril Thornycroft?"

"No," she answered, in the sharp tone of earnest truth, "I swear it was not—I swear it before Heaven. The man bore no resemblance whatever to my brother Cyril; he was at least a head taller."

"Did he aim at Robert Hunter?"

"I cannot say. Robert Hunter was standing with his face towards us then, and I saw him fall back, over the precipice."

"With a yell, did he not?"

"Yes, with a yell."

"What then?"

"I cannot tell what, I believe I shrieked—I cannot remember. I next saw the man running away across the plateau."

"The witness Sarah Ford's evidence would seem to say that he lingered a few moments after firing the pistol—before escaping," interposed the coroner.

"It is possible. I was too terrified to retain a clear recollection of what passed. I remember seeing him run away, and then Sarah Ford came up."

"Should you recognise that man again?"

Miss Thornycroft hesitated. The room waited in breathless silence for her answer. "I believe not," she said; "it was only starlight. I am sure not."

At this moment, an incuisitive juryman spoke up. He wished to know how it was that Miss Thornycroft and the other young lady had never mentioned these facts until to-day, when they had been drawn from them, as it were, by their oath.

"Because," Miss Thornycroft replied, with, if possible, a deeper shade of paleness arising to her face—"because they did not care that their foolish freak of going on to the plateau should come to the knowledge of their friends."

"Glad they have some sense of shame left in them," cried Captain Copp.

The inquisitive juryman was not quite satisfied. He asked to have the maid-servant recalled; and, when she appeared, put the same question to her. "Why had she not told of it?"

Why didn't she tell! was the independent retort. Did the gentlemen think she was going to bleat out to the world what the young ladies had seen, when they did not choose to tell of it themselves, and so bring 'em here to be browbeat and questioned, as they had all been this day? Not she. She was only sorry other folks had ferreted it out, and told.

Very little evidence was forthcoming, none of consequence to the general reader. Supervisor Kyne volunteered a statement about smuggling, which nobody understood, and Justice Thornycroft at once threw ridicule upon. The coroner cut it short, and proceeded to charge the jury. Primarily remarking that, if the evidence was to be believed, Cyril Thornycroft must be held exempt from the suspicion whispered against him, he went on: If they thought a wicked, deliberate act of murder had been committed, they were to bring in a verdict to that effect; and if they thought it had not, they were not to bring it in so. Grateful for this luminous advice, the jury proceeded to deliberate—that is, they put their heads together, and spoke for some minutes in an undertone; and then intimated that they had agreed upon their verdict.

"Wilful murder against some person or persons unknown."

CHAPTER XII

Robert Hunter's Funeral

Filing out of the room in groups, came the crowd who had filled it. The day had changed. The brightness of the morning was replaced by a wintry afternoon of grey sky; the air blew keen; snow began to fall. The eager spectators put up their umbrellas, if they happened to possess any, and stood to talk in excited whispers.

Crossing to the waste land, the roundabout road she chose to take on her way home, was Anna Chester. Sarah had gone striding up the nearest way; Captain Copp had been laid hold of by Supervisor Kyne, whose grievance on the score of the smugglers was sore; and Anna was alone. Her veil drawn over her white face, her eyes wearing a depth of trouble never yet seen in their sweetness, went she, looking neither to the right nor left, until she was overtaken by Miss Thornycroft.

"Anna!"

"Mary Anne!"

For a full minute they stood, looking into each other's faces of fear and pain. And then the latter spoke, a rising sob of emotion catching her breath.

"Thank you for what you have done this day, Anna! I was in doubt before; I did not know how much you had seen that night; whether you had not mercifully been spared all by the fainting fit. But now that you have given your evidence, I see how much I have to thank you for. Thank you truly. We have both forsworn ourselves: you less than I; but surely Heaven will forgive us in such a cause."

"Let us never speak of it again," murmured Anna. "I don't think I can bear it."

"Just a word first—to set my mind at rest," returned Miss Thornycroft, as she stood grasping Anna's hand in hers. "How much did you see? Did you see the pistol fired?"

"I saw only that. It was at the moment I looked out round the wall. The flash drove me back again. That and the cry that broke from Robert Hunter: upon which I fainted for the first time in my life."

"And you—recognised him—him who fired the pistol?" whispered Miss Thornycroft, glancing cautiously round as the words issued from her bloodless lips.

"Yes, I fear so."

It was quite enough. Qualified though the avowal was, Mary Anne saw that she could have spoken decisively. The two unhappy girls, burdened with their miserable secret, looked into each other's faces that sickness and terror had rendered white. Anna, as if in desperation to have her fears confirmed where no confirmation was needed, broke the silence.

"It—was—your—brother."

"Yes."

"Isaac."

Miss Thornycroft opened her lips to speak, and closed them again. She turned her head away.

"You will not betray him—and us, Anna? You will ever be cautious—silent?"

"I will be cautious and silent always; I will guard the secret jealously."

A sharp pressure of the hand in ratification of the bargain, and they parted, Anna going on her solitary way.

"Will I guard the secret! Heaven alone knows how much heavier lies the obligation on me to do so than on others," wailed Anna. "May God help me to bear it!"

Quick steps behind her, and she turned, for they had a ring that she knew too well. Pressing onwards through the flakes of snow came Isaac Thornycroft. Anna set off to run; it was in the lonely spot by the churchyard.

"Anna! Anna! Don't you know me?"

Not a word of answer. She only ran the faster—as if she could hope to outstep him! Isaac, with his long, fleet strides, overtook her with ease, and laid his hand upon her shoulder.

Like a stag brought to bay, she turned upon him, with her terror-stricken face, more ghastly, more trembling than it had yet been; and by a dexterous movement freed herself.

"Why, Anna, what is the matter? Why do you run from me?"

"There's my uncle," she panted. "Don't speak to me—don't come after me."

And sure enough, as Isaac turned, he distinguished Captain Copp at a distance. Anna had set off to run again like a wild hare, and was half-way across the heath. Isaac turned slowly back, passed the captain with a nod, and went on, wondering. What had come to Anna? Why did she fly from him?

He might have wondered still more had he been near her in her flight. Groans of pain were breaking from her; soft low moans of anguish; sighs, and horribly perplexing thoughts; driving her to a state of utter despair.

For, according to the testimony of her own eyes that ill-fated night, Anna, you see, believed the murderer to be her husband Miss Thornycroft had now confirmed it. And, not to keep you in more suspense than can be helped, we must return to that night for a few brief moments.

When Richard Thornycroft darted into the subterranean passage with the intention of warning his brother Isaac, before he reached its end the question naturally occurred to him, Why stop the boats, now Hunter is off? and he turned back again. So much has been already said. But half-way down the passage he again vacillated—a most uncommon thing in Richard Thornycroft, but the episode with Hunter had well-nigh scared his senses away. Turning about again, he retraced his steps and called to Isaac.

A private conference ensued. Richard told all without reserve, down to the point where he had watched Hunter away, under the surveillance of Cyril. "Will it be better to stop the boats or not?" he asked.

"There is not the slightest cause for stopping them, that I see," returned Isaac, who had listened attentively. "Certainly not. Hunter is gone; and if he were not, I do not think, by what you say, that he would attempt to interfere further; he'd rather turn his back a mile the other way."

"Let them come on then," decided Richard.

"They are already, I expect, putting off from the ship."

Isaac Thornycroft remained at his work; Richard went back again up the passage. Not quickly; some latent doubt, whence arising he could not see or trace, lingered on his mind still—his better angel perhaps urging him from the road he was going. Certain it was: he remembered it afterwards even more vividly than he felt it then: that a strong inclination lay upon him to stop the work for that night. But it appeared not to hold reason, and was disregarded.

He emerged from the subterranean passage, lightly shut the trap-door—which could be opened from the inside at will, when not fastened down—and took his way to the plateau to watch against intruders. This would bring it to about the time that the two young ladies had gone there, and Sarah, her apron over her head, had taken her place on the low red stone. In her evidence the woman had said it might be a quarter of an hour or twenty minutes since she met Robert Hunter starting on his journey; it had taken Richard about that time to do since what he had done; and it might have taken Robert Hunter about the same space (or rather less) to walk quickly to the wherry, and come back again. And come back again! Richard Thornycroft could have staked his life, had the question occurred to him, that Hunter would not come back: he never supposed any living man, calling himself a gentleman, could be guilty of so great treachery. But the doubt never presented itself to him for a moment.

What then was his astonishment, as he ran swiftly and stealthily (escaping the sight of Sarah Ford, owing, no doubt, to her crouching posture on the stone, and the black apron on her head) up the plateau, to see Robert Hunter? He was at its edge, at the corner farthest from the village; was looking out steadily over the sea, as if watching for the boats and their prey. Richard verily thought he must be in a dream: he stood still and strained his eyes, wondering if they deceived him; and then as ugly a word broke from him as ever escaped the lips of man.

Thunderstruck with indignation, with dismay, half mad at the fellow's despicable conduct, believing that if any in the world ever merited shooting, he did; nay, believing that the fool must court death to be there after his, Richard's, warning promise; overpowered with fury, with passion, Richard Thornycroft stood in the shade of the Round Tower, his eyes glaring, his white teeth showing themselves from between the drawn lips. At that same moment Robert Hunter, after stooping to look over the precipice, turned round; the ugly fur on the breast of his coat very conspicuous. May Richard Thornycroft be forgiven! With a second hissing oath, he drew the pistol from his breast-pocket, pointed it with his unerring hand, and fired; and the ill-fated man fell over the cliff with a yelling cry. Another shriek, more shrill, arose at Richard's elbow from the shade of the Round Tower.

"So ye cursed sea-bird," he muttered. "He has got his deserts. I would be served so myself, if I could thus have turned traitor!"

But what was it seized Richard's arm? Not a seabird. It was his sister Mary Anne. "You here!" he cried, with increased passion. "What the fury!—have you all turned mad to-night?"

"You have murdered him!" she cried, in a dread whisper—for how could she know that Anna Chester had fallen senseless and could not hear her?—"you have murdered Robert Hunter!"

"I have," he answered. "He is dead, and more than dead. If the shot did not take effect, the fall would kill him."

"Oh, Richard, say it was an accident!" she moaned, very nearly bereft of reason in her shock of horror. "What madness came over you?"

"He earned it of his own accord; earned it deliberately. I held my pistol to his head before, this night, and I spared him. I had him on his knees to me, and he took an oath to be away from this place instantly, and to be silent. I told him if he broke it, if he lingered here but for a moment, I would put the bullet into him. I saw him off; I send Cyril with him to speed him on his road; and—see!—the fool came back again. I was right to do it."

"I will denounce you!" she fiercely uttered, anger getting the better of other feelings. "Ay, though you are my brother, Richard Thornycroft! I will raise the hue and cry upon you."

"You had better think twice of that," he answered, shaking her arm in his passion. "If you do, you must raise it against your father and your father's house!"

"What do you mean?" she asked, quailing, for there was a savage earnestness in his words which told of startling truth.

"Girl! see you no mystery? can't you fathom it? You would have aided Hunter in discovering the smugglers: see you not that we are the smugglers? We are running a cargo now—now"—and his voice rose to a hoarse shriek as he pointed to the Half-moon, "and he would have turned Judas to us! He was on the watch there, on the plateau's edge, doing traitor's work for Kyne."

"He did not know it was you he would have denounced," she faintly urged, gathering in the sense of his revelation to her sinking heart.

"He did know it. The knowledge came to him tonight. He was abject enough before me, the coward, and swore he would be silent, and be gone from hence there and then. But his traitor's nature prevailed, and he has got his deserts. Now go and raise the hue and cry upon us! Bring your father to a felon's bar."

Mary Anne Thornycroft, with a despairing cry, sank down on the grass at her brother's feet. He was about to raise her, rudely enough it must be confessed, rather than tenderly, when his eye caught the form of some one advancing; he darted off at right angles across the plateau, and descended recklessly the dangerous path.

The intruder was Sarah. Miss Thornycroft, passing off her own emotion as the effect of fear at the shot, though scarcely knowing how she contrived not to betray herself, remembered Anna. She lay within the walls in a fainting-fit. Only as they went in was consciousness beginning to return to her. It must be mentioned that at this stage Sarah did not know any one had been killed.

"Who was the man?" asked Sarah of Miss Thornycroft.

"Did you see him?" was the only answer.

"Not to know him, miss; only at a distance. A regular fool he must be to fire off guns at night, to frighten folks! Was it a stranger?"

"Yes." Mary Anne wiped the dew from her cold brow as she told the lie.

They took their departure, Sarah promising not to say they had been on the plateau—to hold her tongue, in short, as to the events of the night, shot and all. But a chance passer-by who had heard the report, saw them descend. It might have been through him the news got wind.

Mary Anne Thornycroft went in. Sounds of laughter and glee proceeded from the dining-room as she passed it, and she dragged her shaking limbs upstairs to her chamber, and shut herself in with her dreadful secret. Anna Chester with her secret turned to the heath, even one more dreadful; for in the momentary glimpse she caught of the man who drew the pistol, as he stood partly with his back to her, she had recognised, as she fully believed, her husband Isaac. Had the impression wanted confirmation in her mind—which it did not—the tacit admission of his sister, now alluded to, supplied it. Miss Thornycroft had opened her lips to correct her, "not Isaac, but Richard;" and closed them again without saying it. Thought is quick; and a dim idea flew through her brain, that to divert suspicion from Richard might add to his safety. It was not her place to denounce him; nay, her duty lay in screening him. Terribly though she detested and deplored the crime, she was still his sister.

And the poor dead body had lain unseen where it fell, in the remote corner of the plateau. The smugglers ran their cargo, passing within a few yards of the dark angle where it lay, and never saw it.

The funeral took place on the Friday, and Robert Hunter was buried within sight of the place from whence he had been shot down. Any one standing on that ill-fated spot could see the grave in the churchyard corner, close by the tomb of the late Mrs. Thornycroft.

None of his friends had arrived to claim him. It would have been remarkable, perhaps, if they had, since they had not been written to. Of male relatives he had none living, so far as was believed. His sister Susan was in a remote district of Yorkshire, and it was a positive fact that her address was unknown to both Anna Chester and Miss Thornycroft. Of course, the Miss Jupps could have supplied it on application, but nobody did apply. His half-sister, Mrs. Chester, was also uncertain in her domicile, here to-day, there to-morrow, and Anna had not heard from her for some months. The old saying that "Where there's a will there's a way," might have been exemplified, no doubt, in this case; but here there was no will. To all at Coastdown interested in the unfortunate matter, it had been a blessed relief could they have heard that Robert Hunter would lie in his quiet grave unclaimed for ever, his miserable end not inquired into. Richard Thornycroft had only too good personal cause to hope this, his sister also for his sake; and Mr. Thornycroft, acting on the caution Richard gave him as to the desirability of keeping other things quiet that were done on that eventful night, tacitly acquiesced in the silence. And Anna Chester—the only one besides who could be supposed to hold interest in the deceased—shuddered at the bare idea of writing to make it known; rather would she have cut off her right hand.

"They will be coming down fast enough with their inquiries from his office in London, when they find he does not return," spoke Richard gloomily the evening previous to the funeral. "No need to send them word before that time."

It was a snowy day. Mary Anne Thornycroft stood at the corridor window, from which a view of the path crossing from the village to the churchyard, could be obtained. Only for a few yards of it; but she watched carefully, and saw the funeral go winding past. The sky was clear at the moment; the snow had ceased; but the whole landscape, far and near, presented a sheet of white, contrasting strangely with the sombre black of the procession. Such a thing as a hearse was not known in Coastdown, and the body was carried by eight bearers. The clergyman, Mr. Southall, walked first, in his surplice—it was the custom of the place—having gone down to the Mermaid with the rest. Following it were Justice Thornycroft and his son Isaac, Captain Copp and Mr. Kyne, who acted as mourners; and a number of spectators brought up the rear. Richard had gone out to a distance that day; he had business, he said. Cyril had not been heard of. Mr. Thornycroft bore the expenses of the funeral. Some money had been found in the pockets of the deceased, a sovereign in gold and some silver; nothing else except a white handkerchief.

Mary Anne strained her eyes, blinded by their tears, upon the short line, as its features came into view one by one, more distinctly than could have happened at any time but this of snow. All she had cared for in life was being carried past there; henceforth the world would be a miserable blank. Dead! Killed! Murdered!—murdered by her brother, Richard Thornycroft! Had it been done by anybody not connected with her by blood, some satisfaction might have been derived by bringing the crime home to its perpetrator. Had it been brought home to Richard—and of course she could not move to bring it—he would have battled it out, persisting he was justified. He called it justifiable homicide; she called it murder.

The distant line of black has passed now, and colours follow: men and women, boys and girls; displaying, if not all the tints of the rainbow, the shades and hues, dirt included, that prevail in the every-day attire of the great unwashed. Mary Anne glided into her room, and sank down on her knees in the darkest corner.

Some time after, when she thought they might be coming home, for the mourners would return to the Red Court, not the Mermaid, she came out again, her eyes swollen, and entered her step-mother's room. My lady, looking worse and worse, every day bringing her palpably nearer the grave, sat with her prayer-book in her hand She had been reading the burial service. Ah, how changed she was; how changed in spirit!

"I suppose it is over," she said, in a subdued tone, as she laid the book down.

"Yes, by this time."

"May God rest his soul!" she breathed, to herself rather than to her companion.

Mary Anne covered her face with her hand, and for some moments there was perfect silence.

"I shall be going hence to-morrow, as you know," resumed Lady Ellis, "never to return, never perhaps to hold further communication with the Red Court Farm. I would ask you one thing first, Mary Anne, or the doubt and trouble will follow me: perhaps mix itself up with my thoughts in dying. What of Cyril?"

"Of Cyril?" returned Miss Thornycroft, lifting her face, rather in surprise. "We have not heard from him."

"Of course I know that. What I wish to ask is—what are the apprehensions?"

"There are none. Papa and my brothers seem perfectly at their ease in regard to him."

"Then whence arises this great weight of care, of tribulation, that lies on you?—that I can see lies on you, Mary Anne?"

"It s not on Cyril's account. The events of the last few days have frightened me," she hastened to add. "They have startled others as well as me."

"Ah, yes; true. And it seems to me so sad that you did not know the man who fired the pistol," continued Lady Ellis, who had no suspicion that Miss Thornycroft had not told the whole truth. "But to return to Cyril. If it be as you say, that they are easy about him, why, they must know something that I and others do not. I have asked your papa, but he only puts me off. Mary Anne, you might tell me."

Mary Anne made no immediate reply. She was considering what to do.

"The thought of Cyril is troubling me," resumed Lady Ellis. "As I lay awake last night, I thought how much I owed him. Were he my own son, his welfare could not be dearer to me than it is. Surely, Mary Anne, whatever you may know of him, I may share it. The secret—if it be a secret—will be sacred with me."

"Yes, I am sure it will," spoke Mary Anne impulsively. "Not that it is any particular secret," she added, with hesitation, framing the communication cautiously; "but still, papa has reasons for not wishing it to be known. He thinks Cyril has gone to Holland."

"To Holland?"

"Yes; we have friends there. And a ship was off lying o here on Sunday night with other friends on board. Some of them, subsequent to the—the accident—came on shore in a little boat, and papa and Richard feel quite certain that Cyril went on board with them when they returned. But there are reasons why this must not be told to the public."

"What a relief!" cried the invalid. "My dear, it is safe with me. Dear Cyril! he will live to fulfil God's mission yet in the world. I shall not see him for a last farewell here, but we shall say it in heaven. Not a farewell there—a happy greeting."

A sort of muffled sound downstairs, and Mary Anne quitted the room to look. Yes, they were coming in in their black cloaks and hatbands, having left Robert Hunter in the grave in St. Peter's churchyard.

For all that could be seen at present he seemed likely to lie there at rest, undisturbed, uninquired after. And the name of his slayer with him.

CHAPTER XIII

Curious Rumours

April. And a fine spring evening.

The weeks have gone on since that miserable January time, bringing but little change to Coastdown or to those in it. Robert Hunter rested in his grave, uninquired for—though as to the word "rested" more hereafter—and Cyril Thornycroft had never returned. Lady Ellis had died in Cheltenham only a week after she went back to it.

That Cyril's remaining away so long and his not writing was singular in the extreme, no one doubted. Mr. Thornycroft grew uneasy, saying over and over again that some accident must have happened to him. Richard, however, had his private theory on the point, which he did not tell to the world. He believed now that Cyril and Hunter had returned that night together; that Cyril had witnessed the deliberate shot, had put off to the ship, and in his condemnation of the act would not come home to the Red Court so long as he, Richard, was in it.

But Richard could not tell this to his father, and Mr. Thornycroft one morning suddenly ordered his son Isaac abroad—to France, to Holland, to Flanders—to every place and town, in fact, where there was the least probability of Cyril's being found. The illicit business they had been engaged in caused them to have relations with several places on the Continent, and Cyril might be at any one of them. Isaac had but now returned—returned as he went, neither seeing nor hearing aught of Cyril. It was beginning to be more than singular. Surely if Cyril were within postal bounds of communication with England, he would write!

The supposition, held from the first that he had gone off in the smuggling boats to the ship that night, and sailed with her on her homeward voyage, was far more probable than it might seem to strangers. Richard and Isaac had each done the same more than once; as, in his younger days had Mr. Thornycroft, thereby causing no end of alarm; to his wife. Cyril, it is true, was quite different in disposition, not at all given to wild rovings; but they had assumed the fact, and been easy. Richard, unwillingly, but with a view to ease her suspense, imparted the theory he had recently adopted to his sister; and she thought he might be right. As Mary Anne observed to her own heart, it was a miserable business altogether, looked at from any point.

No direct confidence had been reposed in Isaac. Richard shrank from it. Isaac had many estimable qualities, although he helped to cheat Her Majesty's revenue, and thought it glorious fun. But he could not avoid entertaining suspicions of his brother, and one day he asked a question. "Never mind," shortly replied Richard; "Hunter got his deserts." It was no direct avowal, but Isaac drew his own conclusions, and was awfully shocked. He was as different from Richard in mind, in disposition, in the view he took of things in general, as light is from dark. The blow to Isaac was dreadful. He could not, so to say, lift up his head from it; it lay on him like an incubus. Now, the coldness with which Anna had ever since treated him was explained, satisfactorily enough to his own mind. As a murderer's brother, her avoidance of him was only natural. No doubt she was overwhelmed with horror at being tied to him. If he could but have divined that she suspected him! But they were all going in for mistakes; Isaac amongst the rest.

As if the real sorrow, the never-ceasing apprehension under which some of them lived, were not enough to bear, rumours were about to arise of an unreal one.

On this evening, in early April, Miss Thornycroft was alone. As she paced her parlour, in the stately mourning robes of black silk and crape, ostensibly worn for her stepmother, the blight that had fallen on her spirit and her heart might be traced in her countenance. The untimely and dreadful fate of Robert Hunter, to whom she had been so passionately attached, was ever present to her; the false part she had played at the inquest reddened her brow with shame; the guilt of her brother Richard haunted her dreams. She would start up in fright from sleep, seeing the officers of justice coming to apprehend him; she would fancy sometimes she saw her father taken, preparatory to the illicit practices he had carried on being investigated before a criminal tribunal. Mingling with this—worse, if possible, than the rest— was the keenest weight of self-reproach. She could not hide from herself, and no longer tried to do it, that her own deliberate disobedience had brought it all about—all, all! But for flying in the face of her father's express commands, in not stopping the visit of Robert Hunter, he had been living now, and Richard's hand guiltless.

All this was telling upon Mary Anne Thornycroft. You would scarcely know her, pacing the lonely drawing-room, pale and sad, for the blooming, high-spirited, haughty girl of two months before. Her father and Richard had gone to London on business, Isaac was out, she knew not where, and she was alone. Her thoughts were dwelling on that fatal night—when were they ever absent from it?—and were becoming, as they sometimes did, unbearable. A nervous feeling came creeping over her; it had done so at times of late, fearless though she was by nature: a horror of being alone; a dread of her own lonely self; of the lonely room and its two candles; an imperative demand for companionship. She opened the door, and glided across the hall and lighted passages to the kitchen, framing an excuse as she went.

"Sinnett, will you—where's Sinnett?"

The maids, three of whom were present, stood up at her entrance. They had been seated at the table making household linen.

"Sinnett is upstairs, miss. Shall I call her?"

"No; she will be down directly, I dare say. I'll wait."

At that moment a sort of wild noise, half shriek, half howl, long-continued and ever-recurring, arose from without—at a distance as yet. Mary Anne Thornycroft turned her ear to listen, her face blanching with dread fear; the least thing was sufficient to excite fear now.

The sounds approached nearer: they seemed to come from one in the very extremity of terror, and, just then Sinnett entered the kitchen. Perhaps it has not been forgotten that the windows, of modern date, looked on the side walk, and thence towards the church and village. The shutters were not yet closed, the blinds not drawn down. In another instant, as the frightened women stood together in a group, one window was flung up, and a form propelled itself in, smashing a pane of glass. It proved to be Joe, the carter's boy; a sensitive, delicate lad, who had recently lost his mother, and was a favourite at the Red Court Farm. He lay for a moment amidst the shivers of glass, then rose up and clasped tight hold of Sinnett, his white face and shivering frame betokening some extraordinary cause of terror.

They put him in a chair, and held him there, he clinging to them. Miss Thornycroft authoritatively stopped all questions until he should be calmer. Sinnett brought him some wine, and the boy tried to sip it; but he could not keep his teeth still, and he bit a piece out of the glass. He looked over his shoulder at the window perpetually in ghastly fear, so one of the servants closed and barred the shutters. By degrees, he brought out that he had "seen a ghost."

Ghosts were rather favourite appendages to Coastdown, as we have read. They were not less implicitly believed in by the lower classes (not to bring in others) than they used to be, so the maids screamed and drew nearer Joe. This ghost, however, was not the old ghost of the plateau; as the boy is explaining, sobbing between whiles; but—Robert Hunter's.

"Nonsense!" reproved Sinnett. "Don't you be a coward, Joe, but just speak up and tell your tale sensibly. Come!"

"I went for the newspaper to Captain Copp's, as sent," answered the boy, doing his best to obey. "Mrs. Copp couldn't find it, and thought the captain had took it in his pocket to the Mermaid. Coming back here to say so, I see a figure in the churchyard hiding, like, behind a tombstone. I thought it were old Parkes, a-taking the short cut over the graves to his home, and I stood and looked at him. Then, as he rose himself a bit higher, I see him out and out. It were Mr. Hunter, with his own face and his own coat on—that black and white thing."

"His own coat!"

"It were," groaned the lad. "I never were thinking of anybody but Parkes, but when I once saw the coat and the face, I see it were Mr. Hunter."

Joe's hearers did not know what to make of this. Miss Thornycroft privately thought she must fall in a fit, too, she felt so sick and ill.

"Was the face—" began one of the maids, and stopped. Remembering Miss Thornycroft's presence, she substituted another word for the one she had been about to speak. "Was the face red?"

"No. White. It—"

At this juncture there came a sharp knock at the window, as if the ghost were knocking to come in. The boy howled, the women shrieked; and the ghost knocked again.

"Who's there?" called out Sinnett through the shutters.

"It's me," answered a voice, which they recognised for that of Sarah Ford. "Is the kitchen a-fire?"

Sinnett went to the entrance-door and called to her to come in. On occasions, when pressed for time, Sarah would give her messages at the kitchen-window, to save going round. She had brought the newspaper, one lent by the Red Court to Captain Copp: Mrs. Copp had found it after Joe's departure.

"He have seen a ghost," lucidly explained one of the maids, pointing to Joe.

"Oh," said Sarah, who had a supreme contempt for such things, regarding them as vanities, akin to hysterics and smelling salts.

"I see it in the churchyard, close again his own grave," said the boy, looking helplessly at Sarah.

"See a old cow," responded she, emphatically. "That's more likely. They strays in sometimes."

"It were Mr. Hunter's ghost," persisted Joe. "He wore that there fur coat, and he stared at me like anything. I see his eyes a-glaring."

"The boy has been dreaming," cried Sarah, pityingly, as she turned to Sinnett. "I should give him a good dose of Epsom salts."

Which prescription Joe by no means approved of. However, Sarah could not stay to see it enforced; and we must go out with her.

Her master had come in when she reached home. It was supper time, and she began to lay the cloth. Old Mrs. Copp was there: she had arrived the previous day (after spending the winter in London) on another long visit. Peering through her tortoiseshell spectacles at Sarah, she told her in her decisive way that she had been twice as long taking home the newspaper as she need have been.

"I know that," answered Sarah, with composure. "A fine commotion I found the Red Court in: the maids screeching fit to deafen you, and young Joe in convulsions. I thought the kitchen-chimbly must be a-fire, and they were trying whether noise would put it out "

The captain looked up at this. He was in an easy-chair at the corner of the hearth-rug, a glass of rum-and-water on a small stand at his elbow: old Mrs. Copp sat in front of the fire, her feet on the fender; Amy was putting things to rights on a side-table near the sofa, and Anna Chester sat back on a low stool in the shade on the other side of the fire-place, a book on her knee, which she was making believe to read.

"Was the chimney on fire?" snapped Mrs. Copp.

"Just as much as this is," answered Sarah, making a rattle with the knives and forks. "Joe was telling them he had just seen Robert Hunter's ghost. They screeched at that."

The captain burst into a laugh: he had no more faith in ghosts than Sarah had. Sea-serpents and mermaids were enough marvel for him. Anna glanced up with a perceptible shudder.

"By the way," said Mrs. Copp, taking her feet off the fender and turning round to speak, "I should like to come to the bottom of that extraordinary business. You slipped out of my questioning this morning, Anna; I hardly knew how. Who was the man that fired the pistol on the plateau? As to saying you did not see him properly, you may as well tell it to the moon. My belief is you are screening him," concluded shrewd Mrs. Copp, watching the poor girl's gradually whitening face.

"If I thought that; if I thought she could screen him, I'd—I'd—send her back to Miss Jupp's," roared Captain Copp, who was still very sore in regard to the part his women-kind had played in the transaction. "Screen a and murderer!"

Anna burst out crying.

"My impression is, that it was Cyril Thornycroft," resumed Mrs. Copp. "If he had not got something bad on his conscience why should he run away, and keep away."

Sarah took up the word, putting a tray of tumblers down to do it. "He may have his reasons for staying away, and nobody but himself know anything about them. But truth's truth, all the world over, and I'll stand to it. I don't care whether it was the King of England, or whether it was old Nick—it was not Cyril Thornycroft."

"She is right," nodded the captain. "He'd be the least likely in all Coastdown to rush on to the plateau at night, armed like a pirate, and shoot a man. It was no more Cyril Thornycroft did that than it was me, mother."

"But, Sarah, what about poor Joe and the ghost?" interposed her mistress gently, upon whom the tale had made an unpleasant impression.

"Some delusion of his, ma'am: as stands to reason. I don't believe the boy has been right since his mother died; he has had nothing but a down, scared look about him. He is just the one to see a ghost, he is."

"Where did he see it?"

"In the churchyard, he says, with its fur coat on."

"Fur coat!" broke in Captain Copp, his face aglow with merriment. "He meant a white sheet."

"Ah, he made a mistake there," said Sarah. And it was really something laughable to see how she as well as her master (mocking sceptics!) enjoyed the ghost in their grim way. In the midst of it, who should come in but Isaac Thornycroft.

He had not been a frequent visitor of late, rather to the regret of the hospitable captain. Set at rest on the score of any surreptitious liking for him on Anna's part—for it was impossible not to note her continual avoidance of him now—the captain would have welcomed him always in his pride and pleasure. Isaac Thornycroft was a vast favourite of his, and this was only the second visit he had paid since his return from abroad. Isaac looked as if he would like to join in the merriment, utterly unconscious what the cause might be.

"It's the best joke I've heard this many a day," explained the captain. "Your boy up at the Red Court—that Joe."

"Yes," said Isaac, the corners of his mouth relaxing in sympathy with the sailor's. "Well?"

"He went flying through the air, bellowing enough to arouse the neighbourhood, and tumbled in at your kitchen window in a fit, saying he had seen Robert Hunter's ghost."

"Breaking the glass and setting the maids a-screeching like mad," put in Sarah. "He saw it in the churchyard, he says, in its fur coat."

A troubled expression passed across Isaac's countenance. Captain Copp, attempting to drink some rum-and-water while he laughed, began to choke.

"What absurd story can they be getting up?" cried Isaac, sternly. "Some rumour of this sort—that Hunter had been seen in the churchyard—was abroad yesterday."

"You never saw a boy in such a state of fright, sir," observed Sarah. "Whether he saw anything or nothing, he'll not get over it this many a week."

"Saw anything or nothing! What d'ye mean?" fiercely demanded Captain Copp, suspending his laughter for the moment. "What d'ye suppose he saw?"

"Not a ghost," independently retorted Sarah. "I'm not such a simpleton. But some ill-disposed fellow may have dressed himself up to frighten people."

"If so, he shall get his punishment," spoke Isaac Thornycroft, with the imperative authority of a magistrate's son.

Captain Copp broke into laughter still. He could not forget the joke; but somehow all inclination for merriment seemed to have gone out of Isaac. He sat silent and abstracted for a few minutes longer, and then took his leave, declining to partake of supper.

"Where's Miss Anna gone?" cried the Captain to Sarah, suddenly missing her. "Tell her we are waiting."

Isaac lingered unseen in the little hall until she appeared, and took her hand in silence.

"Anna, this—"

But she contrived to twist it from him and turned to the parlour. He drew her forcibly to him, speaking in a whisper.

"Are you going to visit upon me for ever the work of that miserable night?"

"Hush! they will hear you."

But there was no other answer. Her face grew white, her lips dry and trembling.

"Don't you know that you are my wife?"

"Oh, heaven, yes! I would rather have died. I would die now to undo that night's work."

She seemed bewildered, as if unconscious of her words; but there was always the struggle to get from him. Had he been an ogre who might eat her, she could not have evinced more terror. Sarah opened the kitchen door, and Anna took the opportunity to escape. Isaac looked after her. If ever misery, horror, despair, were depicted on a human countenance, they were on Anna's.

"I did not think she was one to take it up like this," he said, as he let himself out. And in the tone of his voice, despairing as her face, there was a perfectly hopeless sound, as if he felt that he could not combat fate.

By the next day the story of the ghost, singular to say, had spread all over Coastdown; singular, because the report did not come from Joe, or from any of Joe's hearers. It appeared that a young fellow of the name of Bartlet, a carpenter's apprentice, in passing the churchyard soon after poor Joe must have passed it, saw the same figure, which he protested—and went straight to the Mermaid and protested—was that of Mr. Hunter. He was a daring lad of sixteen, as hardy as Joe was timid. The company at the Mermaid accused him of having got frightened and fancied it; he answered that he feared "neither ghost nor devil," and persisted in his story with so much cool equanimity, that his adversaries were staggered.

"It is well known that the ghosts of murdered people have been seen to walk," decided Mrs. Pettipher, the landlady, "and that of poor Mr. Hunter may be there. But as to the fur-coat, that can't be. It must have been a optical delusion of yours, Tom Bartlet. The coat's here; we have held possession of it since the inquest; for the ghost to have it on in the churchyard is a moral impossibility."

"I'll never speak again if it hadn't got the coat upon it," loudly persisted young Bartlet. "But for that white coat, staring out in the moonlight, I might never have turned my head to the churchyard."

"Had it got that there black fur down it, Tom?" demanded a gentleman, taking his long pipe from his mouth to speak.

"In course it had. I tell ye it was the coat, talk as you will."

This was the tale that spread in Coastdown. When the additional testimony of Joe and the maids at the Red Court Farm came to be added to it, something like fear took possession of three-parts of the community. The ghost of the plateau, so long believed in, was more a tradition than a ghost, after all; latterly, at any rate, nobody had been frightened by it; but this spirit haunting the churchyard was real— at least in one sense of the word. An uncomfortable feeling set in. And when in the course of a day or two other witnesses saw it, or professed to see it, people began to object to go abroad after nightfall in the direction of the churchyard. A young man in the telegraph office at Jutpoint brought over a message for Isaac Thornycroft. He was a stranger to Coastdown, and had to inquire his way to the Red Court Farm: misunderstanding the direction, he took at first the wrong turning, which brought him to the churchyard. Afterwards, the despatch at length delivered, he turned into the Mermaid for a glass of ale, saying incidentally, not in any fear, he had seen "sum'at" in the churchyard, a queer fellow that seemed to be dodging about behind the upright gravestones. He had never seen or heard of Robert Hunter; he knew nothing of the report of the ghost; but his description of the "sum'at" tallied so exactly with the appearance expected, and especially with the remarkable coat, that no doubt remained. Upon which some ten spirits, well warmed with brandy-and-water, started off arm-in-arm to the churchyard, there and then—and saw nothing for their pains but the tombstones. Captain Copp heard of the expedition, and went into a storm of indignation at grown men showing themselves to be so credulous.

"Go out to a churchyard to look for a ghost! Serve 'em right to put 'em into irons till their senses come to 'em!"

Thus another day or two passed on, Mr. Thornycroft and Richard being still absent from home. Fears were magnified; fermentation increased; for, according to popular report, the spirit of Robert Hunter appeared nightly in St Peter's churchyard.

CHAPTER XIV

Robert Hunter's Ghost

It was a gusty night; the wind violently high even for the seaside; and Miss Thornycroft sat over the fire in her own sitting-room, listening to it as it whirled round the house and went booming away over the waste of waters.

Anna Chester was with her. Anna had shunned the Red Court of late; but she could not always refuse Miss Thornycroft's invitations without attracting notice; and she had heard that Isaac was to be away from home that day.

They had spent the hours unhappily. Heavy at heart, pale in countenance, subdued in spirit, it seemed to each that nothing in the world could bring pleasure again. Anna was altered just as much as Miss Thornycroft; worn, thin, haggard-eyed. Captain Copp's wife, seeing the change in Anna, and knowing nothing of the real cause, set it down to one that must inevitably bring discovery of the marriage in its train, and was fretting herself into fiddle-strings. Dinner was over; tea was taken; the evening went on. Quite unexpectedly Mr. Thornycroft and his eldest son arrived; Anna saw also, to her dismay, that Isaac was in; but none of them approached the sitting-room. Hyde, coming in later to replenish the fire, said the justice was not very well, and had retired to rest; Mr. Richard and Mr. Isaac had gone out. And the two girls sat on together, almost hearing the beating of each other's hearts.

"I wonder if the ghost is abroad this windy night!" exclaimed Anna, as a wild gust dashed against the windows and shook the frames.

"Don't joke about that, Anna," said Miss Thornycroft, sharply.

Anna looked round in surprise: nothing had been further from her thoughts than to joke; and indeed she did not know why she said it. "Of course the report is a very foolish one," she resumed "I cannot think how any people can profess to believe it."

"Isaac saw it last night," said Mary Anne, quietly.

"Nonsense!" cried Anna.

"Ah! so I have answered when others said they saw it. But Isaac is cool and practical; entirely without superstition; the very last man I know, save perhaps Richard, to be led away by fear or fancy. He was passing the churchyard when he saw—if not Robert Hunter, some one dressed up to personate him; but the features were Robert Hunter's features, Isaac says; they were for a moment as distinct as ever he had seen them in life."

"Did he tell you this?"

"Yes."

"Could he have been deceived by his imagination?"

"I think not. When a cool, collected man, like my brother Isaac, dispassionately asserts such a thing, in addition to the terrified assertions of others, I at least believe that there must be some dreadful mystery abroad, supernatural or otherwise."

"A mystery?"

"Yes, a mystery. Putting aside all questions of the figure. how is it that the coat can appear in the churchyard, when it remains all the while in safe custody at the Mermaid?"

Anna sat down, overwhelmed with the confusion of ideas that presented themselves. The chief one that struggled upwards was—how should she ever have courage to pass the churchyard that night?

"Mary Anne! why did he not speak to it?"

"Because some people came up at the time, and prevented it. When he looked again the figure was gone."

Precisely so. All this, just as Mary Anne described it, had happened to Isaac Thornycroft on the previous night. Robert Hunter, the hat drawn low on his pale face, the unmistakeable coat buttoned round him, had stood there in the churchyard, looking just as he had looked in life. To say that Isaac was not staggered would be wrong—he was—but he recovered himself almost instantly, and was about to call out to the figure, when Mr. Kyne came past with young Connaught, and stopped him. Isaac and his family had to guard against certain discoveries yet; and in the presence of the superintendent of the coastguard, whose suspicions were already too rife, he did not choose to proceed to investigation.

Silence supervened. The young ladies sat on over the fire, each occupied with her sad and secret thoughts. The time-piece struck half-past eight.

"What can have become of Sarah?" exclaimed Anna. "Mrs. Copp was not well, and my Aunt Amy said she should send for me early."

Scarcely had the words left her lips, when that respectable personage entered head foremost. Giving the door a bang, she sank into an arm-chair. Anna stood up in wonder; Miss Thornycroft looked round.

"You may well stare, young ladies, but I can't stand upon no forms nor ceremonies just now. I don't know whether my senses is here or yonder, and I made bold to come in at the hall door, as being the nearest, and make straight for here. There's the ghost at this blessed moment in the churchyard."

Anna, with a faint cry, drew near to Miss Thornycroft, and touched her for company. The latter spoke.

"Your fancy must have deceived you, Sarah."

"If anything has deceived me, it's my eyes," returned Sarah, really too much put out to stand on any sort of ceremony whether in speech or action—"which is what they never did yet, Miss Thornycroft. When it struck eight my mistress told me to go for Miss Chester. I thought I'd finish my ironing first, which took me another quarter of an hour; and then I put my blanket and things away to come. Just as I was opening the house door I heard the master's voice singing out for me, and went into the parlour. 'Is it coals, sir?' I asked. 'No, it's not coals,' says he; and I saw by his mouth he was after some nonsense. 'It's to tell you to take care of the ghost.' 'Oh, bran the ghost,' says I; 'I should give it a knock if it come anigh me.' And so I should, young ladies."

"Go on, go on," cried Mary Anne Thornycroft.

"I come right on to the churchyard, and what we had been saying made me turn my eyes to it as I passed. Young ladies," she continued, drawing the chair closer, and dropping her voice to a low, mysterious key, "if you'll believe me, there stood Robert Hunter. He was close by that big tombstone of old Marley's, not three yards from his own grave!"

Mary Anne Thornycroft seemed unwilling to admit belief in this, in spite of what she had herself been relating to Miss Chester. "Rely upon it, Sarah, your fears deceived you."

"Miss, I hadn't got any fears; at any rate, not before I saw him. There he was: his features as plain as ever they'd need be, and that uncommon coat on, which I'm sure was never made for anybody but a Guy Fawkes."

"Were you frightened then?"

"I was not frightened, so to say, but I won't deny that I felt a creepishness in my skin; and I'd have given half-a-crown out of my pocket to see any human creature come up to bear me company. I might have spoke to it if it had give me time: I don't know: but the moment it saw me it glided amid the gravestones, making for the back of the church. I made off too as fast as my legs would carry me, and come straight in here. I knew my tongue must let it out, and I thought it better for you to hear it than them timorous servants in the kitchen."

"Quite right," murmured Miss Thornycroft.

"I never did believe in ghosts," resumed Sarah; "never thought to do it, and I'm not going to begin now. But after to-night, I won't mock at the poor wretches that have been frightened by Robert Hunter's."

What now was to be done? Anna Chester would not attempt to go home and pass the churchyard with no protector but Sarah. Hyde was not to be found; and there seemed nothing for it but to wait until Richard or Isaac came in.

But neither came. Between nine and ten Captain Copp made his appearance in hot anger, shaking his stick and stamping his wooden leg at Sarah.

Had the vile hussey taken up her gossiping quarters at the Red Court Farm for the night? Did she think—

"I could not get Miss Chester away," interposed Sarah, drowning the words. "The ghost is in the churchyard. I saw it as I came past."

The sailor-captain was struck dumb. One of his women-kind avow belief in a ghost? He had seen a mermaid himself; which creatures were known to exist; but ghosts were fabulous things, fit for nothing but the fancies of marines. Any sailor in his fo'castle that had confessed to seeing ghosts, would have got a taste of the yardarm. "Get your things on this minute," concluded the captain, angrily, to Anna. "I'll teach you to be afraid of rubbishing ghosts! And that vile bumboat woman! coming here with such a tale!"

"It's my opinion ghosts is rubbish, and nothing better; for I don't see the good of 'em; but this was Robert Hunter's for all that," spoke the undaunted "bumboat-woman." "I saw his face and his eyes as plain as ever I see my own in the glass, and that precious white coat of his with the ugly fur upon it. Master, you can't say that I gave as much as half an ear to this talk before to-night."

"You credulous sea-serpent!" was the captain's retort. "And that same coat lying yet in the tallet at the Mermaid with the blood upon it, just as it was taken off the body! Ugh! fie upon you!"

"If there's apparitions of bodies, there may be apparitions of coats," reasoned Sarah, between whom and her choleric but good-hearted master there was always a fight for the last word. "If it hadn't been for knowing his face, I should say some ill-conditioned jester had borrowed the coat from the Mermaid and put it on."

Away pegged the captain in his rage, scarcely allowing himself to say good-night to Miss Thornycroft; and away went Sarah and Miss Chester after him, as close as circumstances permitted.

As they neared the churchyard Anna ventured to lay hold of the captain's arm, and bent her head upon it, in spite of his mocking assurances that a parson's daughter ought to be on visiting terms with a churchyard ghost; trusting to him to guide her steps. The captain was deliberating, as he avowed afterwards, whether to guide her into the opposite ditch, believing that a ducking would be the best panacea for all ghostly fears; when Sarah, who was a step in the rear, leaped forward and clung violently to his blue coat-tails.

"There!" she cried in a shrill whisper, before the astonished gentleman could free his tails or give vent to proper indignation, "there it is again, behind old Marley's tomb! Now then, master, is that the coat, or is it not?"

The captain was surprised into turning his eyes to the churchyard; Anna also, as if impelled by some irresistible fascination. It was too true. Within a few yards of them, in the dim moonlight—for the cloudy moon gave but a feeble light—appeared the well-known form of the ill-fated Robert Hunter, the very man whose dead body Captain Copp had helped to lay in the grave, so far as having assisted as a mourner at his funeral.

The captain was taken considerably aback; had never been half so much so before an unexpected iceberg; his wooden leg dropped submissively down and his mouth flew open. He had the keen eye of a seaman, and he saw beyond doubt that the spirit before him was indeed that of Robert Hunter. Report ran in the village afterwards that the gallant captain would have made off, but could not rid himself from the grasp of his companions.

"Hallo! you sir!" he called out presently, remembering that in that vile Sarah's presence his reputation for courage was at stake, but there was considerable deference, not to say timidity, in his tone, "what is it you want, appearing there like a figure-head?"

The ghost, however, did not wait to answer; it had already disappeared, vanishing into air, or behind the tombstones. Captain Copp lost not a moment, but tore away faster than he had ever done since the acquisition of his wooden leg, Anna sobbing convulsively on his arm, and Sarah hanging on to his coat-tails. A minute afterwards they were joined by Isaac Thornycroft, coming at a sharp pace from the direction of the village.

"Take these screeching sea-gulls home for me," cried the sailor to Isaac. "I'll go down to the Mermaid, and with my own eyes see if the coat is there. Some land-lubber's playing a trick, and has borrowed Hunter's face and stole the coat to act it in."

"Spare yourself the trouble," rejoined Isaac. "I have come straight now from the Mermaid, and the coat is there. We have been looking at it but this instant. It is under the hay in the room over the stable, doubled up and stiff, having dried in the folds."

"I should like to keelhaul that ghost," cried the discomfited captain. "I'd rather have seen ten mermaids."

Isaac Thornycroft, with an imperative gesture, took Anna on his own arm, leaving the captain to peg on alone, with Sarah still in close proximity to the coattails. He did not say what he had been doing all the evening, or why he should have come up at that particular juncture.

Upon the return of Richard to the Red Court an hour or two earlier, Isaac drew him at once out of the house to impart to him this curious fact of Hunter's ghost—as Coastdown phrased it—making its appearance nightly in the churchyard. Truth to say, the affair was altogether puzzling Isaac, bringing him trouble also. He had seen it himself the previous evening. Who was it? what did it want? whence did it come? That it wore Hunter's face and form was indisputable. What then was it? His ghost?—a kind of marvel which Isaac had never yet believed in,—or a man got up to personate him? Of course what Isaac feared was, that it might lead to discovery of various matters connected with the past.

He imparted all this to Richard. Richard scorned the information at first, ridiculed the affair, would not believe in the fear. Isaac proposed that they should go together to the churchyard, conceal themselves behind a convenient tombstone, watch for the appearance, and pounce upon it. Richard mockingly refused; if he went at all to the place he'd go by himself and deal with the "ghost" at leisure. At present he had business with Tomlett.

They went together to Tomlett's cottage, and sat there talking. The baker's boy came up on an errand; and as Mrs. Tomlett answered the door they heard him tell her that "the ghost was then—then—in the churchyard, his face and his coat awful white."

"The coat has been stolen from the Mermaid," spoke Richard in his decisive tones.

"That fact was easy to be ascertained," Isaac answered. And, rising at once from his seat, he went to the Mermaid there and then. Calling Pettipher, they went up the ladder to the tallet, and Isaac convinced himself that there the coat lay, untouched, and in fact unusable. From thence he went his way to the churchyard, intending to see what he could do with the ghost himself, and thus overtook Captain Copp and his party.

Nothing of this did he say to Anna. Leaving the ghost for the time being, he went on to Captain Copp's. She held his arm, not daring to let it go; her mind in a state of extreme distress. Trembling from head to foot went she; a sob breaking from her now and again.

"What can it be looking for?" burst from her in her grief and perplexity. "For you?"

For the thought, the fear that had been beating its terrible refrain in her brain was, that Robert Hunter's spirit, unable to rest, had come to denounce his destroyer. Such tales had over and over again been told in the world's history: why should not this be but another to add to them?

"Anna!" answered Isaac in a tone of surprise and remonstrance, "you cannot seriously believe that it is Hunter's spirit. Why talk nonsense?"

Which reply she looked upon as an evasive one. "Can you solve the mystery then?" she asked. "That thing in the churchyard wears as surely Hunter's face and form as you wear yours or I mine. It is not himself: he is dead and buried; what then is it?"

"Not his ghost," spoke Isaac. Whether he, the cool-headed, practical, worldly man, who believed hitherto in ghosts just as much as he did in fairies, felt perfectly sure himself upon the point now, at least he deemed it right to insist upon it to his wife.

No more was said. But for Captain Copp's turning back to converse with Isaac (having in a degree recovered his equanimity) he might have striven to get an explanation with his wife there and then.

"Come in, come in, and take a sup of brandy," cried the hospitable captain when they arrived at his house. "That beast of a ghost!"

"Oh, Sarah, what can have kept you!" exclaimed the captain's wife, in as complaining a tone as so gentle a woman could use. "I have had everything to do myself; the gruel to make for Mrs. Copp, the hot water to take upstairs; the—"

"It is not my fault, ma'am," interrupted the subdued Sarah, as she rubbed her shoes on the mat. "Miss Chester was afraid to come home with me alone. There's Robert Hunter in the churchyard."

Amy Copp glanced at her husband, expecting an explosion of wrath at the words. To her surprise, the captain heard them in patient silence, his face as meek as any lamb's.

"Bring some hot water, Sarah, and get out the brandy," said he.

Mixing a stiff glass for himself, Isaac declining to take any, he passed another in silence to Sarah. Anna had escaped upstairs: her usual custom when Isaac was there.

"Much obliged, sir, but I don't care for brandy," was Sarah's answer. "My courage is coming back to me, master."

Amy looked from one to the other, not knowing what to make of either. "Have you really seen anything?" she asked.

"Seen Hunter, coat and all," gravely replied the captain. "Shiver my wooden leg, if we've not! I say, mother," he called out, stumping to the foot of the stairs. "Mother!"

"What's it, Sam?" called back Mrs. Copp, who was beginning to undress, and had not yet taken her remedies for the cold.

"Mother, you know that mermaid in the Atlantic—the last voyage you went with us? You wouldn't believe that I saw it; you've only laughed at me ever since: well, I've seen the ghost to-night; so don't you disbelieve me any more."

Captain Copp returned to the parlour, and in a minute his mother walked in after him. She wore black stockings, fur slippers, a petticoat that came down to the calves of her legs; a woollen shawl, and an enormous night-cap. Isaac Thornycroft smothered an inclination to laugh, but Mrs. Copp stood with calm equanimity, regardless of the defects of her costume.

"What's that about the ghost, Sam?"

"I saw it to-night, mother. It stood near its own grave in the churchyard. And I hope you won't go on at me about that mermaid, after this. It had got long bright green hair, as I've always said, and was combing it out."

"The ghost had?"

"No, the mermaid. The ghost was Hunter's. It looked just as he'd used to look."

Mrs. Copp stood rubbing her nose, and thinking the captain's conversion a very sudden one.

"Is this a joke, Sam?"

"A joke! Why, mother, I tell ye I saw it. Ask Sarah. I called out to know what it wanted, and why it came; but it wouldn't answer me."

"Well, it's strange," observed Mrs. Copp. "Sam's a simpleton about mermaids, but I'd have backed him as to ghosts. But now: you may have observed perhaps, all of you, that I've not said a syllable to ridicule this ghost of poor dead Mr. Hunter, and I'll tell you why. Last June, in Liverpool, a friend of mine was sitting up with her father, who was ill, when her sister's spirit appeared to her. It was between twelve and one at night—twenty minutes to one, in fact, for there was a clock in the room, and she had looked at it only a minute before; the candle—"

"Oh, mother, don't; pray don't!" implored poor Amy Copp, going into a cold perspiration, for she held a firm belief in things supernatural. "This one ghost is enough for us without any more. I shall never like to go up to bed alone again."

"The candle gave as good as no light, for the snuff was a yard long a'most, with a cauliflower on the top," continued Mrs. Copp, who persisted in telling her tale, supremely indifferent to her daughter-in-law's fears and her own robes. "Emma Jenkins, that was her name, heard a rustle in the room; it seemed to come in at the door, which was put open for air, flutter across, and stir the bed-curtains. (Don't you be foolish, Amy!) Naturally, Emma Jenkins looked up, and there she saw her sister, who had died a year before. The figure seemed to give just a sigh and vanish. Now," said Mrs. Copp, applying the moral, "if that was a ghost, this may be."

"You always said, you know, mother, that you didn't believe in ghosts."

"Neither did I, Sam But Emma Jenkins is not one to be taken in by fancy; as stands to reason, considering that she has gone thirteen voyages with her husband, short and long. Sea-going people are not liable to see ghosts where there's no ghosts to see; they have got their wits about them, and keep their eyes open. What are you smiling at, Mr. Thornycroft? Mrs. Jenkins had taken a glass of brandy-and-water, perhaps? Well, I don't know; sitting up with the sick is cold work, especially when they are too far gone to have anything done for 'em. But she always liked rum best."

The story over, Captain Copp plunged into a full account of the night's adventures, enlarging on the questions he asked with the view of bringing the ghost to book, and what he would have done had it only stayed. Sarah gave her version of the sight, both in going and coming. Mrs. Copp, forgetting her cold, plunged into another story of a man who died at sea the first time she sailed with her husband, and the belief of the sailors that he haunted the ship all the while it lay in Calcutta harbour; all to the shivering horror of poor Amy Copp; and Isaac Thornycroft, waking up from his reverie by fits and starts, sat on until midnight, like a man in a miserable dream.

CHAPTER XV

In the Churchyard Porch

Mary Anne Thornycroft had remained at home in a state of mind bordering on distraction. Look where she would, there was no comfort. Surely the death of Robert Hunter had been enough, with all its attendant dreadful circumstances, without this fresh rumour of his "coming again!" Like Mrs. Copp, until impressed with her friend Emma Jenkins's experiences, Miss Thornycroft had never put faith in ghosts. She was accustomed to ridicule those who believed in the one said to haunt the plateau; but her scepticism was shaken now.

She had paid little attention to the first reports, for she knew how prone the ignorant are in general, and Coastdown in particular, to spread supernatural tales. But these reports grew and magnified. Robert Hunter was dead and buried: how then reconcile that fact with this mysterious appearance said to haunt the churchyard? Her mind became shaken; and when, on the previous night, her brother Isaac imparted to her the fact that he had seen it with his own sensible, dispassionate eyes, a sickening conviction flashed over her that it was indeed Robert Hunter's spirit. And now, to confirm it, came the testimony of the matter-of-fact Sarah. Possibly, but for the sad manner in which her nerves had been shaken, this new view might not have been taken up.

"What does it want?" she asked herself, sitting there alone in the gloomy parlour: and certain words just spoken by Sarah recurred to her, as if in answer. "It may want to denounce its murderer." Stronger even than the grief and regret she felt at his untimely fate, at the abrupt termination of her unhappy love, was the lively dread of discovery, for Richard's sake. That must be guarded against, if it were possible; for what might it not bring in its train? The betrayal of the illicit practices the Red Court Farm had lived by; the dishonour of her father and his house; perhaps the trial—condemnation—execution of Richard.

Sick, trembling, half mad with these reflections, pacing the room in agony, was she, when Richard entered. Had he seen the ghost? He looked as if he had. His damp hair hung about in a black mass, and his face and lips were as ghastly as Hunter's. His sister gazed at him with surprise: the always self-possessed Richard!

"Have you come from the village?" she asked.

"From that way."

"Did you happen to turn to the churchyard?"

"Yes," was the laconic reply.

"You know what they say: that his spirit appears there."

"I have seen it," was Richard's unexpected answer.

Miss Thornycroft started. "Oh, Richard! When?"

"Now. I went to look, and I saw it. There's no mistake about its being Hunter, or some fool made up to personate him."

"It has taken away your colour, Richard."

Richard Thornycroft did not reply. He sat with his elbow on his knee, and his chin resting on his hand, looking into the fire. The once brave man, brave to recklessness, had been scared for the first time in his mortal life. The crime lying heavily on his soul had made a coward of him.

He said nothing of the details, but they must be supplied. Shortly after Isaac had quitted Tomlett's, Richard also left, intending to go straight home. As he struck across to the direct road—not the one by the plateau—a thought came to him to take a look at the churchyard; and he turned to it.

There was Robert Hunter. As Richard's footsteps sounded on the night air, nearing the churchyard, the head and shoulders of the haunting spirit appeared, raising themselves behind old Marley's high tombstone. Richard stood still. "There was no mistake," as he observed to his sister, "that it was Hunter." And the eyes of the two were strained, the one on the other. Suddenly the ghost came into full view and advanced, and Richard Thornycroft turned and fled. An arrant coward he at that moment, alone with the ghost and his own awful conscience.

Whether the apparition would have pursued him; whether Richard would have gathered bravery enough to turn and face it, could never be known. The doctor's boy, having been to the heath with old Connaught's physic, ran past shouting and singing; "the whistling aloud to keep his courage up," as Bloomfield (is it not?) so subtly says, was not enough now for those who had to pass the churchyard at Coastdown. The ghost vanished, and Richard strode on to the Red Court Farm.

But he did not tell of all this. Mary Anne, who had been bending her head on the arm of the sofa, suddenly rose, resolution in her face and in her low, firm tone.

"Richard, if you accompany me for protection, I will go and see this spirit. I will ask what it wants. Let us go."

"You!" he somewhat contemptuously exclaimed.

"I will steel my nerves and heart to it. I have been striving to do so for the last half hour. Better for me to hold communion with it than any one else, save you. You know why, Richard."

"Tush!" he exclaimed. "Do nothing. You'd faint by the way."

"It is necessary for the honour and safety of—of—this house," she urged, not caring to speak more pointedly, "that no stranger should hear what it wants. I will go now. If I wait until to-morrow my courage may fail. I go, Richard, whether with you or alone. You are not afraid?"

For answer, Richard rose, and they left the room. In passing through the hall, Mary Anne threw on her woollen shawl and garden-bonnet, just as she had thrown them on the night of Hunter's murder; and they started.

Not a word was spoken by either until they reached the corner of the churchyard. The high, thickset hedge, facing them as they advanced, prevented their seeing into it, but they would soon come in front, where the shrubs grew low behind the iron railings. Miss Thornycroft stopped.

"You stay here, Richard. I will go on alone."

"No," he began, but she peremptorily interrupted him.

"I will have it so. If I am to go on with this, I will be alone. You can keep me within sight." And Richard acquiesced, despising himself for his cowardice, but unable to overcome it. He could not—no, he could not face the man whose life he had taken.

Mary Anne Thornycroft opened the gate and went in. In his place (he seemed to have specially appropriated to himself) behind old Marley's tomb, stood Robert Hunter. How she contrived to advance—contrived to face him and keep her senses, Mary Anne Thornycroft could never afterwards understand.

Is it of any use to go on mystifying you, my reader? Perhaps from the first you have suspected the truth. Any way, it may be better to solve the secret, for time is growing limited, as it was solved that night to Mary Anne and Richard Thornycroft. The ghost, prowling about still, was looking out for Richard, its sole object all along; but it was Robert Hunter himself and not his ghost. For Robert Hunter was not dead.

He had been in London all the while they mourned him so, as much alive as any of his mourners, quite unconscious that he was looked upon as murdered, and that the county coroner had held an inquest on his body. A week since, he had come down from London to Coastdown, had come in secret, not caring to show himself in the neighbourhood, and not daring to show himself openly to the Thornycrofts. He wanted to obtain an interview with Mary Anne; but to want it was a great deal easier than to get it, in consequence of that extravagant and hasty oath imposed upon him by Richard. According to its terms, he must not write to any one of the inmates of the Red Court Farm; he must not enter it; he must not show himself at Coastdown; and he could only hit upon the plan of coming down en cachette, keeping himself close by day, and watching for Richard at night. Not a very brilliant scheme, but he could think of no better; and, singular perhaps to say, there was no bar to his speaking to Richard if he met him; if the spirit of the oath provided against that, the letter did not; and Robert Hunter's business was urgent. So he came down to Jutpoint, walked over at night, and took up his quarters in a lonely hut that he knew of behind the churchyard, inhabited by a superannuated fisherman, old Parkes. The aged fisherman, of dim sight and failing memory, did not know his guest; he was easily bribed not to tell of his sojourn; and the rumours of the ghost had not penetrated to him. In that hut Hunter lay by day, and watched from the churchyard by night, as being a likely spot to see Richard, who used often to pass and repass it on his way to and from the heath, and an unlikely one to be seen and recognised by the public. With that convenient tomb of old Marley's to shelter behind whenever footsteps approached, he did not fear. Unfortunately, it was necessary that he should look out to see whether the footsteps were not Richard's; and this looking out had brought about all the terror. His retreating place, when people had intruded into the churchyard, Isaac for one, was under a shelving gravestone at the back of the church, where none would think of looking. And there he had been on the watch, never dreaming that he was being mistaken for his own ghost, for he knew nothing of his supposed murder.

In little more than half-a-dozen sentences this was revealed to Mary Anne Thornycroft. It was the last night that he could stay: and he had resolved, in the fear of having to go back to London with his errand unexecuted, to accost any one of the Thornycroft family that might approach him, although by so doing the oath was infringed. As their voices were borne on the night air to the ear of Richard, sufficient evidence that Hunter was a living man, a load fell from his heart. In the first blissful throb of the discovery, the thought that surged through him, turning darkness into light, was, "If he is alive, I am no murderer." He ran forward, gained the spot where they stood, grasped Hunter's hand and well-nigh embraced him. He, the cold, stern, undemonstrative Richard Thornycroft! he, with all his dislike of Hunter!

Do you consider well what that joy must be—relief from the supposed committed crime of murder? The awful nightmare that has been weighing us down: the sin that has been eating away our heartstrings! Some of us may have faintly experienced this in a vision during sleep.

"I do not understand it, Hunter," whispered Richard, his words taking a sobbing sound as they burst from his heaving breast in the intensity of his emotion. "It is like awaking from some hideous dream. If I shot you down, how is it that you are here?"

"You never shot me down. Old Parkes has been driving at some obscure tale about young Hunter being shot from the heights; but I treated it as a childish old man's fancies. Mary Anne, too, is wearing mourning for me, she says, though ostensibly put on for Lady Ellis, and came here to have speech of my ghost. I thought ghosts had gone out with the eighteenth century."

All three felt bewildered; idea after idea crowding on their minds: not one of them as yet clear or tangible. Mary Anne could not so soon overcome the shivering sensation that, had been upon her, and caught hold of her brother's arm for support. There was much of explanation to be had yet.

"Let us go and sit down in the church porch," she said; "we shall be quiet there."

They walked round the narrow path towards it. It was on the side of the church facing the Red Court. The brother and sister placed themselves on one bench: Hunter opposite. The moonlight streamed upon them, but they were in no danger there of being observed by any chance passer-by; for the hedge skirting the ground on that side was high and thick.

"That night," began Richard, "after you had gone away, what brought you back again?"

"Back where?" asked Hunter.

"Back on the plateau. Watching the fellows from the boats."

"I was not there. I did not come back."

The assertion sounded like a false one in the teeth of recollection. Mary Anne broke the silence, her low tone rather an impatient one.

"I saw you there, Robert—I and Anna Chester. We were coming up to speak to you, and got as far as the Round Tower—"

"What was worse, I saw you," hoarsely broke in Richard. "After what had passed between us, and your solemn oath to me, I felt shocked at your want of faith. I was maddened by your bad feeling, your obstinate determination to spy upon and betray us; and I stood by that same Round Tower and shot you down."

"I do not know what you are talking of," returned. Robert Hunter. "I tell you I never came back; never for one moment I got to Jutpoint by half-past ten or a quarter to eleven, so you may judge that I stepped out well."

"Did Cyril go there with you?"

"Cyril! Of course not. He left me soon after we passed the village. He only came as far as the wherry. I have been looking for Cyril while dodging about in this churchyard. I'd rather have seen him than you. He would not have been violent, you know, and would have carried you my message."

"We have never seen Cyril since that night," said Miss Thornycroft.

"Not seen Cyril!" echoed Hunter. "Where is he?"

"But we are not uneasy about him," said Richard, dropping his voice. "At least, I am not. We expect he went off in the boats with the smugglers when they rowed back to the ship that night after the cargo was run. Indeed, we feel positive of it. My father once did the same, to the terror of my mother. I believe she had him advertised. Cyril is taking a tolerably long spell on the French coast; but I think I can account for that. He will come home now."

"Still you have not explained," resumed Hunter. "What gave rise to this report that I was shot down?"

"Report!" cried Richard, vehemently, his new-found satisfaction beginning to fade, as sober recollection returned to him. "Somebody was shot, if you were not. We had the coroner's inquest on him, and he lies buried in this churchyard as Robert Hunter."

"But the features could not have been mine," debated Hunter.

"The face was not recognisable; but the head and hair were yours, and the dress was yours—a black dinner suit; and— By the way," broke off Richard, "what is this mystery? This coat, which you appear now to have on, is at this moment in the stables at the Mermaid, and has been ever since the inquest."

Does the reader notice that one word of Richard Thornycroft's—"Appear?" Appear to have on! Was he still doubting whether the man before him could be real?

"Oh, this is Dr. Macpherson's," said Hunter, with a brief laugh. "They were fellow coats, you know, Mary Anne. You did not send me my own—at least, I never received it; and one cold day, when I happened to be there, the professor surreptitiously handed me his out of a lumber closet, glad to get rid of it, hoping madame would think it was stolen. She could not forget the grievance of his having bought them. Why did not mine come with the portmanteau?"

More amazement, more puzzle, and Richard further at sea than ever.

"When you left that night, you had your coat with you, Hunter. I saw you put it on."

"But I found it an encumbrance. I had taken more wine than usual. I had had other things to make me hot, and I did not relish the prospect of carrying it, whether on or off, for five or six miles. So I took it off when we got to the wherry, and begged Cyril to carry it back with him, and send it with the portmanteau the following morning."

A pause of thought; it seemed they were trying to realize the sense of the words. Suddenly Mary Anne started, gasped, and laid her face down on her brother's shoulder, with a sharp, low moan of pain. He leaned forward and, stared at Hunter, a pitiable expression of dread on his countenance, as the moonlight fell on his ghastly face and strained-back lips.

"Cyril said, he was glad of it, and put it on, for he had come out without one, and felt cold," continued Hunter, carelessly. "He has not been exposed to all weathers, as I have. It fitted him capitally."

A cry, shrill and, wild as that which had broken from the dying man in his fall, now broke from Richard Thornycroft.

"Stop!" he shouted, in the desperation of anguish; "don't you see?"

"See what?" demanded the astonished Hunter.

"That I have murdered my brother!"

Alas! alas! As they sat gazing at each other with terror-stricken faces, you might have heard their hearts beat. Poor Richard Thornycroft! Had any awakening to horror been like unto his!

"Murdered your brother?" slowly repeated Hunter.

It was too true. The unfortunate Cyril Thornycroft, arrayed in Hunter's coat; had been mistaken by them for him in the starlight, and Richard had shot him dead. In returning home after parting with Hunter at the wherry, there could be no doubt that he had gone straight to the heights to see whether the work which had been planned for that night with the smugglers was being carried on, or whether the discovery made by Hunter had checked it. It was the coat, the miserable coat, that had deceived them. And there was the general resemblance they bore to each other, as previously mentioned. In height, in figure, in hair, they might have been taken for one another, and had been, even in the daylight, during Hunter's stay at Coastdown. But it was not all this that had led to the dreadful error—it was the fatal and conspicuous coat.

Everything had contributed to the delusion, before life and after death. The face might have been anybody's for all the signs of recognition left in it. They wore, and only they, each a black dress dinner-suit, and Cyril, in his forgetfulness had put away his purse and watch. His money—he generally carried it so—was loose in his pockets: how were they to know that the same custom was not followed by Hunter? The white pocket-handkerchief happened to bear no mark, and his linen was not disturbed. Nothing was taken off him but his upper clothes, the coat and the above-said dinner-suit. It was an exceptional death, you see, not a pleasant one to handle, and they just put a shroud over the under clothes, and so buried him. But for that would have been seen on the shirt the full mark—"Cyril Thornycroft."

Who shall attempt to describe the silence of horror that fell on the church porch after the revelation? Richard quitted his seat and stood upright, looking out, as it seemed; and his sister's head then sought a leaning-place against the cold trellis-work.

"How was it you never wrote to me?" at length asked Robert Hunter, in a low voice. "Had you done so, this mystery would have been cleared up."

"Wrote to you?" wailed Richard. "Do you forget we thought you were here?" stamping his foot on the sod of the churchyard.

"I can hardly understand it yet," mused Robert Hunter.

Richard Thornycroft turned and touched his sister. "Let us go home, Mary Anne. We have heard enough."

Without a word of dissent or approval, she rose and put her arm within Richard's; her face white and rigid as it had been at the coroner's inquest. Hunter spoke then.

"But, Mary Anne—what I wanted to say to you—I have not yet said a word of it."

"I cannot talk to-night," she shuddered. "I cannot—I cannot."

"Then—I suppose—I must stay another day," he rejoined, wondering privately what would be said and thought of him in London. "May I come to the Red Court to-morrow?"

"If you will," answered Richard. "No necessity for concealment now. I absolve you from your oath."

But Mary Anne saw further than either of them; saw that it would not do. Richard walked forward, but she remained, and touched Mr. Hunter on the arm.

"No, Robert, it must not be. You must still be in this neighbourhood— for a time at any rate—as dead and buried."

"Why? Far better to let them know I have not been murdered: and set their suspicions at rest."

"That you have not, but that another has," she returned, resentfully. "Would you have them rake up the matter, and hold a second inquest, and so set them upon my unfortunate brother Richard? His punishment, as it is, will be sufficiently dreadful and lasting."

"Do not speak to me in that tone of reproach," was the pained rejoinder. "You may be sure that I deeply sympathize and grieve with you all. I will continue to conceal myself: but how shall I see you? One more day, and business will enforce my return to London."

"I will see you here, in this place, to-morrow night."

"At what hour?"

"As soon as dusk comes on. Say seven."

"You will not fail, Mary Anne?"

"Fail!" she repeated, vehemently. Then, in a quieter tone, as she would have walked away, "No; I will be sure to come."

Robert Hunter grasped her hand, as if to draw her towards him for a fond embrace, but Miss Thornycroft wrenched her hand away with a half cry, and went on to join her brother. "Good night, dear Robert," she presently called out, in a gentle voice, as if to atone for her abrupt movement: but oh! what a mine of anguish that voice betrayed!

In the midst of the same silence that they had come, they went back again, walking side by side in the road, but not touching each other. Ah! what anguish t was that lay on both of them! We never know; in great affliction we are so apt to think that we can bear nothing worse, and live. It had seemed to Richard Thornycroft and his sister, when they went down to the churchyard, that no heavier weight of misery could be theirs than that lying on them; it seemed now in going back, as if that had been light, compared with this.

"Richard," she whispered, in her great pity, as they passed through the entrance gates of the Red Court Farm, "he is better off; he was fit to go. You know it must be so. Cyril is in heaven with God; it seems now as if he had been living on for it."

Richard hardly heard the words. He was thinking his own thoughts. "The death must have been a painless one."

She was true to her promise. The following evening, when dark fell and before the moon was up, Robert Hunter and Miss Thornycroft sat once more in the church porch. The night was very cold, sharp, raw; but from a feeling of considerate delicacy, which she understood and mentally thanked him for, he was without a great-coat. He rightly judged that the only one he had with him could in her eyes be nothing but an object of horror.

What a day that had been at the Red Court! Mr. Thornycroft had sat on the magisterial bench at Jutpoint, trying petty offenders, unconscious that there was a greater offender at his own house demanding punishment. Richard Thornycroft felt inclined to proclaim the truth and deliver himself up to justice. The remorse which had taken possession of him was greater than he knew how to bear; and it seemed that to expiate his offence at the criminal bar of his country, would be more tolerable than to let it thus prey upon him in silence, eating away his heart and his life. Consideration for his father and sister, for their honourable reputation, alone withheld him. He and Cyril had been fond brothers. Cyril, of delicate health and gentle manners, had been, as it were, the pet of the robust justice and his robust elder sons. The home, so far as Richard was concerned, must be broken up: he would go abroad, the farther distant the better. But for his sister, he had started that day. Something of this she told Mr. Hunter, in an outburst of her great suffering.

"Oh, Robert! even allowing that he shall escape, what a secret it will be for me and my brother Isaac to carry through life!"

"Time will soften it to you. You are both innocent."

"Time will never soften it to me. My dear brother Cyril!—so loving to us all, so good!"

Her hands were before her face as if she would conceal its tribulation from the dark night. Robert Hunter, who had been standing, drew her hands within his, sat down beside her on the narrow bench, and kept them there.

"Time is wearing on, Mary Anne, and I must be at Jutpoint to-night. May I say what I came down from town to say? Though it pains me to enter upon it now you are in this grief."

"What is it, Robert?"

"You have not forgotten that there was a probability of my going abroad? Well, the arrangements are now concluded, and I start in the course of a few days. I did not think of being off before the summer, but it has been settled differently."

"Yes. Well?"

"This alters my position altogether in a pecuniary point of view, and I shall now rest at ease, the future assured. The climate is excellent; the residence out all that can be wished for. In a week from this I ought to take my departure."

"Yes," she repeated, in the same tone of apathy as before. "What else? Make haste, Robert—I must begone; I am beginning to shiver. I have these shivering fits often now."

"I want you to go with me, my love," he whispered, in an accent of deep tenderness. "I came down to urge it; but now that this unfortunate affair has been made known to me, I would doubly urge it. As my wife, you will forget—"

"Be quiet, Robert!" she impetuously interrupted, "you cannot know what you are saying."

"Yes, I do; I wish you to understand I may be away for five years."

"So much the better. You and I, of all people in the world, must live apart. Was this what you had to say?"

"I thought you loved me," he rejoined, quite petrified at her words.

"I did love you; I do love you; if to avow it will do any good now. But this dreadful sorrow has placed a barrier between us."

There ensued a bitter pause. Robert Hunter was smarting with a sense of injustice.

"Mary Anne! Surely you are not laying on me the blame of that terrible calamity!"

"Listen, Robert," she returned. "I am not so unjust as to blame you for the actual calamity, but I cannot forget that you and I have been the cause of it."

"You!"

"Yes, I. When my father heard that I had invited you down, he came to me, and forbid me to let you come. I see now why. They did not want strangers in his house, who might see more than was expedient. He commanded me to write and stop you. I disobeyed; I thought papa spoke but in compliance with a whim of Richard's; and I would not write. Had I obeyed him, all this would have been spared. Again, when you and I told what the supervisor said, that there were smugglers abroad, my father ordered us, you especially, not to interfere. Had you observed his wishes to the letter, Cyril would have been alive now. These reflections haunt me continually; they will be mine for ever. No, Robert, you and I must live apart. If I were to marry you, I should expect Cyril to rise reproachfully before me on our wedding-day."

"Oh, Mary Anne! Believe me you see matters in a false light. If—"

"I will not discuss it," she peremptorily interrupted, "it would be of no avail, and I shudder while I speak. Spare me argument."

"I think you are forgetting that I have a stake in the matter as well as yourself," he quietly said, his tone proving how great the pain was. "Do you not know what, deprived of you, my future life will be? At least, I have a right to say a few words."

"Well—yes, that's true. I suppose I did forget, Robert."

"Forgive me then for reminding you that the sole and immediate cause of Cyril's death, is Richard. I did nothing whatever to help it on; my conscience is clear; the most prejudiced man could not charge me with it. And you? It is certainly a pity—I am speaking plainly—that you disobeyed Mr. Thornycroft in allowing me to come to the Red Court; it was very wrong; but still you did it not with any ill intention, and certainly do not merit the punishment of being condemned to live a lonely life."

"But Richard is my brother. See what it has brought on him."

"What he has brought upon himself," corrected Mr. Hunter. "I do not see that his being your brother throws, or should be allowed to throw any bar upon your marriage with me. You would not say so had he been a stranger.'

"Where is the use of arguing?" she broke in. "I cannot bear it; I will not hear it. All is at an end between us. Do you forgive me, Robert, if I cause you pain? Nothing in the world, or out of it, shall ever induce me to become your wife."

"Is this your fixed determination?"

"Fixed and unalterable. Fixed as those stars above us. Fixed as Cyril's grave."

"Then it only remains for me to return the way I came," he gloomily said. "And the sooner I start the better "

They stood up; looking for a moment each into the other's face. There was no relenting in hers. "Fare you well, Mary Anne."

She put her hand into his, and, overcome by the dead anguish at her heart, burst into tears. He drew her to his breast. None can know what that anguish was to her, even of the parting. He held her to him and soothed her sobs, now with a loving look, now with a gentle action; and then he broke into words of passionate entreaty, that she would retract her cruel determination, and suffer him to speak to her father. But he little knew Mary Anne Thornycroft if he thought that she would yield.

"Say no more; it is quite useless. Oh, Robert, don't you see it is as bitter for me as for you?"

"No; or you would not inflict it."

"Strive to forget me, Robert," she murmured. "We have been very dear to each other, but you must find some one else now. Perhaps we may meet in after life—when you are a happy man with wife and children!"

He went with her to the churchyard gates, and watched her as she turned to her home. And so they parted Robert Hunter retraced his steps up the churchyard, and from behind a gravestone, where he had laid them out of sight, took up his little black travelling-bag, and the rolled-up coat, the counterpart of which had proved so unlucky a coat for the Red Court Farm. He never intended to put it on again—at least in the neighbourhood of Coastdown. Then he set off to walk to Jutpoint, avoiding the road by means of a bypath, as he had set off to walk that guilty night some weeks before.

The night had clouded over, the stars disappeared, the moon was not seen. Drops of rain began to fall, threatening a heavy shower. On it came, thicker and faster; wetter and wetter got he; but it may be questioned whether he gave to it one single thought.

His reflections were buried quite as much in the past as in the present. He murmured to himself the word "RETRIBUTION." He asked how he could ever have dreamt of indulging a prospect of happiness; he almost laughed at the utter mockery of the hope. As he had blighted his wife's life, so had Mary Anne Thornycroft, his late and only love, now blighted his. She—poor Clara—had died of the pain; he, of sterner stuff, must carry it along with him. Amid his days of labour, through his nights of perhaps broken rest, it would, lie upon him—a well-earned recompense! No murmur came forth from his heart or lips; he simply bowed his head in acknowledgment of the justice. God was ever true. And Robert Hunter lifted his hat in the pouring rain, and raised his eyes to heaven in sad thankfulness that the pain his sin had caused was at length made clear to him.

CHAPTER XVI

In the Dog-cart to Jutpoint

But there's something yet to tell of the evening. It was getting towards dusk when Isaac Thornycroft went his way to Captain Copp's intending boldly to ask Miss Chester to take a walk with him, should there be no chance of getting a minute with her alone at home.

The state in which he was living, touching his wife's estrangement (not their separation, that was a present necessity), was getting unbearable; and Isaac, who had hitherto shunned an explanation, came to the rather sudden resolution of seeking it. Although his brother had shot Robert Hunter, it could not be said to be a just reason for Anna's resenting it upon him. Not a syllable did Isaac yet know of the discovery that had taken place, or that Cyril was the one lying in the churchyard.

In the free and simple community of Coastdown, doors were not kept closed, and people entered at will. Rather, then, to Isaac's surprise, as he turned the handle of Captain Copp's, he found it was fastened, so that he could not enter. At the same moment his eyes met his wife's, who had come to the window to reconnoitre. There was no help for it, and she had to go and let him in.

"At home alone, Anna! Where are they all? Where's Sarah?"

Anna explained: bare facts only, however, not motives. It appeared that the gallant captain, considerably lowered in his own estimation by the events of the past night, and especially that he should be so in the sight of his "womenkind," proposed a little jaunt that day to Jutpoint by way of diverting their thoughts, and perhaps his own, from the ghost and its reminiscences. His mother—recovered from her incipient cold—she was too strong-minded a woman for diseases to seize upon heartily—agreed readily, as did his wife. Not so Anna. She pleaded illness, and begged to be left at home. It was indeed no false plea, for her miserable state of mind was beginning to tell upon her. They had been expected home in time for tea, and had not come. Anna supposed they had contrived to miss the omnibus, which was in fact the case, and could not now return until late. How Mrs. Sam Copp would be brought by the churchyard was a thing easier wondered at than told. As to Sarah, she had but now stepped out on some necessary errands to the village.

In the satisfaction of finding the field undisturbed for the explanation he wished entered on, Isaac said nothing about his wife being left in the house alone, which he by no means approved of. It was not dark yet, only dusk: but Anna said something about getting lights.

"Not yet," said Isaac. "I want to talk to you; there's plenty of light for that."

She sat down on the sofa; trembling, frightened, sick. If her husband was the slayer of Robert Hunter—as she believed him to be—it was not agreeable to be in the solitary house with him; it was equally disagreeable to have to tell him to go out of it. Ah, but for that terrible belief, what a happy moment this snatch of intercourse might have been to them! this sole first chance for weeks and weeks of being alone, when they might speak together of future plans with a half-hour's freedom.

She took her seat on the sofa, scarcely conscious what she did in her sick perplexity. Isaac sat down by her, put his arm round her waist, and would have kissed her. But she drew to the other end of the large sofa with a gesture of evident avoidance, and burst into tears. So he got up and stood before her.

"Anna, this must end, one way or the other; it is what I came here to-night to say. The separated condition in which we first lived after our return was bad enough, but that was pleasant compared to what it afterwards became. It is some weeks now since you have allowed me barely to shake you by the hand; never if you could avoid it. Things cannot go on so."

She made no reply. Only sat there trembling and crying, her hands before her face.

"What have I done to you? Come, Anna, I must have an answer. What have I done to you?"

She spoke at last, looking up. In her habit of implicit obedience, there was no help for it; there could be none when the order came from him.

"Nothing—to me."

"To whom, then? What is it?"

"Nothing," was all she repeated.

"Nothing! Do you repent having married me?"

"I don't know."

The answer seemed to pain him. He bent his handsome face a little towards her, pushing back impatiently his golden hair, as if the fair bright brow needed coolness.

"I thought you loved me, Anna?"

"And you know I did. Oh, that is it! The misery would be greater if I loved you less."

"Then why do you shun me?"

"Is there not a cause why I should?" she asked in a low tone, after a long pause.

"I think not. Will you tell me what the cause may be?"

She glanced up at him, she looked down, she smoothed unconsciously the silk apron on which her nervous hands rested, but she could not answer. Isaac saw it, and, bending nearer to her, he spoke in a whisper.

"Is it connected with that unhappy night—with what took place on the plateau?"

"I think you must have known all along that it is."

"And you consider it a sufficient reason for shunning me?"

"Yes, do not you?"

"Certainly not."

Great though her misery was, passionately though she loved him still, the cool assertion angered her. It gave her a courage to speak that nothing else could have given.

"It was a dark crime; the worst crime that the world can know. Does it not lie on your conscience?"

"No; I could not hinder it."

"Oh, Isaac! Had it been anything else; anything but murder, I could have borne it. How you can bear it, and live, I cannot understand."

"Why should I make another's sin mine? No one can deplore it as I do; but it is not my place to answer for it. I do not understand you, Anna."

She did not understand. What did his words mean?

"Did you not kill Robert Hunter?"

"I kill him! You are dreaming, Anna! I was not near the spot."

"Isaac! ISAAC?"

"Child! have you been fearing that?"

"For nothing else, for nothing else could I have shunned you. Oh, Isaac! my dear husband, how could the mistake arise?"

"I know not. A mistake it was; I affirm it to you before God. I was not on the plateau at all that night."

He opened his arms, gravely smiling, and she passed into them with a great cry. Trembling, moaning, sobbing; Isaac thought she would have fainted. Placing her by his side on the sofa, he kept still, listening to what she had to say.

"As I looked out of the Round Tower in the starlight, I caught a momentary glimpse of—as I thought— you, and I saw the hand that held the pistol take aim and fire. I thought it was you, and I fainted. I have thought it ever since. Mary Anne, in a word or two that we spoke together, seemed to confirm it."

"Mary Anne knew it was not I. It is not in my nature to draw a pistol on any man. Surely, Anna, you might have trusted me better!"

"Oh, what a relief!" she murmured, "what a relief!" then, as a sudden thought seemed to strike her, she turned her face to his and spoke, her voice hushed.

"It must have been Richard. You are alike in figure."

"Upon that point we had better be silent," he answered, in quite a solemn tone. "It is a thing that we are not called upon to inquire into; let us avoid it. I am innocent: will not that suffice?"

"It will more than suffice for me," she answered. "Since that night I have been most wretched."

"You need not have feared me in any way, Anna," was the reply of Isaac Thornycroft. "Were it possible that my hand could become stained with the blood of a fellow-creature, I should hasten to separate from you quicker than you could from me. Whatever else such an unhappy man may covet, let him keep clear of wife and children."

"Forgive me, Isaac! Forgive me!"

"I have not been exempt from the follies of young men, and I related to you the greater portion of my share of them, after we married," he whispered. "But of dark crime I am innocent—as innocent as you are."

"Oh, Isaac! my husband, Isaac!"

He bent his face on hers, and she lay there quietly, her head nestling in his bosom. It seemed to her like a dream of heaven after the past; a very paradise.

"You will forgive me, won't you?" she softly breathed.

"My darling!"

But paradise cannot last for ever, as you all know; and one of them at any rate found himself very far on this side it ere the night was much older. As Sarah let herself into the house with her back-door key, Isaac quitted it by the front, and bent his steps across the heath.

In passing the churchyard, he stood and looked well into it. But there was no sign of the ghost, and Isaac went on again. How little did he suspect that at that very selfsame moment the ghost was seated round in the church porch, in deep conversation with his sister! Having an errand in the village, he struck across to it; and on his final return home a little later, he was astonished to overtake his sister at the entrance gates of the Red Court Farm, her forehead pressed upon the ironwork, and she sobbing as if her heart would break.

"Mary Anne! what is the matter? What brings you here?"

"Come with me," she briefly said. "If I do not tell some one, I shall die."

Walking swiftly to one of the benches on the lawn, she sat down on it, utterly indifferent to the rain that was beginning to fall. Isaac followed her wonderingly. Poor thing! the whole of the previous day and night she had really almost felt as if she should die—die from the weight of the fearful secret, and the want of some one to confide in. Richard was the only one who shared it, and she was debarred by pity from talking to him.

There, with the fatal plateau in front of him, and the rain coming down on their devoted heads, Isaac Thornycroft learnt the whole—learnt to his dismay, his grief, his horror, that the victim had been his much-loved brother Cyril; and that Robert Hunter was still in life.

He took his hat off, and wiped his brow; and then held his hat before his face, after the fashion of men going into church—held it for some minutes. Mary Anne in her own deep emotion did not notice his.

"Isaac, don't you pity me?"

"I pity us all."

"And there will be the making it known to papa. He must be told."

"Richard will leave Coastdown for ever. He could not remain in it, he says. I am not competent to advise him, Isaac. You must."

"Richard has never yet taken any advice but his own."

"Ah! but he is changed to-day. He has been changed a little since that dreadful night. I suppose you have known all along that it was Richard who—who did it?"

"Not from information: I saw that you knew; that you were in his confidence. Of course I could not help being sure in my own mind that it must have been Richard. I fancy"—he turned and looked full at his sister—"that Miss Chester thought it was I."

"Yes, I know she did,' was the assured answer. "It was better to let her think so. Safer for Richard, better for you."

"Why better for me?'

"Because—it is not a moment to be reticent, Isaac—Anna Chester once appeared too much inclined to like you. That would never do, you know."

He turned his head away; a soft remembrance parting his lips, a look of passionate love, meant for his absent wife, lighting his eyes.

"You will get wet sitting here, Mary Anne."

She arose, and they went indoors. Isaac was passing straight through to the less-used rooms when his sister stopped him.

Rooms that would never have been closed to the rest of the house, but for the smuggling practices so long carried on by the Thornycroft family. In the rooms themselves there was absolutely nothing that could have led to betrayal, or any reason why they might not have been open to all the household: but it was necessary to keep that part of the house closed always, except to Mr. Thornycroft and his sons, lest it should have been penetrated to at the few exceptional times when the cargo was being run, or the dog-cart laden subsequently with the spoil. When once the cargo was safely lodged in the cavern within the rocks, it might remain there in security to some convenient time for removing it. This was always done at night. Richard and Isaac Thornycroft, Tomlett and Hyde, brought up sufficient of the parcels to fill the dog-cart, which one of the sons, sometimes both, would then drive away with and deposit with Hopley, their agent at Dartfield, whose business it was to convey the booty to its final destination. The next night more would be taken away, and so on. Sometimes so large was the trade done, so swift were the operations, that one cargo would not be all sent away before another was landed. At another period perhaps three months elapsed and no boat came in. With this frequent going out by night with the dog-cart, no wonder the young Thornycrofts got the credit of being loose in their habits, and that the justice encouraged the notion.

The sumptuous dinners at the Red Court Farm (or suppers, according to the convenience and time of year) were kept up as a sort of covering to the illicit doings. When the gentlemen of the neighbourhood, including the superintendent of the coastguard, had their legs under the hospitable board, or the servants subsequently under theirs in the kitchen, they could not be wandering about out of doors, seeing inexpedient things. It was not often of late years Mr. Thornycroft aided in the run; he left it to Richard and Isaac, and stayed with his guests. On the night Lady Ellis saw him he had gone out, found there was a sea fog, and came in again; denying it afterwards to her (as faithful Hyde had done) lest she should next question why he changed his coat and put on leggings.

The late superintendent, Mr. Dangerfield, had allowed rule to get lax altogether, but he had, of course, a certain amount of watching kept up. On the occasion of a dinner or supper at the Red Court (always given when a cargo was waiting to be run), Mr. Dangerfield would contrive to let his men know that he was going to it; as a matter of fact, not a man troubled himself to go near the plateau that night; the Mermaid had them instead; and all too often it happened that one of the young Mr. Thornycrofts would go in and stand treat. No fear of the men's stirring any more than their master. But from the fact of the Half-moon beach being visible only from the plateau, and for the supernatural tales connected with the latter, they had never escaped being seen so long as they did.

The ghostly stories—not of Robert Hunter—had done more than all to prevent discovery. It could not be said that the Thornycrofts raised them in the first place; they did not; but when they perceived how valuable an adjunct they were likely to prove, they took care to keep them up. Report went that the late Mrs. Thornycroft had died from the fears induced by superstition. It was as well to keep up that belief also; but she had died from nothing of the sort. What she had really died of—so to say—was the smuggling. When the discovery came to her at first, through an accident, of the practices carried on by her husband and sons—as they had been by her husband's brother and his father before him—it brought a great shock. A timid, right-minded, refined woman, the dread of discovery was perpetually upon her afterwards; she lived in a state of inward fear night and day; and this most probably induced the disorder of which she died—a weakness that got gradually worse and worse, and ended in death. When she was dying, not before, she told them it had killed her. Had Mr. Thornycroft known of it earlier, he might have given it up for her sake, for he was a fond husband. But he had not known of it; and her death and its unhappy cause left upon them a great sorrow: one that could not be put away. The same grief at the practices, and dread of what a persistence in them might bring forth, had likewise lain on Cyril, and been the secret of his declining to take Orders so long as they should be carried on. Mr. Thornycroft himself was getting somewhat tired of it, as he told Cyril; he had made plenty of money, but Richard would not hear of their being given up.

Perhaps from habit more than anything else, Isaac was passing on to the back rooms, but Mary Anne arrested him. "Stay with me a little while, Isaac; you do not know how lonely it is for me now."

He acquiesced at once. He was ever good-natured and kind, and they turned into the sitting-room, she calling a servant to take her shawl and bonnet. Not empty, as she had anticipated, was the parlour, for Richard was there.

"I have told Isaac all," said Mary Anne, briefly. And Isaac, in his great compassion, went up to his brother and laid his hand on him kindly.

Poor Richard Thornycroft! His eyes hollow, his brow fevered, his hands burning, he paced there still in his terrible remorse. A consuming fire had set in, to prey upon him for all time. He spoke a few disjointed words to Isaac, as if in extenuation.

"I felt half maddened at Hunter's duplicity of conduct that night. I had warned him that I would shoot him if he went again on the plateau, and I thought I was justified in doing so. Why did Cyril put the coat on?"

"Let this be a consolation to you, Richard—that you did not intend, to harm your brother," was all the comfort Isaac could give.

"Had it been any one but my brother! had it been any out my brother!" was the wailing answer. "The curse of Cain rests upon me."

Walking about still in his restlessness as he said it! He had never sat, or lain, or rested since leaving the churchyard the previous night, but paced about as one in the very depths of despair. Mary Anne slipped the bolt of the door, and they began to consult as to the future. At this dread consultation, every word of which will linger in the remembrance of the three during life, Richard decided upon his plans. To remain in the neighbourhood of the fatal scene, ever again to look upon the Half-moon beach where the dead had lain, he felt would drive him mad. In Australia he might in time find something like rest.

"I shall leave to-night," said he.

"To-night!" echoed Isaac, in great surprise. Richard nodded. "You will drive me to Jutpoint, won't you, Isaac?"

"If you must really go."

"And when shall we see you again?" inquired Mary Anne.

"Never again."

"Never again! never again!" she repeated, with a moan. "Oh Richard, never again!"

It was a shock to Mr. Thornycroft, when he drove home an hour later from Jutpoint, to find his eldest and (as people had looked upon it) his favourite son waiting to bid him farewell for ever. They did not disclose to him the fearful secret—either that it was Cyril who had died, or that it was Richard who had shot him—leaving that to be revealed later. They said Richard had fallen into a serious scrape, which could only be kept quiet by his quitting the place for a few years, and begged him not to inquire particulars; that the less said about it the better. Justice Thornycroft obeyed in his surprise, for the communication had half stunned him.

And so they parted. Once more in the middle of the night—in the little hours intervening between dark and dawn—the dog-cart was driven out from the Red Court Farm: not bearing this time a quantity of valuable lace or other booty, but simply a portmanteau of Richard's, with a few articles of clothing flung hastily into it. He sat low down in the seat, his hat over his brows, his arms folded, his silence stern. And thus Isaac, on the high cushion by his side, drove him to Jutpoint to catch the early morning train.

CHAPTER XVII

Ladies Disputing

The next matter to be disclosed was the marriage of Isaac. It was not done immediately. As the reader may have surmised, the sole cause for his keeping it secret at all had its rise in the smuggling. So long as they ran cargoes into the vaults of the Red Court Farm, so long did Mr. Thornycroft lay an embargo, or wish to lay it, on his sons marrying. The secret might be no longer safe, he said, if one of them took a wife.

With the departure of Richard the smuggling would end. Without him, Mr. Thornycroft would not care to carry it on: and Isaac felt that he could never join in it again, after what it had done for Cyril. There was no need: Mr. Thornycroft's wealth was ample. But some weeks went on before Isaac considered himself at liberty to speak.

For the fact was this: Richard Thornycroft on his departure had extracted a promise from Isaac not to disclose particulars until they should hear from him. Isaac gave it readily, supposing he would write before embarking. But the days and the weeks went on, and no letter came: Isaac was at a nonplus, and felt half convinced, in his own mind, that Richard had repented of his determination to absent himself, and would be coming back to Coastdown. With the disclosure of his marriage to the justice, Isaac wished to add another disclosure—that he had done with the smuggling for ever; but a fear was upon him that this might lead to a full revelation of the past; and, for Richard's sake, until news should come that he was safe away, Isaac delayed and delayed. His inclination would have been less willing to do this, but for one thing, and that was, that he could not have his wife with him just yet. Mrs. Sam Copp, poor meek Amy, had been seized with a long and dangerous illness. Anna was in close attendance upon her; Mrs. Copp stayed to domineer and superintend; and until she should be better Anna could not leave. Thus the time had gone on, and accident brought about what intention had not.

May was in, and quickly passing. Pretty nearly two months had elapsed since Richard's exit. One bright afternoon when Amy was well enough to sit up at her bed-room window, open to the balmy heath and the sweet breeze from the sparkling sea, Sarah came up and said Mr. Isaac Thornycroft was below. Anna sat with her; the captain and his mother were out.

"May I go down?" asked Anna, with a bright blush.

"I suppose you must, dear," answered Mrs. Sam Copp, with a sigh, given to the long-continued concealment that ever haunted her.

Away went Anna, flying first of all up to her own room to smooth her hair, to see that her pretty muslin dress with its lilac ribbons looked nice. Isaac, under present circumstances, was far more like a lover than a husband: scarcely ever did they see each other alone for an instant. This took her about two minutes, and she went softly downstairs and opened the parlour door.

Isaac was seated with his back to it, on this side the window. Anna, her face in a glow with the freedom of what she was about to do, stepped up, put her hands round his neck from the back, and kissed his hair—kissed it again and again.

"Halloa!" roared out a stern voice.

Away she shrunk, with a startled scream. At the back of the room, having thrown himself on the sofa, tired with his walk, was Captain Copp, his mother beside him. The two minutes had been sufficient time for them to enter. The captain had not felt so confounded since the night of the apparition, and Mrs. Copp's eyes were perfectly round with a broad stare.

"You shameless hussey!" cried the gallant captain, finding his tongue as he advanced. "What on earth—"

But Isaac had risen. Risen, and was taking Anna to his side, holding her up, standing still with calm composure.

"It is all right, Captain Copp. Pardon me. Anna is my wife."

"Your—what?" roared the captain, really not hearing in his flurry.

"Anna has been my wife since last November. And I hope," Isaac added, with a quiet laugh, partly of vexation, partly of amusement, "that you will give me credit for self-sacrifice and infinite patience in letting her remain here."

Anna, crying silently in her distress and shame, had turned to him, and was hiding her face on his arm, A minute or two sufficed for the explanation Isaac gave. Its truth could not be doubted, and he finished by calling her a little goose, and bidding her look up. Captain Copp felt uncertain whether to storm or to take it quietly. Meanwhile, he sat down rather humbly, and joined Mrs. Copp in staring.

"A ghost one week; a private marriage the next! I say, mother, I wish I was among the pirates again!"

This discovery decided the question in Isaac's mind, and he went straight to the Red Court to seek a private interview with his father. But he told only of the marriage: leaving other matters to the future. Rather to his surprise, it was well received: Mr. Thornycroft did not say a harsh word.

"Be it so, Isaac. Of business I am thinking we shall do no more. And if I am to be deprived of two of my sons—as appears only too probable—it is well that the third should marry. As to Anna, she is a sweet girl, and I've nothing to say against her, except her want of money. I suppose you considered that you will possess enough for both."

"We shall have enough for comfort, sir."

"And for something else. Go and bring her home here at once, Isaac."

But to this, upon consideration, was raised a decided objection at Captain Copp's. What would the gossips say? Isaac thought of a better plan. He wanted to run up to London for a few days, and would take his wife with him. After their departure, Sarah might be told, who would be safe to go abroad at once and spread the news everywhere: that Miss Chester, under the sanction of her mistress, the captain's wife, had been married in the winter to Isaac Thornycroft.

Mrs. Copp, whose visit had grown to unconscionable length, announced. her intention of proceeding with them to London. The captain's wife was quite sufficiently recovered to be left: to use her own glad words, she should "get well all one way," now that the secret was told. So it was arranged, and the captain himself escorted them to Jutpoint.

A gathering at Mrs. Macpherson's. On the day after the arrival in London, that lady had met the three in the crowd at the Royal Academy, and invited them at once to her house in the evening. Isaac, who had seen her once or twice before introduced Mrs. Copp, and whispered the fact that Anna was no longer Miss Chester, but Mrs. Isaac Thornycroft.

"You'll come early, mind," cried, the hospitable wife of the professor. "It's just an ordinary tea-drinking, which is one of the few good things that if the world means to let die out, I don't; but there'll be some cold meat with it, if anybody happens to be hungry. The Miss Jupps are coming, and they dine early. Tell your wife, Mr. Thornycroft—bless her sweet face! there's not one to match it in all them frames—that I'll get in some wedding cake."

Isaac laughed. The jostling masses had left him behind with Mrs. Macpherson, who was dressed so intensely high in the fashion, that he rather winced at the glasses directed to them. However, they accepted the invitation, and went to Mrs. Macpherson's in the evening.

Miss Jupp had arrived before them; her sisters were unable to come. She was looking a little more worn than usual, until aroused by the news relating to Anna. Married! and Miss Jupp had been counting the days, as it were, until she should return to them, for they could not get another teacher like her for patience and work.

Ah, yes: Anna's teaching days were over; her star had brightened. As she sat there in her gleaming silk of pearl-grey, in the golden bracelets, Isaac's gift, with the rose-blush on her cheeks, the light of love in her sweet eyes, Mary Jupp saw that she had found her true sphere.

"But, my dear child, why should it have been done in secret?" she whispered.

"There were family reasons," answered Anna, "I cannot tell you now."

"Since last November! Dear me! And was the marriage really not known to any one? was it quite secret?"

"Not quite. One of Isaac's brothers was present in the church to give me away, and Captain Copp's wife knew of it."

"Ah, then you are not to be blamed; I am glad to hear that," sighed Mary Jupp.

"And now tell me, how is my dear Miss Thornycroft?" cried Mrs. Macpherson, as the good professor, in his threadbare coat (rather worse than usual) beguiled Isaac away to his laboratory. "I declare I have not yet asked after her."

"Had Mrs. Macpherson been strictly candid, she might have acknowledged to having purposely abstained from asking before Isaac. The fact of the young lady's having got intimate with Robert Hunter at her house, and of its being an acquaintance not likely, as she judged, to be acceptable to the Thornycrofts, had rather lain on her mind.

"She looks wretched," answered Mrs. Copp.

"Wretched?"

"She has fretted all the flesh off her bones. You might draw her through the eye of a needle."

"My patience!" ejaculated Mrs. Macpherson. "The prefessor 'ill be sorry to hear this. What on earth has she fretted over?"

"That horrible business about Robert Hunter," explained Mrs. Copp. "The justice has not looked like himself since; and never will again."

"Oh," returned the professor's lady in a subdued tone, feeling suddenly crestfallen. Conscience whispered that this could only apply to the matter she was thinking of, and that the attachment had arisen through her own imprudence in allowing them to meet. She supposed (to use the expressive words passing through her thoughts) that there had been a blow-up.

"It wasn't no fault of mine," she said, after a pause. "Who was to suspect they were going to fall in love with each other in that foolish fashion? She a schoolgirl, and he an old widower! A couple of spoonies! Other folks as well as me might have been throwed off their guard."

Since Mrs. Macpherson had mixed in refined society she had learnt to speak tolerably well at collected times and seasons. But when flurried her new ideas and associations forsook her, and she was sure to lapse back to the speech of old days.

"Then there was an attachment between him and Mary Anne Thornycroft!" exclaimed Mrs. Copp, in a tone of triumph. "Didn't I tell you so, Anna? You need not have been so close about it."

"I do not know that there was," replied Anna "Mary Anne never spoke of it to me."

"Rubbish to speaking of it," said Mrs. Copp. "You didn't speak about you and Mr. Isaac." Anna bent her head in silence.

"And was there a blow-up with her folks?" inquired Mrs. Macpherson, not quite courageously yet. "Miss Jupp! you remember—I come right off to you with my suspicions at the first moment I had 'em—which was only a day or so before she went home."

"I don't know about that; there might have been or there might not," replied Mrs. Copp, alluding to the question of the "blow-up." "But I have got my eyes about me, and I can see how she grieved after him. Why, if there had been nothing between them, why did she put on mourning?" demanded the captain's mother, looking at the assembled company one by one.

"She put it on for Lady Ellis," said Anna.

"Oh, did she, though! Sarah told me that that mourning was on her back before ever Lady Ellis died. I tell you, I tell you also, ladies, she put on the black for Robert Hunter."

"Who put on black for him?" questioned Mrs. Macpherson, in a puzzle.

"Mary Anne Thornycroft."

"I never heard of such a thing! What did she do that for?"

"Why do girls do foolish things?" returned Mrs. Copp. "To show her respect for him, I suppose."

"A funny way of showing it!" cried Mrs. Macpherson. "Robert Hunter is doing very well where he's gone."

Mrs. Copp turned her eyes on the professor's wife with a prolonged stare.

"It is to be hoped he is, ma'am," she retorted, emphatically.

"He is doing so well that his coming back and marrying her wouldn't surprise me in the least. The Thornycrofts won't have no need to set up their backs again him if he can show he is in the way of making his fortune."

"Why, who are you talking of?" asked Mrs. Copp, after a pause and another gaze.

"Of Robert Hunter. He has gone and left us. Perhaps you did not know it, ma'am?"

"Yes, I did," said Mrs. Copp, with increased emphasis. "Coastdown has too good cause to know it, unfortunately."

This remark caused Mrs. Macpherson to become meek again. "I had a note from him this week," she observed. "It come in a letter to the professor: he sent it me up from his laborory."

The corners of Anna's mouth were gradually lengthening, almost—she could not help the feeling—in a sort of fear. It must be remembered that she knew nothing of the fact that it was not Robert Hunter who had died.

"Perhaps you'll repeat that again, ma'am," said Mrs. Copp, eyeing Mrs. Macpherson in her sternest manner. "You had a note from him, Robert Hunter?"

"Yes, I had, ma'am. Writ by himself."

"Where was it written from?"

Mrs. Macpherson hesitated, conscious of her defects in the science of locality. "The professor would know," said she; "I'm not much of a geographer myself. Anyway it come from where he is, somewhere over in t'other hemisphere."

To a lady of Mrs. Copp's extensive travels, round the world a dozen times and back again, the words "over in t'other hemisphere," taken in conjunction with Robert Hunter's known death and burial, conveyed the idea that the celestial hemisphere, and not the terrestrial, was alluded to. She became convinced of one of two things: that the speaker before her was awfully profane, or else mad.

"I know the letters were six weeks reaching us," continued Mrs. Macpherson. "I suppose it would take about that time to get here from the place."

Mrs. Copp pushed her chair back in a heat. "This is the first time I ever came out to drink tea with the insane, and I hope it will be the last," she cried, speaking without reserve, according to her custom. "Ma'am, if you are not a model of profanity, you ought to be in Bedlam."

Mrs. Macpherson wiped her hot face and took out her fan. But she could give as well as take. "It's what I have been thinking of you, ma'am. Do you think you are quite right?"

"I right!" screamed Mrs. Copp in a fury. "What do you mean?"

"What do you mean?—come!—about me?"

"That's plain. I never yet heard of a man who is dead and gone writing back letters to his friends. Who brings them? How do they come? Do they drop from the skies or come up through the graves?"

"Lawk a mercy!" cried Mrs. Macpherson, not catching the full import of the puzzling questions. "They come through the post.'

Mrs. Copp was momentarily silenced. The answer was entirely practical: it was not given in anger; nor, as she confessed to herself, with any indication of insanity. Light dawned upon her mind.

"It's the spirits!" she exclaimed, coming to a sudden conviction. "Well! Before I'd go in for that fashionable rubbish! A woman of any pretension to sense believe in them!"

"Hang the spirits!" returned Mrs. Macpherson with offended emphasis. "I'm not quite such a fool as that. You should hear what the professor says of them. Leastways, not of the spirits, poor innocent things, which is all delusion, but of them there rapping mediums that make believe to call 'em up."

"Then, ma'am, if it's not the spirits you allude to as bringing the letters, perhaps you'll explain to me what does bring them."

"What should bring them but the post?"

Mrs. Copp was getting angry. "The post does not bring letters from dead men."

"I never said it did. Robert Hunter's not dead."

"Robert Hunter is."

"Well, I'm sure!" cried Mrs. Macpherson, fanning herself.

"Robert Hunter died last January," persisted Mrs. Copp, in excitement. "His unfortunate body lies under the sod in Coastdown churchyard, and his poor restless spirit hovers above it, frightening the people into fits. My son Sam saw it. Isaac Thornycroft saw it."

"Robert Hunter is not dead," fired Mrs. Macpherson, who came to the conclusion that she was being purposely deceived; "he is gone to the East to make a railroad. Not that I quite know where the East is," acknowledged she, "or how it stands from this. I tell you all, I got a letter from him, and it was writ about six weeks ago."

"If that lady is not mad, I never was so insulted before," cried Mrs. Copp. "I—"

"There must be some mistake," interposed Mary Jupp, who had listened in great surprise. Of herself she could not solve the question, and knew nothing of the movements of Mr. Hunter. But she thought if he were dead that she should have heard of it from his sister Susan. "Perhaps it only requires a word of explanation."

"I don't know what explanation it can require," retorted Mrs. Copp. "The man is dead and buried."

"The man is not," contended Mrs. Macpherson; "he is alive and kicking, and laying down a railroad."

"My son, Captain Copp, was a mourner at his funeral."

"He wrote me a letter six weeks ago, and he wrote one to the prefessor; and he said he was getting on like a house on fire," doggedly asserted the professor's wife.

"Stay, stay, I pray you," interposed Miss Jupp. "There must be some misunderstanding. You cannot be speaking of the same man."

"We are!" raved both the ladies, losing temper. "It is Robert Hunter, the engineer, who met Mary Anne Thornycroft at my house; and the two—as I suspected—fell in love with each other, which made me very mad."

"And came down to see her at Coastdown, and Susan Hunter was to have come with him, and didn't. Of course we are speaking of the same."

"And I say that he come back from that visit safe and sound, and was in London till April, when he went abroad," screamed Mrs. Macpherson. "He dined here with us the Sunday afore he was off; we had a lovely piece o' the belly o salmon, and a quarter o' lamb and spring cabbage, and rhubub tart and custards, and a bottle of champagne, that we might drink success to his journey. Very down-hearted he seemed, I suppose at the thoughts of going away; and the next day he started. There! Ask the professor, ma'am, and contradict it if you can."

"I won't contradict it," said Mrs. Copp; "I might set on and swear if I did, like my son Sam. You'll persuade me next there's nothing real in the world. Anna Chester—that is, Anna Thornycroft—do you tell what you know. Perhaps they'll hear you."

"Oh, I'll hear the young lady," said Mrs. Macpherson fanning herself violently; "but nobody can't persuade me that black's white."

Anna quietly related facts, so far as her knowledge extended: Robert Hunter had come to Coastdown, had paid his visit to the Red Court Farm, and on the very night he was to have left for London he was shot as he stood at the edge of the cliffs, fell over, and was not found until the morning—dead!

Her calm manner, impressive in its truth, her minute relation of particulars, her unqualified assertion that it was Robert Hunter, and could have been no one else, staggered Mrs. Macpherson.

"And he was shot down dead, you say?" cried that lady, dropping the fan, and opening her mouth very wide.

"He must have died at the moment he was shot. It was not discovered"—here her voice faltered a little—"who shot him, and the jury returned a verdict of wilful murder against some person or persons unknown."

"Was there a inquest?' demanded the astonished Mrs. Macpherson, "on Robert Hunter?"

"Certainly there was. He was buried subsequently in Coastdown churchyard. His grave lies in the east corner of it, near Mrs. Thornycroft's."

"Now you have not told all the truth, Anna," burst forth Mrs. Copp, who had been restraining herself with difficulty. "You are always shuffling out of that part of the story when you can. Why don't you say that you and Miss Thornycroft saw him murdered? Tell it as you had to tell it before the coroner."

"It is true," acknowledged Anna.

"And Miss Thornycroft put on mourning for him, making believe it was for Lady Ellis, who died close upon it," cried Mrs. Copp, too impatient to allow Anna to continue. "And the worst is, that he can't rest in his grave, poor fellow, but hovers atop of it night after night, so that Coastdown dare not go by the churchyard, and the folks have made a way right across the heath to avoid it, breaking through two hedges and a stone fence that belongs to Lord What's-his-name—who's safe, it's said, to indict the parish for trespass. Scores of folks saw the ghost. Anna saw it. My son Sam saw it, and he's not one to be taken in by a ghost; though he did think once he saw a mermaid, and will die, poor fellow, in the belief. Robert Hunter not dead, indeed! He was barbarously murdered, ma'am."

"It is the most astounding tale I ever heard," cried the bewildered Mrs. Macpherson. "What was the ghost like?"

"Like himself, ma'am. Perhaps you knew a coat he had? An ugly white thing garnished with black fur?"

"I had only too good cause to know it!" shrieked out Mrs. Macpherson, aroused at the mention. "That blessed prefessor of mine bought it and gave it him; was took in to buy it. He's the greatest duffer in everyday life that ever stood upright."

"Then it always appeared in that coat. For that was what he had on when he was murdered."

"Well, I never! I shall think we are in the world of departed spirits next. This beats table-rapping. Why, he brought that very coat on his arm when he came on the Sunday to dine with us! The nights were cold again."

"And the real veritable coat has been lying ever since at the public-house where he was carried to. It's there now, stiff in its folds," eagerly avowed Mrs. Copp. "Ma'am, what you saw at your house here must have been a vision—himself and the coat too."

Mrs. Macpherson began to doubt her own identity. The second coat never crossed her mind. It happened that she had not looked into the lumber closet after it, and could have been upon her oath, if asked, that it was there still. Her hot face assumed a strange look of dubious bewilderment.

"It never surely could have been his ghost that came here and dined with us!" debated she. "Ghosts don't eat salmon and drink champagne."

"I don't know what they might do if put to it," cried Mrs. Copp, sharply. "One thing you may rely upon, ma'am—that it was not himself."

"The professor doesn't believe in ghosts. He says there is no such things. I'm free to confess that I've never seen any."

"Neither did I believe before this," said Mrs. Copp. "But one has to bend to the evidence of one's senses."

How the argument would have ended, and what they might have brought it to, cannot be divined. Miss Jupp had sat in simple astonishment. That Robert Hunter had died and been buried at Coastdown in January, and that Robert Hunter had dined in that very house in April, appeared absolutely indisputable. It was certainly far more marvellous than any feat yet accomplished by the "spirits." But Isaac Thornycroft solved it.

He came in alone, saying the professor was staying behind to finish some experiment. Upon which the professor's wife went to see, for she did not approve of experiments when there was company to entertain. Mrs. Copp immediately began to recount what had passed, making comments of her own.

"I have come across many a bumboat woman in my day, Mr. Isaac, and I thought they capped the world for impudent obstinacy, for they'll call black white to the face of a whole crew. But Mrs. Mac beats 'em. Perhaps you will add your testimony to mine—that Robert Hunter is dead and buried. Miss Jupp here is not knowing what to think or believe."

Isaac Thornycroft hesitated. He went and stood on the hearth-rug in his black clothes. His face was grave; his manner betrayed some agitation.

"Mrs. Copp, will you pardon me if I ask you generously to dismiss that topic; at least for to-night?"

"What on earth for?" was the answer of Mrs. Copp.

"The subject was, and is, and always will be productive of the utmost pain to my family. We should be thankful to let all remembrance of it die out of men's minds."

"Now I tell you what it is, Mr. Isaac; you are thinking of your brother Cyril. Of course as long as he stays away, he'll be suspected of the murder, but I've not said so—"

"Be silent, I pray you," interrupted Isaac, in a tone of sharp pain. "Hear me, while I clear your mind from any suspicion of that kind. By all my hope of heaven—by all our hope," he added, lifting solemnly his right hand, "my brother Cyril was innocent."

"Well, we'll let that pass," said Mrs. Copp, with a sniff. "Many a pistol has gone off by accident before now, and small blame to the owners of it. Perhaps you'll be good enough to bear me out to Miss Jupp that Robert Hunter was shot dead."

Isaac paced the room. Mrs. Macpherson had come in and was listening; the professor halted at the door. Better satisfy them once for all, or there would be no end to it.

"It came to our knowledge afterwards—long afterwards—that it was not Robert Hunter," said Isaac, with slow distinctness. "The mistake arose from the face not having been recognisable. Hunter is alive and well."

"The saints preserve us!" cried Mrs. Copp in her discomfiture. "Then why did his ghost appear?"

A momentary smile flitted across the face of Isaac. 'I suppose—in point of fact—it was not his ghost, Mrs. Copp."

Mrs. Copp's senses were three-parts lost in wonder at the turn affairs were taking. "Who, then, was shot down? A stranger?"

Isaac raised his handkerchief to his face. "I dare-say it will be known some time. At present it is enough for us that it was not Robert Hunter."

"I knew a ghost could never eat salmon!" said Mrs. Macpherson, in a glow of triumph.

"But what about the coat?" burst forth Mrs. Copp, as that portion of the mystery loomed into her recollection. "If that is lying unusable in the stables at the Mermaid, Robert Hunter could not have brought it with him when he came here to dinner."

Clearly. And the ladies looked one at another, half inclined to plunge into war again. The meek professor, possibly afraid of it, spoke up in his mild way from behind, where he had stood and listened in silence.

"Mr. Hunter's coat was to have been sent after him from Coastdown; but it did not come, and I gave him mine. He supposed it must have been lost on the road."

It was the professor's wife's turn now. She could not believe her ears. Give away the other coat—when visions had crossed her mind of having that disreputable fur taken off and decent buttons put on, for his wear the following winter when he went off to the country on his ologies!

"Professor! do you mean to tell me to my face that that coat is not in the lumber-closet upstairs where I put it?"

"Well, my dear, I fear you'd not find it there."

Away went Mrs. Macpherson to the closet, and away went the rest in her wake, anxious to see the drama played out. Isaac Thornycroft alone did not stir; and his wife came back to him. Her face was white and cold, as though she had received a shock.

"Isaac! Isaac! this is frightening me. May I say what I fear?"

He put his hands upon her shoulders and gazed into her eyes as she stood before him, his own full of kindness but of mourning.

"Say as little as you can, my darling. I can't bear much to-night."

"Cyril! t—was—"

"Oh, Cyril! Cyril! could he not be saved?"

His faint cry of anguish echoed hers, as he bent his aching brow momentarily upon her shoulder.

"I would have given my own life to save his, Anna. I would give it still to save another the remorse and pain that lie upon him. He put on Hunter's coat that night, the other not wanting it, and was mistaken for him."

"I understand," she murmured. "Oh, what a remorse it must be!"

"Now you know all; but it is for your ear alone," he said, standing before her again and speaking impressively. "From henceforth let it be to us a barred subject, the only one that my dear wife may not mention to me."

She locked an assent from her loving eyes, and sat down again as the company came trooping in, Mrs. Macpherson openly demanding of her husband how long it would be before he learnt common sense, and why he did not cut off his head and give that away.

CHAPTER XVIII

Disclosing it to Justice Thornycroft

Back at Coastdown. Isaac and his wife were staying at the Red Court. Mr. Thornycroft wished them to remain at it altogether; but Isaac doubted. If his sister were to marry, why then he would heartily accede; and Anna could take up her position as its mistress—in anticipation of the period when she would legally be entitled to it. At present he thought it would be better for them to rent a small house near.

Mary Anne had received the news of the marriage with equanimity—not to say apathy. In the dreadful calamities that had overwhelmed her, petty troubles were lost. Cordially indeed did she welcome her brother and his wife home, and hoped they would remain. To be alone there was, as she truly told them, miserable.

A ship letter had been received from Richard, written when he was nearly half way on his voyage. It appeared that he had written on embarking, just a word to tell the name of his ship, and whither it was bound, and had sent it on shore by the pilot. Isaac could only suppose that the man had forgotten to post it.

His destination was New Zealand. Some people whom he knew had settled there, he said, and he intended to join them. He should purchase some land and farm it; but he would never again set foot on European soil. He supposed he should get on; and he hoped in time some sort of peace would return to him.

"I would advise your telling my father the whole, if you have not already done so," the letter concluded. "It is right that he should know the truth about Cyril, and that I shall never come home again. Tell him that the remorse lies very heavily upon me; that I would have given my own life ten times over—given it cheerfully—to save my brother's. Had it been any one out a brother, I should not feel it so deeply. I think of myself always as a second Cain. I will write you again when we arrive. Meanwhile, address to me at the post-office, Canterbury. I suppose you will not object to correspond with me. Perhaps my father will write. Tell him I should like it."

Before the arrival of this letter to Isaac, he had been consulting with his sister about the expediency of enlightening their father. His own opinion entirely coincided with Richard's—that it ought to be done. Mr. Thornycroft was in a state of doubt about Cyril; and also as to the duration of Richard's exile, and restlessly curious always in regard to what had led to it.

One balmy June day, when the crop of hay was being got in, Isaac told his father. They were leaning upon a gate in the four-acre mead, watching the haymakers, who were piling the hay into cocks at the farther end of the field.

Mr. Thornycroft was like a man stunned.

"Hunter not dead! Cyril lying there, and not Hunter! It can't be, Isaac!"

Isaac repeated the facts again, and then went into details. He concluded by showing Richard's last letter. "Poor Dicky! Poor Dicky!" cried the justice, melted to compassion. "Yes, as you say, Isaac, Cyril is in a happier place than this—gone to his rest. And Dick—Dick sent him there in cruelty. I think I'll go in if you'll give me your arm.'

Wonderingly Isaac obeyed. Never had the strong, upright Justice Thornycroft sought or needed support from any one. The news must have shaken him terribly. Isaac went with him across the fields, and saw him shut himself in his room.

"Have you been telling him?" whispered Mary Anne.

"Yes."

"And how has he borne it? Why did he lean upon you in coming in?"

"He seemed to bear it exceedingly well. But it must have had a far deeper effect upon him than I thought, or he would not have asked for my arm."

Mary Anne Thornycroft sighed. A little pain, more or less, seemed to her as nothing.

On the following morning Mr. Thornycroft sent for his son. Isaac found him seated before his portable desk; some papers upon it. The crisis of affairs had prompted the justice to disclose certain facts to his children, that otherwise never might have been disclosed. Richard Thornycroft was not his own son, though he had been treated as such. Isaac listened in utter amazement. Of all the strange things that had lately fallen upon them, this appeared to him to be the strangest.

"I have been writing to Richard," said Mr. Thornycroft, taking up some closely-written pages. "You can read it; it will save me going over the details to you."

Isaac took the letter, and read it through. But his senses were confused, and it was not very clear to him.

"It seems that I cannot understand it now, sir."

"Not understand it?" repeated the justice, with a touch of his old heat. "It is plain enough to be understood. When my father died, he left this place, the Red Court Farm, to my elder brother, your uncle Richard—whom you never knew. A short while afterwards, Richard met with an accident in France, and I went over with my wife, to whom I was just married. We found him also with a wife, which surprised me, for he had never said anything of it; she was a pretty little Frenchwoman; and their child, a boy, was a year old. Richard, poor fellow, was dying, and of course I thought my chance of inheriting the Red Court was gone—that he would naturally leave it to his little son. But he took an opportunity of telling me that he had left it to me; the only proviso attached to it being that I should bring up the boy, as my son. He talked with me further: things that I cannot go into now: and I promised. That is how the Red Court came to me."

"But why should he have done this, sir?" interrupted Isaac, who liked justice better than wrong. "The little boy had a right to it."

"No," said Mr. Thornycroft, quietly. "Richard had not married his mother."

Isaac saw now. There was a pause.

"He said if time could come over again he would have married her, or else not have taken her. He was dying, you see, Isaac, and right and wrong array themselves in very distinct colours then. Anyway, it was too late now, whatever his repentance; and he prayed me and my wife to take the boy and not let it be known for the child's own sake that he was not ours. We both promised; at a moment like that one could not foresee inconveniences that might arise later, and it almost seemed as if we owed the compliance, in gratitude for the bequeathal of the Red Court Farm. He died, and we brought the boy with us to London—he who has been looked upon as your brother Richard. When people here used to say that he was more like his uncle Richard than his father Harry, my wife would glance at me with a smile."

"And his mother?"

"She died in France shortly afterwards. She had parted with the boy readily, glad to find he would have so good a home. Had she lived, the probabilities are that the secret could not have been kept."

"Did you intend to keep it always, father?"

"Until my death. Every year as they went on, gave less chance of our disclosing it. When you were all little, my wife and I had many a serious consultation; for the future seemed to be open so some difficulty; but we loved the boy, and neither of us had courage to say, He is not ours; he has no legitimate inheritance. Besides, as your mother would say to me, there was always our promise. It must have been disclosed at my death, at least to Richard, to explain why you, and not he, came into the Red Court."

"Perhaps his father, my uncle Richard, expected it would be left to him?"

"No, Isaac. We talked of that. Only in the event of my having no children of my own would the property have become his. Richard will take his share as one of my younger children. You are the eldest. I shall at once settle this money upon him; you have read to that effect in the letter; so that he will have enough for comfort whatever part of the world he may choose to remain in."

Isaac mechanically cast his eyes on the letter, still in his hand.

"I have disclosed these facts to him now for his own comfort," resumed Mr. Thornycroft. "It may bring him a ray of it to find Cyril was not his brother."

Isaac thought it would. He folded the letter and returned it to his father.

"There is one thing I wished to ask you, sir, and I may as well ask it now. You do not, I presume, think of running more cargoes."

"Never again," said Mr. Thornycroft. "Richard was the right hand of it, and he is gone. That's over for ever. But for him it would have been given up before. And there's Kyne besides."

Isaac nodded, glad to have the matter set at rest. "May I tell Mary Anne what you have disclosed to me?"

"Yes, but no one else. She may be glad to hear Richard is not her brother."

How glad, the justice little thought. It seemed to Mary Anne as if this news removed the embargo she had self-imposed upon her marriage with Robert Hunter. Perhaps she had already begun to question the necessity of it—to think it a very utopian, severe decision. In the revulsion of feeling that came over her, she laid her head down on Isaac's shoulder with a burst of tears, and told him all. Isaac smiled.

"You must tell him that you have relented, Mary Anne."

"He will not be back for five years."

"He will be back in less than five months; perhaps in five weeks."

She sat upright, staring at him.

"Isaac!"

"He will, indeed. Anna had a letter from him yesterday. It came to Miss Jupp's, addressed to 'Miss Chester.' Business matters are bringing him home for a short while; personal things, he says, that only himself can do. I wonder if he wrote to her in the hope that the information would penetrate to Coastdown?"

She sat in silence, her colour going and coming, rather shrinking from the merriment in Isaac's eye. Oh, would it be so?—would it be so?

"In that case—I mean, should circumstances bring him again to the Red Court Farm—we shall have to disclose publicly the truth about Cyril, Mary Anne. As well that it should be so, and then a tombstone can be put. But it can wait yet."

As she sat there, looking out on the sparkling sea, a prevision came over her that this happiness might really come to her at last, and a sobbing sigh of thankfulness went up to heaven.

Coastdown went on in its ordinary quiet routine. The mysteries of the Red Court Farm were at an end, never again to be enacted. Long and perseveringly did Mr. Superintendent Kyne look out for the smugglers; many and many a night did he exercise his eyes and his patience on the edge of that bleak plateau; but they came no more. Old Mr. Thornycroft, deprived, he hardly knew how, of his sons, lived on at the Red Court, feeling at times a vacancy of pursuit: he had loved adventure, and his occupation was gone. But the land got a better chance of being tilled to perfection now than it ever had been.

Meanwhile the whole neighbourhood remained under a clear and immutable persuasion that the ghost still "walked" in the churchyard. The new right of road had come to a hot dispute; but Coastdown persisted in using it after nightfall, to avoid the graves and their ominous visitor. While Captain Copp, taking his glass in the parlour at the Mermaid, did not fail to descant upon the marvels of that night, when he and that woman-servant of his, who (he would add in a parenthesis) was undaunted enough for a she-pirate, saw with their own eyes the spirit of Robert Hunter. And then the parlour would fall into a discussion of the love of roving inherent in the young Thornycrofts—Cyril lingering away still; Richard also perhaps gone to look after him; and speculate upon how long it would be before they returned, and the glorious dinners were resumed at the Red Court Farm.

MRS HENRY WOOD (aka ELLEN WOOD) – A CONCISE BIBLIOGRAPHY

Danesbury House (1860)
East Lynne (1861)
The Elchester College Boys (1861)
A Life's Secret (1862)
Mrs. Halliburton's Troubles (1862)

The Channings (1862)
The Foggy Night at Offord: A Christmas Gift for the Lancashire Fund (1863)
The Shadow of Ashlydyat (1863)
Verner's Pride (1863)
Lord Oakburn's Daughters (1864)
Oswald Cray (1864)
Trevlyn Hold; or, Squire Trevlyn's Heir (1864)
William Allair; or, Running away to Sea (1864)
Mildred Arkell: A Novel (1865)
The Argosy (1865)
Elster's Folly: A Novel (1866)
St. Martin's Eve: A Novel (1866)
Lady Adelaide's Oath (1867)
Orville College: A Story (1867)
The Ghost of the Hollow Field (1867)
Anne Hereford: A Novel (1868)
Castle Wafer; or, The Plain Gold Ring (1868)
The Red Court Farm: A Novel (1868)
Roland Yorke: A Novel (1869)
Bessy Rane: A Novel (1870)
George Canterbury's Will (1870)
Dene Hollow (1871)
Within the Maze: A Novel (1872)
The Master of Greylands (1872)
Johnny Ludlow (1874)
Bessy Wells (1875)
Told in the Twilight: Containing 'Parkwater' and nine short stories (1875)
Adam Grainger: A Tale (1876)
Edina (1876)
Our Children (1876)
Parkwater: With four other tales (1876)
Pomeroy Abbey (1878)
Lady Adelaide (1879)
Johnny Ludlow, Second Series (1880)
A Tale of Sin and Other Tales (1881)
Court Netherleigh: A Novel (1881)
About Ourselves (1883)
Johnny Ludlow. Third Series (1885)
Lady Grace and Other Stories (1887)
The Story of Charles Strange (1888)
Featherston's Story. A Tale by Johnny Ludlow (1889)
The Unholy Wish and Other Stories (1890)
The House of Halliwell. A Novel (1890)
Ashley and Other Stories (1897)
Victor Serenus (1898)
Johnny Ludlow. Fifth series (1899)
Johnny Ludlow. Sixth series (1899)

Translations

Les Channing. Traduit de l'Anglais par Mme Abric-Encontre (1864)
Les Filles de Lord Oakburn: Roman traduit de l'anglais par L. Bochet (1876)
La Gloire des Verner: Roman traduit de l'anglais par L. de L'Estrive (1878)
Le Serment de Lady Adelaïde: Roman traduit de l'anglais par Léon Bochet (1878)